Also by Julia Brannan

The Jacobite Chronicles

Book One: Mask of Duplicity

Book Two: The Mask Revealed

The Gathering Storm

The Jacobite Chronicles, Book Three

Julia Brannan

DISCLAIMER

Formatting by Polgarus Studio

Cover Model Photography by VJ Dunraven of
www.PeriodImages.com
Photograph of Scotland by Julia Brannan

Cover Design by najlaqamberdesigns.com

In memory of my mother and best friend, Flora Brannan. She taught me to read, and, more importantly, instilled in me a love and understanding of the power and beauty of the written word. She encouraged me to write, to be the best I could be, whilst accepting me as I was and loving me unconditionally. I owe her everything, and miss her every day.

ACKNOWLEDGEMENTS

First of all, I would like to thank my good friend Mary Brady, who painstakingly reads and rereads every chapter as I write, spending hours on the phone with me, giving me encouragement and valuable suggestions as to how to improve the book. I owe her an enormous and ongoing debt of gratitude.

I also want to thank my wonderful partner Jason Gardiner, who puts up with me living in the eighteenth century as I write the books in this series, and who has supported and encouraged me through the long months of writing, and hopefully will continue to do so!

Thanks also to all the friends who read my books and encouraged me to publish them, including Alyson Cairns and Mandy Condon, who has already determined the cast list for the film of the books, and also to all the wonderful people who have read Mask of Duplicity and The Mask Revealed, have recommended them to others, and have given me their valuable feedback and reviews. I hope you enjoy book three as much as you've enjoyed books one and two!

Thank you to the other successful authors who have so generously given me their time, advice and encouragement, especially Kym Grosso and Victoria Danann.

Thanks also have to go to the long-suffering staff of Ystradgynlais library, who hunted down obscure research books for me, and put up with my endless requests for strange information.

I'd also like to thank Najla Qamber, who once again has come up with a beautiful cover design for my book. She's wonderful to work with, and I couldn't do without her.

And to Jason Tobias and Jax Styrna, the models for this cover — thank you for your hard work and professionalism during the photo shoot. You are awesome!

If I've forgotten anyone, please remind me and I will grovel and apologise profusely, and include you in the acknowledgements in my next book!

HISTORICAL BACKGROUND NOTE

Although this series starts in 1742 and deals with the Jacobite Rebellion of 1745, the events that culminated in this uprising started a long time before, in 1685, in fact. This was when King Charles II died without leaving an heir, and the throne passed to his Roman Catholic younger brother James, who then became James II of England and Wales, and VII of Scotland. His attempts to promote toleration of Roman Catholics and Presbyterians did not meet with approval from the Anglican establishment, but he was generally tolerated because he was in his 50s, and his daughters, who would succeed him, were committed Protestants. But in 1688 James' second wife gave birth to a son, also named James, who was christened Roman Catholic. It now seemed certain that Catholics would return to the throne long-term, which was anathema to Protestants.

Consequently James' daughter Mary and her husband William of Orange were invited to jointly rule in James' place, and James was deposed, finally leaving for France in 1689. However, many Catholics, Episcopalians and Tory royalists still considered James to be the legitimate monarch.

The first Jacobite rebellion, led by Viscount Dundee in April 1689, routed King William's force at the Battle of Killikrankie, but unfortunately Dundee himself was killed, leaving the Jacobite forces leaderless, and in May 1690 they suffered a heavy defeat. King William offered all the Highland clans a pardon if they would take an oath of allegiance in front of a magistrate before 1st January 1692. Due to the weather and a general reluctance, some clans failed to make it to the places appointed for the oath to be taken, resulting in the infamous Glencoe Massacre of Clan MacDonald in February 1692. By spring all the clans had taken the oath, and it seemed that the Stuart cause was dead.

However, a series of economic and political disasters by William and his government left many people dissatisfied with his reign, and a number of these flocked to the Jacobite cause. In

1707, the Act of Union between Scotland and England, one of the intentions of which was to put an end to hopes of a Stuart restoration to the throne, was deeply unpopular with most Scots, as it delivered no benefits to the majority of the Scottish population.

Following the deaths of William and Mary, Mary's sister Anne became Queen, dying without leaving an heir in 1714, after which George I of Hanover took the throne. This raised the question of the succession again, and in 1715 a number of Scottish nobles and Tories took up arms against the Hanoverian monarch.

The rebellion was led by the Earl of Mar, but he was not a great military leader and the Jacobite army suffered a series of defeats, finally disbanding completely when six thousand Dutch troops landed in support of Hanover. Following this, the Highlands of Scotland were garrisoned and hundreds of miles of new roads were built, in an attempt to thwart any further risings in favour of the Stuarts.

By the early 1740s, this operation was scaled back when it seemed unlikely that the aging James Stuart, 'the Old Pretender,' would spearhead another attempt to take the throne. However, the hopes of those who wanted to dissolve the Union and return the Stuarts to their rightful place were centring not on James, but on his young, handsome and charismatic son Charles Edward Stuart, as yet something of an unknown quantity.

I would strongly recommend that you read the first two books in the series, Mask Of Duplicity and The Mask Revealed before starting this one! However, if you are determined not to, here's a summary of the first two to help you enjoy Book Three...

The Story So Far

Book One – Mask of Duplicity

Following the death of their father, Elizabeth (Beth) Cunningham and her older half-brother Richard, a dragoon sergeant, are reunited after a thirteen year separation, when he comes home to Manchester to claim his inheritance. He soon discovers that while their father's will left her a large dowry, the investments which he has inherited will not be sufficient for him to further his military ambitions. He decides therefore to persuade his sister to renew the acquaintance with her aristocratic cousins, in the hope that her looks and dowry will attract a wealthy husband willing to purchase him a commission in the army. Beth refuses, partly because she is happy living an unrestricted lifestyle, and partly because the family rejected her father following his second marriage to her mother, a Scottish seamstress.

Richard, who has few scruples, then embarks on an increasingly vicious campaign to get her to comply with his wishes, threatening her beloved servants and herself. Finally, following a particularly brutal attack, she agrees to comply with his wishes, on the condition that once she is married, he will remove himself from her life entirely.

Her cousin, the pompous Lord Edward and his downtrodden sisters accept Richard and Beth back into the family, where she meets the interesting and gossipy, but very foppish Sir Anthony Peters. After a few weeks of living their monotonous lifestyle, Beth becomes extremely bored and sneaks off to town for a day, where she is followed by a footpad. Taking refuge in a disused room, she inadvertently comes upon a gang of Jacobite plotters, one of whom takes great pains to hide his face, although she notices a scar on his hand. They are impressed by her bravery and instead of killing her, escort her home. A secret Jacobite herself, she doesn't tell her Hanoverian family what has happened, and soon repairs with them to London for the season.

Once there, she meets many new people and attracts a great number of suitors, but is not interested in any of them until she falls in love with Daniel, the Earl of Highbury's son. The relationship progresses until she discovers that his main motivation for marrying her is to use her dowry to clear his gambling debts. She rejects him, but becomes increasingly depressed.

In the meantime, the Jacobite gang, the chief members of whom are Alex MacGregor (the scarred man) and his brothers Angus and Duncan, are operating in the London area, smuggling weapons, collecting information, visiting brothels etc.

Sir Anthony, now a regular visitor to the house, becomes a friend of sorts, and introduces her to his wide circle of acquaintance, including the King, the Duke of Cumberland and Edwin Harlow MP and his wife Caroline. Beth does not trust the painted Sir Anthony and thinks him physically repulsive, but finds him amusing. Following an ultimatum from her brother that if she keeps rejecting suitors he will find her a husband himself, she accepts a marriage proposal from Sir Anthony, partly because he seems kind, but chiefly because he has discovered a rosary belonging to her, and she is afraid he will denounce her as a Catholic, which would result in her rejection from society and her brother's vengeance.

The night before her wedding, Beth is abducted by Daniel, who, in a desperate attempt to avoid being imprisoned for debt, attempts to marry her by force. Beth's maid, Sarah, alerts the Cunninghams and Sir Anthony to Beth's plight, and she is rescued by her fiancé. He then gives her the option to call off the wedding, but thinking that being married to him is the best of the limited options she has available to her, she agrees to go ahead as planned.

Book Two – The Mask Revealed

Sir Anthony and Beth marry. The following evening at a function, he has to remove his glove and she sees his hand and its scar for the first time, and remembers where she has seen it before. Having removed his furious wife by force from the company before she can give him away, Sir Anthony admits that he is a Jacobite spy, and that he is really Alex MacGregor. He explains the odd circumstances that led him to follow such a strange double life, and admits that he married her mainly for love, intends to make her dowry over to her and effect a separation, thereby giving her her freedom. She, being of a very adventurous spirit, refuses, stating that she intends to stay with him. He tries to persuade her against this, as his lifestyle is a dangerous one, but eventually he agrees, and they go on honeymoon to Europe together, as Sir Anthony and wife.

He explains that he will be visiting Prince Charles Stuart, son of the exiled King James, as a few weeks ago the Duke of Newcastle, not knowing him to be a Jacobite spy, recruited him on behalf of the Hanoverians, to become acquainted with the prince and report back any useful information.

On the way to Rome, Angus (who has accompanied them as a servant) overhears a private conversation between two French courtiers, in which it is revealed that King Louis of France is secretly planning to invade England, and that one of the men (Henri), intends to give the plans to the British. Alex now decides he must do something to prevent this, but must first carry on to meet Charles and convey the news of the prospective invasion to him. He does, and Beth and Alex are married again in Rome under their real names.

After giving a misleading report of his meeting with Charles to Sir Horace Mann who is the Hanoverian envoy in Florence, Alex, Beth and Angus travel to France, where, at Versailles, Beth becomes acquainted with, and starts to like, the man Henri. Alex, as Sir Anthony, pretends jealousy and challenges Henri to a duel, during which he kills him, as though by accident.

Beth, having not been entrusted with his plans, and also having been kept in the dark about some other things, is very hurt and leaves suddenly, travelling back first to London and then Manchester, on her own, where she settles in with her ex-servants.

Alex's return is delayed as he is held in prison for duelling. He sends Angus to Rome to stop Prince Charles riding to Paris to join the invasion and thereby raising British suspicion and Louis' anger. Alex then returns home to London, where he is expecting Beth to be waiting for him. When he discovers she has left, he follows her to Manchester, where they are reconciled.

STUART/HANOVER FAMILY TREE

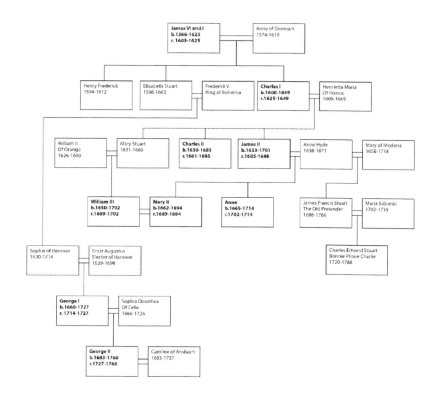

LIST OF CHARACTERS

Alexander MacGregor, Highland Chieftain/Sir Anthony Peters, Baronet
Elizabeth (Beth) MacGregor/Lady Elizabeth Peters, his wife
Duncan MacGregor, brother to Alex
Angus MacGregor, brother to Alex

Iain Gordon, liegeman to Alex
Margaret (Maggie) Gordon, his wife
Simon MacGregor, clansman to Alex
Kenneth MacGregor, clansman to Alex
Dougal MacGregor, clansman to Alex
Robbie MacGregor, Dougal's youngest brother
Alasdair MacGregor, clansman to Alex
Peigi MacGregor, Alasdair's wife
Morag MacGregor
Janet MacGregor

Lieutenant Richard Cunningham, a dragoon and brother to Beth
Lord Edward Cunningham, cousin to Richard and Beth
Isabella Cunningham, Edward's eldest sister
Clarissa Cunningham, Edward's middle sister
Charlotte Stanton, Edward's youngest sister, widow of Frederick

Sarah Browne, formerly lady's maid to Beth
Graeme Elliot, former gardener to Beth
Thomas Fletcher, her former steward
Grace Miller, former lady's maid to Beth
Mary Williamson, childhood friend of Beth's
Joseph, Mary's fiancé

Edwin Harlow, MP and friend of Sir Anthony and Beth
Caroline Harlow, his wife
Freddie Harlow, their infant son

Lady Philippa, cousin to Caroline

Lord Bartholomew Winter
Lady Wilhelmina Winter, his wife
Anne Maynard, an impoverished relative of Lord Winter

William, Earl of Highbury
Lord Daniel Barrington, his son

Thomas Fortesque, MP
Lydia Fortesque, his daughter

Lord Stanley Redburn, an elderly lord, desperate to marry

Gabriel Foley, leader of a band of smugglers

Helen, a beautiful young lady
Percy, a young gentleman
David, a young gentleman

Colonel Mark Hutchinson
John, a captain in the Horseguards
Sergeant Smith, a dragoon

King George II, King of Great Britain and Ireland, Elector of
    Hanover
Frederick, Prince of Wales, eldest son of King George II
Prince George, Frederick's eldest son
Prince Edward, Frederick's youngest son
Prince William Augustus, Duke of Cumberland, second son of
    King George.

Prince Charles Edward Stuart, eldest son of James Stuart (the
    Pretender), exiled King of Britain

Donald MacDonald, of Glencoe, a clansman
Ealasaid MacDonald, Beth's grandmother
Joan MacDonald, cousin to Beth

Meg MacDonald, Joan's twin sister
Robert MacDonald, their younger brother
Allan MacDonald, eldest brother of Joan, Meg and Robert

Nathan Sennet, a Redcoat soldier

John Murray of Broughton

Donald Cameron of Lochiel, Chief of Clan Cameron

PROLOGUE

France, February 1744

The tall, straight-backed figure stood alone on the beach gazing out to sea, the wind toying playfully with his hair and fingering the folds of his heavy winter coat. He had ridden out from the fortified town of Gravelines in the early morning, so early that even the servants had still been abed, and no one had seen the young man with the shock of red-brown hair as he had quietly left the house and made his way to the stables. He had ridden out into the darkness, the cold bite of the wind dispersing the alcoholic haze from the previous evening's revels, leaving him clear-headed and exhilarated.

Tearing his gaze from the sea, he walked aimlessly for a time, the pebbles crunching softly beneath the soles of his fine leather boots, his mind soothed by the soft susurration of the waves. He waited until the sky turned from black to dark grey, then to a lighter pearl-grey, which transformed the sea into a restless sheet of rolling burnished silver.

He turned a pebble over with his toe, marvelling at its smoothness, evidence of the relentless, patient power of the sea, which in time subdued all things, and which could, at a whim, scatter whole navies, driving kings to ruin and despair. A frown etched the fine aristocratic brow briefly, as he thought of the famed ill-luck of his family which had brought so many of his forebears to disaster and a brutal early death.

It would not be so this time, he thought, his brow clearing, the optimism of youth outweighing the legendary superstition of centuries. It was his destiny to change the luck of the Stuarts. He had known that since he was a small child and had first heard the stories, whispered to him by his nurse, that at the exact time of his birth a new star had been seen in the sky, whilst a storm had simultaneously wreaked havoc in Hanover, the home of his despised enemy. The enemy which now sat so smugly and complacently on his father's throne, across that stretch of silver sea.

But not for long. For the time had come at last, the time he had been waiting for, for over twenty long years. It was what he had prepared himself for, putting his body through a punishing regime of diet and exercise, honing his muscles, practising with sword and pistol, with bow and arrow until no one could match his accuracy. He had driven his aching muscles beyond the boundaries of exhaustion and fatigue until his pampered aristocratic companions had whispered in awe that the young prince must indeed be superhuman. Had he not been born on the very eve of the new year, when the old was swept aside and in the depths of winter new hope was born?

He was that new hope, and as he stood on the shore, gazing out across the sea towards his father's kingdom, his kingdom to be, a surge of exhilaration bore him up and over the waves to England. He saw himself, so clearly that it must be a premonition, at the head of an army, riding into London, the cheers of the people resounding in his ears, rose petals falling like velvet rain upon him as the people, his people, went wild with joy at the return of the Stuarts to their rightful place.

A seagull called mournfully and the spell was broken; he was once again standing on the windswept shore, the only sound the gentle shushing of waves on pebbles.

He turned his gaze towards the north-east, where all his hopes were even now being brought to fruition, as the provisions, cannon and the barrels of gunpowder were loaded onto the multitude of ships that would bear the French army and himself to England and to victory. Last night he had disguised himself, and had ridden into Dunkirk, although King Louis, fearful of British spies, had expressly forbidden him to go there. He had gazed in wonder at the multitude of ships, their masts tall and bare like a forest of trees in winter. It was not possible that such a fleet could fail. He had spent the evening in the taverns, drinking with the sailors and soldiers who were now pouring into the town, enriching the pockets of the whores and innkeepers. They had flocked round the charming, generous young Frenchman from Paris, eager to tell him tales of their bravery in combat, which grew ever more extravagant as the alcohol flowed. It had been a good evening, one to amuse his courtiers with from the comfort of St James's Palace, from the throne where his grandfather had sat, where his father would sit, and where he too would be enthroned, when the time came.

He was Charles Edward Stuart, eldest son and heir to King James the Eighth of Scotland and Third of England. He would use his looks, his strength and above all his enormous charismatic powers of persuasion to regain the throne for the Stuarts. He had friends, many friends in England, and even more in Scotland. The clans were loyal to him. He was, after all, one of them, a Scot by blood if not birth, and they did not cast aside the bonds of kinship lightly. If this French invasion failed, which it would not, could not, then he would call on the allegiance of his kinsmen.

His whole life had been lived for this single purpose. This was his destiny, and by God, he would fulfil it, if he had to row across the channel single-handed to raise his subjects. They *would* rise for him. It was unthinkable that they would not. In all his young life, he had never been denied, and he would not be denied now. The crown was his, if his father did not want it, and he would win it, or die in the attempt.

CHAPTER ONE

Late February 1744

Alex and Beth managed to keep the fact that they had returned to London a secret for a whole week, until Beth was unfortunately seen looking out of her window, after which the calling cards began to trickle in, forming a small pile on the table in the hall. The trickle quickly became an avalanche as the rumour that Sir Anthony Peters and his wife were apparently reconciled spread like wildfire among society. It was unbelievable. After all, hadn't Lady Peters engaged in a passionate affair with both King Louis of France *and* his servant? And hadn't Sir Anthony, in a fit of jealous rage, challenged the servant to a duel, where he had accidentally killed the man? It was also rumoured that the baronet had intended to call Louis himself out, had the king not had him thrown into prison before he could do so. It was so exciting! Everyone wanted to be the first to interview the couple and find out the truth of the affair.

Beth and Alex ignored the mountain of cards, unwilling to return to the empty whirl of concerts, dinners and card parties. Then Beth received a somewhat wordy letter from her cousin Isabella, in which she expressed a wish to visit the following day to discuss the arrangements for a dinner party she intended to hold next Wednesday to welcome her dear cousins home.

They bowed to the inevitable, and while Beth penned an insincere reply, stating that she and her husband were delighted at the honour Isabella was according them, Alex gloomily combed and curled his wig, and unearthed his cosmetics from the bottom of his travelling trunk.

At Smith Square, the Cunningham sisters were beside themselves with joy. Their dinner party would be the first occasion on which Sir Anthony and Lady Elizabeth would appear in public since their return from France, and everyone wanted to be invited. Isabella pondered the enormous list of would-be guests for a time, then tentatively approached her brother for his advice.

Lord Edward was no help at all, declaring that he would have nothing to do with the organisation of this ridiculous dinner, being neither partial to his cousin or her husband, although he did agree to be present at the meal itself. After all, Sir Anthony had promised to put in a good word for the peer with the king, and a dinner would be an excellent opportunity to remind him of his promise. He just hoped that Sir Anthony had made it very clear to his wife that he would not tolerate such wanton behaviour as she had engaged in in France, if all the rumours were true. It was almost impossible to imagine that ridiculous apology for a man actually challenging anyone to a duel, let alone killing him. Hopefully it had given him the courage to tame his headstrong wife. She certainly needed it.

Left to her own devices Isabella, with an unerring talent for the inappropriate, invited all the people Beth would least want to spend an evening with, only adding Edwin and Caroline to the list after Beth insisted quite forcefully that they be included. Sir Anthony, resplendent in royal blue satin, an ingratiating smile plastered on his chalk-white face, said that he would be quite happy to attend any dinner of Isabella's, no matter who was invited, as he was on good terms with almost everybody he could think of, and for himself he would trust to the excellent Cunningham taste to ensure the guests were of a suitably eclectic mix to provide an entertaining evening.

The three sisters had beamed, and the sycophantic Sir Anthony had then been dragged straight round to the Harlows' house by Beth to personally deliver the invitation, which was for six o'clock, three days hence. And to see the sweet, docile angel of a baby with the most beautiful blue eyes and most endearing smile, that Sir Anthony had enthused about to Isabella.

When they were shown into the drawing-room, Caroline was pacing up and down the carpet, rocking the tiny angel in her arms, now christened Frederick John, Sir Anthony having had no objections to her using his middle name, which was common enough not to cause problems later, although he had steadfastly refused to be a godfather. She looked up at her guests.

"Now might not be the best time to visit," Caroline roared to make herself heard over the sweet, docile baby's furious screams. "He's got wind, and he's not in the best of moods. And neither am I, to be honest."

"Nonsense!" shouted Sir Anthony amiably, arranging himself gracefully on the sofa. "It's never a bad time to visit friends."

Caroline hoisted the baby impatiently onto her shoulder and tapped his back wearily. His roars doubled in volume, his face turning bright red and his tiny fists waving angrily about in the air. Beth looked at her husband uncertainly.

"Isn't he gorgeous?" Sir Anthony enthused, with absolute sincerity.

Both Caroline and Beth looked at him with disbelief.

"Yes, he's beautiful," Beth agreed lamely, thinking she had never seen such a hideous crumpled thing in her life, although she would not have admitted that to Caroline, even under torture. She sat down next to her husband. "We've come to invite you to a dinner next…"

"What?" cried Caroline. "I can't hear a thing, I'm sorry. God, I love him dearly, but he's driving me mad today. At times like this I wish I *had* hired a nurse, as everyone keeps telling me I should."

"Here," said Sir Anthony, to Beth's surprise. "Let me try. You sit down for a minute." Without waiting for Caroline's permission, he deftly removed the screaming bundle from her arms and cradled it to his chest, the tomato-coloured face resting on his shoulder.

Caroline plopped herself down next to Beth, watching with interest as the baronet paced slowly across the room, alternately patting then rubbing the baby's back with a firm circular motion. There was something very endearing about a large man holding a tiny infant with such infinite tenderness, as Sir Anthony was doing. The two women watched him for a short while, mesmerised. The racket continued.

"I'm sorry," Caroline said into Beth's ear. "This isn't a good introduction to him. He's normally quite placid."

"Yes," said Beth doubtfully. "Anthony said he was a very quiet child."

The cries stopped abruptly, replaced by a loud burp and an ominous sound that Caroline recognised immediately. She leapt up, just in time to see a copious trickle of white liquid emerge from the child's mouth and pour thickly down Sir Anthony's immaculate royal-blue back.

"Oh, God!" said Caroline. "I'm sorry. I'll get a cloth."

"It's all right, my dear. Stop apologising, it's natural," he reassured her. "There, there now, that's better, isn't it?" he crooned to the child, whose cries had subsided to whimpers now the source of pain had gone. Its face was changing slowly from red to pink. The baronet continued to pace slowly round the room, crooning to his charge, unfazed by the mess on his coat. He used the proffered cloth to carefully wipe the child's mouth and chin.

"Er...we came to invite you to a dinner party," Beth said, eyeing her husband with continued amazement. She had never seen him with children before, had no idea he was so accustomed to them.

"Oh," said Caroline, "you're throwing a party! Of course I'll come. I'm not sure about Edwin though. He's virtually living at Parliament at the moment, with the French crisis."

"No, it's actually Isabella's dinner party, but she wants you to come."

"Does she?" Caroline asked. "Really?"

"Well, she doesn't have any objections, anyway," Beth revised. "But I want you to come. You *have* to come. She's throwing it for me and Anthony, and you can't imagine the people she's invited."

"I think I probably can," Caroline said with a grimace.

"Please, you must come. I'll need some respite from the endless questions about my affair with King Louis, and the duel. I assume you know about the duel?"

"As much as I need to, yes. Yes, I'll come," Caroline replied, looking at Sir Anthony. He had stopped pacing now, and the baby had ceased crying completely, his eyes drooping, ready for sleep.

"There you are," Sir Anthony smiled, placing the child in his startled wife's arms, before straightening and carefully removing his coat. He eyed the damage, which had now soaked into the expensive satin. Caroline winced.

"Oh, I think that can be cleaned," he said carelessly, hanging the somewhat smelly item over a chair in the far corner of the room, before coming back in shirtsleeves and waistcoat to take a seat adjacent to his wife.

Beth was sitting preternaturally still, the infant held awkwardly in her arms. Now relieved of wind and excess milk, he did actually look rather cute, she thought, with smooth rose petal skin and a tiny pursed mouth. His ears were like little shells, but his eyes were more green than blue. She smiled, and looked up from the baby to see Caroline and Anthony watching her with amusement.

"He's not a bomb, my dear," said Sir Anthony. "He won't explode if you make a sudden move."

"I don't know," said Caroline. "He might. He seems to spend half his life exploding, from one end or the other. If he suddenly screws his face up, prepare yourself."

"He *is* beautiful, isn't he?" Beth said, with such astonishment in her voice that Caroline burst out laughing. "I'm sorry," Beth said, blushing. "I didn't mean…"

"That's all right, I'm not so easily offended. He *is* ugly when he's crying. And I should have expected your reaction anyway, Beth."

"You should? Why?" asked her friend.

"Because one thing you two have in common is unpredictability. Men are usually very uncomfortable with babies. I should have expected, therefore, that Anthony would be relaxed with them, but it still came as a surprise. Whereas women are usually accustomed to children and know exactly what to do. But you look as though you've never held a baby before in your life. Have you?"

"Yes," said Beth, a little put out. "Once or twice. But you're right. I haven't had many dealings with babies. I didn't have any younger brothers or sisters, or any other relatives with children, as you know. I like them, but I'm a bit frightened of them, too, to be honest."

"Whereas I had three younger sisters," said the baronet smoothly. "And I lived in France for a time. The French are very child-orientated."

Beth thought of a marble headstone in an icy country churchyard in Switzerland, and then of a baby Angus with slate-blue eyes and ridiculous eyelashes, and a fuzz of fair hair, gazing mischievously up at his eight-year-old brother, anticipating the volatile, action-packed years to come.

"Didn't one of your servants have a baby?" Sir Anthony asked, breaking into her thoughts. She realised she was smiling foolishly, and bestowed the smile on the infant in her arms, where it would be understandable.

"Martha," Beth said. "Yes, she did, but when she got pregnant she was disowned by her father, and went away to her aunt's to have the child. It was over a year before Thomas managed to track her down, and Ann was nearly two before Martha could get away from her aunt. She was a horrible woman, insisted that Martha owed her a lifetime of slavery because she'd allowed her to have her bastard child in the house. Children are quite different when they're two," she pointed out.

"So I assume Martha's not gone back there then," Sir Anthony asked.

"No, that was the first place Thomas asked. She's just vanished. It's very odd."

As Caroline was looking confused, Beth explained about Martha's resignation after an altercation with Richard, and her inexplicable disappearance.

Little Frederick, or Freddie as Edwin was already calling him, had now gone to sleep on Beth's knee.

"I'd like to get accustomed to babies," she said wistfully, looking down at him.

"My advice is to take your time," Caroline said. "Get to know each other first. Because once a baby arrives, you'll have no time for anything else."

"Unless you hire a nurse," Anthony said.

"Yes. But I didn't want to do that, not straight away, at any rate. Your attitude is a relief, to be honest, Beth. I thought I was the only woman in the world who didn't know much about babies. I've been learning as I go along. It's fun, but exhausting, too. I though Edwin would be able to help more than he has. He really wants to, but what with the gin tax, all the argument about whether England should be paying for Hanoverian troops who are doing nothing at the moment, and now the imminent invasion, we hardly see each other."

"How is the invasion?" Sir Anthony asked, as though enquiring after the health of a mutual acquaintance.

"Still imminent, as far as I know," Caroline answered. "I'll worry about it when the French are hammering on the door. To be honest, by the time Edwin gets home he's too tired to talk about it, and I'm too tired to listen. But there was a letter from a spy at Louis' court which pretty well detailed the whole plans, and gave a list of Jacobites who have since been rounded up. A lot of troops are being mobilised, and the navy is preparing. Or is prepared, probably, by now. Oh, and the king has written to Louis to demand the removal of the Pretender's son from French soil."

"Louis will like that," Beth said.

"He did. He's written back, basically saying 'go to hell'. Something on the lines of 'you abide by your treaty with us, and we'll abide by ours with you,' you know the sort of thing. And more than that I don't know, but I'm sure you'll find out at the dinner. I thought you'd already know everything anyway, Anthony. You're normally very well-informed."

"Ah, but I've been out of the country for six months, my dear. I am completely ignorant of current developments."

"But not of how to stop babies crying. Before you go, just show me exactly what you did to bring the wind up so spectacularly."

He did, and Caroline bent over to relieve Beth of the burden of the child.

"Have you got any silver, Anthony?" Beth asked suddenly.

"Why do you need silver?" Caroline asked.

"I must give the baby some." The baronet having come up with nothing, Beth unclasped the slender chain from around her neck, and pressed it into the baby's hand. "It's a Scottish custom, very unlucky if you don't," she explained. "My mother told it to me. You'll have to take it off him straight away, though. I don't want him to swallow it."

Caroline looked at Sir Anthony, who was debating whether to don his soiled coat or put up with the cold for the short journey home. She was clearly remembering that he too had given the child a silver coin on his previous visit, saying only that it was a family custom. He smiled vacuously at her, then slung his coat over his arm, and opened the door.

* * *

To Beth's relief, not only Caroline, but also Edwin turned up for the meal. He looked tired and a little harassed, but he was there. Which was as well, when you looked at the other 'dear friends' of the Peters' that Isabella had thoughtfully included. Lord Bartholomew and Lady Wilhelmina Winter; Anne Maynard; Lydia Fortesque and her father Thomas, who Beth had met briefly once, and who Edwin spoke highly of. And an elegant man in late middle age of medium height with intelligent brown eyes, who she had never met before, but who nevertheless looked vaguely familiar, and who was soon introduced by Sir Anthony as William Barrington, Earl of Highbury.

Daniel's father.

It seemed, Isabella gushed, delighted at being able to count such a distinguished name amongst her guests, that the earl had arrived in London only yesterday, but had kindly agreed to make up the numbers. The party was informal, and Beth had already decided to seat herself between Caroline and Anthony, and opposite Edwin, if possible. Or some similar arrangement. She whispered as much to Caroline, and made sure she was in their company, firmly glued to her husband's side for the pre-dinner drink in the salon.

"Oh, Sir Anthony!" exclaimed Anne Maynard, materialising from nowhere at his side, and laying her hand shyly on his arm. "I cannot tell you how happy I am that you and your dear wife are reconciled! I must confess I felt partly responsible for your separation, having foolishly divulged that you had challenged Monsieur Monselle." Her brown eyes were genuinely pleased and embarrassed, as they passed from Beth to Anthony. He patted her arm.

"Nonsense, my dear Anne!" he trilled. "It was nothing more than a misunderstanding. Beth and I were never separated. We had a slight disagreement before the duel, that is all. She merely returned home early to conduct some business for me in Manchester. I joined her as soon as I was able. People will misconstrue the most innocent actions," he added, glancing at Lady Winter, who refused to meet his eye. She, after all, had been the main promulgator of the rumour that Beth had had an affair with King Louis and that the marriage was over.

The bell rang for dinner, and all Beth's hopes were overturned in an instant, as her husband carefully tucked Anne's hand under his elbow and led her into the dining room, leaving Beth unchaperoned. It appeared merely thoughtless of him, but it wasn't, Beth was sure, and was puzzled. Edwin was about to come to the rescue by offering her his spare arm, when a hand descended lightly on her shoulder.

"If I may have the honour?" the earl said. Reluctantly Beth surrendered her arm to him, and Caroline and Edwin walked ahead, Caroline casting a sympathetic glance over her shoulder at her friend as they went.

They were the last to enter the dining room, and just as they were about to cross the threshold, the earl held back, forcing Beth to halt as well.

"May I have a brief word, before we go in?" he said, to Beth's surprise. She had intended to politely avoid him all evening, as far as that was possible at such a small gathering, and had expected him to do the same. Instead he seemed to be set on the opposite course of action. She nodded her head in acquiescence and waited for him to speak.

"I would just like to say that I was utterly appalled by the conduct of my profligate wastrel of a son with regard to yourself. His behaviour was despicable and inexcusable."

"Yes, it was," said Beth, impressed by his bluntness, and returning it. "But he is a grown man, my lord, and should make his own apologies."

"Indeed he should, but will not. I wish therefore to apologise for him, as I must assume some responsibility for how he has turned out, being his father."

"Children are influenced, but not wholly made by their parents," she replied, thinking of Richard. "When they are adults they must take responsibility for their own actions. But I will admit, I did feel a little awkward tonight and your apology has put me at ease. Thank you."

They entered the dining room.

"I would also like to say that I feel you have made a far wiser choice in taking Anthony to husband than Daniel. He is a quite remarkable man," the earl continued.

"Do you know Anthony well, my lord?" Beth asked. Her husband had never mentioned the earl as being a particular friend of his.

"I would go so far as to say that I know him better than most people, your good self excepted, of course," he replied, leading her to the only two vacant seats left, near the top of the table, where the highest ranking guest would be expected to sit.

The first course arrived, a mutton broth, and, as is the case at most dinner parties, the conversation began, hesitantly at first, and then more enthusiastically as the half-eaten soup was removed and the second course of roast beef was served. Glasses tinkled, wine, thankfully of good quality, was poured, cutlery clattered, and the earl listened with amusement as Beth gave detailed replies to Lady Wilhelmina's carefully probing questions about her sudden return to England and subsequent time in Manchester, without revealing anything of moment at all, to that lady's frustration. The noise level grew. Lord Winter, having listened to Sir Anthony extolling the virtues of Manchester, began to expound, tactlessly and at length, about the merits of the southern towns of England over the north. Edwin and Thomas Fortesque, both MPs, seemed to be continuing a debate begun earlier that day in Parliament, and Anne and the Cunningham sisters were happily discussing curtain material, Lydia reluctantly joining them.

"Ah, that is one of the advantages of breastfeeding, Anthony. It has given me a cleavage," Caroline declared into one of those odd sudden silences that naturally punctuate any lively gathering. Edwin looked up, startled. The eyes of every male in the room rested involuntarily on his wife's bosom. She reddened. A brief unnatural silence descended on the table. During this Sir Anthony had been attempting to cut a potato, which now startled him by sliding from under his knife and skidding from his plate across the table, almost overturning Clarissa's wineglass. The previous potato the baronet had tried to halve had subsided sullenly into a pile of pale yellow slush at the first touch of his knife.

"I must say, Lord Edward, that the food tonight is remarkably…English," he said, retrieving the runaway vegetable from the damask tablecloth and returning it to the edge of his plate.

"Thank you," replied the lord. "Yes, I have finally managed to convince Isabella of the impossibility of retaining a French cook in the current climate. Why, one cannot welcome spies into one's house at any time, let alone when one is at war!"

"You thought the man to be a spy, Lord Edward?" asked the earl.

"There was no proof, of course, my lord. These people are too clever to leave evidence lying around. But the man was a Frenchman, and a Papist. And I like to think I have a nose for deception. One can recognise spies, my lord, by their very desire not to be noticed. Andre was such a man, very quiet and deferential. A sure sign that he was up to no good." Caroline and Edwin, who were aware of the baronet's brief flirtation with espionage in Rome, and the earl, who was not, all glanced at Sir Anthony.

"I would have thought modesty and deference to have been the sign of a good servant, myself," the baronet responded.

"It is difficult to explain, sir. There is a certain slyness about those involved in espionage, which one as…ah…ingenuous as yourself might fail to see. And I am proved right. The scoundrel has persuaded our plain cook to abscond with him. We have been compelled to engage another at short notice."

"Yes, Susan was an excellent cook. I am afraid the food is not up to our usual standard. I am most terribly sorry," said Isabella.

"The excellent company makes up for any small imperfections in the meal, my dear Isabella," Sir Anthony reassured her, patting her hand. "You have made a very patriotic gesture. The man would most likely have been arrested before long anyway. I hear that suspected Jacobites are being taken into custody, and Catholics are now severely restricted in their movements."

"It's quite ridiculous," snorted Thomas Fortesque. "Edwin and I were just discussing that very subject. The arrest of known Jacobites is all well and good, but persecuting Roman Catholics and other dissenters for no good reason does us no credit."

"I am surprised to hear you say that, sir, and you a Whig," said Lord Winter. "Why, it is well known that Papists are Jacobites to a man. They should all be clapped in irons, in my view."

"It is hardly surprising that Catholics look to the Stuarts to redress the wrongs done them, when Hanover persists in its bigotry," said Edwin.

"Are you inclined to the Roman faith yourself, Mr Harlow?" asked the earl.

"No, my lord," bristled Edwin, a devout Anglican. "I am inclined to religious tolerance, which is quite another thing."

"I hear you were almost seduced by the Catholics, Sir Anthony, whilst at Versailles," said Lord Edward with poorly-veiled disgust.

"Not at all," replied the baronet calmly. "I merely engaged in some interesting theological discussions with Roman priests. I will discourse with anyone, on any subject, as is widely known. I find it extremely tedious to converse only with those who hold the same opinion as myself, or in fact hold no intelligent opinion at all." He smiled meaningfully at his host.

"Nevertheless, it can be dangerous to fraternise with some sections of the community," Edward replied, oblivious.

"Only when one lives in a country which does not enjoy freedom of speech, thought and action. I was unaware that England was such a country."

"It is not, sir," put in Thomas, "providing you believe that we should be supporting useless troops in Hanover, and that we should be stirring Catholics and Tories as well to an even greater fervour to see the Stuarts restored, by exacting repressive measures against them."

"We have had a frustrating few days in Parliament," explained Edwin. "Ministers are wasting a good deal of time, in our view, arguing as to whether the author of a recent pamphlet denouncing the funding of Hanoverian troops should be hunted down and arrested, and discussing how to enforce the unenforceable Act against Catholics, when both Thomas and I, and a good many others feel we should instead be addressing the long-term implications of this action of France, who as we speak, is loading her ships with cannon, guns and men, and preparing to sail against England. In fact by now, news travelling as slowly as it does, they may well be engaged in battle."

Anne paled noticeably, and Charlotte gave a little scream of fright.

"Is it not just a feint to distract Britain while France strengthens its troops in Flanders?" asked the earl.

"That is possible. But the Pretender's son is in France, and has been seen near Dunkirk. In view of that one must take seriously the possibility that Louis means to put the Stuarts back on the throne, and act accordingly, as we are. Admirals Norris and Matthews are now in place, and ready for anything," said Thomas. "But we must address the wider issues as well. I still think that the Pretender would have less support if, instead of suppressing dissenters, we allowed them to practise their faith openly, and gave them less cause to support James and his son."

"I disagree," said Lord Winter. "One cannot guard too strongly against the perfidies of the Roman Church, which on the surface appears so attractive, and seduces the young and impressionable. And you malign our monarch. King George is far more tolerant of dissenters than the Pretender would be. At least they are not forced to recant, and tortured if they refuse."

"The Pretender has an Anglican chapel at his palace in Rome," Beth dropped casually into the conversation. "It is for the use of his Protestant servants." She looked down the table. Everyone except her husband and the earl looked deeply shocked.

"How do you know that, Lady Elizabeth?" asked the latter.

"I met an Anglican minister in Rome," lied Beth smoothly. "He told me he is employed at the Palazzo Muti. It would seem that James is more tolerant than is bruited about." She smiled, and determinedly speared a carrot with her fork.

"I don't believe it," breathed Lady Winter.

"You must be mistaken, Elizabeth," said Lord Edward patronisingly.

"Oh, it's quite true, my dears," put in Sir Anthony, as Beth's colour rose. "I heard the man say so myself. And the Anglican chapel is very tastefully appointed, quite devoid of the icons and other paraphernalia of which Catholics are so fond."

Attention now transferred to the baronet.

"Are you sure this is not just a rumour put about by the supporters of the Pretender?" asked Thomas, who had just managed with difficulty to swallow a particularly large piece of gristle.

"No, not at all. I saw it myself. Attended a service, in fact. It was most refreshing."

"Why didn't you tell us this before, Anthony?" asked Edwin.

"It quite slipped my mind. The conversation at your house

recently has been somewhat dominated by your son and heir. And quite rightly so. A divine child!" he replied serenely, seemingly unaware that he and his wife had just demolished one of the main objections to the replacement of the House of Hanover by that of Stuart. If it was true.

"You and your husband will make Jacobites of us all, Lady Elizabeth," said the earl in a low voice which was nevertheless heard by the whole table, which was still in a state of shock.

"God forbid!" declared Thomas. "If what you say is true, then I believe it to be no more than a publicity exercise by James."

"Possibly. Although you would think, if that is the case, that James would make it more widely known that he employs Anglican servants and ministers," the earl said thoughtfully.

"Clearly he has decided to do so, by inviting gullible tourists to visit the Palazzo Muti, hoping they will spread his insidious lies unwittingly," Lord Edward said tactlessly, forgetting that he was supposed to be ingratiating himself with the baronet.

"The dispute over the Stuart restoration is about more than religious tolerance, though, isn't it?" said Caroline. "It is about the divine right of kings to rule as they wish without interference, which is what James wants."

"He might want it, but do you think he would get it, if he was restored?" Sir Anthony asked.

"I doubt it, but he would certainly fight for it, and so would his supporters. We have had enough of civil war in this country, I think."

"Better the devil you know," said the earl, smiling.

"Yes. Exactly. Caroline is right. At least we know George's virtues and failings," Thomas said. His daughter sighed. She had enough of political conversation at home, and had hoped this dinner would provide a respite. But everyone else seemed fascinated, except for Isabella and her sisters, who looked confused, and worried. "But these repressive measures enacted by the king play into the Pretender's hands. George is not greatly liked, even by his supporters."

"Come, sir!" said Lord Winter, shocked. "How can you say this, when only a few days ago the merchants of London led a huge procession to St. James's and offered the king six million pounds? You speak treasonably!"

"They offered him a *loan* of six million pounds," Thomas said dryly. "No my lord, I speak honestly. It is no secret that the king is not popular with his subjects. He knows it himself. There are many who long for a more exciting court. I do not see you, my lord, or any of the aristocracy for that matter, flocking to George's entertainments. Indeed he rarely provides any. It is what he represents that we support. The king has not the kind of personality which endears men to him. Unlike the Pretender's son, who, if rumour is true, does. Many still think George favours Hanover over Britain. And his public estrangement from the Prince of Wales does not enhance his standing in the eyes of the public."

"So what you are saying," said Sir Anthony, "is that if George allowed people to worship as they wished, and allowed Tories to enjoy the fruits of their offices, perhaps they would not be so inclined to favour the Stuarts, in spite of Charles's charisma?"

"That is exactly what I am saying," said Thomas. "Contented men are rarely willing to risk their lives for a mere principle. It is only when life becomes intolerable that they are roused to rebellion. Scotland is where the main danger lies, I think, as it always has done."

"Ah, because the Scots see James Stuart as one of their own?" Sir Anthony asked.

"Partly. The Stuarts are of Scottish origin. But also because overall the Scots didn't want the Act of Union, and feel that they have not benefited from it. Many of them might feel they have nothing to lose by rising for the Pretender. And the king's hostile attitude towards his northern subjects does nothing for his popularity there. I feel that we would do better to address some of their grievances, so they feel they are prospering under George. Then they would be less likely to rebel."

Beth had by now decided that Thomas Fortesque was a man to be admired. And a man who could be very dangerous to the chances of a Stuart restoration, were his ideas to be heeded.

"Speaking of rebellions, it seems that we left France just in time," said Lord Winter, eyeing with some trepidation the pasty suet pudding sparsely dotted with raisins which had just been presented to the company by way of dessert.

"We did. The French are impounding British boats, including

the mail packet. It would be difficult now to obtain a passage home," said Sir Anthony absently. He was looking at a footman, who was heading in his direction. The man bent and whispered something to him. The baronet nodded, and the man left the room. "Although I doubt Louis is going so far as to arrest innocent tourists, as yet," he continued. "He has not, after all, formally declared war on us."

"I am sure that, no matter what the situation between France and England, Sir Anthony, you would have been unharmed," said Lady Winter acidly, still piqued by his comment in the salon. "Your lady wife enjoying such…ah…*cordial* relations with King Louis." She smiled sweetly at Beth, who smiled back, and prepared for war.

She was prevented from deploying her weapons by the surprise entrance of Duncan in full livery, who approached Sir Anthony with the deference befitting a servant, and handed him a paper, which that man scanned with a neutral expression, before nodding and dismissing his employee.

"Is it bad news, Sir Anthony?" asked Isabella. It was unusual for a servant to interrupt a dinner party, unless it was important.

"No. Well, yes, a little. It concerns a friend of mine from my university days, who is ill. I have been awaiting news of his health, and told my man to bring any message from him to me immediately."

"And is his health then deteriorating?" asked Clarissa.

"It seems so, although not as rapidly as I had feared," replied the baronet, folding the missive and putting it in his pocket. "But if you have no objections, Elizabeth and I will leave directly the meal is over. I would like to get an early start in the morning, and go to visit him. I could not possibly contemplate a long journey and a possibly traumatic visit, without a good night's sleep. My nerves are already shattered from my experiences in Paris. You will understand, of course." He smiled around the table.

Of course they all understood, except Beth, who knew what the message was about and was expecting Sir Anthony's friend to have deteriorated dramatically, not merely a little, and thought to make a two mile journey to Blackwall, not a long one. She made her farewells casually with no sense of urgency, as did her husband, who paused to exchange a few quiet words with the earl, before, to Beth's utter frustration, offering Thomas and Lydia a lift home, as it was on the way. He chatted merrily with Thomas, while Beth seemed to give her full attention to praising Lydia's hairstyle, which was one of Sarah's confections, while her mind raced through the possible implications of the letter.

They had barely entered the house before she pounced.

"What's happened?" she said, beside herself. "Are the French at Blackwall?"

"No," said Alex, throwing his coat to Duncan, and his wig on the chair in the hall. The others had all been listening for the coach, and were waiting to hear the news. "I dinna ken what's happened, but it's no' the invasion. Something's wrong, but it doesna seem urgent. Foley's in Tilbury."

"D'ye want me to go, and find out what's happening?" Angus asked, his eyes alight.

"I'll come with you," Duncan said without waiting for Alex's reply.

"No," countermanded Alex. "That is, ye can both come, but I'm going, too." He looked at Beth's disappointed face. "Wear something plain and practical," he said to her. "And cover your hair. It's your most distinctive feature."

They rode through the night, arriving in Tilbury the following morning, and were shown into the dimly lit cellar from which Gabriel Foley was temporarily conducting his business. The bull-like man was dishevelled, and had obviously slept in his clothes, but his eyes were alert as he surveyed the visitors, two of whom were unknown to him.

"Mr. Foley," said Alex. "I came as fast as I could."

"There was no need to rush, although there are things you need to know," Foley replied carefully.

"Ye ken Jim," Alex said. "And this is Murdo, another friend of mine, and a trusted one." Duncan smiled briefly at the smuggler, who assessed him before moving on to the other stranger. Beth stepped forward into the light, and his eyes widened appreciatively at sight of the startlingly beautiful young woman in the travel-stained, faded brown woollen dress.

"Mrs. Abernathy," she said by way of introduction. "I have heard a great deal about you, Mr Foley. I'm delighted to meet you, at last." She held out her hand. He took it and she grasped and shook it firmly, before he could raise it to his lips. He was shrewd, recognising what she was saying by this; she knew about him, therefore her husband trusted her. And she did not want Gabriel Foley to treat her as a feeble woman.

"I thought it time you became acquainted with my wife, Gabriel," Alex said. "You may well have to deal with me through her, if I am otherwise occupied."

She endured Foley's scrutiny calmly. After a moment he nodded, then turned away.

"Sit down. You must all be tired. Fetch some bread, cheese and ale," he called to the shadows. One of them took shape, became a man and left the room. The MacGregors distributed themselves on various items of illicit merchandise, and waited. "We have to be careful," the smuggler said. He sounded tired. "There are dragoons scattered along the coast, waiting to arrest anyone suspicious. That's why I'm here rather than at the Hope. But I can ride there in less than a day, if the French fleet's sighted." The food arrived. They ate, gratefully.

"It's miscarrying," Gabriel said suddenly, and swore, expressively, something he would never normally do in the presence of a woman. Beth was gratified.

"What's happened?" said Alex calmly.

"I'm sorry. I'm frustrated. And angry. Very angry," said Gabriel. "I'll start at the beginning. You all know what's been arranged?"

"They know everything I do," Alex said.

"Well, then. It was decided that a man we'll call 'Mr Red' was to gather together the English pilots with special knowledge of the waters around Dunkirk and sail there to join the French. Except that the bloody stupid so-called leaders panicked when they heard that all the Jacobites are being arrested, and decided in their cowardice that English pilots couldn't be trusted not to give them away. So they sent Mr Red to France with instructions to pick up some suitable pilots in the Picardy ports."

"That could work," said Duncan. "They'll ken the waters as well as the English pilots, if not better."

"Yes, it could work. But there was a problem."

"What's that?" asked Beth, chewing steadily. She hadn't eaten anything since the indigestible meal of the previous evening, and was starving.

"They insisted Red go alone, none of the rest of us being worthy of trust," Foley continued, his beefy fists clenching. "Overlooking the small but significant fact that Mr Red speaks only English, and as they didn't tell the French of their change of plan, no one was looking out for him. Can you believe it? He's just arrived back after spending three days looking for, and failing to find, the prince or any of the English contacts who had no idea he was there. It's like a bloody stage farce."

"Except it's no' funny," Alex said. "What possessed Mr. Red to agree to go to France alone, if he canna speak the language?"

"I have no idea," said Foley. "The man's a bloody idiot. The problem is that I'm now waiting to guide a French fleet up the Thames, which has no one to guide it from Dunkirk to the Hope. I'd go myself, except I'm not familiar enough with the tides in that part of France. I usually operate from Calais. I've not come to the worst of it, yet, though."

"It gets worse than this?" Angus said.

"It does. Rumour now has it that Louis is contemplating abandoning the whole venture, putting the blame on Prince Charles for riding to Paris and giving the game away to the British."

"Christ, maybe I should have knocked him on the head and dragged him back to Rome, after all," said Angus. Gabriel looked at him with curiosity.

"Jim rode to try to stop the prince coming to France, but met him en route and ended up accompanying him to Paris instead," Alex explained. "It's no' Charlie's fault. A spy at Louis' court has handed the invasion plans to the British. If Louis decides to blame the prince, it's because he's changed his mind and is looking for an excuse to back out without losing face."

"Why would he do that?" asked Beth.

"There could be all manner of reasons," said Alex. "Maybe he thinks he canna win, now the element of surprise is gone. Or maybe his ministers have convinced him that he'd be better concentrating all his forces in Flanders and Germany. It's never easy to tell what a devious bastard like Louis is thinking."

"Whatever he's thinking, it's not going to help if at the slightest hint of danger, all Charles's so-called supporters run for the hills in panic," said Gabriel disgustedly.

"Yet you're still here," Duncan said quietly, from the nest he had made in some burlap sacks. He had the ability to look relaxed and at home, wherever he was and whatever his true feelings.

"Yes, I am, Murdo. I'm not so easily scared, and neither are my men. I don't need to see James actually crowned before I come out to support him, like most of the English seem to, God rot them," Gabriel replied. "And I don't pay heed to rumours, although I listen to them. I'll not return to Hastings until I'm sure I won't be needed. The weather's getting up, though, which won't help the French chances of sailing."

"What do we do now?" Beth asked. They all looked at Alex.

"We gang away hame," he said simply. "I've been neglecting certain of my acquaintance of late. I think it's time I remedied that. I'll send ye word, Gabriel, when I have anything of interest to report."

"Would one of the acquaintances you've been neglecting be the Earl of Highbury, by any chance?" Beth asked as they rode home. She was exhausted. They had spent the daylight hours hidden in the basement room, where Alex, Duncan and Angus had shown themselves to be true Highlanders by throwing themselves down on a few sacks and going instantly to sleep, ears attuned to pay heed only to sounds which represented danger. Whereas Beth had tossed and turned on her makeshift bed of sacks and a horse blanket, kept awake by the comings and goings of the smugglers and now cursing the fact that Gabriel had clearly taken it that she wanted to be treated like a man in every respect. A woman would surely have normally been offered a more comfortable resting place.

"No, it wouldna. It was Geordie I was thinking of," said Alex. "Why do you say that?" He veered expertly to the left as her horse nudged his side. "Will ye pay heed to your riding, Beth? Ye'll have us off the road."

"Sorry," she said tiredly, pulling on the reins. "The earl said he knew you well, but you've never mentioned that you were a friend of his. And you engineered it so that I had to go into dinner with him. Why was that?"

He grinned.

"I thought ye'd noticed that," he said. "Aye, he's a friend, but I dinna see him often. I help him keep an eye on his son, on occasion. He knew I'd married, and was interested in meeting you. Particularly as ye'd captivated Daniel before me."

"Hmm," said Beth. "Is he a friend of Sir Anthony, or Alex?"

Alex looked at her.

"He is probably the best friend Sir Anthony has," he said. "Now will ye stop your blethering, woman, and look to your horse?"

After a while he gave up, and leaning over, hoisted her across onto his saddle and settled her in front of him, giving the care of her horse to Angus. Too tired to object, she drew comfort from the warmth of his body and his arm wrapped securely round her waist and after a while, lulled by the steady motion of the horse, she relaxed back into his chest, and slept.

It took several days to secure an audience with his Imperial Majesty King George the Second, or 'yon wee German lairdie,' as he was more frequently and irreverently called in the MacGregor household. The aim was to find out as much information as possible about what was happening in France, and Beth was warned to keep her temper no matter how rudely she was treated by George.

"Your job," said Alex, "is to occupy Prince William, who is likely to also be there, while I re-establish my rapport wi' Georgie."

"How do you advise me to do that?" she asked.

"Oh, I dinna ken. Use your feminine wiles. Ye did well enough last time. He was very impressed by you."

"He wanted to have sex with me," Beth said bluntly. "So, you want me to seduce Cumberland then, while you chat with George and discover what the British are up to?" she said.

"Christ, no! I'll throttle ye, an ye do that," he growled. "No, keep him talking. Let him flirt wi' ye, a wee bit, if he wants. A very wee bit," he added warningly.

Which put Beth in the enviable position of having to appear flattered whilst a man she found physically repulsive and had formed an instinctive antipathy towards, flirted with her, while her jealous husband glowered at her from the corner, and then no doubt took her to task for every gesture he found inappropriate when they got home. Wonderful. She couldn't wait.

In the event, she was not treated rudely by George. She was not treated at all, but completely ignored. And Sir Anthony had no need to re-establish his rapport, having hardly completed his bow before being seized by the arm by the king.

"*Ah, mein freund, ich habe heute sehr gute Nachrichten bekommen! Komm, ich zeige dir!*" And so saying, he dragged his friend off to the same large table she had seen on their last visit, still covered with maps and diagrams, although they were presumably not the same ones as last time, the geographical location of the current conflict differing from the previous one.

Prince William, Duke of Cumberland was, as expected, present, clad in beige, his jewelled waistcoat buttons straining over his stomach. He slid smoothly to her side the moment her husband had left it.

"Do you speak German, Lady Elizabeth?" he asked.

"No, I have not that privilege, Your Highness," she replied.

"We have received excellent news this very morning, regarding the situation with the French. Are you aware of what is happening?" he said.

Beth adjusted quickly to the fact that every comment was going to be addressed to her breasts, whose outline was clearly visible through the rose silk bodice of her court gown, in spite of the lace fichu that she had employed to cover her cleavage.

"I think everyone in the country must be aware of the terrible threat posed by the perfidious French invasion," she said. Was that too much? Apparently not. The duke laughed. His chin wobbled. His belly shook. She reflected on the fact that he was the same age as Prince Charles. She stopped her lip from curling.

"A threat no more, madam," he said. "But I will not bore you with tedious news of war. Would you care to take a stroll in the gardens? The weather is not inclement."

Sir Anthony lifted his head from the map he was perusing and shook his head minutely, although Beth had not been going to agree, anyway.

"I do not find news of war tedious, Your Highness," she replied. "What has happened? Or is it confidential?"

"No. It is not yet publicly known, but will be as soon as we have rounded up any of the remaining Jacobites waiting on the coast for the French to arrive."

Oh, God. This was going to be worse than she had envisaged, for reasons she had not envisaged.

"Do not keep me in suspense, I beg you," she pleaded, smiling coquettishly.

"Very well." He smiled, laying his podgy hand on her arm and moistening his red lips with his tongue. "The French are defeated. A report has arrived this morning from Admiral Matthews. It has been known for some time of course, that the French had assembled and provisioned a fleet at Dunkirk under Saxe, and another at Brest, under Roquefeuil. On the eighth, Roquefeuil's fleet was sighted by Matthews, who gave chase and managed, in spite of the storm that was rising, to get within three guns' shot of them by dusk. The following morning he set off to engage them, with Rear-Admiral Rowley leading the van, but he realised after a short time that the French had no intention of doing battle."

"The cowards!" exclaimed Beth.

"No, madam, their intention was to draw us away, and so leave the way open for Saxe to cross the Channel and invade, by way of the Thames, most likely. Once he realised this, Rowley then gave up chasing the French, and instead engaged the Spanish, who were supporting the French, under Admiral Navarro. The Spanish had some excellent gunners, I must admit, and they shot mainly at the masts and rigging of our ships to disable them, with the result that only nine of our men were killed, and some forty or so wounded... do you find this tedious?" He stopped.

"No, not, at all!" Beth cried, searching for the right words. "How could I find the deeds of our brave men tedious? And you explain it in such plain terms, so that even I can understand! Please continue."

"If you are sure...the Spanish were defeated, and we managed to take one of their ships, although we could do nothing with it, as all its masts were destroyed. Rowley engaged three of the French ships, but most of them kept their distance. During the night the French succeeded in recapturing the Spanish ship, although they still would not engage." Cumberland's eyes were sparkling, and Beth could see him running through the complex manoeuvres of the ships, even as he simplified it for her. He was a born soldier, that was clear, enthralled by war. He had even forgotten to speak to her bosom. "The following morning we set to chasing the French again, recapturing and firing the Spanish ship, but we could not catch them, and the weather was so bad by then that the admiral had to put into Port Mahon. Are you still following me, Lady Elizabeth?"

Yes, you condescending pig.

"I think so," she said. "It is all very exciting. But you said earlier that the French were defeated. What of Saxe's fleet, and those of Roquefeuil that you did not engage?"

"Ah, yes. If we needed proof that God is on our side, we have it now. The weather has done most of our job for us. Saxe's troops were loading at Dunkirk when a terrible storm arose, which destroyed eleven transports and countless other ships, along with all their supplies, and rendered it impossible for them to sail. Indeed, the same storm damaged several of Norris's ships, too. And some of Roquefeuil's as he sailed back to Brest. But it is now reported to be impossible for the invasion fleet to sail, although our ships are still ready for them if they do foolishly attempt to. And we have four detachments of Dragoons searching the river from London to the estuary. If they do succeed in getting any ships through, which is doubtful, they will find no one to navigate them up the Thames."

Across the room Beth saw her husband clap his hands and exclaim in joy at the ruination of all their hopes. King George had been explaining events in much more detail to Sir Anthony than Cumberland had to her, punctuating his torrent of German with stabs at the maps.

On their way home, her husband filled her in on the details, and also gave her the joyous news that the long-postponed Handel concert was to take place in two weeks, and they were invited. The coach was filled with gloom.

"Do you think it's as bad as the Elector and Cumberland have made out?" Beth said, lowering her voice.

"Yes, it probably is," the baronet replied. "I must send Angus as soon as we get back, to warn Foley about the search parties. He probably already knows what's happened, but just in case....he said the weather was getting up, and if the French fleet has been damaged, it'll give Louis the perfect excuse to call the whole thing off. I'm starting to think William was right."

"William?"

"Highbury. When he said it was just a feint to distract the British. If it was, and Charles finds out, he'll be livid. I just hope he keeps his head. But there's not much I can do about that. I can't risk going to France at the moment, and I'm probably better off here, trying to find out what I can. He has advisors there. I just hope they know how to handle him."

CHAPTER TWO

On the fifteenth of March 1744, King Louis XV officially declared war on Britain, giving as his reason that the King of England had persecuted France under the pretext of defending Austria. In Louis' opinion, the abortive invasion attempt had been successful, in that it had, as intended, diverted a great many British and Dutch troops to England to await the French attack, leaving the Low Countries vulnerable. Louis now started the redirection of his coastal troops to Flanders and Germany. Then he promised to allow the Stuart prince to gain valuable military experience by fighting with the French in Flanders if he did as he was told, which was to leave the coast, make his way incognito to the rural house of the bishop of Soissons and lie low there until sent for.

Charles Edward Stuart, being a prince of the blood royal, was accustomed to giving orders, not obeying them, and had never laid low in his life. He had no intention of doing so now, either. Instead he remained on the coast at Gravelines, raising several pertinent and uncomfortable points with Marshal Saxe regarding the failure of the first invasion, and encouraging him to attempt another. Then, when he realised this was not to be, he looked around for alternatives. Recognising that the flames of British Jacobitism were burning brightly at the moment, and not wishing to lose the impetus generated by recent events, Charles suggested sending the Irish Brigade, currently fighting for France, to Scotland. Or, if all else failed, he would go to Scotland himself, alone. The clans had assured him of a hearty welcome whenever he arrived. They at least would rise for him, he said.

His advisor, the aloof and imperious veteran Jacobite Earl Marischal, poured cold water on every exuberant suggestion.

What Charles needed at this time was empathy and tactful understanding. What he got was unrelenting gloom and defeatism. Marischal found only fault with everything Charles suggested, and expressed his doubts in the way most likely to alienate the prince. Their relationship had never been good; now it became catastrophic, his attitude bringing out all the rebellious qualities in Charles that Alex had hoped would be contained. In the midst of this, the prince discovered that King Louis had ridden off to Flanders without him, having never intended to allow Charles to fight with him. It had been a sop to keep him quiet, no more.

Turning his back on Marischal, and ignoring Louis three-times-repeated command to travel to Soissons, Charles, now justifiably convinced that the king had just been using him to accomplish his own political ends, did, finally, leave the coast. He did not, however, take quiet refuge in a country retreat as Louis wanted, but instead rode straight to Paris.

If Alex had known what was going on in France, far from thinking he would be of more use in England, he would have swum the Channel unaided if necessary to get to his prince and attempt to limit the damage. But, news travelling slowly, he was unaware of what was going on until it was too late, and was currently engaged with other matters.

"I had no idea ye hated Anne that much," he said.

"I don't hate her at all," Beth retorted. "I feel sorry for her. How could I not feel sorry for someone who has to depend on the Winters for her livelihood? This is a chance for her to escape. I'm trying to help her."

"Ye're mad," he said, with Marischal-like pessimism. "Dinna waste your time. It'll never work."

"It could," she replied enthusiastically, "if I have your help. And Caroline's. And Edwin's."

"Well then, go ahead and ask them. If they agree, I'll go along wi' ye. But they've more sense than you have. They'll say the same as me."

"Hmm. You know, it might just work," Caroline said thoughtfully. "But it won't be easy."

"Are you mad?" said Edwin, echoing his friend's words of the previous evening. The friend in question was now lolling in his favourite spot on the sofa, eating tiny strawberries from a plate by his side.

"My sentiments exactly, my dear boy," he said, chewing blissfully. "I can't believe you've managed to acquire strawberries in March, Caroline. Wherever did you get them?"

"From Aunt Harriet," she said. "She's the one with the enormous pile in Hertfordshire."

"How very uncomfortable for her, poor dear," Sir Anthony remarked, disposing of another strawberry.

Caroline shot him a withering look.

"She's the one with the enormous mansion in Hertfordshire," she amended. "And a huge hothouse. And nothing better to do with her days than force strawberries for gluttonous and vulgar acquaintances of mine to devour in March."

"Aunt Harriet didn't disown you then, when you married Edwin?" Sir Anthony asked. Caroline's extremely aristocratic family had turned their backs on their wayward relative when she had, upon reaching the age of twenty-one, blithely announced her intention to marry a mere untitled MP, against all their wishes. They had been even more annoyed when Caroline had shown complete and genuine indifference to their attitude. She was in love with Edwin, had married him, and had never had any reason to regret her decision.

"Aunt Harriet couldn't care less about anything or anyone," Caroline said. "As long as I show an interest in her exotic plants, she wouldn't care if I'd married the pope. She's very sweet, but quite mad."

"Clearly it runs in the family then," Edwin said. "You can't really think that marrying Lord Redburn off to Anne Maynard is a sensible proposition. He's a ridiculous, drunken old fool, and she's…" he trailed off, unable to think of a suitable adjective.

"Colourless," Sir Anthony supplied. "But I still wouldn't try to foist Redburn off on her, poor child."

"You're being unfair," Beth said. "The 'poor child' is the same age as you, Anthony. And he's not that bad. He's just a lonely old man who needs someone to look after him in his declining years."

"That's not what you used to think, dear heart. After all, you even went to the desperate measure of marrying me to avoid being forced into a union with him."

Beth coloured.

"Yes, I did," she said, trying to sound as though she regretted her choice. "But I'm not cut out for looking after an invalid. Anne is. Don't forget, she nursed both her parents through their last illnesses. It would make her feel wanted, which she needs. And when he dies, probably quite soon, he'll leave her stinking rich, and with a respectable widow's status, unlike her parents, who left her in penury. It's perfect. He's desperate for a wife, she's desperate for a husband. No one else will have them."

She did have a point.

"If you're so eager to marry her off, why not consider Edward?" Edwin suggested. "At least he's younger, and better-looking. And could give her a child. After all, the Cunningham estate needs an heir desperately, and Richard shows no sign of marrying."

Beth and Caroline both looked at Edwin with disgust.

"I wouldn't wish that pompous fool of a cousin of mine on my worst enemy," Beth said. "I'm trying to get her away from Lord Winter, not shackle her to a younger version of him. God, she'd just fade away completely. No, I think caring for Lord Redburn will bring her out of herself, give her some responsibility. I can take care of Anne, with Caroline's help. But I need you two to extol her virtues to Redburn, and make sure he doesn't get incapably drunk at his next ball."

"Which is in only two weeks," said Sir Anthony. "Three days after the tiresome Handel concert." He sighed dramatically.

"Don't you want to go, Anthony?" Edwin said. "There are plenty who would willingly take your place."

"Are you volunteering?" the baronet asked hopefully.

"No," came the hasty reply. "I know how dull the Court can be. You could always make an excuse though, surely?"

"One cannot refuse the monarch, Edwin," replied Sir Anthony, expressing deep shock at his friend's lack of patriotism. "Besides, Beth wishes to pursue her torrid affair with Cumberland, and who am I to refuse her anything?"

"You want to refuse your assistance in my matchmaking plans, though," Beth pointed out, ignoring his jibe about the duke.

"*Au contraire,* my love. If you wish to waste your time, far be it from me to prevent you. I agree to all you ask. I will sing the praises of Miss Maynard to the highest heavens. I am sure Edwin will assist me. But it will be a waste of time, I do assure you. Even when drunk and desperate, Redburn has never so much as noticed the invisible Anne before, let alone been inclined to propose to her."

"Would you like to make a wager on that?" said Beth, with conviction.

* * *

The plot gathered pace. Beth, visiting the Winters, wore a particularly close-fitting woollen jacket she had recently purchased, which drew, as she had hoped, a great deal of admiration from both Lady Winter and Anne, who exclaimed at length over its military cut, with its brass-buttoned mariner's cuff and tasselled frogging.

"It is quite the latest thing," Beth said, in conscious imitation of Sir Anthony. "All things military are, and of course it keeps one in mind of our brave soldiers fighting in Europe."

"It's lovely," said Anne sincerely. She would never have the courage to wear such a garment.

"Here," said Beth casually, handing her the jacket and coming to the point of the whole exercise. "Try it on."

Anne recoiled as though being offered a large and particularly hairy spider.

"Oh no, I couldn't possibly," she said. "It is too…" *Masculine* was the word that came to mind, but that would be offensive. "Small," she finished timidly.

"Nonsense. We are not dissimilar in stature," Beth said firmly. "It will pass, I think. Go on, try it on."

Anne tried it on.

"Although she's only an inch or so taller than me, she's a lot longer in the body and shorter in the leg than I am," Beth said to Caroline later. They were casually arranged on cushions on the floor, surrounded by a rainbow of silks and velvets. "She has a remarkably small waist, as small as mine, we can maybe make something of that, but the jacket was loose around the chest. It fitted perfectly on the shoulders and arms, though. She's really quite dainty."

"She hasn't got a chest," Caroline remarked candidly. "But with careful positioning of lace, we should be able to conceal that. If we can persuade her to wear heels, that will make her legs look longer. Now, what colour do you think? The burgundy? Purple? Blue?"

The two conspirators examined the materials.

"I don't know," Beth said after a while. "I never really think about what colour to wear. To be honest, in Manchester I only had two formal gowns. One of them was a hideous shade of yellow, and about thirty years out of date." She laughed. "I still remember Isabella desperately trying to think of something nice to say about it the first time I visited her, after Richard came home. Before that I spent most of my time in loose-fitting woollen dresses. They were lovely. Really comfortable." Comfort was the most important quality in a garment, to her mind. Most of her current wardrobe failed to meet the mark.

"Yet you always look the height of fashion," Caroline noted. "It must be being married to Anthony, I suppose. You wouldn't dare look otherwise."

An idea occurred to them both at the same moment. They looked at each other, and smiled.

"The emerald green," he said after a cursory glance at the fabrics. "And the silk, not the velvet."

"That was a quick decision," said Caroline suspiciously. "You're not just saying anything so you can get back to your chess game with Edwin, are you?"

"Not at all. I'm losing. And Freddie's just woken up. Edwin's walking around with him, trying to get him off to sleep again. Although the bottle of burgundy is a temptation…" Sir Anthony shrank back in mock terror at the ladies' threatening looks. "No, I know how much this ridiculous plan means to you both. The green. It will bring out the colour of her eyes. They are not really mud brown as everyone thinks, you know, but more hazel, like yours, Caroline. It's the hideous colours she wears that deaden them."

Beth looked at her friend's beautiful almond-shaped hazel eyes, and then incredulously at her husband.

"Trust me," he said.

Two days later, the silk dress now taking shape on the dressmaker's dummy, Beth paid a further visit to the Winters', where the conversation was carefully steered onto the subject of shoes.

"Really," she said, sinking gratefully into a chair. "I wish Anthony wouldn't insist that I wear such ridiculous heels." She lifted her skirt gracefully, displaying a shapely ankle and a pair of red leather shoes with a three-inch heel. "He thinks I am short."

"Oh, no," said Anne, looking at the delicate foot with admiration, and the height of the heel with horror. "You are petite, and Sir Anthony is tall. You look perfect together."

"I wish you could convince him of that, Anne," Beth replied. "You cannot believe the agony I am in half the time, just to please him. Here, put these on and take a turn around the room. You will see what I mean."

"She could hardly even get her toe in the shoe. She has the most amazingly big feet," Beth said later.

"Lk mn?" Caroline mumbled through a mouthful of pins. Beth looked at the foot placed before her for her inspection.

"Well, yes," she admitted. "They are like yours. But your feet are in proportion to the rest of you. Anne is six inches shorter than you."

"It doesn't matter," said Caroline more distinctly, having deftly pinned up the hem of the new dress. It was looking very promising. The dark green silk brought out the colour of Caroline's eyes, anyway. Beth hoped Anthony was right. "Her feet will be hidden under the dress. And if they're the same size as mine, then I have a pair of shoes she can borrow."

"I don't think even we'll be able to persuade her to wear heels," Beth said. "I've never seen anyone look so horrified at the sight of a mere shoe."

"Oh we will, believe me, if I have to strap her into them. I'm not going to all this effort for nothing."

"What's he interested in?" said Sir Anthony thoughtfully, repeating his wife's question of a moment before.

"Food," said Edwin unhelpfully. "And claret."

"And brandy," added the baronet. "And food, and more claret."

"Oh come on," said Beth, exasperated. "You're supposed to be being helpful. He must have some interests, something we can coach Anne in, so they can have at least a brief conversation before he proposes to her."

"You're very confident, aren't you?" Edwin said. "Have you told Anne what you're up to yet?"

"God, no, don't be ridiculous," said his wife. "She'd never agree, if we did. And even if we did manage to get her to the ball, she'd be a complete wreck if she thought someone was going to propose to her. She'd ruin the whole thing."

"You mean you're not going to tell her *at all?*" said Edwin, appalled.

"Gout," said Anthony suddenly. "He's always looking for cures for the gout. And all the other illnesses he thinks he's got."

"What illnesses would those be, then?" Beth asked.

"Oh, I am sorry to hear that," said Anne, strolling through the Winters' garden with Beth. "The gout is such a painful thing. My father was a martyr to it. Your friend really ought to consider a milk diet. It is quite effective, if persevered with. It involves drinking one third of milk mixed with two thirds of water, twice a day. And of course no liquor…"

"Oh dear, my friend…James… would never agree to that. You know what men are like with regard to alcohol," said Beth. "Is there nothing else?"

"Well, yes, a rub of the feet and legs with a woollen cloth before going to bed and again in the morning helps to relieve the pain. Quinine or laudanum should only be used sparingly, of course."

"I never would have thought of that," said Beth admiringly. "You are very knowledgeable about health matters."

Anne blushed patchily.

"I cared for my parents for many years," she said shyly. "It is the only thing I know anything about. I'm afraid I can add nothing to general conversation. People are not interested in discussing ailments."

"You would be surprised," replied Beth. "Now, could you recommend anything for piles?"

"She could be a physician," she informed her husband and friends that evening. "Honestly, she knows an awful lot more about illnesses than any doctor I've ever met. And where to get all the potions. And how to make up the ones you can't buy. They're made for each other, I'm convinced of it."

"I think we'd better try to steer her away from telling him about the milk diet for gout though," Caroline said. "At least until after they're married."

"I do wonder what sort of tyrants her parents were," Beth mused. "She's got absolutely no self-confidence at all. I've never met anyone so timid in my life. But she's very sweet-natured. She hasn't got a bad word for anyone. Lady Winter must find her extremely tiresome."

"I find *you* extremely tiresome, my dear," said Sir Anthony, glowering . "Did you really have to tell her I'm a martyr to piles? I'll have to remember to wince every time I sit down for the next month."

Beth smiled nastily.

"Serves you right for making fun of Caroline's poor Aunt Harriet. And eating all the strawberries, without offering me one. Now, the dress is ready, the three of us have an appointment with Sarah on the morning of the ball, and she knows what it's all about. The next step is to start praising Anne to Lord Redburn. That's up to you two," Beth said, looking at the two reluctant male conspirators. "I suggest you pay him a call tomorrow, share a bottle of wine or something, then introduce the subject of the delights of marriage."

"You'll have to tell me what they are," said the baronet gloomily. "I can't think of any at the moment."

Edwin nodded in morose agreement.

"We can't visit him tomorrow though, at any rate," he said, brightening suddenly and looking at Beth and Anthony.

"Why not?" asked Caroline.

"You two have got this musical do at St James's, haven't you?"

Now it was Beth's turn to look miserable.

"Oh, damn," she said. "I'd forgotten all about that."

Beth stood politely by the side of the Duke of Cumberland, listening with half an ear to an anecdote he was telling her about training country boys to ride horses, the rest of her mind absorbed by the forthcoming ball. What should she and Caroline wear?

They had to look as plain as possible. Beige, or grey, perhaps. She half-wished she still owned the hideous yellow affair. The dress she was wearing now, although, or perhaps because, it was the latest fashion, was hideously uncomfortable. The lace at the elbows was particularly rough. Her arms would be raw by the end of the evening. Still, at least the insane width of the skirts was keeping Cumberland several feet away from her. It was worth the discomfort for that. She realised belatedly that the duke had stopped speaking, and was waiting for her response.

"My wife would understand the need for novice cavalrymen to initially learn to ride bareback, I am sure," Sir Anthony said, coming to her rescue. "She is a most remarkable horsewoman, herself." His hand circled her arm in a seemingly affectionate gesture, his fingers tightening warningly. Concentrate. Give him your full attention.

"Are you really?" the duke said, seemingly surprised that this beautiful flower could know anything about horses.

"Yes," she replied, taking the warning on board. "It does teach you to control your mount perfectly. I learnt to ride bareback myself, in fact."

"Good God," exclaimed the duke.

"Do not be deceived by the apparent fragility of my wife, Your Highness." Sir Anthony smiled. "She is as tough as any man, in many ways. She is much like the Princess Emily."

"Emily?" asked Beth. She could think of no princesses of that name.

"My sister Amelia," explained Cumberland affectionately. "Emily is our pet name for her. She's an excellent woman, loves the hunt, riding, that sort of thing. She calls a spade a spade. Has an informed opinion on any topic of importance."

For topic of importance read military affairs. Beth wondered idly if the duke would speak affectionately of *her* if she called a spade a spade. Or an ass an ass. No, probably not. And he wasn't an ass at all, as Alex had reminded her. Just devoid of charm, which was not the same thing.

"Of course, I learnt to ride as a child, on a docile pony," she said. "It must be quite a different matter to be faced with a warhorse as your first mount. Do many recruits refuse?"

"No," Cumberland replied. Clearly no one dared to, if he was around. "It is a requirement of every soldier to face danger and obey orders without question or hesitation."

"Yet it must be terrible to be a young boy coming from a village or a farm, and to be expected to leap fearlessly onto a charger. Are many injured or killed, learning?" Sir Anthony asked.

The duke shot him a look of distaste. He did not share his father's favourable opinion of the baronet, finding the paint he wore ridiculous. One would think the man a molly, were he not married. Perhaps he was anyway.

"Yes, some are hurt," he said indifferently. "But one should not enlist, if one is a coward. The army soon sorts the wheat from the chaff."

Poor boys. Sir Anthony made his excuses and drifted off in search of Lord Edward. He had managed to secure his cousin-in-law an invitation for this evening, to the lord's delight and gratitude, but he needed to be carefully monitored, if he was to make a favourable impression.

"The concert was quite wonderful, very stately," Beth said, changing the subject before the duke could continue expressing his contempt of fearful country boys, who deserved sympathy rather than derision, in her view. "Mr Handel is very talented. The kettledrum was particularly rousing."

"Indeed. Of course the *Dettingen Te Deum* was composed to celebrate my father's victory last year, in the battle of the same name."

Beth sighed inwardly, smiling up at the podgy prince. Every conversation was steered with unerring accuracy back to war. She gave in to the inevitable.

"In which of course you played no small part yourself, I believe, Your Highness. Are you planning to lead your forces in the Low Countries this summer?" she asked. She might as well try to find out something useful.

"Of course my father and I would be delighted to. But the threat from the Pretender's son is not yet over. We must look to our own shores as well."

"Really?" she said, trying to sound worried rather than hopeful. "You told me the French invasion force had been defeated. Are they planning another attempt?"

"No, I do not think so. Louis is moving his troops away from the coast. But the Pretender's son has not returned to Rome. In fact our informants tell us he is still at or near Dunkirk. We must therefore assume he is plotting some action of his own. A landing in Scotland seems most likely. If I had my way…" He hesitated, and she wasn't sure whether he wondered if he was boring her, or had been about to commit an indiscretion.

"Don't leave me in suspense, I beg you," she said sincerely. "What would you do?"

"What should have been done after the '15 rebellion," he replied, seeing she was genuinely interested. Quite a remarkable woman. He warmed to her. "My grandfather was far too magnanimous in dealing with the rebels then. They should have been crushed, not given pardons and allowed to continue their treasonous plottings. The whole country is a hotbed of Jacobitism."

"Yet are not several Scottish regiments fighting for His Majesty?" she pointed out. "Pulteney's and Campbell's, for example?"

He beamed down at her. She did know her stuff.

"Yes, you are quite right. But they are in the main lowland regiments. I should not have said Scotland as a whole, but rather the Highlands. The Highlanders are illiterate lawless barbarians, operating to their own ridiculous savage codes, looting and massacring each other on a whim. It is high time they were taught the ways of the civilised world, and brought in line with the rest of Britain."

"Although if they are massacring each other on a whim, surely if left alone they will solve the problem by exterminating themselves?" she commented innocently.

"Yes, if they didn't breed like rabbits, they most likely would. And if they did not persist in their support of the Stuarts, it would probably not be worth the cost of sending an army to pacify them."

"You plan to lead an army against them, then?" she said.

"No, it is not possible at the moment. Our forces are all committed in Europe. But if I have my way, once the war is over we will have to look closely at the problem of North Britain."

"God, the man's insufferable!" she exploded later, at home. "I've never known anyone so sure of himself. He knows everything.

I'm sure he believes he can walk on water. He's unshakable."

"Ye didna try to shake him, did you?" said Alex.

"Of course not. I'm supposed to be an admirer. No, I just fluttered my eyelashes and looked enthralled while he insulted my countrymen and told me of all his brave deeds at the front, which he hopes to repeat at the earliest opportunity. I wish him luck, and I hope the man who shot him at Dettingen repeats his brave deed as well, but aims a little higher next time."

Duncan smiled, and handed her a glass of brandy. Alex reached down her back and undid her laces.

"Thanks," she said to both of them, deftly collapsing her hoops and trapping them under her armpits so she could sit down, almost disappearing altogether in a billowing cloud of lilac silk. She pushed it down impatiently. "I shouldn't drink this, really," she said, taking a mouthful. "I've had enough already tonight. But I deserve it, I think. He tested my acting skills to the limit. I don't know how I kept my temper."

"Ye did verra well," Alex said sincerely. "I was proud of ye."

She smiled.

"Thank you. But I doubt I can keep it up for much longer. I can't stand the man, Alex. Please tell me I don't have to see him again. He makes my skin crawl. Do you know you're an illiterate savage, by the way?" she said to Duncan, who had stopped reading a copy of *The Iliad* to pour her brandy.

"I couldna care less what the German lairdie's son thinks of me," he replied amiably. "Myself, I think it isna a bad thing when the enemy underestimates you. He's going tae feel an awfu' fool when he finds out he and his father have been taken in by one of those illiterate savages and his wife."

Beth hadn't thought of it like that. It made her feel a lot better.

"Aye," said Maggie. "As long as he finds out after James is on the throne and no' before."

"If we all continue to do as well as we are, there's no danger of that," replied Alex. "I'm sorry though, Beth, I canna promise that you'll no' see him again. He likes you. And you're finding out useful information."

"His opinion of my kinsmen, and what he intends to do about it," she said. The other useful, relieving thing she'd found out was that Cumberland was in no way another Henri. This enemy, at least, was easy to hate. She did not mention this.

"Aye, but other stuff too. Like the fact that he and Geordie intend to go back to Europe as soon as they can. If we find out exactly when, we can let Charles know in advance. If he can persuade the French to assist him again after the recent mess, the best time to do it would be while the Elector and his son are abroad. But there is something else ye need to bear in mind, Beth."

"What's that?" she asked.

"Some of what you said about the duke applies equally to Charles. He's also over-confident, and would be very surprised if more than his shoes got wet when he was halfway across the lake. It's a common fault among princes. The difference is that Charles has the looks and charisma to carry it off, and Cumberland doesna."

She kept in mind what he said. But she didn't believe him, not then.

The concert over, attention reverted back to the imminent ball and the crown of all their matchmaking hopes. Or Beth and Caroline's, anyway. Their spouses were far more doubtful that the enterprise would succeed.

"Seeing as you managed to worm your way out of visiting Lord Redburn the other day," Beth said to Sir Anthony as he was assisting her on with her cloak on the afternoon of the ball. "You'd better both do a good job this evening. And don't let him get falling-down drunk."

"If your enterprise fails, my sweet," replied her husband. "It will not be due to any failing on mine or Edwin's part. We will play it to the hilt, I assure you."

"You know, I really think that Sir Anthony is starting to exert a positive influence on his wife, at last," Lady Winter was saying at the same moment, sipping tea at Isabella's. "She has visited us numerous times in the last weeks, and has shown a great interest in clothing and hairstyles and other subjects far more befitting a baronet's wife than her former interests. She is cultivating quite a friendship with Anne, too. They are at this very moment attending Miss Browne's establishment, in preparation for the evening's entertainment at Lord Redburn's."

"Do you think she was perhaps shocked by the dreadful occurrence in Paris?" Isabella asked.

"I think Sir Anthony was more shaken by that, poor thing," said Lady Winter. "It must be terrible to kill a man by accident."

"Indeed, he reminds me of my poor dear Frederick," sighed Charlotte.

Her companions stared at her. They had all known poor dear Frederick, and someone less like the baronet would be hard to imagine. Diminutive in stature and personality in life, he had been elevated to greatness only in his widow's mind.

"In what way, Charlotte?" asked Clarissa kindly, before Lady Winter could say something tactless.

"He also abhorred killing of any sort. And he was once challenged to a duel, in his youth."

"Was he?" said Lady Winter, wondering if he had perhaps stood on a box to fight his challenger. "What happened?"

"I don't know," replied Charlotte sadly. "He would not talk about it. He said duelling was not a fit subject for feminine ears."

This was most unsatisfactory, thought Lady Winter. One should not embark upon a potentially interesting story unless one could finish it.

"Yet he rode to hunt on his little horse, did he not? He could not have abhorred killing that much," she retorted spitefully.

Charlotte had never thought about the connection between the sport of hunting, and killing, before. She fluttered, confused.

"Perhaps Beth has realised the consequences of her flighty actions," Isabella interposed hurriedly, "and has been persuaded to behave in a more restrained manner. She did have a rather free childhood. And Sir Anthony is such a refined man. It would be impossible to live with him for any length of time and not be influenced by him."

This was true, although she was not being influenced in quite the way that Isabella envisaged. Beth was, of necessity, learning the arts of duplicity and manipulation, and was currently attempting to use them in as altruistic a way as possible. Anne, having been manipulated into a chair at Sarah's slowly flourishing beauty house, was gazing shyly at herself in the looking glass.

"It's amazing!" she said breathlessly, raising a timorous hand to the shining brown confection of hair piled elaborately on top of her head, about a third of which was her own, the rest consisting of padding and hairpieces. But it *appeared* to be all her own, which was the main thing. "How did you do it?" she asked.

With a great deal of skill and effort, Sarah's expression said.

"It is not difficult, when one has such lovely raw material to work with. Your hair is very lustrous." *And thin, and mousy coloured.* "Now," she continued, "we must see what we can do to enhance your beauty."

"Oh, I could never make any claims to beauty," Anne said. "Indeed, Mama always said she could never understand where my plainness had come from, as both she and her sister were quite lovely."

Beth could have killed Mrs Maynard on the spot, were she not already dead.

"Papa said it was a blessing that I was ugly, because of course, both being infirm, they needed someone to look after them and my lack of looks ensured that I would not be tempted away from my duty by a procession of suitors." There was no trace of sadness or self-pity in Anne's voice. She was merely stating facts, had accepted her fate as an ugly spinster. *Well, she can just unaccept it,* the three women standing around her thought.

Sarah reached for the glass pots in which she kept her cosmetics.

"Oh no!" cried Anne. "I never wear paint. Great-uncle Bartholomew says that only harlots wear paint."

"I do not intend to use it in the way your uncle means," Sarah said, tipping two small carmine balls into a dish and expertly pulverising them to powder with a spoon. "Excessive use of paint only makes you look ridiculous." She caught Beth's eye and repressed a laugh with difficulty. Sir Anthony *did* look ridiculous. "But a little subtle use of creams to bring a becoming colour to the cheeks and lips and enhance the beauty of your eyes is a different matter altogether. If you do not like it, you can wash it off immediately."

"Well, I don't know," wavered Anne.

"Your eyes are a lovely shade of hazel," continued Sarah, adding a quantity of pomad and briskly stirring. The powder slowly dissolved into the wax and rosewater mixture, producing a smooth crimson cream. The three women watched, fascinated. "What colour is your gown for the evening?" Sarah asked.

"Brown," said Anne.

"Green," said Caroline and Beth together.

Anne looked up at them, perplexed.

"It was to be a surprise," Beth said. "But you might as well know now. We have purchased a dress for you. It is a present. For your birthday."

"But my birthday is not until July," Anne said. "I couldn't possibly accept such a gift. I have not the means to reciprocate..."

"You had better take it up with Anthony then," said Beth, knowing Anne would never have the temerity to tackle him. "He bought it, and will be most disappointed if you reject his kind gesture."

Crushed by the formidable army ranged against her, Anne subsided, defeated. So defeated that when she later tried on the beautiful green dress with its gold lace trimming, she uttered barely a murmur when it was discovered that the hem was exactly three inches too long, and there being no time to alter it, Caroline helpfully produced a pair of soft green leather shoes with heels of exactly three inches. Anne slipped them on without complaint, and engaged with looking in the mirror, missed the twin triumphant expressions on Caroline's and Beth's faces. The final test was yet to come. What would a masculine eye make of her?

"Bloody hell!" said Edwin, as Anne gingerly made her way down to the Harlows' hallway, terrified of plummeting headlong down the stairs in the unaccustomed heels.

"My darling Anne, what a vision you are!" trilled Sir Anthony, as Edwin coloured under his wife's glare. "You look quite beautiful."

She looked down, blushing, fingering the expensive silk of her dress with reverence.

"Oh, Sir Anthony, I really cannot..." she began.

"I am deeply honoured that you agreed to accept my small gift. It becomes you so, and brings out the colour of your eyes to perfection." He threw an I-told-you-so smirk at his wife, who smiled back. He was right. Anne's eyes *were* hazel. But the final victory would be hers and Caroline's. She was sure of it. Edwin's reaction had told her that.

So did the response of everyone at the ball who was already acquainted with Anne, when they arrived. Beth had willingly surrendered her husband's arm to her protégée, knowing that if Anne were to suddenly panic or try to flee under the attention she was bound to receive, he not only had the tact, but also the strength to restrain her and soothe her, without causing a scene.

Once she was safely ensconced in the room, and the initial stunned reaction of her acquaintance had subsided, Sir Anthony and Edwin abandoned the women, and as promised, retired with Lord Redburn.

The evening wore on. Anne, smothered in compliments and unaccustomed attention, blossomed. Her small eyes, made to look larger by Sarah's skill, aided by a few drops of atropine, shone. Her thin lips, made more full by the expert application of rouge and gloss, smiled happily. She looked, not beautiful, her mother had been right in that she could never be that, but attractive. Definitely attractive.

At precisely one a.m., an hour earlier than normal, Lord Redburn made his appearance. His cheeks were flushed and he limped when he walked, but that was due to the gout and high blood pressure rather than inebriation. Sir Anthony and Edwin, impressed by the herculean efforts of their wives, had clearly played their parts to perfection. The lord made his way directly to the trio. The ladies stood and curtsied as he approached.

"You are already acquainted with my wife and Lady Elizabeth Peters," Edwin said, thereby making sure Redburn knew to which lady he was to address his attentions. "Allow me to introduce Miss Anne Maynard." She curtsied again, blushing scarlet. Lord Redburn beamed, but did not speak. It was clear he found her attractive, but not overly so. *Really, he ought to look in a mirror,* Beth thought crossly. Why did ugly men think they would be attractive to beautiful women? There was a silence.

"Miss Maynard has only recently entered society, my lord," said Beth. "She is living with her relatives, Lord and Lady Winter, following the tragic death of her parents. She nursed them both for many years, through a number of illnesses. Including the gout."

"Really?" Lord Redburn said, looking at Anne with new interest. "And what means did you employ to relieve the symptoms?"

"Well, we found the milk and…" Anne began.

"Miss Maynard told me that briskly rubbing the affected limbs with a linen cloth was most efficacious," Beth interrupted hurriedly.

"A woollen cloth," Anne corrected timidly. "Yes, Papa found it brought him relief from the pain, as it helps to dissipate the humours, bunches and knots, which otherwise become fixed in the joints."

"Really?" said Lord Redburn again, offering her his arm. "You must tell me more. Why don't we take a stroll? The gardens are well lit, and I am sure you will not mind if we walk slowly."

She took his arm.

"Oh, no, my lord," she said. "I often used to accompany my father. A little exercise is of course good for the circulation, and…"

They wandered off sedately, arm in arm. Beth waited until she got home to do a triumphant and credible approximation of the Highland fling, if an amused Angus was to be believed.

The next morning the crested carriage of Lord Redburn was to be seen outside the London residence of Lord and Lady Winter. And again, two days later.

"They aren't actually married yet," Edwin protested. "Wasn't the wager only if they married?"

"Stop splitting hairs, Edwin. You're not at Westminster now," Caroline said. "He's proposed, she's accepted. The wedding is in June. We won. Give in and pay up. Now."

"Better do as she says," Sir Anthony sighed. "I think we must accept defeat on this one, and seek a more sure thing for our next wager."

"I will never make another bet with you two again," said Edwin, depositing five sovereigns into his wife's waiting hand. "I'm shocked by your deviousness, the pair of you. I don't know why the king doesn't pack you both off to Europe directly. Between you, I'm sure you could persuade Frederick of Prussia to give up his claim to Austria, and stop the war overnight."

"I must confess though, that I am not sorry you won the bet, my dears," Sir Anthony said to the two grinning women. "You were right. They are remarkably well suited."

Edwin watched the victors as they retired with their spoils.

"Just pray they never let women into Parliament, Anthony," he said. "The day they do, we men are doomed."

"We are already, dear boy," the baronet replied, eyeing his wife with admiration. "We let them into our hearts, and that's a far more dangerous place."

Sarah was also happy that her former mistress had won her bet, and that she had subtly spread the news that it was Miss Browne who had performed the amazing transformation of Anne Maynard. She was so inundated with customers that within a month she had to take on an assistant, and was contemplating the happy prospect of looking for larger premises.

CHAPTER THREE

August 1744

"Oh, that's nice," said Beth.

"What is?" asked Angus. "For God's sake, if it's something nice, share it with us. There's no' much that is at present."

Angus's uncharacteristic gloom was occasioned by the latest news filtering through from Paris, where Prince Charles was still resolutely residing against the wishes of the French King, who, as Charles's cause was of no current use to him, wanted nothing more than to be rid of the embarrassing Stuart prince. Vague promises had been made and broken; Charles had initially been told that his requirement to remain incognito would be lifted in June, and then no later than the end of July, then that it must continue a while longer. The prince was not stupid: he no longer believed that he would be allowed to serve in Louis' forces. Neither did he feel that he should bow his neck to the will of France, as his father's frantic letters from Rome kept advising him to do. In his view he had been treated badly by Louis.

And not only in his view, but also in the view of most of the royal families of Europe, his followers in Scotland and elsewhere, and even the pope, who tried never to take sides between Catholic monarchs. Forced to negotiate with Louis through the minister least sympathetic to Jacobite affairs, Philibert Orry, Comte de Vignory, Charles expressed his frustration by attending a series of high-profile balls and parties in Paris, making almost no effort to mask his identity, eliciting sympathy for his plight among the elite of France, and generally getting up Louis' duplicitous nose.

The reason for the current pessimism in the MacGregor

household was because although the prince's attitude was understandable, alienating the monarch of the country most likely to support your family's restoration was not the best of ideas. The latest news was that John Murray of Broughton, who Alex and Beth had met briefly in Rome, had now gone to Paris to discuss the possibility of a Scottish rising, a plan to which Alex was vehemently opposed, unless it was accompanied by substantial French support, which did not seem likely at the moment.

Beth looked up from the letter she had been reading to see Angus, Iain and Maggie expectantly awaiting this 'nice' news. At that moment, Alex and Duncan joined them, Alex freshly scrubbed clean of makeup, and both of them stockingless and barefoot.

"What's amiss?" said Alex immediately.

"Nothing," replied Maggie. "Beth has received some good news, that's all."

"Have you?" said Alex, smiling and coming to squash himself between Angus and Maggie on the sofa. "What's that, then?"

Beth felt awkward at the triviality of the news which had caused her earlier comment, in view of the eagerness now surrounding her.

"Em…well, it's nothing important, only that Jane and Thomas have offered Mary and Joseph the use of their house for their wedding feast."

"Better than a stable," Duncan commented. Beth pulled a face.

"I don't think they'd thank you for a comment like that," she said. "They must have heard them all by now. It's nice because they're limited as to where they can go, with them and many of their guests being Catholics. Both Mary and Joseph's landlords are Anglicans. They might turn a blind eye to their tenants' faith, but they'd never agree to them holding a party. Particularly in the current climate." The Act restricting the movements and activities of Catholics, revived the previous year, was still in force.

"Aren't Jane and Thomas Anglicans?" Alex asked.

"Yes, but they're very open-minded, I've already told you that. They know I'm Catholic. Graeme's Episcopalian, and so is John. Grace and Martha are Presbyterian. We were a real mish-mash. It made for very interesting conversation. But I'm sorry, my news was only really nice for me. It doesn't concern the rest of you at all. The wedding's in two weeks, so I'll have to leave next Wednesday if I'm to be sure of being there in time."

"It concerns me," said Alex. "I was included in the invitation too, was I no'?"

"Yes," said Beth. "Or rather Sir Anthony was. But I didn't think you'd want to come."

"Why ever not, my dear?" he replied in the baronet's affected tones. "Sir Anthony is well-known for his non-partisan attitudes. A Catholic wedding attended by Anglicans, Episcopalians and Presbyterians would be just the thing! In fact," he continued, reverting to his own rich Scottish accent. "I was thinking, if it's acceptable to everyone, tae combine a trip to the wedding wi' a wee journey home. I'm after thinking it's about time my wife became acquainted with her clan."

"Whether that's a good idea or no' depends on who's included on this wee journey home," said Iain.

"Aye. Well, Sir Anthony will certainly need both his personal manservants," he said, nodding to Duncan and Angus. "And a footman, in case any doors need opening. And it wouldna be fitting for my wife to travel wi' only men for company, so I suppose Maggie'll have to come along. We'll shut the house up for a month or so. We can use the wedding as an excuse to leave, and once that's over we can head officially north to somewhere near the border, and then Sir Anthony can disappear for a while. I can get news as well from home as here, maybe even easier, as there's nae chance of an English invasion at the minute, but a considerable likelihood of a Scottish one."

Angus leapt to his feet, dragging Maggie from the sofa and spinning her round the room in a joyous little dance.

"I think we can say that the news was nice for all of us after all, Beth," he said, beaming.

"Aye, mebbe," said Iain, trying unsuccessfully to scowl. "But it doesna give ye the right to make free with my wife, ye wee gomerel. Leave her be."

Angus ignored him, completed his turn round the room, bowed formally and escorted Maggie courteously back to her seat.

"We'd best start packing, then, had we no'?" he said, blue eyes sparkling.

They set off the following week, Sir Anthony, Beth, and her maid Margaret in the coach, Iain acting as coachman, and Angus and Duncan following on behind with a cart laden with provisions and gifts, ostensibly for the lucky couple, but in reality destined to continue to Scotland. With one or two exceptions.

"Oh, I can't believe it!" cried Mary, upon opening Sir Anthony and Beth's wedding present. Folded carefully in layers of tissue was a full tea set in green and white Sevres porcelain. There were also more practical gifts; bedding, pans, and kitchen utensils. But this was the one Beth had chosen carefully, as a personal present for her friend, who loved the expensive beverage, but rarely got to drink it. At the bottom of the box was a pound of the finest Bohea tea. Mary gave a little cry of delight, and lifted a cup from its wrappings, handling it with the utmost reverence.

"Now you don't have to borrow a tea set from your employer any more when guests call," Beth said.

"I won't have an employer from Monday," Mary replied, her gaze still firmly fixed on the delicate cup. "Mrs Chesters believes most firmly that a married woman's job is to stay at home and look after her husband."

"Quite right too. I expect my meals on the table on the dot when I come home, or there'll be trouble," said Joseph with mock severity. Beth had met him for the first time earlier that day, and had liked him immediately, sensing that his affection for her friend was genuine. Mary pulled a face at her beloved.

"I told her that he was quite used to looking after himself, and that I could continue to work for her until I had my first child, but she wouldn't change her mind. It's ridiculous."

"Will you be able to manage?" Beth asked.

"Yes," she said. "Thanks to your generosity, my lord." She smiled shyly at the baronet, quite overcome by the idea of having a titled personage at her wedding. Although she had invited him, she had not really thought he would condescend to actually attend her modest affair.

"Please, my dear, I am not a lord, and have no wish to be," he replied. "And if you stand on ceremony with me all weekend, you will most certainly spoil your happy occasion, and mine. I intend to let my hair down a little at this merry affair, being far from the Capital and gossip, and would far prefer it if you stop reminding me of my title. Anthony is my name, and you will be doing me the utmost service if you address me by it."

She tried. She really tried, but did not succeed fully until the following evening, when much the worse for several glasses of wine. The wedding service had been conducted clandestinely by Father Kendal, witnessed only by Mary and Joseph's Catholic friends. Alex had declined to attend, pointing out that he would not be able to make the correct responses without arousing suspicion, and that Mary would be worried that he felt out of place.

"They're a lovely couple," he said. "I want them to enjoy the ceremony, without worrying about their pseudo-aristocratic guest."

Instead he sat with his brothers and Iain, later joined by Graeme and Thomas, chatting and lending a hand to move tables, chairs and other furniture when required, while the non-Catholic women ran around preparing the substantial wedding feast, which was laid out in one of the two rarely used reception rooms.

The subsequent dancing was held in the other room, and was a very jolly, if somewhat cramped affair, with Sir Anthony and Beth demonstrating the menuet they had danced at Versailles, and Angus and Duncan later leading Beth and the blushing bride in a Scottish reel, while Iain scraped merrily away on the fiddle he had wrested from its owner, who was providing the music for the evening, but knew no Scottish numbers.

Wine flowed freely and Beth took Angus to one side, warning him that Grace, who was quietly falling under his spell, was a good girl and if he did any more than dance with her, she'd make sure he never did anything again, with anyone. He did not abandon her for alternative prey after this warning as he could have done, there being several unattached ladies present who would have laid all their favours willingly at his feet. Instead he continued to lavish attention on Grace, to her delight, behaving like a perfect gentleman and leaving her at the end of the evening feeling like the most beautiful woman in the world, but most definitely unsullied.

"Oh, I cannot remember when I have been so happy!" Mary said to Sir Anthony and Beth, as the evening drew to a close. She seemed unconcerned by the fact that there was little chance of her union being consummated this night, as the groom, brown hair tousled and handsome face flushed from dancing and wine, had unwisely embarked upon a drinking wager with Angus and Iain. Judging by the state of him at the present moment, and Angus's reputation, Joseph would be spending his wedding night under the table. Still, the couple had many more nights to spend together, but the wager with Angus and Iain could not be repeated. They were leaving in the morning.

"It has been a wonderful occasion, my dear Mary," agreed Sir Anthony. "And no doubt bodes well for your marriage. Joseph is an excellent fellow."

"And thanks to you and Beth, Anthony, we have not had to wait any longer. I thought we would never be able to save enough to marry."

"And I thought you would persist in treating me like the king all night. But at last you have addressed me as Anthony, without a Si..or my Lo…before it. Thank you, my dear."

"Ah, now," she said, swaying a little. "As for treating you like a king, that would depend on which king you are speaking of."

"Is there more than one?" asked Beth, who was equally tipsy. "A German idiot may be wearing the crown, but that does not make him the king."

Mary raised her glass, slopping wine carelessly on the floor in the process.

"A toast to King James!" she cried. Across the room, Graeme also raised his glass, along with several others. His eyes flickered to Angus, whose hand had moved automatically upward, before he remembered where he was and disguised his gesture by pretending to admire the ruby glow of the wine in the candlelight. Graeme noted this, then looked closely at Sir Anthony. And then back at Angus.

Sir Anthony gently took Mary's hand and straightened the glass.

"I think I will leave you to your toasts," he said smilingly, and, making his way across the room, caught Iain neatly as he fell sideways off his chair, lowering him carefully to the ground. The remaining two competitors eyed each other across the table. Sir Anthony looked from Joseph's drooping grey eyes to Angus's lucid, wide-awake blue ones.

"Be gentle with him, Jim," he advised, before leaving the room and making his way to bed.

By the time Beth decided to join her husband, Joseph was indeed settled under the table for the night, and several other men had joined him, a hard floor seeming a better option than the walk home in the rain. Graeme intercepted her in the hall, taking the candle off her before she could set fire to herself.

"Here," he said gruffly. "I'll see you to your room."

She took his arm gratefully, aware that she had drunk more than was perhaps wise, certainly a lot more than she normally drank in mixed company. She stumbled on the landing, and he transferred his arm quickly to her waist, narrowly stopping her from falling on her knees.

"Thank you," she said, giggling a little and regaining her balance with difficulty. "Goodnight, Graeme."

"Beth, how drunk are you?" he said suddenly, seriously.

She tried to focus on him, vaguely aware that there seemed to be something wrong, and forced herself to concentrate, pushing away the alcoholic haze a little.

"Pretty drunk," she admitted. "But not incapably so. Not quite, anyway. What's wrong?"

"You're leaving in the morning. I doubt I'll get a chance to talk to you alone again. Are you all right, lass? Are you sure of this man you're married to?"

"I have never been more sure of anyone in my life," she said, enunciating each word with exaggerated care. The pattern on the rug shifted a little to the side, then back again. She blinked several times, but when she looked back at it, it was still moving. "Why do you ask?" she said, forcing her mind back to the subject in hand.

"He's not what he seems, Beth. I don't know what he is, and he seems nice enough on the surface, but...I'm worried about you, all the more because you're so taken with him."

She laughed suddenly, joyously, then hiccupped, putting a hand to her mouth.

"You're right, I am." She grinned. "And he's taken with me, too. Don't worry about me, Graeme. I've never been happier. Alex is the most wonderful man I've ever met. He'll look after me, really he will."

Graeme watched her as she weaved her way into the bedroom, and then watched some more. Then he made his way slowly to his room, where he sat sleeplessly until the morning, worrying.

"Are you angry with me?" Beth said to her husband as they clattered along the road the following morning. She couldn't remember how she had got to bed last night, and her head was aching horribly, but at least she was not alone in that. Duncan and Maggie both seemed somewhat delicate, and Iain was positively green. Only Angus, damn his soul, was unaffected, smiling cheerily and leaping up onto his horse without giving the slightest indication that he had drunk more than any of the others the previous night.

"No, *a ghràidh*," said Alex after a delay. He had been thinking about Graeme. On the surface his farewell to Sir Anthony had been friendly, normal, but there had been an obvious reluctance to part with Beth, and he had felt the gardener's eyes burning into his back as he had climbed into the carriage. He dismissed Graeme from his mind, with an effort. "Why would ye think I was angry with ye?" he said. He couldn't wait to get to Carlisle and be rid of this disguise. At least he could drop the accent, though, with Iain driving the coach.

"You know, drinking a toast to James, and calling George a German idiot. It was a bit indiscreet. I'm sorry."

"Aye, but it didna do any harm. After all, all your friends here ken well that you're a supporter of James. Now they think that I'm an indulgent husband, who doesna mind who ye support. It's certainly enhanced Sir Anthony's reputation in their eyes, and didna compromise me. That's why I didna join you in a toast, much as I wanted to. Christ, I canna wait to be home!" he burst out suddenly.

"How long has it been?" Beth asked.

Alex thought.

"Over a year, now," he said. "I paid a flying visit there just before I proposed to ye, but I havena had the chance since. Sometimes the hardest thing about being Sir Anthony is having to be away from Scotland for long periods. I'll be so happy when this is all over, and I can go back to stay. D'ye think you'll feel at home in Scotland?" he asked. His tone was casual, but she knew how important her answer was to him. Nevertheless, she would not insult him by lying.

"I don't know," she said. "But I'm willing to give it a chance."

"Would you rather live in Manchester, d'ye think?"

"How can I know that until I've seen the alternative?" she pointed out logically. "But even though most of my friends live in Manchester, and I'll want to visit them regularly, I still have a powerful incentive to like Scotland, and to want to make my home there."

"Your mother's blood," he said.

"No, you fool," she answered, looking askance at him. "You. And all the rest of my MacGregor clan, if they're as wonderful as the ones I've met so far."

The fool grinned like one, and leaned across to kiss her, thoroughly.

"And if you tell the swollen-headed Angus that I said he was wonderful, I'll deny it, and kill you," she finished a little breathlessly, her face liberally smeared with white paint.

After Carlisle, although Beth was still in severe danger of being kissed regularly by her increasingly buoyant husband, there was no longer any risk of being daubed with makeup, as Alex had finally and ecstatically abandoned both Sir Anthony and his coach, neither of which would be seen again for some six weeks, the latter being stored safely away, and the former now riding at Beth's side in plain woollen breeches and shirt, and a well-cut, but sober coat. His wife and companions were similarly attired in practical clothes, as befitted a gentleman of modest means and his family. Beth's memorable hair was decently covered, her dress, thankfully, comfortable rather than fashionable.

This was the transitional stage. Although no longer the foppish Sir Anthony, Lady Elizabeth and servants, neither were they the MacGregor chieftain and his family. That would have to wait until they actually arrived in MacGregor territory. Their plaids remained safely tucked away in their saddlebags. But the anticipatory mood of elation that infused all the Scots once they crossed the border did not leave Beth unaffected, although as they picked their way along roads and then lanes, and then finally across narrow tracks, she became increasingly nervous.

"What have you told them about me?" she asked without

preamble on the third day in her mother's native land. The scenery was lovely, the mountains purple and yellow with heather and gorse, the slopes thickly wooded. They were not far from Loch Lomond now, Angus had said merrily on waking that morning, unknowingly striking fear into his sister-in-law. That was where the MacGregors were currently making their home, in the thickly wooded terrain on the northern side of the loch.

"Nothing," said Alex, knowing to what she was referring. She had been unusually quiet and thoughtful all morning.

"Nothing?!" she echoed.

"Well, they ken your name, and that your mother was a MacDonald of Glencoe."

She waited, until it became apparent he wasn't going to add any more.

"Is that all?" she said.

"Aye. I want them to make up their own minds. But they'll be inclined to like ye anyway, as you're my wife. Dinna fash yourself, Angus and Duncan like ye well enough, there's no reason why the others shouldna."

"He's right," agreed Duncan, reining in beside Beth. "It's hard no' to be impressed by a lassie who dirks ye the first time she sets eyes on ye, and throws herself wantonly at ye the second."

"So what you're suggesting is that on arriving at the MacGregor enclave I should lay waste to the clansfolk with a broadsword, and then seduce all the survivors?"

Duncan considered her suggestion with due gravity.

"They'd no forget ye for a long time, anyway, an ye did that. And ye'd certainly be accorded a reception of some sort, that's for certain," he said.

"Aye, and if the cuckolded wives didna finish you off, I would," said Alex. "Just be yourself, that's all."

They all rode along quietly for a time, Alex, Beth and Duncan side by side, Angus directly behind, and Maggie and Iain bickering good-humouredly at the rear. Everyone seemed happy and carefree. Except Beth. It was ridiculous to be so worried, she told herself. She'd met kings and princes and all manner of important people without more than a slight qualm. But she hadn't cared about them. She did care about these people who were Alex's family, his life. No, she amended, she had been nervous when meeting Prince Charles, had wanted him to like her. And look what a mess she'd made of that, losing her temper and slapping the guard in the face. It had all ended well, though. Even so, she was far more nervous now, knowing that if Charles hadn't liked her, it wouldn't really have mattered that much, not in the long term. She was unlikely to meet him again, after all. But if Alex's clansmen and women didn't like her, it could have enormous repercussions. And if Alex was forced to choose between her and his clan, who would he choose? His clan, of course. Oh God. She realised she was making herself more nervous, brooding like this.

"Did you write to tell them we were coming?" she asked.

"No," Alex replied calmly. "I thought we'd give them a wee surprise."

A wee surprise?

"I would think it'll be one hell of a shock, surely, if the chieftain, after a year's absence, suddenly appears in their midst without warning?"

"Oh, there's nae danger of that," Angus said cheerfully. "They've kent since at least yesterday that we're on the way. I'm hoping they'll have something good tae eat waiting for us. I'm famished."

"I thought you said you hadn't told them we were coming," Beth said, thoroughly confused.

"No more I have," said Alex. "But we passed wee Davy yesterday forenoon, and, being able to cut across country, he'll have arrived home in the evening."

"Dinna forget young Jamie this morning, either," added Duncan.

"Jamie?" said Alex, with surprise. "I didna see him. Where?"

"Shortly after the eagle, remember?"

"Aye, well, he's getting bigger now, and cannier, I suppose. Even so, I'm impressed. I didna mark him at all."

Beth remembered the eagle. She also remembered thinking how sparsely inhabited the countryside seemed to be, because apart from themselves she had not seen a living soul in two days. Not even an innkeeper. The weather being fine, they had slept under the stars, which Beth, uncomfortable though it had been, with every sharp stone and twig seeming to migrate under her restless body, had nevertheless seen as a great adventure. There was something extremely romantic about being safely nestled in the loving arms of a large warm man, while staring at the stars.

"I didn't see anyone at all," she remarked. "Not Davy nor Jamie either."

The three men looked at her.

"Well, no, an ye had've done, ye being used to the Sasannach ways, I'd have had a word to say to their fathers, and them, about it," Alex said. "The whole point is no' to be seen. No' by strangers to the clan anyway," he added with an unusual lack of tact. "I'm sorry," he said, seeing her expression. "But you're no' used to our ways yet. Ye dinna ken what to look for. Give it time. The next time we come home, ye'll be able tae spot a MacGregor hiding in the heather half a mile away. And dinna forget, forbye, *I* didna see Jamie, either."

She was not reassured.

The sun was low on the horizon when the MacGregor settlement first came into view. At first Beth didn't see this either, from a distance, but that was because, in spite of what she'd been told by her husband and his brothers, she had still been expecting houses in the English sense, brick or stone-built affairs; whereas what she was confronted with was a series of turf huts with thatched roofs, which being scattered among the trees and made of unpainted natural materials, blended in very well with the surrounding landscape. In view of the MacGregors' lifestyle, this was probably a great advantage. One of these, slightly larger than the others, and which was not only built of stone but boasted a rudimentary chimney, was their house, Alex pointed out with pride. A thin spiral of smoke drifted lazily from the roof, telling her that he had been right. They *were* expected, and someone had taken the time to light a fire to welcome them home.

As they rode down the final slope to the settlement, figures started to emerge from the huts. There were a couple of men, dressed in shirts and plaids in muted shades of green and brown, but mainly, as far as Beth could see, the clan MacGregor seemed to consist of women and children, the women clad in patterned woollen dresses belted at the waist, and the children in an assortment of ragged bits of tartan cloth. Most of them were barefoot.

They surrounded the horses as their chieftain and his entourage finally arrived amongst them, laughing and chattering in a Gaelic so rapid that Beth could follow little of it, other than that they were glad to see him home, and that the menfolk, apart from Kenneth, Dougal and Sandy, who had remained behind in case of trouble, were mainly at the droving, but should be home from market tomorrow, which explained the preponderance of women, at any rate.

Beth was aware of being observed discreetly, but no one addressed a comment to her directly. They were waiting for Alex to introduce her, that was clear. She waited too, thinking that it would probably be a mistake to perform her own introductions.

After a minute or so of this he swung himself down easily from the saddle, reaching to lift her from her horse and placing her by his side.

"This is my wife, Beth," he said simply.

She smiled in what she hoped was a welcoming and friendly way, although she felt almost paralysed with fear. The children were staring up at her as though she had two heads. One of them started to cry, and although it wasn't due to the sight of Beth, but because his brother had slyly pinched him, it didn't make her feel any better.

"Christ, Alex," came a deep booming voice from behind her, "she's tiny. Ye didna tell us ye'd married a wee bairn."

The wee bairn, ever sensitive about her diminutive stature, spun round on her heel, her fear temporarily replaced by indignation, to be confronted by the tallest man she had ever seen in her life, who had only now belatedly emerged from his hut. He topped even Alex by a head, and was as well-built as his chief, in due proportion. She tilted her head back to look him in the face, which, framed by a shock of long red hair, was rugged and merry, although his light blue eyes were shadowed and there were deep lines of care etched into his forehead.

"My God," she said, amazed. "I haven't believed in giants since I *was* a wee bairn. I'll never doubt their existence again. Where's the beanstalk?"

The giant responded with a grin, impressed by her fearlessness, although he had no idea what she meant by her last sentence, having never heard the fairytale. "Are all the English as wee as you, then? If so, I'll take half a dozen men wi' me the night and march directly on London."

"If all the Scots are as big as you, you'll probably be successful," she replied.

"Dinna underestimate her, Kenneth," advised Duncan. "She nearly did for me the first time I met her."

"And she favours her MacDonald mother rather than the English side, so she tells us," added Angus.

"Do ye so?" said the giant.

"Yes, I do," said Beth. "And if you'd met my English brother and cousins, you'd be very glad I don't favour them, believe me."

"Beth, let me introduce ye to your clan," Alex said. "Even though this loon has ruined the formalities. This is my wife, Beth, as I was saying afore I was interrupted. Ye'll make her welcome, and treat her as she deserves."

Whatever that might mean. Beth's fear started to return. She swallowed it down, and spoke to them all, although she didn't know if she should without being invited to.

"This is my first visit to Scotland," she said, "although my mother told me a lot about it, and I understand the Gaelic, if you speak slowly. I want to learn your ways, and I will, if you'll help me. If I do something I shouldn't, please tell me so I can learn. If I offend anyone, it's likely to be unintentional, and if it's not, I'll tell you so, and why."

She looked at her husband nervously, aware that she'd said more than she'd intended to. Had she sounded too arrogant? She had no idea what she was expected to do, and realised now that Alex had not, in all the long ride here, given her any pointers as to how to behave. That this had been deliberate, in the hope that she would behave naturally rather than follow a list of instructions, she was not aware. His clanspeople were down to earth, honest, and did not appreciate artifice. Alex was certain they would like Beth. How could they not?

Her involuntary sigh of relief as the formal silence and non-committal faces were transformed into smiles and expressions of welcome told him and the others, how uncertain she was. She was led away by her husband to view her house, and much as they wanted to regale their chieftain with all that had happened in his absence, his people left him and his wife alone for a time, so that she could form her first impressions of her new home. Then they would join the rest of the clan for a meal. A cow had been killed in honour of the occasion, for which Angus was truly grateful, his stomach having rumbled loudly at intervals for the last hour. He went off with Duncan to Iain and Maggie's house, to wash and change.

The clan's first impression of her was, on the whole, favourable. She was feisty enough. See how she'd stood up to Kenneth Mòr, the mere sight of whom could strike the fear of God into the bravest man? There were plenty of reservations about her physique, though. Aye, she was bonny, right enough, and no doubt well suited to an English drawing-room. But awfu' frail looking. A general doubt was expressed as to whether she'd be capable of performing the hard manual tasks generally expected of Highland women, of giving birth to the next chieftain, or even of surviving a Scottish winter, for that matter. Only time would tell. In the meantime there was a feast of sorts to be had. There would be a greater one when the men returned safely, and time enough to worry whether Alex had made the right choice or not later.

Unaware of this speculation, Beth was examining her new home with interest. Inside it consisted of three rooms; kitchen, pantry and living room downstairs, and upstairs a loft, accessed by a ladder, where the chief, his wife and his two brothers would sleep on heather-filled mattresses. Someone had tactfully erected a partition of wattle across the middle of the loft, to afford Alex and Beth a little privacy.

The kitchen fire was in the centre of the floor and there was a hole in the roof to allow the smoke to escape. There was also a table which doubled as a surface for preparing food, several wooden stools, and a cupboard to store the wooden plates, pots, pans and other utensils. After examining the room, Beth moved into the sitting room, which boasted the chimney, and the peat fire. The walls were painted white, which enhanced the waning light coming through the small window. By the fire were two chairs, with another two and a bench by the far wall. The only other furniture was a cupboard, a chest for blankets which could double as a table and a few shelves, stacked with books. On one of the fireside chairs a large ginger cat had taken up residence, and eyed his new mistress doubtfully through his one remaining eye.

"MacGregor," said Alex suddenly. It was the first sound he had made since they'd entered the house. He had watched intently from the door as she investigated the rooms, trying to assess her reaction. Her mother had told her how Highlanders lived, and he had told a few tales of his own in the year they'd been married, but nothing could prepare you for the reality.

Beth, in the act of moving to examine an object hanging on the wall, stopped and turned back with a puzzled expression.

"The cat," he elaborated. "MacGregor's his name. He's getting a wee bit old now, but he's still a good mouser."

"Isn't that a bit confusing, with everyone else being named MacGregor as well?" she said.

"Aye, well, everyone else is addressed by their first name or a nickname, generally. And like all cats, he doesna answer to his appellation anyway, unless he's a mind to." MacGregor, presumably satisfied that the intruder wasn't going to eject him from his cosy spot, closed his eye.

"Is that yours?" she asked, pointing to the circular studded leather and wood shield she'd been heading for before Alex spoke.

"The targe? Aye, now. It was my father's. I dinna use it any more."

"It looks a bit bashed about." There was a chunk missing from one edge, the leather was badly scraped in places, and there was a neat hole punched through the middle of it.

"It's been well used. It stopped its owner being bashed about, which is the point of it."

She reached up and ran her hand lightly across the worn leather.

"Is that how he died?" she asked, her fingers halting at the hole. "I'm sorry, I shouldn't have asked that."

"Why not? No, it's no' how he died. The musket ball went between his arm and his body and killed the poor soul behind him. Da died in his bed, wi' no warning. Just said he wasna feeling so well, went to sleep and didna wake up. It's no' how he'd have wanted it, but we canna choose the way of our passing."

She turned away from the targe to look at him. He didn't seem sad, but then his father had been dead for eight years. He did seem uneasy though, hovering by the door as though seeking an opportunity to leave. She thought this strange. After all, this was his house; she was the one who should feel awkward. And then she realised.

"Do you have another pressing appointment then, or are you thinking of staying a while?" she asked.

The corners of his mouth lifted slightly, and he took two steps into the room.

"Did you think I wouldn't like it?" she asked softly, taking his hand.

"Well, it's no' quite what ye're used to," he said.

"Nothing about my life since I've been married to you is what I was used to," she pointed out. "That's why I love it so much. It's a fine house, Alex. It's well built, warm, dry and comfortable. It's better than I expected it would be, to be honest, after all your stories about sleeping in the bracken and suchlike. I was expecting a couple of poles tied together with a blanket thrown over them at best."

The upturned corners became a wide smile.

"I wanted ye to be prepared, so ye wouldna be too disappointed," he said.

"It worked," she affirmed. "I'm not. It's lovely, Alex. But I still haven't examined the most interesting piece of furniture in the place."

"What's that?" he asked. He thought she'd seen everything there was to see.

"This," she murmured, moving closer.

There was a brief pause in the conversation, during which MacGregor, disgusted at what his master and mistress were doing, uncurled himself and leapt down from the chair, stalking haughtily and unnoticed from the room.

"Please tell me," Beth said from the floor a few minutes later, her voice somewhat muffled by her skirts, which had just been tossed unceremoniously over her head, "that the whole clan are not about to descend on the house with the welcome feast." She pushed at the material with her one unoccupied hand, freeing her face and looking into her husband's eyes, which seemed almost black at the moment, the pupils wide with arousal.

"No," he mumbled, not really caring at the moment if a full regiment of redcoats was about to ride through the room. "They're giving us some time alone together. And if they did come in, at least they'd know ye're more than capable of fulfilling one of the duties of a wife, anyway."

She meant to ask him what he meant by that odd comment, but became somewhat distracted by subsequent events, and later forgot all about it.

CHAPTER FOUR

The men returned home from driving the cattle to market two days later, but upon realising that the chieftain and his new wife were intending to stay for several weeks, it was decided to celebrate both his recent marriage and his return together, at a feast to be held in a couple of weeks.

"That'll give ye the time to settle in a wee bit, and get acquainted wi' people," Alex explained to Beth as they sat by the fire on the evening of the men's return. There had been many ribcracking hugs and much good-humoured railing of the chieftain by his men, who they said they had feared was becoming seduced by the pampered English lifestyle, he'd been away for so long.

The reception his wife had received was less familiar; that was to be expected, as she was an unknown quantity, and a Sasannach too. Alex had watched his clansmen carefully as they greeted her, and was, on the whole, satisfied. They had been welcoming, warm even, obviously appreciating her beauty and open friendly greetings of them. Alex had known she would not hesitate to accept the embraces of travel-stained men who smelled somewhat less than pleasant to say the least, after several days of herding cattle across the hills. He also knew that she would have coped well with any good-humoured ribbing, although there was none.

He could do nothing about the concerns he saw in their eyes regarding her size, slender build and apparent unsuitability to the rigours of the Highland life. He had not chosen her for her ability to perform heavy manual labour or give birth to twenty children with ease; he had chosen her for her independent free spirit, her intelligence and trustworthiness, because he could not bear to see that spirit stifled, and because he loved her. Most of all because he loved her.

He was of course aware that she was small and slight; how could he not be, when he towered over her? In an English drawing room, however, her fragility was not incongruous with the surroundings, and her spirit detracted from her physique. But here, as he saw her in conversation with the other women of the clan whilst they prepared a communal meal for the homecoming men, he realised for the first time just how pale and delicate she appeared when compared to the robust tanned MacGregor clanswomen, and started to have misgivings of his own as to how well she would cope with the lifestyle.

He looked at her now sitting opposite him, brow creased in concentration as she attempted to knit a pair of stockings.

"Ye're holding the wool wrong," he said. "Here, gie it tae me." He took the needles from her and demonstrated, looping the wool over his index finger and letting it trail across his palm. "You see, this way the tension stays even." He knitted a row quickly, then showed her the stitches, loose and even on the bone needle, unlike hers, which had been so tight she had to stop at regular intervals to force them along the needle. He handed the work back to her, and she sighed. "Ye dinna have to learn everything at once," he said. "The clan'll no' reject ye if ye canna knit a pair of stockings. I can knit my own, anyway. Most of the men can."

"I know that," she replied. "But we're only here for a few weeks and I want to learn as much as I can in that time. And anyway, I *can* knit. Or I could. My mother taught me when I was a child. I'm just out of practice. I didn't like it much, because it involved sitting still and I wasn't very good at that then." She looked up in time to see him grinning, and smiled back. "Well, yes, I'm still not very good at it, but at least I'm trying." She put the uneven piece of work to one side. "I'll use that to practice on until I get it right."

Before she could lean back or find something else to do he grasped her wrist and hooked her deftly from her chair onto his knee. Angus and Duncan were out, and he was glad she'd stopped knitting. He knew what clan life was like; he would not have a lot of time alone with his wife, and when he did get her to himself he wanted all her attention. It was childish, but he didn't care. She settled comfortably into him, her head resting against his shoulder.

"I'm looking forward to the wedding feast," she said. "Are the men annoyed that you got married away from the clan, without asking them?"

"No," Alex replied. He was their chieftain. They would not expect him to ask their permission to marry, as they would ask his. "They consider it an honour that the prince was a witness to our wedding. They'll enjoy the celebration anyway. It isna necessary to have the ceremony first. And it saves the trouble of locating a priest to perform it. I was thinking," he continued, tracing the line of her cheek with one long finger, "of sending to Glencoe, to see if any of the MacDonalds would care to come. Would ye like that?"

She sat up.

"Are you serious?" she said, her eyes alight.

"Aye. I was going tae do it as a surprise, but wasna sure if ye'd welcome it, so I thought I'd ask ye first."

"I'd love it!" she said. "My grandmother had a couple of sisters and a brother who had children. They'd be my cousins, I suppose. I know my grandmother didn't have any more. She didn't remarry after my grandfather died in prison after the massacre, and my mother was her only surviving child. She had six others, but they all died young, one way or another. Of course," she said, smiling up at Alex, "I suppose, technically speaking, the whole clan are my family."

More than technically speaking, thought Alex. Although they would consider the MacGregors to have first claim on her now that she was married, in the event of any problems she could turn to her MacDonald family for help. Not just technically, but in actuality. And Highland life was so precarious, particularly for the proscribed MacGregors...

He wrapped his arm around her suddenly, protectively, and pulled her into him, inadvertently crushing her face against his body. She gave a small chirp of protest and pulled back a little, then kissed the hollow at the base of his neck, inhaling the unique warm masculine scent of him, smiling as he made a deep, inarticulate sound in his throat that she knew was the precursor to other things. She was very happy. The clan had not rejected her. He would not have to choose between them.

She continued to be very happy for a couple of days. She thoroughly enjoyed being able to abandon hoops and elaborate hairstyles in favour of comfortable woollen and cotton dresses and simple braids. She was enjoying caring for three men too, much preferring the honest labour of housekeeping and the company of jovial, down-to-earth people to that of looking merely decorative and trying to appear interested in trivial chatter in the company of malicious gossips.

Having rearranged the house to her liking, she decided to set about the weed-clogged piece of ground outside the back door, intending to turn it into a herb patch, with perhaps a few cabbages and suchlike. The fact that they would not be staying long enough for her to reap the fruits of her labours, as Duncan pointed out, was beside the point. She would at least have made a start. Perhaps someone else would tend the plot while she was absent, and when they returned permanently, as she hoped they would, and soon, they would be thankful for the extra food, which would provide some variety from the staple diet of oatmeal.

She pulled up the lightly rooted weeds, scythed down the rest, and had just resigned herself to making a start on the heavy work of digging, when Rob MacGregor poked his nose round the side of the cottage.

"Would ye be wanting some help with that?" he asked. "It's awfu' heavy work."

She planted the spade in the soil and smiled at him. Fourteen years old, and indolent, with the black hair and grey eyes of his three brothers and deceased sister Jean, he was not one to normally volunteer for anything, although Beth did not know that. She did know that fourteen-year-old males are usually permanently hungry.

"I'll do you a deal," she said. "I've just made a batch of oatcakes. You turn this patch over, and you can eat as many as you want."

In the end the fourteen-year-old had proved himself so hungry that she had to make another batch of oatcakes for the three ravenous men who descended from the mountain that evening, having spent the whole day practising their sword skills. It looked to her as though they had spent the day rolling in the mud and getting as dirty and torn as they possibly could, so she shooed them out to wash in the loch while she tried to remember how Jane had gutted and prepared rabbits for the pot.

She was still trying to remember when they returned, clean, their hair dripping, and while Duncan expertly turned the furry corpses into pot-sized chunks of meat, Beth, Alex and Angus went outside to survey the prospective herb plot.

Angus whistled through his teeth.

"You've done an amazing job," he said, eyeing her with admiration. "I wouldna have expected ye to do half of that in one day."

"Yes, well, Rob helped me," she admitted. "I cleared all the weeds, and moved most of the stones," she pointed to a pile of rocks, "and he did the digging. And ate all the oatcakes I'd made for the four of us."

"Rob?" said Alex incredulously. "Ye dinna mean Robbie Og?"

"Yes," she said. In a group where almost everyone had the same surname, and a great many owned a Christian name in common too, people were usually identified by an additional appropriate adjective. Hence Rob Og, or young, being the youngest of his family. Alex Mòr, or tall, for her husband, Angus Ban, or fair, for her brother-in-law. And so on. She was merely Ealasaid, which was Gaelic for Elizabeth, as there were no others of that name.

"Now that I'd like to have seen," Angus said. "Your oatcakes are good, I'll give ye that, but I still wouldna have thought them good enough to get Robbie Og off his arse."

She thought nothing of it, then. Nor did she think anything amiss the following day when Simon offered to carry the buckets of water back from the river for her. Until later in the day when she noticed Simon's pregnant wife Janet struggling back with two brimming pails while he sat chatting with a couple of other men.

"They think you're frail," Angus said with tactless honesty when she asked him if it was normal for clansmen to treat the chief's wife differently to the other women.

"Frail?" she said. She hadn't expected that.

"Well, look at ye, compared to the other women. Ye are smaller than them."

"Janet's the same size as me," Beth pointed out indignantly. "Or nearly, anyway. And she's pregnant!"

"Aye, but she's wider through the shoulders and hips than you. And she's strong, and used to the life."

"I'm strong, too," she protested. They were walking back from the river together. And he was carrying the water for the evening. He looked down at her and she saw the doubt in his eyes. She stopped walking, and when he would have carried on, she grabbed his arm, causing him to slop some of the water on the grass.

"Does everyone think I'm frail?" she said. "Even you?"

He put the buckets down, and looked uncomfortable.

"Aye, well, I hadna thought much of it before," he said. "But ye are delicate, are ye no'? I ken that ye're a lot stronger than ye look," he added hurriedly, seeing the look on her face that in her husband would presage a physical assault, and attempting, belatedly, to be tactful. "Ye just need to build yourself up, slowly, that's all." He bent down to pick up the buckets, and she slapped his hands away crossly, hoisting them up herself and striding off across the grass.

"I said I'd carry those for ye!" he protested when he caught up with her.

"Yes, well, I won't get to build myself up if everyone insists on doing everything for me, will I?" she said through gritted teeth.

"Beth, there's nae reason to take on so," he said placatingly, snatching at one bucket and succeeding in prising it from her fingers. "Ye canna help it that ye're weak, ye've no'…"

Whatever he'd been about to say was lost in a gasp as the contents of the other pail of water hit him full in the face.

"Thank you for telling me the clan thinks I'm a feeble, exotic flower, about to expire at the slightest exertion," she said. "I can, now you've explained it, understand why *they* might think so. You, however, have known me for over a year. You've seen me ride for three days at a time with hardly any sleep, drag Sir Anthony's trunks full of clothes up and down stairs, and lug endless buckets of water upstairs for baths, since the only other help we have at home is Maggie. I thought you, at least, would have known better!" She glared at the empty bucket, and turned back to the river. "Leave the water there and go home," she called back over her shoulder. "Make sure the stew doesn't boil dry. I'll be there in a few minutes, when I've calmed down."

He left the water there and went home, dripping, to be greeted by the amused grins of his brothers, which soon disappeared as he told them how he'd come to be drenched.

"Ye could have put it a wee bit better," Duncan said, revealing that he also agreed with Angus with regard to his sister-in-law's physical state.

"Aye, well, I've no' got your gift for tact, man, and I didna think she'd take it so amiss. After all, she *is* tiny, is she no'?"

Alex rubbed his hands through his hair.

"She is. But she's verra sensitive about it, too."

"I ken that, now," said Angus dryly, dragging his sopping shirt over his head.

"She's spent her whole life no' being taken seriously on account of she's wee, being patted on the head and treated like a bairn by patronising men. She'd no' appreciate thinking that the whole clan feels that way about her," Alex said, not admitting his own doubts. "She wants to be accepted on equal terms."

"Will ye have a word wi' her about it?" Duncan said.

"No, not unless she raises the subject," Alex replied.

He was not being a coward. Now she knew, it would be interesting to see how she dealt with the problem herself.

* * *

Peigi MacGregor paused in her labours, tucking a wayward strand of hair behind her ear before pressing her fingers into the base of her back. She remained like that for all of ten seconds, before diving across the room and out of the door to wrestle a large and wriggling worm from her son's hand before he could succeed in his intention of putting it in his mouth.

"Yeuch!" she cried, then softened her voice as the child's face began to crumple. "Ye dinna want tae eat that, *a leannan.*" She picked the infant up for a moment, swinging him high in the air to take his mind off the tasty treat he'd just been deprived of. His twin, still sitting on the blanket, made a mew of complaint at the attention his brother was receiving and lifted his arms to her to be picked up. Peigi sighed. This was impossible. Normally Alasdair would look after the bairns, or someone else with nothing to do would. But today everyone was busy, and she had, insanely, thought she could make butter and keep an eye on her two normally placid babies, who today had become possessed by some demon and seemed intent on crawling off the blanket she'd placed them on and into as much mischief as possible.

A shadow fell across her, and she squinted up to look into the smiling face of the chieftain's wife.

"Hello, Peigi, isn't it? I was told you're making butter, and I've come to see if I can be of any help."

Peigi put the baby down and admonished him to stay there in her sternest voice. Then she stood, and eyed her helpmate dubiously.

"Aye, well, I was just about to drain off the buttermilk, when this wee loon decided tae eat a worm." She went over to a pail of water and washed her hands briskly. "Ye can keep an eye on they two while I carry on, an ye want."

Without waiting for a reply, she went over to the churn and removed the plug, draining the buttermilk into a clean bucket. When this was done, she filled an identical bucket to the same level with water, and poured it into the churn.

"I expected you to have a dash churn," Beth said, eyeing the barrel-shaped churn on its metal cradle with approval. "We had one like that in Manchester, but I've never seen another."

"It was made for us by a cooper," explained Peigi. "He'd been in America, and seen them there, but he was awfu' homesick, and came back in the end. It's still hard work, mind," she added, as she saw that Beth had no intention of minding the twins, but had instead pushed her sleeves up and taken a hold of the crank.

"I know," Beth replied. "I used to make the butter at home. You have a rest. The twins'll prefer their mother to look after them anyway. They don't know me."

Peigi's back was aching and she was tired. The twins were teething and fractious and had kept her awake for most of the previous night. A rest would be lovely.

"All right, then, if you're sure," she said. "Let me know when ye get tired though, and I'll take over."

She sat down on the blanket outside in the sunshine and waited for Beth to call her, in about fifteen minutes or so, she thought. The children, appeased by the undivided attention of their mother, crawled into her lap. The weather was lovely, wall-to-wall blue skies. Perfect harvesting weather. Alasdair and the other men had gone to see if the oats and barley were ready, and to fish for trout. A large bumble bee buzzed drowsily in a nearby patch of clover. Peigi closed her eyes, just for a moment.

When she opened them the sun had declined considerably in the sky and the blanket was now in the shadow. The twins had fallen asleep on her knee, and one of her legs had gone to sleep. Remembering, she moved the babies off her lap onto the blanket, taking care not to wake them, and stumbled into the dairy shed, wincing at the pins and needles in her leg as the blood started to circulate again.

Beth was at the table, working the last of the butter into pats with the grooved wooden 'Scotch hands,' used to expel the excess water after churning. She looked up and smiled.

"You looked so peaceful there," she said cheerfully. "I thought I'd let you sleep. Is this for sale, or are you storing it for winter?" She cast a glance at the pile of earthenware jars, freshly washed and ready to one side.

Peigi stared at Beth with amazement. She showed not the slightest sign of fatigue, in spite of the fact that butter-churning was an exhausting task for even the brawniest of the women, and she had the slenderest arms Peigi had ever seen. Yet the butter was perfect; she could see that.

"It's to be stored," she said. "We'll have to leave it for a couple of hours, then roll it again. I'll away off and put the bairns to bed, then come back and finish off. Thank you," she added belatedly, stunned.

"It was nice to do a bit of hard work for a change," said Beth. "I'm ready for my meal now. I just hope Alex managed to catch some trout, that's all."

She walked back to the house, smiling, while Peigi's eyes followed her, watching for any sign of backache or soreness.

While Angus cooked the trout, Alex massaged Beth's aching arms and shoulders, working his fingers deep into the muscles and gently teasing out the knots. Duncan sat watching, but made no comment as Beth alternately winced and sighed with pleasure as the overworked muscles relaxed.

"Do ye no' think it was just a wee bit stupid, to churn all that butter yourself, without a rest?" Alex said after a few minutes. The smell of frying trout drifted from the kitchen, making Beth's mouth water. She was starving.

"No, I don't," she replied. "Like I said to Peigi, I used to do it at home."

"On your own?" Alex said.

"Well, no," she admitted. "John used to help me. In fact, he used to do most of the churning. I don't care, though. If it makes them stop treating me as if I was made of glass, it'll be worth it."

"Ye'll be sorry in the morning," he said, finishing his ministrations by planting a kiss on her shoulder. "Ye'll no' be able to move."

"I haven't got a lot to do," she said. "Apart from fetching water without looking as though it hurts. Which I'll do myself," she added, as Angus walked in with a large plate on which were three expertly-cooked trout.

"I've nae intention to help ye," he said, putting it on the table. "No' after the thanks I got last time. I'll be out in the fields with everyone else, anyway."

"Why?" she asked, liberating a piece of fish from the plate and popping it into her mouth. "What's happening tomorrow?"

"The harvest," said Alex. "The oats and barley are ready. Everyone helps. Except yourself. Ye'll be in no fit state to."

The three brothers, along with much of the rest of the clan, kept an intermittent eye on the young woman with the pale gold hair who was wielding her sickle with dexterity and no sign of discomfort. The women sang a song to help them keep the rhythm, and their voices were sweet and melodious on the warm late summer air.

"How the hell is she doing it?" said Duncan quietly to Alex, when there was no danger of them being overheard. "She must be in agony."

"Or an awfu' lot stronger than we thought," remarked Angus, his voice laced with admiration. He *had* seen her drag trunks up and down stairs, and lug buckets of water upstairs. But not for twelve hours at a stretch, for two days. After churning butter for several hours the day before that.

"She's in agony," said Alex with certainty, although there was no sign of pain on his wife's features as she laughed and joked with the other women. It was working, he had to give her that. The others had relaxed noticeably around her as they accepted there was more to her than met the eye. Only Alex knew that that 'more' was nothing to do with physical strength.

"She's no' strong, she's bloody-minded," he said now to his brothers. "But dinna tell anyone I tellt ye that. Least of all her."

In the distance Beth paused for a minute, stretched her arms and rotated her shoulders a few times, then continued, quickly re-establishing the rhythm.

"She is that," agreed Duncan with due reverence. "But even the most bloody-minded man canna continue when his strength gives out. Are ye no' going tae stop her, afore she injures herself?"

"No' today, no," replied Alex. "It's getting late, anyway, and she needs to prove herself. She'd never forgive me if I made her stop now in front of the whole clan, and she'd be right. But ye're right, too. She canna continue like this for another day."

"She doesna need to, as far as I'm concerned," Angus said.

Judging by the general attitude, that was the view of the whole clan. Alex felt justified in what he was about to do.

"What do you mean, I'm not allowed out of the house?" Beth said, hands on hips, glaring at her brother-in-law. Exhausted, but in pain, she had found it difficult to get to sleep and had consequently woken late, by which time Angus and Alex had already risen silently, breakfasted and gone.

"They'll be finished by noon, anyway," Duncan reasoned. "There's no' much left to do."

"Fine," she said. "Then I'll be out there doing not much with them till noon." She made a move and Duncan set his back to the door. They eyed each other for a moment.

"He's got no right to do this," she said. "He can't keep me here against my will."

At this point Angus would no doubt have told her that Alex was her husband and could therefore do anything he wished to her, short of murder. Duncan did not, which was why he had been chosen for this unenviable task.

"Ye've proved yourself, lassie," he said instead. "Ye dinna need to do more."

"But all the other women are out there reaping, aren't they?" she said.

He nodded.

"Then I need to be out there with them, Duncan, or all my work'll be for nothing! Let me go, please," she pleaded.

He did not move.

"You cannot keep me here against my will!" she cried, almost in tears. Her muscles were cramped and sore. It had taken her ten minutes to dress, but if she didn't put in an appearance now everyone would know she wasn't as strong as the others.

"Aye, I can," he said logically. "But I dinna want to. Everyone kens ye churned butter all day, Peigi's tellt them she fell asleep. There isna a woman out there who wouldna jump at the chance of a rest. Ye've done it. Did ye no' ken that by the way they acted towards ye yestereve?"

She did, and had rejoiced. Even so…

"Has Alex told them that I'm too sore to work today?" she asked.

"No. Give him some credit. Ye're needed here tae make the bannocks and get things ready for tonight. So am I. We always have a wee feast to celebrate getting in the harvest. It's normal, Beth. If it wasna me and you, someone else'd have tae do it."

It was clear he was not going to let her go, so she sat down. Even if she had full use of her arms, she couldn't overpower him. As it was, she didn't even know if she could manage to make the bread, she ached that much. Duncan moved away from the door and sat down opposite her.

"They've accepted ye, Beth. They think ye're accustomed to such work. If ye go out there today and collapse, they'll ken that ye've overreached yourself, and why ye've done it. They'll still admire ye, mind, but that's no' what ye want, is it?"

"No," she said. "I just want them to stop treating me differently, that's all."

"Well, then," he said. "Stop now, while ye're ahead. And ye dinna need to pretend to me that ye're no' hurting. I'll no' tell a soul, and neither will Alex or Angus." He smiled winningly, and she gave in. He was right.

"I'm not sure I can even knead the bread dough," she admitted in a small voice.

"Dinna fash yourself," he said, rolling up his sleeves. "I'm an expert. Away off back to your bed for a couple of hours. It'll be a long night, if things go as normal, and ye'll want to be awake to see the fruits of your labours."

* * *

Once the harvest was in it rained for a few days and then the sun came out again. Everyone made the most of it; it was September by now, and was probably the last time they'd see the sun, or the warm sun at any rate, for some months. The grain had been ground, peat for the fires dug, the cattle brought down from the hills, and the knowledge that their diet would be supplemented by the generous provisions Alex had brought from England rendered the MacGregors carefree and relaxed. Whatever problems the winter brought this year, starvation would not be one of them.

Today the clan was occupied in various leisure pursuits. Most of the children were swimming in the loch, their mothers watching and chatting, some of the men had gone hunting, and Alex, Duncan, Angus and Dougal, the lazy Robbie's eldest brother, had gone off into the hills to practice fighting. Beth had asked if she could accompany them, as she had no children to watch, and had never seen Highland swordplay.

Permission having been granted, Duncan, Alex and Beth were sitting on a large flat sun-warmed rock, observing Angus and Dougal as they went through their paces.

"It seems awfully realistic," Beth observed, as Angus ducked just in time to avoid being decapitated by Dougal's broadsword. He drove his targe into the other man's stomach, temporarily winding him, and then paused to allow Dougal to get his wind back.

"There isna any point in holding back," Alex explained. "If ye canna hold your own against one man who'll give ye the time to recover yourself, ye'll no' last five minutes on the battlefield. Ye're slipping, man," he said to Dougal, who had regained his feet. "In a real fight Angus would ha' finished you off now."

"He's improved since I last fought him," Dougal acknowledged.

The two men circled each other for a moment before closing in again, Dougal more wary now. They had stripped off their shirts and their muscles bulged and rippled as they thrust and counter-thrust at each other. Even Beth could see they were well-matched, in size and strength, at least. As far as technique went, she had no idea, but they both seemed pretty accomplished and ferocious to her.

"He's put on bulk," Alex said, eyeing his youngest brother's muscularity with admiration.

"Aye, he's a man now," observed Duncan. "In the body, at least."

Beth sat between her husband and brother-in-law, watching closely. She had expected some sort of fencing competition with rules, not the free-for-all battering and gouging contest she was now witnessing. She waited with trepidation for the blood to spurt, and wished she'd thought to bring some bandages with her.

"Do people often get injured in these play fights?" she asked.

"Oh aye," Duncan said nonchalantly. "But it's no' normally that serious."

Alex looked down at his hand.

"That's how I got yon wee scar there, that gave my identity away to ye," he said.

Beth looked at the 'wee scar', and wondered what a big one would look like.

"Who were you fighting?" she asked.

"Me," replied Duncan. "We were eleven and thirteen, and thought we were men. So we borrowed da's claymore, without telling him of course, and went away off tae play at soldiers. Keep your arm up, man, ye're tiring!" he shouted suddenly to Angus, making Beth jump. Dougal's sword smashed into the younger man's targe with arm-numbing force, and Angus leapt nimbly backwards out of striking distance.

"Ye could hae taken him then, Angus, his right side was unprotected!" Alex said, shaking his head. Angus acknowledged the truth of this with a rueful smile, not taking his eyes off his opponent, and shook his head. Droplets of sweat flew in all directions.

"What happened?" Beth said after a minute.

"What? Oh, well, we took it in turns to use the claymore, swinging it about like mad things while the other one leapt away or used his dirk to parry. Christ, we were stupid, were we no'? It's a miracle one of us wasna killed." Duncan smiled at his brother, remembering.

"So you hit him with your father's claymore?" Beth asked.

"No," Alex cut in. "He did it wi' his dirk. We'd both had them as presents a few weeks before, and we were awfu' proud. We kept them razor-sharp. Well, a claymore's a mighty heavy weapon, around fifteen pounds or so, but da used to wield it as though it was a feather. After a wee while of swinging it around and running at him, I got tired, so I planted the sword in the ground for a wee rest."

"Just as I went for him wi' my dirk. He couldna get his arm up in time, and I laid his hand open to the bone," Duncan said. "I thought I'd cut it off at first, there was that much blood."

"Aye, and while I was bleeding to death on the grass, all he could think of was that Da'd kill him when he found out what we'd been up to!" Alex laughed.

"I did tear up my best shirt to bind it up with!" Duncan protested. "Ma never forgave me for that. And I've still got the scars from the flogging I got, too."

Alex looked at him sceptically.

"Scars of the mind," Duncan said firmly.

"We both got those," Alex said. "Da flogged Duncan that evening. I thought I'd get away wi' it, being injured an' all, but he just waited till my hand was healed before he beat me. That was worse. Not only did I get a beating, but I got to look forward to it for a week as well. And that wasna the end of it, either."

Duncan creased his brow in puzzlement.

"I dinna remember anything else from it," he said.

"Aye, well, ye werena there when the scar got me a broken nose, were ye?" Alex said, looking at Beth, who coloured violently.

"You asked for it," she said. "You should have told me who you were before you married me."

"I didna get the chance, wi' Isabella and co fluttering around morning, noon and night. And anyway, I needed to have the legal power as your husband to lock ye away if ye'd taken exception to marrying a Jacobite traitor."

"Would you really have done that?" she asked.

"I dinna ken. Aye, probably. For a while. Anyway, it's irrelevant. You're here, and you're happy, are ye no'?"

"I suppose so," she said, with intentional insincerity. She *was* happy. In fact she could not remember when she'd been happier. She thought she'd like nothing better than to live like this for the rest of her life, looking after Alex and his brothers, enjoying the affectionate bickering, sitting round the fire at night drinking whisky and telling stories, before returning to her own home to make love to her strong, gentle husband. Of course life was not always peaceful like this, she was continually being told. Hence the 'playfighting' between the two sweating protagonists in front of her, which now appeared to have turned into a wrestling contest, their weapons having been abandoned on the grass. Dougal had just managed to trap Angus's arm over his shoulder, and was in a perfect position to break it, although he obviously had no intention of following through and doing so, to Beth's relief.

Duncan leaned over and picked up the skin of ale from the shadow at the side of the rock.

"This is where Angus should really kick Dougal in the balls," he explained to Beth, taking a deep pull from the flask before passing it to her.

Both combatants heard the advice, and Angus shifted position slightly.

"You try it, ye wee gomerel, and it's your neck I'll break, no' your arm," Dougal growled.

The two brothers on the rock groaned in unison, half a second before Angus did just what he'd been warned not to do, as they'd known he would. Dougal let go of his adversary, twisting his lower body to deflect the blow, which caught him on the thigh. Then he leapt at Angus, gripping him round the waist and driving him backwards to the edge of the grassy clearing. The two men teetered on the edge of the slope for a moment, then lost their balance and fell over the side, rolling off down the hill in a flurry of oaths, green and brown plaid and bare buttocks, before disappearing out of sight.

Beth let out a cry of alarm, and dropping the flask, made to run after them. Alex deftly caught the flask with one hand and Beth's arm with the other, pulling her back down onto the stone.

"Leave him," he said. "He'll be all right. He'll no' appreciate a nursemaid." He lay back on the stone, keeping a hold of his wife's arm. Duncan followed suit.

She looked from one brother to the other, both of them wearing unconcerned expressions.

"It's a long way to the bottom of the hill," she pointed out. The way they'd fallen, there was also a sheer drop half way down onto jagged rocks fifty feet below. Why weren't they worried? Hadn't they remembered? Angus and Dougal would be killed, or at least badly injured. She tried to get to her feet again, but Duncan caught her other arm and she was trapped between them.

"They'll no' get as far as the cliff edge," he said, showing that he had remembered. "They'll stop in a minute, ye'll hear them."

"How can you possibly know...?" she began.

Her sentence was cut off by an agonised shriek from the side of the hill, followed by a torrent of cursing in Gaelic that proved Duncan right. Whatever had happened, Angus and Dougal were definitely not dead, nor, by the strength of their voices, about to be.

"Gorse," explained Alex, closing his eyes. "A wee bit prickly," he added with spectacular understatement.

"Aye, they'll think twice before they launch themselves off the hill again," Duncan observed.

Unable to do anything else, Beth lay back between the two men.

"Aren't you being a bit heartless?" she said, smiling now. The torrent of swearing had now diminished into irritated bickering as the two men presumably tried to extricate themselves from the spikes. A peal of youthful laughter drifted upwards on the warm air, by which Beth surmised that Angus had been successful in freeing himself, at least, and that Dougal had not.

"We're being practical," Alex said drowsily. "It's essential to know the terrain of any battlefield. Choosing the place that makes the most of your army's particular skills is one of the most important jobs of any general. If he gets that wrong, you're fuc...ah...lost. And when he's chosen the site any soldier worth his salt will go out and familiarise himself with it before the battle, if he's the time to. Many a battle's won or lost by the terrain rather than the army. Next time they two'll think about the ground as well as the enemy."

"Mmm," murmured Duncan blissfully. "What a rare day. Let's hope it keeps like this for the wedding party."

Silence reigned for a while. Alex's arm slid under Beth's neck, pulling her head into his shoulder. She closed her eyes. Time passed. Alex's hand roamed warmly up her leg under her skirt and she started, looking round. Duncan had gone. They were alone. Alex was propped up on one elbow, looking down at her, his eyes dark and smiling. He cupped one firm buttock and put his other arm round her shoulders, moving her smoothly off the stone onto the soft grass, bunching her skirts up round her thighs as he did so. As was normal, he wore nothing under his kilted plaid; there was no clumsy fumbling at breeches to interrupt the smoothness of his action as he sheathed himself in her in one fluid movement. She gasped softly.

"What if…?" she began.

"Wheesht," he murmured. "There's no one here. And even if there was, it's natural."

He began to move, subtly, tantalisingly, driving all worries about being disturbed from her mind. So successful was he that she did not notice when Angus and Dougal finally reappeared at the top of the hill, saw what was happening, retrieved their weapons silently and wandered off, smiling.

It *was* natural. That was something else she had to get used to. In such a close-knit community, privacy was virtually unheard of. People wandered in and out of each other's houses without knocking or being introduced by footmen. Whole families slept in one room, and no one turned a hair if two of the occupants of the room decided to become intimate under their blanket. Or slid off into the shadows of the communal fire at night. Providing they were married to each other, of course.

In a similar fashion, ideas of decency in dress could not be further removed from that of London society. Beth smiled as she remembered Isabella's shock at seeing the servant Abernathy bare-legged and minus his waistcoat.

What they would make of the sight of women wading in the river, skirts kilted up past their knees, or the not infrequent glimpse of a pair of male buttocks or genitals as the wind gusted or his plaid became disarranged, Beth could not imagine. Nobody thought anything of it. Regardless of their semi-nudity, everyone behaved with absolute decorum. Her mother had been right. All

Highlanders considered themselves to be gentlemen or ladies, and their state of dress or undress did not detract from the natural dignity with which they carried themselves and which was the birthright of every clansman or woman.

Fine clothes do not a gentleman make. Who had said that? Ah, yes, Lord Winter, Beth remembered, at Versailles, referring to Louis XIV. It was true, although Sir Anthony would dispute it vehemently. Alex, standing now in front of the fire clad only in a thin shirt which left little to the imagination, would not.

She had almost forgotten Sir Anthony and the life she had to return to in a few weeks. Gloom suffused her, and she instead forced herself to concentrate on the task she was supposed to be giving her full attention to. She leaned forward and carefully extricated a vicious-looking thorn from her brother-in-law's backside.

He craned his head back over his shoulder to see how she was doing.

"Christ, have ye no' finished yet? I thought we'd got them all out on the hill," he said, his face flushed scarlet with embarrassment, made all the more acute by the unsympathetic grins of his siblings and the cool one-eyed scrutiny of MacGregor, sitting by the fireside, tail waving slowly from side to side.

"Nearly," she said. "You'll be sorry if I miss one and it goes nasty. I'm sure Dougal's going through the same ordeal even as we speak."

"Aye, but it'll be Dougal's wife doing it for him, which is a different thing entirely. Now, if it was Morag doing the honours…"

"You keep your lecherous paws off her," Alex warned. "I'm no' judging in a dispute between you and her father, Ye touch her, ye marry her. Or preferably the other way round."

Angus cast a look of outraged innocence at his brother.

"I havena so much as kissed the lassie," he said. "I'm no' ready for marrying yet. I ken the rules. Anyway, I'm waiting to see what the MacDonald lassies are like. They'll be here in a day or so."

"Tomorrow," said Alex. "And you'll keep your lecherous hands off them, as well. The MacDonalds are our friends, and we've few enough of them. I'd keep them so. Ye can dance wi' them, ye can talk wi' them, and that's all, d'ye understand?"

"There," said Beth, delivering a smart slap to Angus's bottom before pulling down his plaid, causing him to screech in surprise. "Finished. You'll have no trouble sitting down tomorrow, anyway. Now if you're thinking of doing anything else, I'd better inspect the other parts as well." She smiled evilly, brandishing the tweezers and eyeing the parts she had in mind, now decently covered by tartan wool.

"No," he said hurriedly, backing away. "I've checked them myself already. And it seems I'll no' get a chance to use them anyway until we go back to London, wi' you lot watching me like hawks."

"Abstinence is good for ye," said Alex in his best strict parental tone. "When I was your age, I was…"

"Whoring your way around Paris," interrupted Angus. "I was only twelve at the time, but I understood enough to get the general idea when ye came home and were whispering wi' Duncan about what ye'd been up to. I learnt a lot frae those conversations. In fact, it was because of you that I ken how to…" He broke off as Alex made a threatening gesture, and skipped lightly off into the kitchen, chuckling.

Beth and Duncan laughed in unison at Alex's blood-red face. It was rare for Angus to turn the tables so neatly on his older brother.

"Aye," said Duncan, looking after him. "He's becoming a man all right."

"No, it doesn't bother me," Beth said later that night, in bed. "You didn't get the pox, did you?"

"No," he said. In spite of the darkness, she could feel the heat of his blushes, and smiled to herself.

"What you did before you married me is no concern of mine," she said. "I'd have been surprised if you hadn't been with the odd prostitute. You're a red-blooded male, after all." Now it was her turn to blush as she thought of just how she knew that. "I'd rather you did that than get some girl pregnant, then abandon her."

"I'd never have done that!" he retorted.

"I know. And I don't think Angus will, either. He knows where to draw the line. He might be reckless at times, but he's not an idiot. Neither are you, I hope. Because now we are married, and if I ever find out you've been…"

He put a finger lightly on her lips.

"There's nae danger of that, I've tellt ye already. I take my wedding vows seriously. Forsaking all others. Unlike yourself."

"What!"

"Ye promised to obey, as I remember."

"Oh, that," she said, relaxing back. "Well, I do, mostly. Some of the time, anyway. I have good intentions."

"Do ye now?" he said. "Well I dinna. And I'll thank ye to obey me, by…"

The rest of the sentence was muffled as he drew the blankets up over them both. Feminine giggles drifted out from under the covers as she did, indeed, obey him for once, with enthusiasm. With the result that they both overslept the following morning.

CHAPTER FIVE

The MacDonalds arrived the next day. Beth had expected maybe two or three of her nearest relations to come, but as they started to make their way down the hill to the MacGregor settlement, led by their piper and clad in plaids of various hues, a sprig of heather in their bonnets and armed as though for war, she realised that there were a good many more than that; about thirty or so, at a rough estimate. They greeted the MacGregor chieftain warmly, allaying Beth's fears that they had come to raid rather than celebrate, then turned to Beth.

"You'll be the bride, then," one of them, a stocky swarthy man with dark hair and beard said to her. It was not a question, and she wondered how he knew, because Alex had not yet introduced her, and she was standing amidst a group of other women. The MacDonald saw her perplexity and smiled.

"Ye've the look of the clan about ye," he explained.

As all the members of the clan so far appeared to be brown or red-haired, and stocky of build, this puzzled Beth even more.

"What Donald means is you look like your mother, and your grandmother, and all her kin," clarified his wife, who had made her way to his side, a small child balanced comfortably on her hip. "They all have the same hair, and are small and feeble-looking, like yourself. We used to say they were changelings."

Alex cast his wife a warning look, willing her not to react, but she hardly noticed the comment, being so delighted that there were others who resembled her amongst the clan, even if they had chosen not to attend the wedding celebrations.

"They're no' feeble, though, whatever their appearance," remarked another man. "Christ, they can be stubborn, vicious bastards when crossed!"

"That's Beth's family all right, then," said Angus from somewhere in the background, and everyone laughed.

Formal greetings over with, the MacDonalds repaired to the various homes they were to stay in to freshen up and have something to eat. Beth wandered off with Alex to their house, with Duncan and Angus following behind. The actual wedding party was fixed for tomorrow, but there would be a good deal of alcohol drunk tonight. Alex had a dual purpose in inviting the MacDonalds; as well as pleasing his wife, it would improve cordial relations between the two clans, always a good thing when the mutual Campbell enemy was so strong and numerous. Having said that, Beth's look of ecstasy as she skipped along beside him was on its own worth all the extra food and whisky that would be consumed over the next couple of days.

"It's a shame that none of my actual direct blood kin could come," Beth said as they arrived home.

"They are coming," said Alex. "They've just taken the longer route, that's all."

"Are they?" cried Beth. "That's wonderful! I wonder why they've taken the long route?"

"Because one of them's as bloody-minded as yourself," Alex said, but in spite of her cajoling, would not explain further, saying only that she would see why for herself in an hour or so when they turned up.

She did. When they arrived there were five of them, two men and three women, and they were in a carriage of sorts, which was why they'd taken the long way. Any thoughts that this might be due to some misguided delusion of grandeur was dispelled when the two men, both flaxen-haired and slender of build, leapt down from the coach, and with great care and tenderness assisted a woman down to the ground. The other two women jumped down unassisted. They were also blonde, although their hair was more honey-coloured than silver.

The woman they were assisting was silver-haired, but this was due to her extreme age. Even so, once safely on the ground she stood unaided, frail but erect, her blue eyes shrewd and intelligent as she surveyed the settlement and the people who had come out to greet her on hearing the coach. Beth, who was amongst them, and who in fact had been glued to the doorway listening for their arrival ever since Alex's enigmatic words, gasped. This woman was so like her mother, or like her mother would have been had she lived to old age, that the sight of her brought tears to Beth's eyes. She felt Alex's comforting hand on her shoulder and swallowed back the tears. Then she moved forward to greet her relation, trying to work out who she could possibly be. Her mother, who would have been fifty-four now, had she lived, had had no sisters, and this woman was older than that anyway, maybe seventy. Her great-aunt, perhaps? Yet Beth's grandmother, after whom Beth was named, had been thirty when Ann was born, and had been the youngest of her family.

"*Fàilte. Tha mi toilichte ur coinneachadh,*" Beth began. She *was* pleased to meet the old lady, even if she didn't know the exact relationship between them.

The woman smiled warmly. Her face, although deeply lined still showed clearly that she had once been beautiful, had looked like the young woman standing before her. As Beth would no doubt one day look like her, if she was lucky enough to live so long.

"*Halò, m'ogha. Tha mi toilichte do coinneachadh cuideachd.*"

Beth's eyes widened in disbelief. She could not have heard right. The blond man standing at the old lady's side spoke now for the first time.

"*Seo do sheanmhair, Ealasaid,*" he said gently.

Her grandmother?

"But I thought you were dead!" Beth cried, and then blushed. "I mean…"

"I'm no' dead yet." Beth's grandmother laughed. Her voice was clear and strong. "Although I thought at times the road would finish me off. I think I would have done better to ride, after all! No, *mo chridhe,*" she continued in a softer voice, "I was transported to the colonies a few years after the massacre of '92, because I wouldna accept what the authorities had done and be grateful to be allowed to return to my ravaged home. I only came back a few years ago. But we can talk of this later. We have a lot to say to each other, I think." She reached out and gently caressed Beth's cheek with a trembling hand. "You are so like Ann," she whispered.

And then they were embracing, and crying, after which Alex offered the old lady his arm, and gallantly led her to his house, where she was assisted upstairs to gratefully lie down for a time on the bed which was normally shared by Angus and Duncan, but which they had temporarily vacated in favour of Iain and Maggie's house. The MacDonalds would have been insulted if such an honoured guest had not been accommodated in the chieftain's house.

"I'm just glad that Alexander didna come," said Alex an hour or two later. "If he had, he'd have had to be accommodated in our house as well, being the chief, and it would have been a wee bit difficult."

They had gone out for a while, ostensibly to leave the old lady in peace, but also to have a little time together to talk before the wedding and the duties of hospitality swept away all chance of any time alone for several days. They were sitting on a fallen tree near the lochside, watching the sun set over the water.

"We could have slept downstairs," Beth said.

"Aye, but that's no' what I meant," Alex replied. "Ye'll be wanting some time to chat quietly wi' your grandmother, I'm thinking, and the MacDonald is a braw man, a brave warrior, and a great wit. But he's a wee bit larger than life, if you take my meaning, and no' one for quiet chats by the fire."

"I can't believe she's still alive," said Beth, dismissing the MacDonald chief from her mind. "She must be eighty-five. Mother told me that she was arrested in 1694 with some others, for killing a group of government soldiers, and died in prison of a fever. Mother was brought up by her aunt after that. I can't understand it. Why weren't they told if she was transported? And why didn't she let the clan know she was alive?"

"It's probably because the situation was verra sensitive at the time. The government were seriously embarrassed when the news got out that they'd at least condoned, if not actually ordered the massacre of the MacDonalds, who had, after all already submitted to the crown. King Billy had intended to transport all the survivors to the colonies, but there was such an outcry he changed his mind. No doubt it was more politic to let the world know that the arrested MacDonalds had died of natural causes rather than that they were being transported for taking revenge against those who had butchered their kin. But as for why your grandmother didna tell anyone she wasna dead, ye'll have to ask her that yourself."

"I will," Beth said, "as soon as I get the opportunity."

She sat for a moment in silence, swinging her legs. Alex put his arm round her shoulder. It was warm and comforting. She felt safe, contented.

"She's certainly not weak and feeble, is she?" she said after a time.

"No, she isna. And neither are you. And everybody kens it well, and would have done even if your granny hadna come to the wedding, Beth. Ye dinna need to prove yourself any more."

She smiled.

"I know," she said. "Do you know what makes me really happy? It's the fact that now I've established myself a bit, that I don't have to pretend to be something I'm not. And that you are truly relaxed for the first time since I married you."

He looked down at her.

"Why, am I normally tense?" he asked.

"I never noticed that you were when we were in London, or Europe. You just seemed normal, or as normal as you could be, having two completely different identities. It's only since we've been here that I've seen the difference in you. You're at home here, and at ease, somehow. Not so alert for trouble all the time. It's subtle, but …oh, I don't know how to explain it. You don't rub your hand through your hair very often, anyway. I'm not married to a porcupine any more. It's nice."

He laughed.

"Aye, you're right. This is my home. You're seeing us at a particularly peaceful time, mind. There have been times when I've been tearing my hair out by the roots. But I dinna have to watch my back all the time to see if anyone's about to stick a knife in it, or no' anyone of my own clan, anyway. Being with your own folk, those ye love, in the land of your heart is the best thing there is."

"Yes, it is, isn't it?" she said happily.

"Do ye really mean that?" he asked.

She had said it without thinking, but now she realised that she had spoken no more than the truth.

"Yes," she said slowly. "Yes, I do. I could quite happily spend the rest of my life here, I think. I know it's not all roses, but I like adventure, as you know. Yes, then, in answer to the question you asked before we came here; I do feel at home here. I miss nothing at all of the London life. I'm dreading going back, to be honest. I'd be quite happy if I never saw Sir Anthony again, amusing as he is at times."

He felt as though he was dancing on air, ecstatic. He had prayed she would be happy here, that she would be content to make her life amongst his people, but in spite of her assertions that she hated society life, he had wondered if the novelty of being the chieftain's wife would wear off after a time, and she would start to yearn for her old way of life, the opera or the theatre, or even for more variety of foodstuffs. Once again he had underestimated her, he realised. She did not apologise unless she was sorry. And she did not make claims lightly. When she had told him she hated the restrictions and duplicity of society life, she had truly meant it. He should have believed her. He curled his arm closer round her shoulders and drew her in to him. She put her arm around his waist, hooking her thumb under his swordbelt. The sun was low over the hills now. Soon it would disappear behind them and the temperature would cool dramatically. They sat in silence, just enjoying the sheer joy of being together in a beautiful place, in their home, young and healthy and in love. A nightingale sang melodiously in a nearby tree. Life was perfect.

"What's wrong?" Alex said suddenly and inexplicably. Beth was about to answer that nothing was wrong, that on the contrary nothing had ever been more right than this moment, when she realised that he wasn't speaking to her, but to Duncan, who had approached with the customary silence of the MacGregors and now moved round the side of the tree into sight.

"Nothing," he said. As Duncan was the last person to intrude upon another's private space without good reason, Alex raised a disbelieving eyebrow and waited for his brother to explain his unusual behaviour.

"It's just that with it being the eve of your wedding, as far as the clan are concerned, that is, them considering the fact of ye's being already married as a mere formality, so to speak, they asked me to come down here and have a wee word wi' ye both regarding certain customs to be followed at this special time…"

This long-winded preamble was so alien to Duncan's normal way of speaking that even Beth began to be somewhat suspicious.

"What're ye blethering on about, man? Out wi' it," Alex interrupted.

"Of course, ye'll maybe no' ken the tradition, Beth, unless your mother tellt ye about it," continued Duncan pleasantly to Beth, as though Alex hadn't spoken. "It's no' an English custom, I'm thinking."

"What isn't?" asked Beth.

Duncan's grey gaze wandered absently over Beth's shoulder to the trees behind her, as he thought of how to explain the custom.

"Well," he said after a moment. "Normally, on the evening before the wedding, it's customary for a washing of the feet to take place…"

Alex launched himself from the log and hit the ground running, almost dislocating Beth's thumb in the process, which had still been hooked through his swordbelt. He hurtled through the trees, making straight for the loch, unbuckling his belt en route and letting his sword and dirk fall to the ground. Duncan and Beth followed his progress with interest for a moment, before the sound of a great number of feet in pursuit drew her attention away from her husband's flight. Half the men of the clan charged into the woodland after him, whooping with glee. Beth turned her attention back to Duncan, who had made no move to join them. She realised that his seemingly absent glance over her shoulder had been to judge the proximity of the pursuit.

"Aye," he continued amiably. "It's a verra ancient custom, and likely something to do wi' our Lord washing the feet of the disciples. A sign of respect and friendship, if ye like."

There was a splash as Alex dived into the loch and struck out strongly for the other side, then several more as his pursuers joined him.

"That's nice," said Beth insincerely. Alex would never have reacted like that to a simple washing of the feet. Clearly there was something far more sinister involved. There was obviously nothing she could do to help him, and however unpleasant this was likely to be for him, it was unlikely to be life-threatening. Hopefully. "Do all the men have their feet washed before they get married?" she asked.

"Oh, aye. And no' just the men, but the women too," said Duncan.

"What?" she said.

"It's normal that the men wash the groom's feet, and the women wash the bride's," Duncan said, catching hold of her hands as she jumped down from the log, and refusing to relinquish them when she tried to pull free. A yodelling cry of triumph came from the direction of the water. Alex had presumably been overtaken by the others. The giant Kenneth had been leading the pursuit. If it was him who'd caught up with the prey, Alex didn't stand a chance.

"Ah, now, dinna fash yourself, lassie," said Duncan soothingly. "Alex is overreacting. It's no' that bad. We wouldna do it to ye if we didna think of ye as one of us now." He smiled reassuringly.

Beth was not reassured. This time when Duncan looked over her shoulder, Beth twisted in his grip to see what he was looking at. A file of women was making its way towards her. Beth didn't know whether to be comforted or not by the fact that Maggie was indeed carrying a bowl, which could be used for washing feet.

"Well," said Duncan as the women reached them. "I'll away off and see how my brother's doing. I wish ye a pleasant night." His brother had been hauled unceremoniously from the loch, having put up a ferocious struggle, during which he had swallowed a considerable amount of water, and as Duncan relinquished Beth to the brawny arms of Peigi, Maggie and the other females, the men began to make their triumphant way back through the trees carrying their reluctant and dripping chieftain by the arms and legs.

Duncan picked up the discarded swordbelt and made his way leisurely after the other men, whistling softly as he went, and leaving his sister-in-law to the tender ministrations of her recently adopted clanswomen.

* * *

"Honestly," said Beth much later that evening, in the house. "I don't know why you made such a fuss, running off like that. I was frightened to death. I thought they were going to flay me alive, the way you reacted."

Beth had been firmly pinioned and had had her feet and legs thoroughly 'washed' in soot and some sort of smelly paste which had left her lower limbs an interesting shade of mustard yellow, even after repeated washings with soap and water. The women had reassured her as they passed the whisky around, that the colour was harmless and would fade in a day or so. Alex wouldn't be put off performing his marital duties by having a wife who looked half-chinese, they laughed, and if he was, she should look for an alternative man. This comment had led to some more ribald observations about sex, and on the whole, in spite of her yellow legs and slightly malodorous smell, she had enjoyed herself.

"Aye, well, it all depends on what they decide tae wash ye with," he said, scrubbing furiously at his shins to remove the final traces of shoe blacking from his skin. "And which bits they decide tae wash." He had cleaned his private parts down by the loch, in spite of his men's suggestions that he get his wife to do it for him. That would have been very pleasant indeed were he not playing host to her aged grandmother at the moment.

The old lady was sitting in a chair by the fire, her face wreathed in smiles.

"He's right," she said now, briskly wringing out a cloth in a bowl of water and passing it to him. He thanked her and began to wash between his toes. "Ye've got off lightly. They often use manure, and the more it reeks, the better," she said.

"Even if they had used manure, there was still no reason to hare off like that," said Beth. "And you could have warned me that I was in danger too."

"Aye, you're right, I'm sorry. But I kent as they wouldna do anything bad to you. Whereas I thought Duncan might take the opportunity to get his revenge for what I did to him on his wedding eve."

"Duncan?" said Beth, surprised.

"I was a lot younger then, ye understand, and more like Angus, a wee bit stupid at times. I'd only been the chieftain for a few months, and hadna grown into the responsibility of it. I wouldna do such a thing now."

"What did ye do?" the old lady asked.

Alex stopped scrubbing and looked up, the wicked gleam in his eye saying clearly that whether he would do whatever it was now or not, he certainly didn't regret having done it then.

"We tarred and feathered him," he said.

Beth's mouth fell open, whilst her grandmother hooted with laughter.

"Oh, the poor bairn!" she cried. "Ye used proper tar, then?"

"Aye," Alex said. "And feathers from the hens we kept at the time. I canna even say it was a spur of the moment thing. I'd been saving the feathers for weeks. Of course we only did his legs and arms, ye ken. We didna tar his…er…other bits. Even so, Mairi, his wife that was, was awfu' angry."

"Well, I'm no' surprised!" said Ealasaid.

Alex laughed.

"It took him ages to scrape and scrub it all off, and his arms and legs were brown for days. I had tae keep away from Mairi for weeks after that. I couldna even claim it was someone else's doing. It's no' easy, being the chieftain at times," he said ruefully. "Ye have tae take the blame for everything."

"I didn't know Duncan had been married," said Beth.

"Ah. I wasna sure if he'd tellt ye or no'. He doesna talk about it overmuch. It was all over a long time ago. He was only nineteen when he married."

"What happened?" asked Beth. "Didn't they get along together?" She couldn't imagine anyone not getting along with Duncan. He was so easy to be with.

"Christ, no! It wasna that. They loved each other like…well…like you and I do. No, she died."

Beth was so surprised at finding out that Duncan had been married, she didn't notice the finality of tone that said Alex didn't want to pursue the subject further.

"Oh, that's terrible," she said. "How did she die?"

Childbirth was the most likely cause, she thought.

"Er…it was an accident, in a manner of speaking," he said.

She heard the reluctance in his voice now, and saw his uneasy glance at her grandmother.

"I think it's best we dinna talk of it now," he said.

"I ken what happened, laddie, if that's what you're worried about," the old lady said. "I didna get back from the colonies till it was all over, but Glencoe holds no grudges now. He thought ye dealt with it well, ye being so young an' all."

"That's good to hear, *sheanmhair*," he said, "but it isna polite tae speak of a blood feud between your clan and that of the one you're hosting."

"It's your wife's clan too," pointed out the old lady, smiling at his addressing her as grandmother. He was a courteous man. "She has a right to know of it, unless ye're thinking your brother would have an objection."

Beth's eyes were burning with curiosity, but she wouldn't push Alex into pursuing the subject unless he wanted to.

Alex sighed, and abandoned his ablutions.

"No," he said. "Duncan wouldna object, although he wouldna volunteer the information himself. He thinks very highly of Beth."

"Well, then. I'll no' be offended. And it'll no' be brought up outside these walls," Ealasaid said.

"Verra well, then. D'ye want to hear it?" he said to Beth.

"Not if you don't want to tell me, no," she replied, giving him the chance to back out.

He stood and went to the shelf in the corner, taking down a bottle of wine and three glasses. He shared them out, then sat down and stared into the fire for a short time.

"I suppose your grandmother's right, Beth," he said finally. "You should know, and it'll give ye some idea of how things are up here when it isna all milk and honey, as it is now.

"Well then, as I said, Duncan was nineteen when he married Mairi, and she was seventeen. She was a bonny lassie, a Cameron. She had a fearful temper on her when roused, but Duncan could calm her, he's always had that way wi' people. Anyway, they'd been married for about six months, when the MacDonalds decided to raid our cattle."

"I thought you said the MacDonalds and MacGregors were friends!" Beth said.

"We are, but that doesna stop ye raiding each other. Everyone does it, it's no' a matter for hatred, more a warning that ye should be taking better care of your animals. We'd hae done the same. There wasna any ill feeling over that. Well, no' much, anyway. We didna live here then, ye ken, but a wee bit further north. Anyway, they made off wi' thirty head of our cattle from the hills, and Mairi had been watching over them."

Beth suddenly wished that she hadn't asked how Mairi had

died. A terrible dread filled her.

"Did the MacDonalds kill Mairi when they took the cattle?" she asked apprehensively.

"God, no. They took her along wi' them. No, they didna harm her at all. Anyway, as I said, she had a fearful temper, and she was determined they were no' going to have an easy time of it, so she hamstrung three of the calves wi' her knife to slow them down. Of course the mothers wouldna carry on without their babies, and so the MacDonalds had to stop to try to sort it out. She was hoping to run away in the confusion and tell us so we could send a party out tae get them back." He drained his wine and refilled the glass.

"She might have managed it, too. Certainly the MacDonalds were concentrating so much on the cattle that they didna hear the MacFarlanes until they were almost on them. There was somewhat of a stramash, and Mairi was caught in the crossfire and killed. Two of the MacDonalds were killed as well, and three of the MacFarlanes. The MacDonalds got the better of it, and brought the cattle and Mairi's body back to us the next day."

"That was awfu' brave of them," Ealasaid commented.

"Aye, it was," Alex agreed. "All the more so because we MacGregors are no' renowned for our reasonable natures, and they didna ken what manner of chief I was, being so new to the job, as it were. They even admitted that they didna ken if it was them or the MacFarlanes that had killed her, things being somewhat frantic at the time. I admired their courage and agreed to leave it to Glencoe to decide their punishment, although I tellt them I would be visiting him to make sure that justice had been done."

"It was," the old lady said. "Alexander had them flogged. He tellt me that himself."

"So it *was* an accident," Beth said. "God, poor Duncan. He must have been heartbroken."

In spite of Beth's earlier comment about the disappearance of the porcupine, Alex now scrubbed his hand viciously through his hair. She leaned over and captured his hand as he was about to repeat the gesture.

"You don't have to tell me any more if you don't want to," she said, aware that there was clearly more to the story and that it was not pleasant.

"I'd as soon get it over with now I've started," he said. "I'm all right."

The old lady stood up suddenly, with surprising agility.

"Well, an ye'll excuse an old lady's rudeness," she said. "It's been a long day, and if ye've no objections, I'll away to my bed."

Alex and Beth stood to wish her goodnight and Alex gallantly escorted her up the steps. Beth heard a short whispered exchange between her grandmother and husband, and then he came back down alone, his eyes strangely moist. He pulled his chair closer to Beth's and she took his hand again. He continued with the story, his eyes dark with remembered pain.

"I sent the raiders off home, and then I called Duncan in, and tellt him what had happened. He was always the reasonable one of us three, always the peacemaker. He still is. I kent he'd be verra upset, but I was sure he'd understand that it was a tragic accident, too."

"But he didn't understand, did he?" Beth said.

"No, he didna. He went wild with grief, said he was going to kill every MacDonald in Scotland, and…I've never seen him so, and hope I never will again. I ended up having to lock him up for two days until he calmed down. I thought that would be long enough. I didna understand then. I do now."

"Understand what?" Beth said.

"What love can do tae a man, how it can drive him beyond reason. MacDonald of Glencoe understood it, thank God. But I'd never been in love then, had no idea…Christ, Beth, if I even think about anyone hurting ye, it makes my blood boil. I'd kill any man who laid a violent hand on ye, ye ken that."

She did.

"Do I ken him?" he asked suddenly.

"Who?" she asked, thoroughly confused.

"The man who hurt ye? I'll no' force ye to tell me who he is, until ye want to, but if I ken the man, it's a whole different matter, ye understand."

She was paralysed by the sudden change of subject. What could she say? If she admitted that Alex did know her assailant, he would insist on her identifying him. She had no idea what Duncan had done to his wife's killers, but she could imagine all too clearly what Alex would do to Richard.

She had sworn not to lie to him. She could not tell him the truth. She sat there, stricken, speechless.

"I'm sorry," Alex said. "I didna mean to remind ye of him and what he did. I can see I've upset ye. But I couldna stand it if I'd spoken pleasantly to the man unawares, and him having hurt ye so."

She made her decision, and summoned up everything she had ever learned from Sir Anthony and everyone else she had had to dissemble with.

"No," she said. "You don't know him." She looked him straight in the eyes as she said it, because if she did not he would know she was lying. He had to believe her, but when she saw by his expression that he did, she felt sick with shame and self-loathing.

"Well, that's all right then. I'll speak no more of it. I'm sorry," he said.

She wanted to crawl away into a corner and die. He trusted her. He was sorry. For a moment she thought she was going to be sick, and she forced herself to concentrate on the continuing tale of Duncan until the feeling passed.

"Duncan waited for three days after Mairi had been buried, then he left. He said he wanted to be by himself for a while, to think things over, and I believed him. He'd never lied to me before," Alex said.

Beth closed her eyes. She felt genuinely ill. How could this have happened? Three hours ago they had been sitting on a tree deeply in love, and now she had betrayed his trust. She swallowed, thankful that the story he was telling her was distressing enough to account for her behaviour.

"What did he really do?" she asked.

"He killed five of the MacDonalds who'd raided the cattle. The last one wounded Duncan in the side before he died. He was away for a week, and when he came back he was in a bad way, for the wound was turning bad."

"But you said it was an accident," Beth said.

"Aye, so it was, but Duncan didna see it that way. Whoever had killed Mairi, he blamed the MacDonalds, because they'd taken her hostage and should have looked after her. Well, of course I had some sympathy for him, but I also kent that I had maybe fifty men at best and Glencoe has nearly four times that number. If he chose to make a blood debt of it, which I was pretty sure he would, we didna have a chance."

"What did you do?"

"I discussed it wi' the clan, and then decided that the only way to avoid annihilation was to go to Glencoe and ask him if he'd be happy to settle the matter by single combat. And then I made the mistake of telling Duncan what I intended to do. I thought he was too sick to say anything against it, but his fever had broken and he insisted that if anyone was going to die because of his actions, it would be him, no' me, and that he would go and challenge the MacDonald chief himself. I couldna let him do that. I was in full strength and in all honesty didna rate my chances of survival very highly. Glencoe was a formidable man. Duncan, weak as he was and only nineteen, wouldna have had a hope."

The candle guttered in the sudden draught, but Beth hardly noticed it.

"What happened?" she asked, thoroughly engrossed in the story again.

"He broke my wrist," Duncan said from the doorway. His voice, normally soft and well-modulated, was flat and hard.

Beth started violently and turned to the door.

"I came to fetch my best plaid for the morrow," he said, taking two paces into the room and then stopping.

"Would ye rather I didna…?" Alex began.

Duncan waved a hand in the air.

"No, I dinna mind if she kens about it," he interrupted, then turned to Beth. "Ye'll understand why I did it, I think," he said. "Alex does, now. I was wrong, but I couldna say that if it happened now I wouldna do the same thing again." He sat down heavily, his eyes guarded. "Go on," he said to his brother. Alex searched Duncan's face for a moment, then continued.

"As Duncan said, we argued and I broke his wrist. I couldna think of anything else to do. I couldna get him to see reason, and I wasna about to lose my brother as well as my sister-in-law."

"Couldn't you have just locked him up again?" Beth said. "You'd already done that once."

"Aye, I had, but things were different by then. For one thing, he'd just killed five of the MacDonalds. There were those in the clan who resented the fact that he was risking a blood feud for the sake of personal vengeance over an accident. Others thought he had the right to challenge Glencoe himself. And quite a few didna see why their chieftain should risk his own life to save his idiot of a brother." He smiled fondly at Duncan. "If I'd locked him up there was a good chance that the minute I left for Glencoe, someone would hae let him go."

"I'd have made sure they did," agreed Duncan.

"But you were the chieftain. Isn't your word law?" Beth said.

"Aye. It is, now. But ye've got the wrong idea about chieftainship, Beth. The chieftain isna God. Nor is he the king. When the king dies, his eldest son takes the throne, no matter what kind of dribbling idiot he is. When my da died, I had the right to take his place – but I had to prove myself worthy of it. If I hadna, the clan would have found someone else more suitable. It was made harder for me by the fact that I'd been away in France for two years. There were those that thought I might have gone soft while I was there, and I'd no' been the chieftain long enough to prove I hadna, when all this happened." Alex paused, searching for the right words to try to justify his action. "We're a violent clan, Beth," he said finally. "All the clans are violent when they have tae be, but the MacGregors are more so, being proscribed, because we have no recourse to law. Often, when I'm faced wi' a problem, the first solution I think of is the violent one. It's second nature. Then I think again and often I'll come up wi' another way. And sometimes I won't."

"Like with Henri," Beth said.

"Aye. I had to kill him. And I had to make sure that there was no point in Duncan following me. And the only way I could do that was to make sure he couldna fight the MacDonald, and wouldna be able to for quite a while."

"He was right, Beth," said Duncan. "I'd have done the same in his position."

"Go on then," said Beth. "What happened next?"

"I went to MacDonald," said Alex, "and I tellt him everything, including what I'd done to Duncan, so that he wouldna think Duncan didna have the courage to meet him. He agreed to the single combat, but said that if I didna take it amiss he'd no' fight me himself, lately having been ill, but get one of his clansmen to do it instead. I didna take it amiss, as I couldna think of any member of the clan I'd be afraid to fight, excepting the chief himself."

"But you would have fought him, if you'd had to," Beth said.

"Aye, of course I would. It isna cowardly to be afraid. It isna cowardly to run away either, if you're faced wi' impossible odds. It's common sense. Unless you're betraying others by doing so. Of course now I realise that Glencoe hadna been ill at all, but admired my courage and understood why Duncan had acted as he had. He didna want a blood feud either, which could have escalated tae include other branches of the MacGregors and MacDonalds in time. So he chose a man who was well-matched to me in size and strength, and we fought. He was a bonny fighter. Malcolm, his name was." Alex stopped and looked at Duncan. A look of such intensity passed between them that Beth had to turn away.

"Needless to say, Alex killed Malcolm, and there has been mutual respect between Glencoe and us ever since," Duncan took up the story. "And I'm alive, although for a long time I didna thank my brother for that blessing. And your clan and mine are no' embroiled in a bloody and pointless feud, but instead are going to enjoy a great celebration of the joining of a MacGregor and a MacDonald."

"I'm so sorry, Duncan," Beth said helplessly.

"Dinna be sorry, lassie. Just love each other, like Mairi and I did. Ye do, I can see that. And treasure every day as though it'll be your last. If I'd have…" he stopped, and his face contorted for a moment, then he stood.

"I'll be taking my plaid, then," he said. "And I'll wish ye a good night." He moved across the room to the chest where all their clothes were kept and which doubled as a seat, and busied himself, his back turned to them. Beth opened her mouth to speak, her eyes brimming, but Alex folded his hand over hers and she remained silent. Duncan closed the lid of the chest and walked to the door, a bundle tucked under his arm. He nodded once and was gone.

Alex's eyes remained on the door, dark with a multitude of emotions Beth could not even begin to identify.

"I'll no' speak of it again, if it's all the same to you," he said, "unless ye've any questions?"

She had no questions, and when they went to bed they did not make love, by mutual consent, being too emotionally distressed to do so, although the reasons for their distress were not entirely the same. Instead they curled up together wrapped in each others' arms and silently waited for sleep to come.

It was a long time coming, particularly for Beth, whose head was reeling, not just with the news of Duncan's tragic marriage and the knowledge that the wound it had inflicted on him had not even begun to heal after eight years, but also with the awareness that she had betrayed her husband's trust in her, and broken her own vow not to lie to him. She felt justified in doing so; much as she hated Richard, she would not be directly responsible for his death, as she would be if she told Alex what he had done to her. That Alex would succeed in killing Richard if he wished to, she did not doubt for one moment. But she could not live with the death of her brother on her conscience. After all, he had come off worst in the encounter between them. They were even, in her view, although Alex, with the pride of the Highlander, would not see it that way, she knew.

No, she reasoned, she could not have done other than she did. The thought should have comforted her, but it did not.

Alex had been breathing softly and regularly for a long time before tiredness overwhelmed Beth's conscience and allowed her to join him in sleep.

When Beth awoke in the morning Alex was kneeling down near the side of the bed, clad only in his shirt. She watched him for a while through half-open eyes as he prepared his *feileadh mhor*, laying the long piece of faded green and brown material on the ground over his belt, then deftly pleating the long length of it, leaving a small amount at each end unpleated. He was unaware that he was being observed, and moved quickly and gracefully, performing the habitual actions automatically and expertly. She felt a small thrill of pleasure, seeing the heavy muscles of his shoulders and arms perfectly defined through the thin material of his shirt as he bent over his task, the strong wrists and long capable fingers, remembering the heavy, comforting warmth of him in the bed during the night as he had held her close to him.

The material prepared, Alex lay down on top of it, folded the unpleated material over his stomach, and buckled his belt tightly round his waist. When he got to his feet the lower width of the material had become a kilt, reaching to his knees, the upper part trailing over the belt almost to the floor. He reached behind, gathering the surplus material in loose folds, drawing it over his left shoulder and pinning it in place with an ornate silver brooch. It was a remarkable garment, she realised. A simple length of woollen material could become a kilt, a cloak, a blanket, even a shelter. This clothing, coupled with an imperviousness to hunger and even the most extreme weather made the Highlander a formidable foe; armed with pistol, broadsword, dirk, targe and bag of oatmeal, he could travel all day across country, unimpeded by the cumbersome baggage wagons containing tents and other provisions considered so essential to the average soldier. He could sleep anywhere, wrapped in his plaid, perfectly camouflaged, and materialise from the heather as if by magic at a moment's notice to hurl himself at his unsuspecting, terrified enemy.

She had once been terrified of him, she remembered, in a disused room in a Manchester alleyway. She continued to watch him as he sat down on a wooden stool near the bed to pull on his hose. She was not afraid of him any more, although she respected him; it was impossible not to. He radiated confidence, authority and a carefully leashed power that could erupt into violence when challenged. Not against her; she knew that he would never raise his hand to her. But against anyone who threatened him or those he loved. It was a powerful aphrodisiac, having such a formidable man on your side, protecting you, loving you.

It was also the reason she had been compelled to lie to him last night. He would never intentionally hurt her; but what he would do to Richard if she told him the truth did not bear thinking about. She did not need Alex to fight this battle for her. She had fought Richard and got the better of him. They had made an agreement; she would marry the foppish Sir Anthony, and he would obtain his military commission and disappear from her life. They had both kept to the bargain, and as far as she was concerned she had got the better of that, too. Looking at her magnificent husband as he finished pulling up his hose and looked around for his shoes, she was sure of her victory. She put Richard and her deception firmly to the back of her mind. This was her wedding day, in a manner of speaking, for the third time. She intended to enjoy it.

"They're under the bed," she said.

He looked at her and smiled, his eyes crinkling at the corners, and she lifted her arms to him. He came willingly, folding her to his chest, and she snuggled into him, inhaling the scents of linen, wool, and healthy young male. His brooch was cool against her cheek and she shifted her head slightly.

"You're not wearing that for the celebrations, are you?" she said, fingering the soft worn wool of his kilt.

"God, no," he replied. "The clan would disown me if I did. It's the full garb of the chieftain for me tonight. I have the MacDonalds to impress, ye ken. No, I thought I'd away off for a wee walk, leave ye to talk to your kin in peace. They're all downstairs, having breakfast."

Beth, intoxicated by the part of his scent that was young and male, had been about to suggest some dual activity rather more enjoyable than 'a wee walk', but now shot up in bed.

"What?" she cried. "They're all downstairs now? Why didn't you wake me?"

"Relax," he said soothingly, maintaining his hold on her. "A few minutes more'll make nae difference. Duncan is looking after them."

"But shouldn't I be making breakfast for them?" she asked. "What sort of a chieftain's wife will they think me if I leave my guests to fend for themselves?"

"One that doesna burn the porridge, or make it too thin," Alex said wryly. Beth's repeated failure to successfully prepare a dish as simple as porridge was a cause for hilarity throughout the clan. It was ridiculous; she could make oatcakes and bannocks, could, now that Duncan had taught her, skin and prepare a rabbit and make various other dishes to perfection. But porridge, a simple dish of oatmeal and water, escaped her. It was either thin and runny, or cement. She had accepted the jokes about slices of porridge and filler for the gaps in walls with good humour, and given up. The three men she shared a house with were all excellent cooks anyway. Highlanders did not consider cooking women's work, as the English did. And she could not be good at everything, as Alex had said. Even so…

"At the very least I should be down there entertaining them instead of making love to you," she said, breaking free of him and swinging her legs out of bed.

"Who said anything about making love?" Alex asked, accepting his shoes as she bent down and pulled them out from where he'd kicked them the night before.

"Ah, well…" she said, colouring prettily. "I had thought…but that was before I knew there were half a dozen MacDonalds sitting directly underneath the bedroom." She dodged neatly out of his way as he made a grab for her.

"You're a hard woman, Beth," he said mournfully, "raising a man's hopes like that."

"Well, I've heard it called a lot of things, but never a 'hope'. You'll just have to lower it again until later. Have a cold swim in the loch. That should do the trick."

She emerged from donning her shift to find him a lot closer to her than she'd thought. Too close to dodge. He grabbed her, pinning her arms, and kissed her long and deep, smiling as he felt her body respond automatically to him. His hand slid smoothly up under her shift, caressing the inside of her thighs. She sighed, her legs turning to water, the MacDonalds forgotten.

"Until later, then," he said, releasing her suddenly with a mischievous grin. "I'll no' forget."

Neither would she. It took her five minutes after he'd gone to compose herself before she could go down to her family.

Duncan had done them proud. The porridge had been cooked to perfection, the oatcakes were warm and dripping with butter and honey, and he had even brewed coffee for them, two of them never having tasted it before. Judging by the grimaces on their faces, they wouldn't want to taste it again.

"I tellt ye that ye wouldna like it," Ealasaid said. "We drank it all the time in America. It's an acquired taste."

"Euch," said Meg. "I'll leave it to the Americans and the Sasannachs tae acquire it, then."

They had repaired to the lounge once breakfast was over, and once Beth's grandmother was comfortably settled in the chair by the fire, her young relatives scattered themselves casually around her.

"The Sasannachs drink tea mainly, now," Beth said. "At least the rich ones do. It's very expensive, so you have to pretend to enjoy it even if you don't, if you're not to be thought of as ill-bred."

"D'ye miss it?" asked Joan. Meg and Joan were nineteen and twins. Allan, at twenty-one, was their eldest surviving brother, and Robert at sixteen, the youngest. They were Beth's cousins, the grandchildren of Ealasaid's older sister, long dead.

"I've brought some with me. I quite like tea," Beth said, misunderstanding.

"I didna mean the tea, I meant the rich life, the fancy dresses and suchlike," Joan clarified.

Beth had to tread carefully. None of the MacDonalds knew about Sir Anthony. They only knew that Alex had met her in London, and that her English cousin was a lord.

"No," she said firmly. "I hate that life. The fancy dresses are itchy and uncomfortable, and all the people are horrible and false."

That was unfair.

"Well, not all the people," she amended. "I've got a few friends and they're wonderful, but in general you have to watch everything you do or say, and even then rumours spread round London like wildfire. You can't make a wrong move without everyone knowing about it within an hour."

"It's no' so different here," said Robert, looking at his great-aunt sourly. "I hadna so much as exchanged two words wi' Morag afore ye knew it and were thrashing me within an inch of my life."

"Ye'll become accustomed to Robbie's exaggerations soon enough, Beth," Ealasaid said, unperturbed by the allegation of unwarranted brutality. "What he means is that he was caught halfway to imperilling his immortal soul wi' the lassie, and I gave him a good thrashing wi' my tongue. And if you do it again, laddie, ye'll have cause to regret it. I'll use more than words next time."

Robert's blue eyes glittered with rebellion. Both the brothers, although of only average height and slender build, were wiry and powerful. And strikingly handsome. In spite of possessing Beth's silver-blond hair and cornflower blue eyes, there was nothing feminine or fragile about the brothers. Their features were strong and masculine, and they could both clearly handle themselves, although Robert was not as self-possessed as his older brother. Ealasaid was clearly concerned that there would be trouble later, if Robert attempted another seduction. His expression made it clear he had every intention of doing so. Her expression made it clear that she considered him a troublemaker, was regretting having allowed him to come, and would not normally have done so, had she not wanted Beth to meet her family.

"Have you met Angus yet?" Beth said casually. "You'd probably get on well with him. You seem to have a lot in common."

Robert's face creased with concentration.

"I'm no' sure," he said. "What does he look like?"

"He looks like Alex," she said. "They're brothers. He's got the height and build of Alex, but his hair is more the colour of Joan's. I'll introduce you later, if you like. He's a vicious fighter," she added, as though that was one of the things she thought they would have in common. "And he's very fond of Morag, too."

It was clear from his sudden pallor that Robert now remembered who Angus was. He glanced hopefully at Allan, and was greeted with an implacable glare that told him he could expect no help from that quarter if he antagonised the MacGregor chieftain's brother. Ealasaid hid her smile behind a handkerchief, and Beth continued talking as though she had not noticed the youth's reaction.

"What was life like in America, *sheanmhair*?" she asked.

"Hard, at first," her grandmother said. "But not as hard as the crossing. Nothing could be as bad as that. Nearly half of us died before we ever saw the land. And then your quality of life depended on who hired ye, ye ken. They tellt ye ye were sentenced to life as an indentured servant. But there isna any difference between that and being a slave. It's just a fancy word tae make it sound better."

She settled back in her chair, and her family gathered eagerly round her. The others, Beth excepted, had heard the story before, but it lost nothing in the retelling.

"When I was arrested, I thought they'd hang me. I wanted them to. I did shoot the Dragoon, after all, and I never tried to deny it. I was a wee bit crazy, I think. Once I knew that Ann would be well-cared for by my sister, I had nothing left to live for. I couldna believe it when they tellt me I was to be transported. Of course, there was such a fuss caused over the massacre, even in England, that they didna dare to hang a woman for revenging herself on the soldiers who'd murdered her kin. I was verra beautiful then, ye ken, like yourself," she said, smiling at her granddaughter, "and I had my last speech all prepared. There'd hae been a riot, and the authorities knew it. So they shuffled me quietly off to America. Well, the crossing might have weakened my body, but it didna hurt my spirit, and I'd decided I'd be no man's slave. I spent the first two years being beaten by my first master, before he gave up on me and put me up for hire again."

"Ye should see the scars, Beth," said Joan, shuddering.

"No, she shouldna," replied the old lady before one of her great-nieces suggested she bare her back for her granddaughter. "I'm no' proud of them. I was stupid. I couldna win, and I should have given up and accepted the life God had planned for me. He wasna such a bad man, that first one. Summerville, his name was. If I'd have accepted that I was to be a servant, I think I'd have had a far better life. He'd probably have released me, in time. But I was impossible. I tried to kill him three times before he gave me up for lost, and even then he didna give me up to the authorities as he should have done. It wasna his fault that the next man who bought me was an animal. Most of my scars are from him. He enjoyed wielding power, and the whip. He saw me as a challenge and he won, in time, in a way. He broke me, although I never let him see it."

She passed a hand over her face.

"Aye, well, I dinna talk about it. After he died, I was put up for hire again, and a sorry sight I was, too, all skin and bones and crawling wi' lice. It was a Campbell, of all things, who bought me after that."

"A Campbell?" said Beth. "God, that must have been terrible!"

It was the Campbells who had massacred the MacDonalds at Glencoe.

Ealasaid leaned forward in her seat.

"I'll tell ye something, lassie," she said earnestly. "For ye've the same spirit as myself. I can see it in ye. You need to ken when you're beaten, when the only person you're hurting by resisting is yourself. I should have stayed at home, brought my daughter up myself. I'll always regret no' doing that. Ye need to learn when it's wise to compromise. And ye need to learn that there's good and bad in everyone. Including the Campbells. Ye must judge each man as ye find him, no' by his name or his nationality. Archibald Campbell and his wife Annie were the best thing that ever happened to me. They were kind, they nursed me back to health, they put up with my insults, and then they gave me the offer of my freedom and a small farm on their land, at a very reasonable rent. I've never met such good people in my life. They shamed me into thinking about my behaviour. For the next thirty years or more I lived on the farm and was content, in my way. But I didna want to die in America. It wasna home. So when I thought my time was coming, I took my savings and booked my passage home. That was in '38 and here I am still waiting to die." She laughed. "I got that wrong, too. Ye never ken when your time's coming, only the good Lord knows that. Ye see, I'm still arrogant, in spite of it all."

"I'm glad you got it wrong," Beth said fervently. "At least I've had the chance to meet you. I wish my mother was still alive. She thought you were dead. We all did. Why didn't you write to us, tell us you were alive?"

"I was ashamed, for a long time. And by the time I wasna, there seemed no point, somehow. Most of those I'd loved were dead, killed in the massacre." The old lady's voice sunk to a whisper, and Beth, who was sitting at her feet, was the only one who heard the next sentence. "And I didna have the courage to face my daughter, knowing I'd abandoned her for a pointless revenge."

She reached down, stroked her granddaughter's cheek.

"It makes my heart proud to see what ye've come to. Married to a chieftain in front of the prince himself, and a fine man ye've got for yourself too, if my instincts are still true."

"They are," said Beth firmly. "He's wonderful, and I love him."

"He's awfu' handsome," said Meg wistfully.

"His brothers are awfu' handsome too," said Joan, "and they're available," she added practically. "Ye said Angus favours Morag, did ye?"

"Aye, well, she canna favour him that much, if she'd let Robbie…" Meg cast a quick glance at her great-aunt's face and subsided, blushing.

But Duncan's no' courting, is he?" persisted Joan, starry-eyed.

"No," said Beth. "Duncan isn't courting." Duncan could look after himself, she knew that. He was a born diplomat.

Angus was another matter altogether. In spite of his comments about not being ready to marry and seeing what the MacDonalds had to offer, he *was* sweet on Morag. That was obvious by the way his face lit up every time they met. The beautiful blonde blue-eyed MacDonald twins had been batting their eyelashes at him for two days and he'd done no more than give them an appreciative look and a few friendly words. She could only hope that Robert had taken her warning to heart, and would leave Morag alone.

CHAPTER SIX

The wedding celebration got off to a good start, with everyone eating their fill and chatting merrily in small groups. The original intention to hold the feast outdoors had been defeated by the inclement weather, and the barn, which was large enough to comfortably accommodate the guests, had been appropriated instead. Benches, stools and tables had been brought from every house for those who needed to sit, and piles of hay had been left in the corners for those who wanted to sprawl; later they would make a bed for the children too young to stay awake, and possibly for some of the adults too.

At the moment the children were almost sick with excitement and good food, and after having repeatedly got under the feet of every adult present, were taken outside by Iain and Angus in spite of the intermittent rain, to play a boisterous game which would no doubt result in several scraped knees and elbows and not a few tears, but which would at least deplete their energy a little.

Alex, as he had promised, was clad in the full garb of the chieftain; tall, broad and magnificent in red and black *feileadh mhor* and hose, armed with basket-hilted broadsword, dirk and *sgian dubh*, which weaponry, tonight worn only for show, he would abandon later when the dancing started. His blue bonnet was adorned with the pine sprig of his clan and two eagle feathers denoting his status as chieftain, and he wore his hair loose, falling to his shoulders in rich chestnut waves. The right sleeve of his white linen shirt was rolled up in preparation for the impromptu arm-wrestling contest that was about to take place. A crowd of impressively-clad clansmen had gathered round and a cheer arose from the assembly as Simon took his place opposite his chieftain.

The two men locked arms, shifting elbows on the table to achieve the best position, and at a mutual nod the contest began. The men closed around, obscuring Beth's view, but she had no fears that Alex would lose this bout.

There was only one man here who could best his chieftain, and she looked around the room for him, finally locating him in another corner, armed with a large hunk of beef and a pewter cup of wine, his tree-trunk legs stretched out in front of him. He looked in no rush to join the proceedings and was instead watching the musicians of both clans, who were choosing a suitable spot to sit and were chatting amiably, getting to know each other. He sensed Beth's gaze on him and looked up, smiling appreciatively at her beauty which was enhanced by the simplicity of the white dress she wore, belted with a sash of the same red and black pattern that her husband was wearing. Her hair was also loose tonight and floated around her hips in a silver cloud. She walked across to join him and he moved to one side to make a place for her on the bench.

"Do you think he'll win?" she asked.

Kenneth swallowed his mouthful of beef and nodded.

"Aye," he said. "Simon's a bonny fighter, but he's no' got the strength of Alex." He scanned the assembly quickly. "There's no' a man here that'll take him, I'm thinking, although one or two would gie him a challenge."

He caught her surreptitious glance at his enormous arms, as thick as her thighs, and smiled sadly.

"It's an awfu' shame that I canna challenge him mysel'," he said. "But I'm too long in the arm, ye ken."

She looked up at him.

"And if you weren't too long in the arm, you'd no doubt have strained a muscle this very day, unfortunately rendering you unable to participate," Beth commented.

Kenneth laughed, a deep rich giant's boom.

"Aye, something of that nature. At least while the MacDonalds are here. But even so, it's still the truth that ye do need to be somewhere close tae each other in arm length. There's no' many men alive I can wrestle with."

That had to be true. She had never met anyone who came even close to his stature. *He must be near seven feet in height,* she estimated.

She normally avoided standing close to him. Accustomed as she was to looking up at people, especially her husband, who topped her by a full foot, she still felt somewhat ridiculous talking to somebody whose belt buckle was approximately on a level with her eyes. She wondered how tall Jeannie had been and felt a sudden rush of sympathy for this mountain of a man who had almost been destroyed by his wife's stupidity. Duncan had told her the details of the story of her death and Kenneth's subsequent distress and had warned her not to speak to him of it. Kenneth didn't notice her changes of expression as these thoughts crossed her mind, being too busy scrutinising the other occupants of the room.

"Now take yon wee gomerel there for example, yon's the sort of idiot that'd insist on taking Alex on, although he's too short in the arm for a fair contest. Then he'd take it badly when he lost," he said scathingly.

Beth followed Kenneth's gaze across the room to where Robert MacDonald was sitting, chatting enthusiastically and seemingly innocently with an enraptured Morag. Beth wondered whether it was a blessing or not that he was too preoccupied to entertain challenging Alex, in view of what that preoccupation was.

"Sorry," said Kenneth belatedly and insincerely. "He's your kinsman."

"He is," replied Beth, resolving to keep an eye on her cousin. "But you're still right. He's got all the rebelliousness of the family without the sense. He's very young though, in fairness, only just turned sixteen."

"Let's hope he finds the sense quickly, then, or he'll no' grow much older," said Kenneth roughly, reminding her of Graeme in his bluntness.

A somewhat damp Iain and Angus re-entered the barn, pied-piper-like, trailing a line of rather subdued and dishevelled but grinning children, just as a roar arose from the table and Simon emerged, red-faced but smiling, rolling down his sleeve.

Angus, who had been about to make his way over to the food along with all his small companions, instead veered away and joined his brother, just as one of the MacDonald visitors, Alasdair, took the place of the defeated Simon.

"Now there's one who'd gie Alex a contest," said Kenneth, burrowing his enormous paw into the hay at his side and producing a bottle of the finest claret, provided courtesy of Sir Anthony Peters and his mysterious benefactor. He uncorked it with his teeth and took a deep swig before passing it to Beth.

"Do you think so?" she said doubtfully, eyeing the MacDonald's wiry arms. She didn't think he had a hope, herself. He was a good ten years older than Alex, and by the way he held himself Beth recognised the early signs of rheumatism.

"No' him, he hasna a chance. I'm talking about Angus," said Kenneth. "Maybe no' the now, he's too impatient and careless forbye, but he's growing into his strength, and fast."

As they watched the contest started, and Angus removed the single eagle feather from his own bonnet, brandishing it like a sword near Alex's armpit in a distinctly threatening tickling gesture. Alex's right arm dipped suddenly, and with lightning speed he drew his dirk left-handed, slashing it at Angus's hand and slicing the feather neatly in two, to the riotous applause of the assembly. Angus withdrew, sucking his finger, from which Alex had also accidentally shaved a sliver of skin. He smiled ruefully at Beth as he passed and made his way to the food table.

"There's another one who needs to find sense quickly," said Beth, watching him affectionately as he engaged in a mock battle with two of the older children for a choice piece of meat, his injured finger already forgotten.

"Angus? No, not at all. He's sense enough when it's needed. He's just high-spirited is all. He reminds Alex of what he used to be before he had to take on the chieftainship. And he stops him getting too serious about it at times. Angus is what Alex wishes he could still be. And Alex is what Angus wants to be, some day."

Beth looked up at the big man, who was watching Angus carefully as he walked past Morag and Robert seemingly without noticing them, a wriggling child tucked under his arm, the choice piece of meat shared between the protagonists and already half consumed.

"How long have you known them?" Beth asked.

"Since they were born. I'm older than I look, lassie," Kenneth said. "It's the soft pampered life of the MacGregors that does it. I turn forty next winter."

Beth was surprised. She had put him in his very early thirties, at most. He had all his own teeth still, and the smooth skin and lithe step of a much younger man.

"What about Duncan, then?" she said.

"Duncan? Ah, well now, he's the odd one out. Second-born sons often are. He was sent down to mediate between the two firebrands, I'm thinking, and stop them acting on impulse too often. He holds his brothers in check, helps to tame their wildness. Alex has learned to tame himself now, to some degree. Angus'll learn too, in time. But ye ken that already, do ye no'?"

She did on a subconscious level, but hadn't thought about it until now. She looked for Duncan, saw him expertly and sensitively fending off the attentions of Joan MacDonald.

"Yes, I do. They're very close, as brothers. It's nice to see. I'm not at all close to my brother," she said, grimacing.

"They're more than close, they're parts of a whole. If one was gone, the others'd be diminished. Ye're doing well, lassie," he said suddenly, pale blue eyes twinkling down at her. "I kent it'd take a particular sort of woman to fit in wi' them without causing strife, and ye've done it. Most women would feel threatened by the closeness between them."

She looked at him, puzzled.

"Why would I feel threatened by Alex's brothers?" she said. "The love of a man for his wife is a different thing altogether from that of a man for his blood kin. I feel protected by Angus and Duncan, not threatened. They're the brothers I longed for and never had."

"Aye, that's the way it should be. Ye'll be a fine wife to him, Ealasaid, and it's no' just me who thinks so. I'd take my hat off to ye, if I could remember where I'd put the damn thing." He felt around at his side fruitlessly.

Beth exploded into laughter.

"It wasna that funny," he began, and then followed her gaze to where Angus had appeared behind Duncan, bending over to whisper something to him. Then he straightened and passed on, fiddling briefly with his bonnet. When he put it on, its beautiful intact eagle feather waved proudly above his left ear. Duncan, oblivious, still verbally fencing with the tenacious Joan, now sported the mutilated remains of what had once been a magnificent plume and briefly a tickling stick.

Beth and Kenneth watched as Angus approached with jaunty step.

"The musicians'll be ready in a minute," he said as he came within earshot. "That'll give Alex the excuse to stop before he starts to tire."

"He'll kill you when he finds out," Beth commented. They both knew she was talking not about Alex, but Duncan.

Angus threw himself down in the hay at Kenneth's side.

"No he willna, he'll be too busy throttling you," he said. "Joan's just tellt him it was you who said he's no' courting at the minute."

"I didn't actually *tell* her he wasn't," Beth said defensively. "I just confirmed it when she asked."

"Aye well, ye've made his job awfu' difficult. Christ, is it a MacDonald family trait to never take no for an answer?"

"I don't know," said Beth. "You know my family as well as I do. Allan and Meg seem very reasonable." Allan and Meg were sitting with her grandmother, and seemed content just to eat and drink and watch the proceedings.

"That's two out of five reasonable ones then, at least," he said, tarring Beth with the same brush as Joan and Robert while casually observing the latter, who had slung one arm across the back of the bench seat behind Morag. "Will ye have the first dance wi' me, then?" he asked as the drone of the pipes announced the commencement of the music.

For a moment she was tempted to say yes. It would at least take his attention away from Robert.

"No, I've to have the first dance with my husband, as you well know," she said. "I'll save you the second. Don't use me to get your revenge on him for decapitating your feather. How's your finger, by the way?"

"Desperate sore," he whined, hoping to elicit sympathy.

"Good," she replied. "Have a drink to dull the pain. Kenneth's got three bottles of claret stashed in the hay under you. I'll be back after the first dance."

She wandered off into the waiting arms of her husband, leaving Kenneth to reluctantly unearth the carefully secreted bottles of claret, and bemoan with Angus over the unsympathetic and far too observant nature of the chieftain's beautiful wife.

Beth ended up having the first three dances with Alex, after which Duncan intercepted her as she dashed off to get a breath and a drink before the next dance started.

"I'm sorry," she said, before he could speak. "I didn't actually tell her you were unattached."

"What? Oh, that. I can deal wi' Joan, she's a bonny lass anyway. It's no' that I want to speak to ye about," he said. "Ye'll have seen wee Robert, I'm thinking."

"Yes, I've been watching him, as far as I can," she said. It would be difficult to keep a close eye on him all night, as she had to circulate, being the chieftain's wife as well as the bride.

"Aye. He tried to seduce Morag yesterday, and by the looks of him he's hoping to complete the conquest tonight. She's only just fourteen, and even if Angus wasna soft on her, I've nae intention to let her be ruined. Or Robert be killt, either."

"Grandmother warned him she'd thrash him if he didn't leave her alone," Beth said. "Hopefully he's just talking to her. Providing they stay here, there'll be no harm done. And Angus doesn't seem too bothered, anyway." He had seemingly given up on dancing with Beth and was taking the floor with another woman.

"Dinna be fooled by his casual attitude. I ken him well. He's watching their every move. And he's no' impressed. But he's got no claim on Morag and he kens it. That doesna mean he'll no' cut the throat of anyone that harms her."

"What do you want me to do?" she asked.

"Nothing, at the minute. I'll keep an eye on them. I'm in a better position to do that than you. But if I call for ye, will ye come straight away?"

"Yes, of course," she said.

The dancing continued, the claret flowed, ran out, was replaced by whisky. Night came and lamps were lit. The older people gathered in small groups to watch the younger ones dance and to reminisce about their youth. The very young ones started to wilt, and subsided drowsily into the hay. Everyone was in great spirits, the music good, the drink and food plentiful and excellent, the mood friendly. Morag and Robert had danced together twice, then returned to their seats. They showed no signs of sneaking off.

There was a short break while the musicians rested, drank and discussed the next tunes they were going to play. One of them produced a wooden whistle from his pocket and played the first bars of a jig. The others nodded, confirming that they knew it, and it was added to the repertoire.

"Oh!" said Beth, who was passing by. "I've not seen one of those for years!"

"Do ye play?" asked the man, a short stocky dark-haired MacDonald, whose preferred instrument was the fiddle.

"I used to," she said, eyeing the instrument wistfully. "My mother had one and she taught me and my father to play a few songs. I lost it a few years ago, though."

The fiddler held it out to her.

"Here ye go," he said. "Gie us a tune."

She took it hesitantly.

"I'm not sure I can remember how to play it," she said.

"Have a go," said Alex, who was standing behind her. "No one'll laugh at ye if ye canna."

She raised it to her lips, played a scale, then a few random notes. Then she smiled, half to herself, tapped her foot and struck up a short tune. By the end of it she'd played no more than two or three bad notes and had attracted the attention of several of those nearby, who called for an encore.

She tried it again, more sure of herself now, playing it through once without error, then a second time, when to her surprise her audience started singing along:

'There came a fiddler out of France,
I wat nae giff ye kend him
And he did you wi' our good wife,
Geld him, lasses, geld him!'

Beth took the whistle from her lips amidst cheers, blushing furiously, and made to hand it back to the fiddler.

"Christ, what manner of woman have I married?" came the teasing voice in her ear. "Where the hell did ye learn that?"

"My mother taught it to me," Beth said, scarlet. "The tune, that is. I didn't know the words until now. I had no idea."

Alex laughed.

"Do ye ken any more?" he asked.

"Yes. But I'm not sure if I should play them, after that," she said, glancing at her grandmother, who she was sure would be offended. The old lady laughed and beckoned her to play another.

She braced herself and struck up a jig. She knew the name of this, 'The Blythsome Bridal', and prayed that the lyrics didn't go into the intimate details of the wedding night.

They didn't, although they did dwell somewhat on the desire of the groom to take the bride's maidenhead in advance of the wedding.

There was great applause, after which Beth firmly handed the whistle back to the fiddler and walked away before she could be persuaded to play any more.

"I thought ye said ye couldna play an instrument," Alex said, his arm round her waist.

"I can't as far as the English are concerned. Can you imagine Clarissa's face if I asked her to accompany me in 'Geld him, lasses, geld him' on the harpsichord?" She giggled. "Maybe I should do a turn at the next Handel concert. That'd liven things up at Geordie's Court a bit. With a bit of luck he'd have an apoplexy on the spot."

"I doubt it, but it's worth a try. How many tunes d'ye ken?"

"Quite a few, though I'm out of practice. The ironic thing is that I didn't play the one I remember best, because I know the title and am sure that one's a bit rude. I had no idea about the others."

"What's the title, then?" Alex asked.

"'Piss on the grass'," said Beth.

He hugged her to him.

"I wish I'd kent your mother," he said sincerely. "She must have been one hell of a woman."

"She was," said Beth. "And so is my granny." Ealasaid, in spite of her age, had stood and was demonstrating the steps to a complicated ancient dance no one else could remember, a short line of youngsters watching her feet and attempting to copy her. Joan and Meg were amongst them, as was Angus and Allan. Robert was not. Nor was Morag.

"And so are you," murmured Alex in her ear, managing a brief kiss before he was swept away by a group of his clansmen to officiate in a good-natured dispute.

Duncan came up behind Ealasaid, and whispered a few words in her ear. She faltered momentarily in the steps, nodded her head at whatever he'd said, and continued. From there he went to another woman, one of the MacDonald visitors, a black-haired buxom girl with laughing brown eyes. Then he moved to Kenneth, still sitting by the hay, although the claret was long consumed.

Finally he came to Beth, taking her arm as she was just about to accept a cup of whisky.

"Are ye drunk?" he said.

"No not at all," she replied, following as he led her across the room. "I've been dancing, not drinking. Although I intend to remedy that as soon as possible."

"Good," he said. "They've gone."

She did not ask who had gone. Ten seconds later they were out of the barn, standing in the starry darkness, the wind grabbing at their clothes and causing Beth's hair to snake around her head Medusa-like. Duncan removed his bonnet before it could blow away, registered the decimated feather with a brief smile, and then started explaining.

"She left about ten minutes ago, and he followed her no more than a minute since," he said as he hurried her across the clearing in the direction of the stables.

"How do you know they'll be in the stable?" she said.

"It's warm and dry, and there's plenty of soft hay. Small noises'll no' be heard among the horses snuffling. It's where I went to do my illicit courting. It's where everyone goes. They'll be there."

As they got near to the building, he slowed.

"Beth, d'ye think ye can handle this on your own?" he asked.

She stopped, surprised. She knew why he didn't want Alex to handle it. As the chieftain, he would have to deal with it on an official basis and it would become an inter-clan matter. But she thought Duncan intended to sort things out himself and had asked her to accompany him only because there was another woman involved.

He saw the uncertainty in her face, and the puzzlement.

"Robert's your kinsman, Beth, and you're the MacGregor chieftain's wife. And a woman. He's a stupid wee loon wi' no morals and no respect for the rules of hospitality. If I go in there,

I've nae doubt his pride'll make him challenge me and force me to fight him. I've nae wish to become involved in another blood feud between the clans. He canna challenge you, and Morag'll no' be so embarrassed at ye finding them as she would be if I did. Can ye do it? I'll be outside in case he does get nasty, though I canna believe even he'd be that stupid."

She gathered herself, trying to think of the right words to say at a moment's notice, then abandoned the effort. She would deal with events as they unfolded.

"Yes," she said, because he was right and she really had no choice. "I can do it." She hesitated for a moment, then slipped silently in through the door of the stable, which the lovers had left ajar.

In the barn Angus had given up trying to learn the new dance, and had noted the absence of Morag and Robert. He was just turning towards the door when he was accosted by a young black-haired woman.

"Will ye dance wi' me?" she said, laying her hand on his arm.

He hesitated, searching for an excuse that would not sound rude.

"I'm a wee bit…" he began.

"Only I havena a partner, and you're an awfu' bonny dancer. I've been watching ye. I'd be honoured," she said, persisting, and taking a firm grip on his sleeve.

He could not refuse the MacDonald girl without causing offence, and Angus was at all times aware of the proprieties. He swallowed his frustration and smiled down at her.

"The honour will be mine," he said gallantly, leading her to the floor as the fiddler struck up a reel. Kenneth, who had moved forward in his seat, leaned back again, watching the dancers with lazy interest.

The stable was lit only by a single lantern, but Beth saw the couple immediately, because they were lying directly beneath it, Robert half on top of Morag, his hands busy around her bodice, his silver hair falling over his face.

"I'm no' so sure…" she was saying as Beth stepped silently towards them.

"Come on," he cajoled, slightly breathlessly. "It's fun. I love you, I've tellt ye that. And there's nae harm in it."

"You're wrong, Robert," said Beth loudly and clearly.

The couple exploded apart. Beth noted with relief that while Robert had clearly made some headway in the area of Morag's breasts, one of which she was hastily tucking back into her dress, her skirts were undisturbed.

"There's a whole lot of harm in it. I suggest you tidy yourselves up and go back to the barn now. Separately," Beth advised.

For a moment she thought it would be that easy. Then the initial shock of discovery left Robert's face and was replaced by rebellion.

"She's willing," he said. "I've done nothing wrong."

"Not yet," agreed Beth. "But you're well on the way to it. She's barely fourteen."

"I'm a woman!" said Morag indignantly, emboldened by her lover's attitude. "Have been these last two months!"

"Well, you need to act like one, then," said Beth. "Womanhood brings responsibilities, as I'm sure your mother's told you."

"We werena doing anything wrong," Robert said sullenly.

"I'm glad to hear it," said Beth. "Then you can just go and do nothing wrong back in the barn, in public."

"I dinna have tae listen to you," persisted Robert. "Ye've no authority over me."

"You're right, I haven't," said Beth, to his surprise. "Shall I go and get the chieftain, then? He does have the authority. You're on his land, abusing his hospitality and trying to ruin his clanswoman."

Morag blanched.

"Ye wouldna do that, we're kin," said Robert with the smug confidence of the spoiled youngest child whose previous indiscretions have always been covered by his family.

"We are. But you're forgetting something. The MacGregor is my husband, and I owe my first allegiance to him and his clan. And as your kinswoman, your action here is bringing disgrace on me, to say nothing of the rest of the MacDonalds. Now if you want me to, I'll call the chieftain and we'll make it official. Likely you'll be flogged, if you're lucky. Alex has a nasty temper on him, and it'll not be improved by him being dragged from his wedding celebrations to pass judgement on one who ought to know better. And after that you'll have your great-aunt to deal with. Are you willing to go through all that for a quick tumble in the hay? Unless you're serious about the girl. You said you love her. Do you intend to marry her, then?"

Morag looked at him, clearly expecting him to say he did. She had a lot to learn, Beth thought sadly, seeing her look of distress at Robert's horrified expression.

"It was just a wee bit of fun, that's all. We've no' done anything to give cause for marriage," he said sulkily.

"No you haven't. And because I'm your cousin, and I've no wish to cause my grandmother distress, or tarnish Morag's good name, if you go back now, we'll say no more about the matter. But you'd better not abuse my clan's hospitality again, Robert, for I'll give you no second chances."

He stood, reluctantly, brushing the hay from his kilt, then reached out a hand to Morag, clearly intending to escort her back and make a defiant entrance into the barn. Angus would crucify him, if Duncan's judgement was right.

"No thank you," said Morag, crossing her arms over her chest, her eyes blurred with tears. "I'd as soon ye didna speak to me again."

He glared at Beth for a moment, then he spun away, kilt swirling out around his legs, and strode out of the barn.

The dance finished, Angus escorted Isobel, as he now knew she was called, back to her seat and made his escape before she could find another reason to detain him. He was almost at the door when he was arrested by a pull on his kilt as he strode past a group of the older folk. So desperate was he now to find out what Morag and Robert were doing, that he pretended he hadn't noticed and tried to march on. The resultant deathgrip on his attire nearly disrobed him. He stopped and looked down into the delicate face of Beth's grandmother. The tiny fragile hand held onto his kilt like a limpet.

"Angus," she said pleasantly. "I'm afraid I need to go to the privy. Would you be so kind as to escort me? It's a wee bit embarrassing, but as we're kin now I kent ye wouldna mind. And ye're a braw laddie. If I stumble, ye'll have nae trouble catching me, I'm thinking."

Angus now most definitely smelt a rat. This old lady who had just been demonstrating the steps of a remarkably vigorous dance, had no more need of being assisted to the small shed out the back than he did. And she did not seem the sort to be embarrassed by something as natural as going to the toilet, having joined in lustily with 'Geld him lasses, geld him,' and then led the chorus of the extremely bawdy song Angus had taught Sir Horace Mann's clerks several months ago in Florence. He looked around. Alex was in one corner with several other men, all much the worse for drink, trying to balance his sword on his nose. Duncan was nowhere to be seen. Neither was Beth.

Praying that they had gone where he was trying to, and that they would stop Robert and Morag before any harm was done, he gave his arm to the suddenly frail old lady, assisting her to rise. He would deal with the wee yellow-haired shite later, if he'd dishonoured Morag.

"I'm sorry, Morag," said Beth when Robert had left.

"Dinna be sorry," replied Morag, sniffing loudly and valiantly attempting to fight back the tears. "I should be thanking you. He tellt me he loved me. He tellt me he just wanted to be alone wi' me for a wee while. He tellt me I was beautiful." A tear trickled slowly down her cheek.

Beth knelt down beside her in the hay.

"You are beautiful, Morag," she said softly. It was not true. The girl was pretty enough, but no more than that. But now was not the time for fine distinctions.

"No, I'm not," said Morag sadly. "I'm daft in the heid, that's what I am, tae believe him."

"You're not daft, Morag, you're young is all," said Beth. "You've got to learn that a man'll tell you anything if it'll get you to lift your skirts for him. It takes time to fall in love with someone, more than two days, anyway. You're not in love with him, are you?"

"Not any more I'm no', the bastard," she replied with feeling, wiping her eyes on her skirt. "He made me feel awfu' good, though. Sort of special and warm inside. How d'ye ken the difference? How d'ye ken if he's the right one?"

Beth sighed. She had no idea. She had fallen in love with a spoilt brat who'd threatened to cut her fingers off, and married a man she didn't like who had turned out to be the love of her life.

"It's not easy," she said after a minute. "You need to take the time to get to know him, to feel that you can relax with him, tell him anything, trust him. Men can be very convincing though, when they're aroused. But if a man really cares for you he'll not try to take your virginity before you're married. Or rather, he might try, because sex is a powerful urge, you understand. But if you say no he won't try to make you."

"He would have, would he no'?" said Morag, starting to recover now.

"Yes, I think so, if I hadn't found you. I'm not saying he didn't like you, Morag, and he certainly desired you. But he should have respected you too, and he wasn't doing that."

"No, you're right, he wasna," she said. "Oh God, I don't think I'm ever going to find the right man!"

Beth suppressed a smile. Life is very serious when you're fourteen.

"There are lots of nice young men in the clan. Give it time, Morag, you've only been a woman for two months. You're very young to be marrying."

"My ma was fourteen when she married Da," Morag pointed out. "And she'd known him for years before. I dinna ken anyone worth marrying!"

"What about Angus? He seems to like you," Beth said without thinking, then wished she hadn't.

"Angus?" said Morag, snorting. "Angus still thinks of me as a wee bairn. He's more likely to duck me in the loch than invite me to the stables."

Beth could not dispute this, knowing Angus.

"Do you like him, though? Can you tell him anything, and do you feel relaxed around him?"

"Well, aye," said Morag, reassessing the relationship before Beth's eyes. "Or at least I could. But since he's come back this time he's been different. Sort of stiff, a wee bit formal like. I dinna think he likes me any more."

Beth could have gone into the likely reasons why Angus would be suddenly awkward around Morag, but realised that her life would not be worth living if she did and Angus got to find out. Better the girl find it out for herself.

"I wouldn't be so sure of that," she said instead, standing. "But I am sure of one thing. If you stay away much longer you'll be missed. Are you ready to go back yet?"

Morag accepted Beth's hand and stood. Her eyes were still a bit pink, but that could be put down to the drink, if anyone noticed.

"Aye," she said. "I am. And I'll no' forget this night in a hurry."

When Robert emerged from the stables Duncan shrank back into the shadows so as not to be observed. He watched the boy walk across the clearing, then, only feet from the barn, change his mind and veer away, heading instead for the lochside, his steps slowing as he went. A bare ten seconds after he'd disappeared into the trees Angus appeared, heading purposefully for the stables. Duncan moved forward to meet him halfway across the clearing. Behind Angus, Kenneth emerged from the barn, started to run, saw Duncan and stopped.

"It's over," said Duncan as he reached Angus. "There's nae harm done."

"No' yet," said Angus, "But there will be when I get my hands on the wee shit." He moved to pass Duncan, who grabbed him by the arm.

"He's no' there," he said. "Beth's dealt wi' it. Robert's gone and Beth's comforting Morag. Ye'll do nothing but harm if ye play the avenging angel now."

"Ye let Beth deal wi' it?" Angus said.

"Aye, she's fully capable, as ye well know. I didna want the wee gomerel to challenge me."

"Did ye no'?" replied Angus hotly. "Well, I'd be delighted if he challenged me. Where is he?"

"He's away off to the loch tae think things through. He didna hurt her, Angus. There's nae cause for a fuss."

"He tried to rape her, did he no'?" cried the young man, losing his temper. "He enticed her there and then he tried to rape her, and ye say there's nae cause for a fuss?"

"She went there of her own free will, and he tried to seduce her. Beth got to them in time. It…"

"Christ, Duncan, ye're going soft," spat Angus contemptuously. "He's sullied the clan and disrespected a wee lassie and ye're willing tae let it pass? Well I'm not!"

Duncan's fists clenched at his side, and he only refrained from hitting his younger brother by reminding himself that this display of temper was inspired by his fondness for Morag. Angus spun away in the direction of the trees, then stopped suddenly, arrested in his pursuit of Robert by Kenneth, who had approached unheard and now wrapped his arms around the young man, pinioning him. Angus froze.

"Let me go," he said through gritted teeth. "Let me go, Kenneth, or I'll kill ye when ye do."

"Hear your brother out first," said Kenneth softly, "and then ye can do as ye wish an' I'll no' stop ye."

There was no point in struggling and losing his dignity. No one man could match Kenneth's strength. No two men could.

"Right then," Angus said, glaring at his brother. "Say your piece, and then let me go. I'll no' kill the bastard, if that's what's worrying ye. I'll just make him wish I had."

Now he had a captive audience, Duncan realised he had no idea how to calm Angus. He thought for a moment. Morag. She was his weak spot.

"He didna rape her, Angus. He didna seduce her either. They did no more than have a wee kiss and a cuddle before Beth disturbed them. Morag was already changing her mind. Likely she's had too much wine and let herself be sweet talked. Ye ken all about sweet talk, Angus, ye're a master of it."

"Aye, I am," agreed Angus. "But I'd no' use it to try to dishonour a bairn!"

"She's no' a bairn anymore, as ye well know, man. She's a woman, although a very young one. She's feeling the power of being a woman for the first time and what it can do to a man. It's a mighty thing, and ye're feeling the effects of it yourself, if I'm right."

Angus blushed, but didn't say anything.

"Aye, well, that's another thing," continued Duncan. "Tonight she made a mistake. At the moment, as far as she's aware, only

Beth, Robert and herself ken that. Robert'll be gone in a day or so, and he'll no' say anything in the meantime, or his auntie'll thrash him. Beth is sensitive, she'll no' say anything either, and Morag kens that. She's still got her maidenhead, and she's still got her dignity. Now let's say ye go and burst in on them…"

"I've nae intention tae do that," said Angus, shifting experimentally in Kenneth's grip. The iron-hard arms tightened, and Angus subsided. "I wouldna hurt her for the world. It's him I've a reckoning with."

"Aye, I see that. So let's say we let ye go, and ye go and beat Robert to a pulp, as I've nae doubt ye can. Let's put to one side the problems it could cause between us and the MacDonalds. If ye do that everything will come out. Alex'll have to get involved, and the whole clan, both clans, will ken that Morag was stupid enough to let a wee laddie take her to the stables and fondle her. She'll be mortified, her confidence'll be crushed, her reputation needlessly tarnished and she'll hate ye for the rest of her life, and rightly so. Now if that's what ye want, fine. Let him go, Kenneth."

Kenneth let him go.

"I've nae more to say to ye," Duncan said. "Do what ye will. But dinna ever accuse me of going soft again for being considerate, or ye'll regret it."

He turned and walked away, followed by Kenneth, leaving Angus standing in the gusting wind, his kilt swirling around his legs, his hair blowing into his eyes. He stayed there for a while, making no attempt to brush the hair from his face. Then, slowly, he walked away.

"Will he heed ye, d'ye think?" said Kenneth as they reached the barn.

"If he cares for Morag as much as I think he does, aye, he'll heed me," answered Duncan, blinking as they entered the warmth and light of the barn. The atmosphere was wonderful; it was clearly the best ceilidh there had been for some time. The music was continuing, although the dancers were flagging a bit. Simon had succeeded in balancing his sword on his nose to the count of ten, beating Alex and redeeming himself for his defeat in the arm-wrestling. The party would continue for a while yet, no one wishing to bring such a happy occasion to an end. Unless Robert staggered in through the door in half an hour, covered in blood.

That would dampen the merriment somewhat. Duncan did not think he would. He prayed that Angus would see sense.

Angus saw sense. After a few minutes Beth and Morag returned, acting as though they had popped out for some fresh air. Robert also returned briefly, his handsome face petulant, only to be scooped off almost instantly by Ealasaid and Allan, to assist her to bed. He did not reappear, and Duncan thanked God for giving Beth such a sensible grandmother.

Angus came back some time later, subdued and windswept, nodded once in apology to Duncan as he passed and continued into a corner, where he sat alone. His uncharacteristic behaviour was not commented on, even by the normally astute Alex, now much the worse for drink. The party was subsiding into a storytelling session, as was customary when everyone became too drunk or too weary for more boisterous entertainment.

The children were all fast asleep in the hay, except for Peigi and Alastair's twin babies, who Alex had volunteered to take custody of while their parents stole off for some rare undisturbed time alone. The infants were sleeping soundly, one in the crook of each arm, a corner of Alex's plaid tucked tenderly around them. They made a lovely picture. Beth had, as she had intended, made up for her earlier abstinence and now sat between Kenneth and Duncan on a bench, Kenneth's hand periodically moving to her back to stop her toppling backwards.

"There's a question I've been meaning to ask ye for a while," he said, in the lull between the end of one story and the start of the next.

"What's that?" said Beth, blinking up at him.

"The first time we met, ye asked me where my beanstalk was. What did ye mean?"

She laughed, swaying back into the security of his hand.

"Ah well, that's a fairy story. Haven't you heard the story of Jack and the Beanstalk?"

Several ears pricked up. Everyone had heard all the stories told tonight many times before; tales of the deeds of the clans, of kelpies and the *ban-sidhe*. They were comforting, familiar. Nevertheless the chance to hear a new one was a rare treat indeed. There was a clamour for her to tell it, and she thought for a minute, trying to remember the details through the blur of alcohol.

"Once upon a time there was a young boy and his mother," she began.

"What time was that?" Janet asked.

"Sorry?" said Beth.

"What time was it upon?" she said.

"I don't know, it's just a way of starting a story," Beth replied. "It was a long time ago, anyway. Er…a hundred years."

Everyone settled down.

"Anyway, this young boy Jack and his mother lived alone in a little cottage in the woods," Beth continued, "and they were very poor, because his father had died."

"What had they done wrong?" interrupted Simon.

"Nothing," said Beth, confused.

"Why were they living alone, then, instead of wi' their clan?" he said.

"They were Sasannachs," Alex said, coming to her rescue. "They didna have a clan."

There was a murmur of sympathy from the assembled crowd.

"So, they were Sasannachs, and they lived alone," said Beth. "All they had left was a cow, and one day Jack's mother told him they'd have to sell the cow because they needed the money, and they'd sold everything else of worth, their furniture and suchlike."

"What for'd they dae that?" said Joan. "What the hell use is money? Ye canna eat that. Ye're no' poor while ye've got a cow. There's the milk, and ye can always bleed it in the winter if ye're desperate and mix the blood wi' a wee bittie oatmeal. And if ye're really starving, ye can kill it. One cow'd feed a woman and a bairn through to the spring."

Even through the alcoholic haze Beth realised that if she was ever going to finish this story, she'd have to adapt it. Once she got to the magical bit she'd be all right, she knew that. They'd accept any amount of giants and talking harps without a murmur. It was the practical stuff they'd query.

"The cow was diseased, although it didn't look it," improvised Beth. "And the woman knew there was a market coming up where lots of her enemies would be. The ones who'd killed her husband. So, not wanting to wait until Jack was old enough to avenge his father's death, she thought she'd get her revenge early by selling them a diseased cow."

There was a murmur of understanding from the listeners. Beth ignored Alex's amused face and continued.

"So, Jack was a bit daft in the head, and lazy too," she said. "And on the way to market, he met this man, and they got into conversation. And the man persuaded him to accept five magic beans for the cow, so he did, because he couldn't be bothered to walk ten miles to market."

"Are ye sure his name wasna Robbie Og instead of Jack?" someone called from the back, and everyone laughed. Beth took a deep draught of whisky, swayed, coughed, and settled down to the rest of the story.

"That was really interesting," said Alex an hour later, trying to manage two comatose and remarkably heavy babies, whilst supporting both himself and his extremely inebriated wife on the way home. "I've heard the story before, of course, but I had nae idea the giant was a Campbell, or that he spent his evenings counting his bottles of whisky."

Beth squinted up at him, somewhat cross-eyed.

"Oh shut up," she said. "I'd still have been there now trying to justify why they were selling the cow, if I hadn't changed things a bit. Anyway, they enjoyed it."

"Aye, they did," he agreed. "So I hope ye're now aware that ye'll have tae tell every Sasannach story ye ken, adapted for a MacGregor audience, before we leave."

"No problem," she said with the confidence of the extremely drunk, waving a hand airily around before losing her balance and landing on her bottom on the grass with a thud. She giggled, and Alex left her there for a moment while he delivered the twins safely to their grateful parents, who had spent the time, although they didn't yet know it, creating the next child.

When he returned Beth was lying on her back in the wet grass gazing dreamily at the moon.

"Do you know," she said, as he approached and squatted down unsteadily beside her. "I can see the hare in the moon. I've never been able to see it before. I've always seen the man instead. Isn't that amazing?" Her voice was full of childish wonder and he smiled, enraptured, turning his head up to look skywards and regretting it instantly as the world tilted dizzyingly. He looked back down at her instead, her silver hair and white dress rendering her ethereal in the moonlight. She could have been *sidhe* or fairy herself, so beautiful was she.

"Oh, I do love you!" she cried, launching her upper body at him and wrapping her arms round his neck with a suddenness that unbalanced him and sent him toppling forward. He got his elbows down just in time to save his whole weight from crashing down onto her and she laughed, winding her arms tighter round his neck.

"Make love to me, Alex," she said, trying unsuccessfully to free her legs from her skirts and wrap them round his waist.

It was tempting, and his body told him he was capable of complying with her request, in spite of the copious quantity of alcohol he'd consumed. But it was cold and windy and the ground was soaking. What was more, a warm and cosy bed awaited. If they were quiet, they would not disturb the old lady…

His decision made, he untangled himself from her and managed, with some difficulty, to lift her from the ground, walking somewhat erratically in the direction of his house while she mumbled away dreamily in his arms.

"Until later," she said suddenly as they reached the door and he opened it quietly. The room was in darkness, but the fire had been burning all evening and it was pleasantly warm. He placed her carefully on her feet, keeping an arm round her waist.

"What did you say, *mo chridhe?*" he asked softly, leading her to the stairs.

"Until later," she said loudly and clearly. "You said you wouldn't forget. I haven't."

Neither had he.

"*Isd,*" he said softly. "If we're quiet we'll no' disturb your granny, and we can have our 'until later'."

"Mmm. Oh yes, I forgot. Granny." She hiccupped and giggled. "Sshh!" she hissed, loud enough to wake those in the next hut.

He managed to light a candle from the fire and manhandle his wife, alternately giggling and shushing herself, up the stairs and into the bedroom, where she turned immediately into his arms.

"Oooh, I want you," she said. "I've wanted you all day. You

look wonderful in your chieftain's *feil*…ah…your…this," she said, grabbing at the front of his kilt and narrowly missing squashing his left testicle.

He swerved, and laughed. She was lovely, her hair tangled, her blue eyes soft and unfocussed with whisky and desire. Her back was soaking wet and cold. He put the candle down on the little wooden stool next to the bed.

"Come, lassie," he whispered. "Let's get ye out of these wet clothes first and into bed. We dinna want you to catch your death."

"Death," she echoed. "No. Better with no clothes on anyway." She laughed as he untied the sash round her waist and tried with great difficulty to pull her dress over her head. It would have been a little easier if the material hadn't been sodden and clinging, and a lot easier if she wasn't trying to disrobe him at the same time as he was disrobing her. They weaved around the room, making far more noise than was desirable. If Ealasaid had stayed asleep through this racket it would be a miracle.

Finally naked she fell backwards on to the bed, watching as he unpinned his brooch and unbuckled his belt, bracing himself against the wall with one hand in what he hoped looked like a nonchalant pose, but which was in fact stopping him from sliding down it. Alcohol-induced tiredness washed suddenly over him, and he fought it, hard.

"Hurry up," she said impatiently from the bed. "This is our third wedding night, and I want my marital rights this time! It's a husband's duty to satisfy his wife!"

A snort of laughter came from the adjoining room, quickly stifled. He was both disappointed and relieved in equal measure. He was very tired, and so drunk he was not sure he'd be able to complete the act if he started it. Better to wait until tomorrow, when they'd both slept off some of the whisky. He attempted to fold his plaid, gave up, dropped it on the floor and climbed into bed.

"Shh," he whispered. "We've woken your granny. Go to sleep, *a ghràidh*."

"Have we?" she said. "Sorry, Granny. Are you all right?"

"Ah…aye, thank ye for asking," came the voice from the other side of the partition, bubbling with suppressed laughter.

"Goodnight,"

"Goodnight," said Beth, turning happily back to Alex. "It doesn't matter, though, does it?" she continued. "It's natural. Everyone does it, everywhere. You said so yourself that day on the hill when you…"

He kissed her, desperately, cutting off the rest of what she'd been about to say, his face burning. A peal of remarkably youthful laughter floated from the next room and was not suppressed this time.

"Gie her what she wants, laddie," Ealasaid said shakily. "Ye'll get no peace until ye do."

If he'd been unsure before, he wasn't now. He couldn't. Under no circumstances. He ended the kiss, and pushed his wife gently back onto the pillows, hoping she'd close her eyes and go to sleep.

She closed her eyes, and was silent for a moment. Then she opened them again and made a sudden grab for the mattress.

"Oooh," she said in quite a different tone of voice. "I think I'm going to…"

He leapt from the bed, tripping over the discarded plaid and grabbing at the basin as he fell. He twisted round and managed to get it in place just in time. Shuffling forward, he knelt at the side of the bed and held her until she had finished retching. Then he wet a cloth and wiped her mouth and face, before easing her gently back into bed. He toyed with the idea of taking the bowl back downstairs, made a realistic assessment of the capability of his legs to get down and back up again, then abandoned the idea, placing it in the farthest corner of the room instead.

He returned to the bed, gathering his now shivering, clammy and far from amorous wife in close to his side, crooning softly to her as though she was a child until the shivers ceased and she slept. Only then did he relax himself. His eyes started to close.

"Is she all right, laddie?" said the old lady softly.

"Aye," he said. "Just verra, verra drunk. She'll regret it in the morning, I'm sure. She drank an awfu' lot of whisky verra quickly."

"She did you proud tonight. It's a fine woman you're married to, MacGregor, even if she is my granddaughter."

"I ken that well, *a sheanmhair.*"

"And it's a fine man she's got herself, too. Ye'll cherish her and protect her, I've nae doubt of that."

"With my life," he said. "Thank ye."

"It's no more than the truth. I'll let ye get your sleep. Ye've performed your husbandly duty for tonight, even if it's no' the one she was hoping for. Goodnight."

"Goodnight," he said.

Pause.

"Ealasaid?" he said.

"Aye?"

"It's a fine grandmother she's got, too. Your daughter would have understood what ye did, and been proud of ye, I'm certain. I'm sure she is, if she can see ye now."

There was a short silence.

"Thank ye, laddie. Goodnight," the old lady said, her voice shaky again, but not with laughter this time.

He closed his eyes, and let sleep take him.

CHAPTER SEVEN

Alex's prophecy was correct, and Beth did indeed deeply regret her overindulgence the following morning. While the rest of the MacGregor and MacDonald clans enjoyed a communal breakfast before settling down to a serious political discussion, Beth remained in bed wishing she was dead, and for a time believing she was about to be so.

By mid-morning however, it was clear she was not about to shuffle off the mortal coil and she managed, with much wincing and holding of her head, to dress and make her way downstairs, where she settled herself in a chair by the fire with a cool damp cloth on her forehead. After a time she heard the door open and lifted the cloth from her eyes.

"Go away," she said, when she'd identified the intruder. "The last thing I need right now is a visit from someone who is completely unaffected by alcohol."

She replaced the cloth over her eyes and clenched her stomach, waiting for the joke about greasy breakfasts, delivered with head-splitting loudness.

"I'm sorry," said Angus softly. "I'll leave ye in peace, then."

She lifted the cloth from her face again. He was indeed going away, quietly.

"Angus," she said. "What's wrong?"

"Nothing important," he replied unconvincingly. "I'll come back later, when ye're feeling better."

"No, come in," she said, sitting up and then immediately wishing she hadn't. "I am better. Or I will be, soon. It's all right."

He moved further into the room.

"Ye look terrible," he said.

"Thank you, that makes me feel a lot better," she answered sarcastically.

"Have ye eaten yet?"

"No," she replied firmly, hoping to close the topic.

"Ye should have a wee bit of bread or something, to get your stomach working. And drink as much water as ye can," he said. "Wait a minute, I'll get you some." He disappeared into the kitchen.

There really was something wrong. Not that Angus could not be sympathetic when someone was really ailing. But nobody was sympathetic over hangovers. They were common, self-induced, and always a cause for leg-pulling.

He returned with a cup of water and a slightly stale bannock. She took a few sips, and bit off a tiny corner of the bread. He sat down on the edge of the chair.

"What's the matter, Angus?" she asked when he showed no sign of volunteering the information. To her surprise, her stomach had not rebelled at the introduction of the morsel of bread. She took a larger bite.

"I…er…I've come to thank ye, for last night. And to apologise," he said. He looked very boyish this morning, his dark gold hair flopping untidily over his forehead, his blue eyes anxious.

"Well, that's very kind of you, but it's not me you should be thanking," she replied. "Janet, Moira and Peigi did the food, and Sir Anthony provided the drink, or most of it. And if you did anything you should be apologising for, you must have done it late on in the night when I was too drunk to remember it, so I'd forget it, if I were you." She smiled palely at him and took another sip of water.

He looked at her intently.

"Duncan hasna told ye, has he?" he said.

"Duncan hasn't told me what?"

He sighed, sat back, contemplated for a moment, then told her what had happened the previous night.

"I thought he'd have tellt ye about it. I said sorry to him this morning, and I thought I'd get my apology to you over wi' at the same time," he finished.

"I see. Well you can thank me if you want, but there's no need to apologise. After all, I can understand why you were angry, even if, as you say, you've got no claim on her, but you didn't act on it, so there's no harm done."

Angus took a deep breath.

"You walked in on them," he said. "Had he….was he…emm…?"

"No," she said. "He wasn't, and he hadn't. They'd had a kiss, that was all, and she was already telling him she didn't want to go further." She pushed the image of Morag's young breasts, pink from Robert's attentions, firmly to the back of her mind. "You like her, don't you?"

"Aye," he said, reddening slightly. "Aye, I do."

"Why don't you tell her, then?" Beth asked. "Make a claim on her, if you think that much of her."

"Christ, I couldna do that!" he said. "She's just a bairn. Anyway, she kens well enough that I like her."

"You weren't thinking of her as a wee bairn when you were fantasising about her pulling thorns out of your backside," said Beth.

Angus blushed to the roots of his hair.

"Aye, well, I was only jesting about that," he muttered. "I was forgetting how young she was."

"You weren't joking, Angus, and you were right," said Beth gently. She had finished the bannock and the water, and her stomach was settling, although her head still pounded. "She's a woman now. Robert saw that, he wouldn't have been interested otherwise. And she doesn't know that you like her."

Angus looked at his sister-in-law, incredulous.

"She must do!" he protested. "We've been friends for years, since we were both tiny wee things. I used to gie her piggy backs everywhere, when she got too tired to walk. We had a secret hideout away up the glen. I taught her to swim!"

"Yes, she said you'd be more likely to dunk her in the loch than invite her to the stables." Beth smiled. "She also said you'd changed towards her recently, and were more distant now."

"Aye well, it's difficult," he said, looking very uncomfortable. "She's different. Maybe you're right. She is becoming a woman. And I canna throw a woman in the loch, or play fight wi' her. That's what we used tae do. And then when we were tired, we'd sit and talk."

"I don't see why you can't," said Beth. "You play fight with me. I've got the bruises to prove it. And you'd throw me in the loch without a second thought, if the mood took you."

"I would, if ye could swim," he said, grinning mischievously for a moment. "But that's different. You're no' a woman. Well, ye are," he amended immediately. "But you're more like a sister than a woman. There's a difference."

"Alex would throw me in the loch as well," she persisted. "And he *definitely* doesn't think of me as a sister."

"Aye, but when ye're husband and wife, it's no' the same. All that touching between a man and a woman leads tae other things. Things I canna do wi' Morag." He was blushing furiously now, and she took pity on him. He did have a point, too. Most of her and Alex's friendly tussles ended up in them making love.

"Angus," she said. "You've acknowledged she's a woman. That's why you're behaving differently around her, although she doesn't understand that. Women need to feel desired, attractive, and protected. But they still need friends too, people they can feel relaxed with. And friends often turn into lovers. Take a tip from me and Alex. We were friends before we fell in love."

"Are ye truly suggesting I follow my brother's example and court Morag by pretending to be a completely different person, blackmailing her into marrying me, and then punching her on the jaw and abducting her?" he asked, grinning broadly now.

Beth laughed, and then regretted it. The hammer pounded with renewed vigour behind her eyes, and she closed them for a moment until the pain subsided a little.

"No," she said, still smiling, which didn't hurt as much as laughing. "I'm suggesting you treat her like a friend, as you used to. Relax with her. Let her know you like her. Tell her she looks lovely in that dress, or with her hair in a particular way. You do it with me. Hold her hand, that sort of thing. Pay her some attention. But most of all, be yourself. You're a wonderful person Angus, although I'll only say it the once," she said. "You'd make any woman a good husband. Morag likes you, now. But if you carry on keeping your distance, she'll look elsewhere for what she needs."

"Like she did last night," said Angus sourly.

"Exactly like that," agreed Beth. "Make the most of the time we've got left, before we go back to London."

"You're right," he agreed, all sunshine and smiles again, the Angus she knew. "I will."

"Good," she replied. "Then please, go away and make a start. I know how much you drank last night, and it's doing me no good whatsoever to see you looking so healthy."

He grinned, planted a kiss on her cheek, and went away.

* * *

The MacDonalds left the next day. Beth shed some tears at the departure of her grandmother, promising to visit Glencoe as soon as possible. It surely could not now be long, she thought, before Sir Anthony could be permanently abandoned and they could come back to live in Scotland for good.

The exchange of political news had been interesting, if not enlightening. Since the aborted French invasion attempt there had been little or no news regarding developments in the Jacobite cause. As far as everyone knew, the prince was still in France, urging a further invasion; but William MacGregor, or Drummond of Balhaldie, who was with the prince and was supposed to be keeping the Scottish Jacobites informed of developments, remained ominously silent. In July a letter had been received by Doctor Barry, a Jacobite ally in London, in which Balhaldie asked him to send British pilots, but not specifying where to, or why they were needed. No further explanation had been forthcoming.

In August John Murray of Broughton had finally travelled to France himself, to try to find out what was going on. He had not yet returned, but was expected back in early October at the latest. Alex told Beth that as the weather would force them to leave by that time anyway if they were not to be snowed in for the winter, they would visit Edinburgh on the way back to London and try to meet with Broughton.

Beth would have been quite happy to be snowed in for the winter, but she had accepted that it was not to be, could not be. The longer they were away from London, the more explanations would be needed for their absence; and a spy cannot collect information effectively if he is four hundred miles away from its source.

They all put the inevitable departure to the back of their

minds, and settled to enjoy what time they had left. Angus renewed his friendship with Morag, Alex settled disputes, spent as much time as possible with his wife, and became more and more carefree and relaxed. When Beth was, inevitably, thrown in the loch, after a cheeky retort and a brief struggle, it was by her husband and not her brother-in-law. His subsequent offer to teach her to swim had been met by a spluttering refusal as icy as the waters of the loch, and he had had no choice but to carry her home and make love to her, both to warm her physically and reconcile her to him. They made love a lot, in those weeks.

Maggie and Iain were also spending a lot of time with each other, and with the other members of the clan. They did not consciously avoid Beth and Alex; but they knew that they would soon be returning to London with them. There was no need to spend time together now which could be better spent with those they would soon have to leave.

The days wore on, and the nights became longer and cooler, and one day in mid October, Alex looked up at the sky and announced with great reluctance that they would have to leave in a couple of days.

"It's coming on to snow," he said. "We've waited too long already, really. We canna wait any longer."

The day before they were due to depart Angus and Morag went off for a picnic in the hills; the fact that her parents had allowed it, providing they came back well before dark, was a very good sign. Angus had been glowing with happiness, in spite of the imminent separation. Duncan and Alex went off with some of the other men for a last bit of serious sword practice; once they were in London opportunities to practice would be rare and would have to be conducted more in the style of Sir Anthony than Alex, in case they were observed.

Beth ensured that they took bandages and salve with them, and then, after having desultorily packed a few of their clothes, gave up, took her warmest cloak and went for a walk on the pretext of fetching water, but in reality to say goodbye to the landscape she had made her own in the last weeks.

She walked slowly and aimlessly, knowing that by following the stream she could not get lost, and ended up walking further along it than she ever had before. There was a definite chill in the air; Alex was right, snow was imminent. The hawthorn and rowan still sported a few berries, red as blood in the otherwise predominantly brown landscape. A few stubborn leaves clung to the trees, fluttering tenaciously in the breeze, but most of them had fallen now, and Beth kicked her way through them, lifting great clouds of them with her feet, watching in delight as they floated back down, red, brown, copper, bronze and gold. The previous week the children and some of the adults had collected an enormous pile of leaves in the centre of the settlement, clearing the forest for a considerable distance. Then they had thrown themselves into the pile, burying themselves and each other, plaiting them into their hair, seeing who could find the biggest leaf. Beth had, delightedly, found a leaf that exactly matched the colour of her husband's hair, and he had obligingly worn it weaved into his chestnut locks until bedtime.

If we stay here much longer, Beth thought, smiling to herself, *we will all become little children again.* She tried to keep in mind what Alex had said, that life was not always this carefree. Maybe not, but the irrepressible good humour of the MacGregors was infectious, irresistible. If there was pleasure to be found in something, they would find it. She did not want to leave.

She sighed, and stopped at a point where the stream bubbled merrily over an outcrop of rocks. She contemplated whether it was worth negotiating the boulders, many of which were wet and looked slippery, and decided against it. She had walked far enough. Instead she sat down on one of the drier rocks and stared moodily at the stream for a while, lost in thought. Then she stood and picked her way carefully down to the edge of the water, bending to cup her hands in the icy flow and drink.

A flash of scarlet caught her eye and she froze immediately. It was too bright to be hawthorn or rowan, and in any case the patch of colour was too extensive for berries, and in the wrong place. She turned her head with infinite slowness in the direction of the bright splash, and found herself looking into the frightened brown eyes of what was unmistakably a British soldier, who had wedged himself between two boulders.

She should have run, as fast as possible, praying as she went that his musket wasn't loaded and that he was not fast enough to overtake her. Part of her mind told her to do just that, and she jerked backwards, then stopped. The rest of her mind told her that he had been there all the time she was sitting brooding, and must have known she was there; she had not been quiet. If he had wanted to kill her, he would already have done so. His eyes indicated that he was more terrified of her than she was of him, and the pale strained face around the eyes told her that he was no more than a boy, in spite of the military garb.

Seeing her indecision, he raised his hand in supplication.

"Please," he said, his voice soft and etched with pain. "I won't hurt you. Please, don't tell anyone I'm here."

Beth straightened slowly, moved a few steps closer, then stopped. She was still far enough away to run if he made a move, but from her new vantage point she could see that he was not going to do that. He was slumped against the rock, half sitting, his legs stretched out in front of him, the lower half of the left one canted at an unnatural angle. He had clearly made an effort to take his boot off, and had given up.

She approached him now without fear, and squatted down a few paces away from him.

"It's all right," she said. "You're injured. What happened?"

His eyes widened in amazement.

"You're English!" he said. "Is there a regiment camped nearby?"

He clearly assumed she was a soldier's wife or a camp follower. Yet his voice held no optimism at the thought of being in close proximity to a British regiment, as she would have expected it to.

"No," she said. "Not as far as I know. I am not with the British. This is clan country." That was as much information as she was willing to give. He must already know it was clan country, and could surmise what he wished from her presence in it. She looked at him, made a decision, drew her knife from her pocket slowly, and saw him flinch.

"I'm not going to hurt you," she said. "Your leg is broken, I think. If you will let me take your boot off, I can have a look at it."

"I've tried already," he said. "I can't get it off. My leg's too swollen."

"I can cut the boot off if you'll let me," she replied. "But you must stay still so I don't cut you by accident." Even so, it would hurt, although she did not tell him that. He nodded, and she moved closer.

The stench that hit her nose was so sudden and so overpowering that she heaved, screwing up her face in disgust and turning away to try to hide her revulsion.

"I'm sorry," he said, shamed. "I've…"

"It's all right," she interrupted. "It's understandable. I just wasn't expecting…it's not that bad," she lied, breathing through her mouth.

The smell was appalling. She could only think that he must have soiled himself, badly. The smell of faeces was unmistakable, mixed with another odour that she could not identify.

"How long have you been here?" she asked.

"Since yesterday," he said. "I fell off my horse and he ran away, so I crawled in here to get out of the wind."

She quelled her stomach and set to work on his boot.

"Your accent is from the south, isn't it?" she said, hoping to engage him in conversation and take his mind off the pain she could not avoid causing him.

"Yes," he said. "I'm from Dorset."

"How did you come to be here, then?" she asked.

It was the question he must have wanted to ask her, but to her relief, he did not.

"My regiment was sent here two months after I enlisted," he said. "We're on our way to reinforce Fort William in case of a rebel…" his voice trailed off as he realised he'd said more than he should.

The knife, razor sharp, was making easy work of the boot, but she had to go slowly because of the swelling.

"You're very young, if you don't mind me saying," she observed, pretending she hadn't noted the import of what he'd just said. "What made you want to enlist in the army?" Probably the glamour of the uniform and the promise of travel and adventure.

"I didn't really want to," he said to her surprise. "It was a mistake. Oh!"

She had cut the leather down to the sole, and now pulled the boot gently from his leg, which had hurt, and had caused his exclamation. She looked at the injury.

"Mother of God," she said softly under her breath.

"Is it bad?" he asked.

It was definitely, most definitely, broken. The shattered tibia had pierced the skin and was poking through his stocking, which was soaked with blood, the jagged end of the bone clearly visible through the thin material. The whole leg was terribly swollen.

"Yes," she said. There was no point in lying. "I need to take your stocking off to get a better look at it. Do you mind?"

"No," he said bravely. "But won't it make you feel sick, if it's very bad?"

She looked up at him and smiled. She thought nothing could make her feel more sick than the smell emanating from him, but did not say so. It was not his fault. In the state he was in, he could hardly wander off in search of a latrine.

"Yes," she said. "But if I want to help you, and I do, I've got no choice."

She took the time to steel herself by taking his empty water bottle and refilling it from the stream. Then she came back and handed it to him, before setting to work on his leg again.

"Why was it a mistake?" she asked. "Enlisting, I mean."

"I was drunk," he said. "I'd been doing bits of jobs on Johnson's farm for years, you know, casual stuff, helping out with the harvest, a bit of weeding, that sort of thing. Anyway, when I turned fourteen, he said that I was such a good worker he'd take me on permanent, like." He stopped, shuddering with the pain as she eased the stocking from his leg, bravely trying not to cry out.

"Is that what you wanted to do, be a farmer?" she asked.

"Yes," he said, his voice strained. "One day I'd like to have my own place. I was really pleased to have the job, because Mr Johnson was a good master, strict but fair, and I knew I'd learn a lot from him and he'd pay my wages on time. Which was the problem."

"Why?" Beth lifted her skirt slightly, tore a strip off her petticoat, and wetting it, started to carefully clean the worst of the blood away from the wound.

"At the end of six months he paid me, and I took the money to my parents. My dad gave me a shilling back. A whole shilling! So I went to a tavern in Poole to celebrate with some of the other farm boys."

"What happened?" she asked. The wound had stopped bleeding, which was good. At least he was not going to bleed to death. She wanted him to continue talking, to take both his mind and hers off the horrible mess of his leg. He obviously appreciated the company, having had a whole day alone to brood on his injury.

"I got in with some dragoons, who started telling me what a great life it was, how it made a man of you. They bought me a few drinks, started telling me about Dettingen and what a glorious victory it had been. It sounded fantastic."

"Is that why you enlisted, then?" she asked.

"No," he said. "I never wanted to travel to fancy places. Like I said, I want to be a farmer. No, they got me drunk, and when I woke up in the morning I found that I'd enlisted, though I don't remember it. I tried to tell them it was a mistake, but they said I'd accepted the king's shilling, and that was that."

"At fourteen?" she said, incredulous.

"Fifteen now," he corrected her. "It was my birthday two weeks ago." He tried to pull himself up a little and then thought better of it and subsided, his face white. A fresh wave of foul odour emanated from him. "How's the leg?" he asked faintly.

"It's stopped bleeding," she said. "But I can't set it myself." Or amputate it, as seemed to be the more likely treatment. She did not say that. "I need to go and get help."

His eyes filled with panic instantly, and he clutched convulsively at her dress.

"No!" he cried. "Don't tell them I'm here! They'll hang me if they find me!"

What was he talking about? Was he delirious?

"No one's going to hang you for falling off a horse," she replied soothingly. "You're injured. You can't stay here, and I can't move you on my own. I've got to get help, you must understand that."

"No. You can't. I…I…ran away," he said, shamefully.

Understanding dawned.

"You mean you're a deserter?" she asked.

"Yes," he whispered.

He bit his lip and looked away, unable to bear the open contempt he knew he would see on her face.

Very gently she detached his hand from her dress.

"I am not going to ask the redcoats for help," she assured him. "I don't blame you for deserting. They should never have made you join in the first place. It's their fault, not yours."

She took her cloak off and laid it gently over him, and then stood.

"I'll be as quick as I can," she said. "I'll leave the water with you, and I'll bring food and someone who can help you. Don't try to move, you'll only start bleeding again if you do. I won't betray you, I swear it."

Without waiting for his answer, she turned and began to pick her way carefully across the rocks. It was afternoon. Alex would surely be back by now. He would understand, and would know what to do.

She ran most of the way, her legs strong and fit after two months of daily exercise, but even so it took her over half an hour to get back to the settlement. She paused in the trees to get her breath, not wanting to arouse concern. Then she strolled towards the house. No smoke came from the chimney, which was not a good sign.

"Is Alex back?" she asked the passing Janet casually.

"No, not yet," came the reply. "They should be down any time now though."

Beth carried on to the house. Duncan was with Alex, but Angus might be back from his picnic by now. She opened the door and walked in. The house was empty. She stood there for a minute, undecided, trying to work out what to do.

She couldn't go and find him. She wasn't sure where the men had gone to practice. It could be any one of half a dozen different venues. She had no idea where Angus was either, and even if she could find him he would not appreciate her spoiling his last chance to be alone with Morag.

So the only sensible thing to do was to wait, which was something Beth was not good at doing. She sat down, stood up, lit the fire and sat down again. After maybe ten minutes she got up again and went into the kitchen, gathering together some oatcakes, a piece of mutton, some cloth for bandaging, and whisky. He would need that to dull the pain when Alex moved him. She realised she had not asked the boy his name, and spent a few minutes trying to guess what it might be. The sound of masculine voices came from outside and she ran to the door, forcing herself to open it slowly. Several men were walking past, dirty and tired-looking. One of them had a makeshift bandage round his head. Alex was not there, nor Duncan.

"Are they on their way?" she asked, leaning against the doorpost.

"No, they've gone away off for a wee walk," said William, the injured man. In spite of her casual tone, he caught the expression that clouded her features, and thankfully misinterpreted it.

"Have ye got their meal ready for them?" he asked, assuming this would be the most likely cause for anger. She seized on it.

"No," she said huffily. "And it's just as well, isn't it? Did they say how long they'd be?"

"No," replied Alasdair. "But they'll be back before dark, I've nae doubt."

Beth retired back into the house, seething with frustration. She could not ask anyone else to help. The boy was a redcoat, after all, and she was not certain whether the clansmen would be sympathetic to his plight or not. Alex would be. She was sure of it. Damn it! Why did they have to go for a walk, when she needed them? She couldn't wait until they returned, hours from now. The boy would think she'd deserted him, or betrayed him.

She had to go back. She gathered together the provisions, bundled them up in a blanket and set off, skirting the settlement to minimise the chance of meeting someone who would ask where she was going with such a large parcel. She would take him the food and the whisky, bind his leg as best she could, and get a small fire going to warm him until she could return again with Alex.

She couldn't run this time, encumbered as she was, and the sun was much lower in the sky when she finally reached him. He was still where she had left him, his mouth taut with pain, his eyes dark smudges in the pallor of his face.

"You came back," he said, relieved.

"Of course I did," she replied, bracing herself against the stench, which if anything, had grown stronger. "I couldn't bring help yet," she said, squatting down beside him. "The people I trust weren't there, but they'll be back later. I've brought you some food and a blanket, and something to dull the pain. I'll make you as comfortable as I can, and then I'll go back and fetch the person who can help you."

"You've helped me," he said. "You're very kind."

His voice slurred as though he was drunk, and she realised that he was only half conscious. She felt his forehead, expecting it to be hot and fevered, but his skin was cold, too cold, and clammy, and his lips were tinged with blue.

"You must stay awake and eat something," she said, trying to hide the alarm she felt at the deterioration in his condition since she'd been away.

"I'm not sure it's a good idea for me to eat," he said, attempting to smile at her. "You see I…" he stopped with a gasp and his eyes widened, fixing on a point over her shoulder. Then he moved, clawing at her dress with his left hand and fumbling frantically for his sword with his right.

She had unwrapped the blanket, and was unpacking the oatcakes, but looked up at this unexpected movement. Following the direction of his gaze, she turned and looked behind her.

For a split second she saw the two men as the boy must have done, tall, broad and ferocious, half-naked, bristling with weapons, their long hair wild and tangled on their shoulders, bare arms bulging with muscle, their faces fierce and implacable. Then they became simply Alex and Duncan, and she almost fainted, so great was her relief.

"It's all right, they're friends," she said, turning back to the boy and stroking his arm reassuringly, moved beyond measure by the fact that he had been trying, in spite of his pain and the impossibility of the task, to put her behind him and defend her against these savages.

"Have you told him your name? Or ours? Or anything about us?" Alex asked, in Gaelic.

"No," she replied in the same language. "Of course not. I'm not stupid. I've told him nothing at all. His leg is broken, and I don't know how to set it. Can you help him?"

To her surprise, instead of examining the boy he scrutinised her first, taking in the scarf covering her hair, the grubby dress, the work-reddened hands, and the scuffed shoes. Then he moved forward and squatted down beside the boy. His nostrils flared suddenly, and he grimaced.

"He smells very bad," she explained, still in Gaelic, but this time to spare the boy's blushes rather than for any secretive purposes. "He's been here two days."

Alex ignored both her and the boy's leg, instead examining his face. The young soldier remained silent, frozen with fear.

"It's all right, laddie," said Alex softly. "I'm here to help ye, like the lady says." Like Beth, he laid a hand on the boy's forehead, then nodded to himself, and with great care he removed the cloak she had laid over him and began to unbutton the scarlet coat. Beth retched suddenly, the smell overpowering her control, and Alex waved a hand behind him at his brother.

"Take her," he said, and Duncan moved forward, grasping Beth by the shoulders and drawing her backwards a short distance, where the air was untainted. She inhaled gratefully, taking several deep breaths.

"I'm all right now," she said, making an attempt to return to the boy's side. Duncan kept hold of her shoulders, restraining her gently.

"Wait," he said. "Let him look to the laddie."

Alex had shifted position, the breadth of his shoulders completely blocking the boy's upper body from her view. All she could see were his legs, one encased to the knee in black leather, the other bare, twisted and swollen. They were talking together, the man's voice deep and musical, gentle and soothing as he asked questions, the boy's voice higher pitched, still slurring slightly, nervous at first, then slowly relaxing.

She couldn't hear what they were saying, only the tone. Then the boy began crying softly, and Beth started in Duncan's grip, trying to move forward to comfort him. Had Alex just told him he would have to amputate the leg? If he had, how did he know? He had given the limb no more than a cursory glance.

"No," Duncan said, transferring his arm to her waist. "Trust him Beth, he kens what he's doing."

The conversation continued for a while, and the youth stopped crying. There was a pause, then Alex's hand moved to his waist.

Beth saw his arm move back, bent at the elbow, but it was only as he drove it forward again, hard, that she realised what he was doing.

"No!" she screamed, tearing at Duncan's arm, which tightened round her waist, lifting her off her feet, his other hand clamping over her mouth. He moved backwards, to the edge of the river, and she fought him wildly, kicking back and tearing at his restraining arm with her nails until he released his grip on her waist briefly to capture her hands, pulling her back into him.

It was over very quickly. The boy's legs jerked convulsively once as Alex drove the dirk into his chest, and then went limp. Alex remained motionless for a moment, then he wiped the blade on the grass before sheathing it, and leaned forward over the body, closing the eyes and crossing himself.

Then he stood, slowly, as though it cost him great effort, and turned to where his wife and his brother were still struggling.

She froze immediately as he advanced towards her. Her chest was heaving, her eyes huge and horrified above Duncan's muffling hand. Duncan removed the hand, and setting her back on her feet, let her go.

Beth and Alex stared at each other for a moment. An expression of unbearable distress flitted across his features too quickly for her to make sense of it, then it was gone and his face became neutral and cold.

"Ye ken what to do," he said to Duncan. "I'll send Angus to help ye. Come on."

He seized Beth's arm and set off, picking his way over the rocks with ease and then striding off across the heather at such a pace that Beth was forced to run to keep up with him. Several times she stumbled, and once she fell. He stopped then and picked her up, gently. Then he set off again before she could get enough breath back to speak, keeping hold of her arm.

He strode across the clearing, opened the door of the house and drew her inside. She clung to the wall, fighting for breath, and Angus, who was sitting by the hearth, MacGregor curled cosily on his knee, looked up in surprise.

"Duncan needs help," said Alex shortly. Angus lifted the cat off his lap and stood, looking from Alex to Beth.

"Ye'll need a spade," Alex added. "There's a burying to be done. Down by the burn, near the twisted oak. Now," he said brusquely, as Angus hesitated.

He nodded his head, cast a concerned look in Beth's direction and left, closing the door carefully behind him.

Alex turned his attention to his wife, who had almost regained her breath. He reached out to touch her and she drew away from him, taking several steps backwards. He made no move to follow her.

"Does anyone else ken about the dragoon?" he asked.

She stared at him as though he'd spoken to her in Greek.

"Ye came back to get food for him," he said. "Did ye tell anyone what ye were doing?"

"He was fifteen," she said, her face white.

"Answer me, Beth," he said, still softly. "Did ye tell anyone about him?"

"He was fifteen," she repeated. "Just two weeks ago."

"Beth, did ye tell any of the clan ye were going to help a dragoon?" he said, slowly and clearly.

"He didn't even want to be a soldier," she said, as if to herself. "He was…"

"Answer me!" he roared.

She jumped violently and flinched backwards, as though she expected him to hit her.

"No!" she shouted. "No, I didn't tell anyone! I found him, and he was a child, and hurting, and I couldn't help him, and I came back to get you because I thought you would know what to do! But you weren't here, and William said you'd gone for a walk. I didn't know what time you'd be back and I couldn't leave him alone, so I went back to him." The words rushed from her mouth, falling over each other as they came out, so he could only just understand what she was saying. "I thought you'd help him!" she cried, her eyes filling with tears. "Jesus Christ, Alex, I thought you'd help him!" Her voice rose hysterically, and she stopped and turned her head away, swallowing hard, trying to fight back the tears and bring herself under control.

"Beth, d'ye ken what ye almost did?" he said to her softly. "Ye almost undid everything ye've worked so hard for over the last two months. Duncan and I saw ye sneaking off through the trees. We followed you because you looked furtive. If it had been any of the other clansmen who'd followed you instead and seen what ye were doing, ye'd have had to start all over again to win their trust."

"Is that why you killed him?" she cried. "So the clan wouldn't think I was a government spy? Well to hell with the clan, if they think that helping a terrified, injured child makes me a traitor!"

"Beth," he said, moving towards her, "I killed him because…"

"Keep away from me!" she screamed. He stopped, his hand raised towards her, his face unreadable. "Don't tell me you killed him for me," she continued, her voice ragged, harsh. "Don't you dare tell me that. You told me before that the first solution that comes to you when you're faced with a problem is usually a violent one, didn't you? 'We're a violent clan.' That's what you said. Well you've excelled yourself this time, killing a young frightened boy who couldn't fight back. I hope you're proud of yourself. To hell with you, too."

"Beth," he tried again, "I didna kill him because he was English, or a dragoon, or for you. He was dying."

"No," she said, shaking her head. "No. He had a broken leg. Maybe it could have been set or maybe you'd have had to amputate it, I don't know. But people don't die of a broken leg."

They did, but now was not the time to quibble about medical details. Alex sighed. At least she had managed to control her own incipient hysteria. That was something.

"He was dying, Beth. Did ye no' smell him? Of course ye did, it nearly made you sick."

"You'd have smelt, if you'd been lying in one place for two days," she said. "He'd soiled himself. He couldn't help that."

"Yes he had, but it was more than that, ye must have smelt it. That sweetish sort of stink? That's corruption, Beth. He'd been…"

"No," she interrupted, her face set. "I washed his leg myself. It was a mess, but it hadn't gone bad. You can't use that as an excuse."

Besieged as he'd been in the last two hours by strong emotions; suspicion, concern, horror and grief, he fought now to remain calm, not to lose his temper with this woman who would not listen to him, and he succeeded only partly. He leaned forward, gripped her arm and ignoring her protests, dragged her outside again and over to the stables.

The sturdy Highland ponies or garrons were not stabled, as they were able to fend for themselves, but the more highly bred horses that Alex and the others had arrived on needed more care. One of the stalls was already empty. Alex threw a halter over the chestnut mare's head and led her out of her stall. Then he threw his wife unceremoniously onto its back and mounted behind her.

"Where are we going?" she asked after a moment, having abandoned the idea of trying to leap off the horse mid-gallop.

"Ye'll not believe me until I show ye," he said icily.

They rode without speaking, the hostility between them palpable. She would never believe the boy's leg was infected. It had been clean, the flesh pink and healthy, no ominous red streaks or blackened flesh, in spite of the swelling.

By the time they arrived the sun was setting, but the light was still good enough to easily make out Angus, covered in dirt and standing by a speedily but efficiently dug grave. A hobbled horse grazed contentedly nearby. Duncan was crouched over the boy's body, folding his arms respectfully on his chest. Both men looked up surprised as Alex dismounted, helped Beth down, and led her over to them.

"I've put his effects to one side," said Duncan, gesturing to a pitifully small pile nearby. Beth could see a brightly coloured pebble, some silver coins, a horse chestnut on a string. A child's toy. Her eyes brimmed.

"She doesna believe me," Alex said coldly. "She needs to see for herself."

Duncan looked at Beth's defiant white face and tear-filled eyes, and nodded curtly. He stood and backed away.

Alex bent down over the corpse and unbuttoned the coat, as he had done on first meeting the boy.

"Come here," he commanded, gesturing to her. "Look."

She came, and looked, and turned away, green-faced.

The lead ball had entered the young soldier low in the abdomen, lodging somewhere in the soft tissue. The wound was small and had not bled a great deal. But the smell, which was indeed overlaid with a sweetish sickening odour, was intense, and was emanating from the wound she had known nothing about.

"He was gut-shot, Beth. His sergeant shot him as he was galloping away," explained Alex emotionlessly. "You wouldna let me tell ye. He would have died anyway, in time. And in agony."

She looked at her husband's face as he tidied the boy's

disarranged clothing, folding the arms back in place with infinite care, and was aware that she had done him a terrible, unforgivable injustice.

"I…I didn't know," she faltered, her voice hardly more than a whisper. "He didn't tell me…"

"That was what the smell was," Alex continued matter-of-factly. "I recognised it straight away. I thought you had, too, but of course ye wouldna. Ye've had no experience of battle, how could you know? Even so, I thought ye trusted me enough to ken I wouldna kill a bairn without need, enemy or no."

She looked away from his face, which was cold and set. She felt sick again, but not because of the smell.

"Well," Alex said to his brothers, standing. "I'll leave ye to it." He jerked his head at his wife. "Are ye coming?"

He sounded as though he didn't care whether she came or not. She went over to the horse, and they mounted in silence. She had no idea what to say to him, and thought to use the time travelling home to think. But her mind refused to focus, and when they got back she had no more idea of what she could possibly say to repair the damage than she had when she had knelt by the corpse and realised what she had done.

"Are ye hungry?" he asked, once the door was closed behind them.

She shook her head, and he moved towards the kitchen.

"Thirsty, then?" he said. The politeness of his voice was chilling.

"Alex," she said. "I don't know what to say."

"Sorry would be a good start."

She only apologised when she was truly sorry. They both knew that.

"I'm sorry," she said. "God, I'm so sorry." Her face crumpled suddenly and she sank down into a chair, burying her head in her hands. Instinctively he lifted a hand to comfort her, then lowered it again and went into the kitchen, returning a few minutes later with some whisky, which he needed badly, and some food, which he did not. He sat down opposite and waited until she brought herself under control before he spoke.

"We need to talk, Beth," he said. "I thought we'd sorted out all the problems between us in Manchester, but I can see now I was wrong. Ye told me I didna trust ye over Monselle, and ye were right. I didna, and I was wrong not to. I trust ye now."

He looked at her. She had stopped crying and was looking down at her lap. But she was listening.

"I trust ye with my life, my secrets, the secrets of my clan. I trust ye with my strengths, and my weaknesses. I love ye, Beth, ye ken that already, but what I feel for you goes a lot deeper than that. I canna explain it rightly, but I thought I didna need to. I thought you felt it too. When I saw ye sneaking off through the trees I followed you, not because I didna trust ye, but because I thought ye might be in trouble. I didna call out to ye because it was clear ye were trying to move silently and I didna ken why. I wanted to be near to help you, if you needed it. When I saw you with the boy, I didna think ye'd changed sides for a minute. I asked ye if ye'd tellt him anything, because I ken how easy it is to let something slip when you're upset. I checked you over to make sure your hair wasna showing, because that's the memorable part of ye, the part that's most likely to identify you. At that point I had every intention of blindfolding the boy and bringing him back here to treat his wounds. The clan may be violent, but they're no' heartless. They'd have understood if I'd found the laddie. They'd have understood if you had, too, and why you'd kept it secret, eventually, but it would have taken time, and we're leaving tomorrow. I made the decision to kill him because I had no choice. I explained it to him and he understood and agreed wi' me. I'd not have done it else. I knew ye'd be upset." He paused and ran his fingers through his hair, slowly, wearily, before reaching for the whisky flask. "It didna occur tae me for one minute that ye'd think I'd done it from malice. If our positions had been reversed, I may have asked ye why ye did it, I may not have agreed with your decision, even, but I would never have doubted that you had good reasons for what you'd done, and I'd have listened to them before I judged ye. I wouldna have condemned you out of hand, as ye've just condemned me, Beth. I canna tell ye how much that hurt."

He didn't have to. It was written on his face, and Beth felt a huge wedge of despair rise up in her throat, choking her. She stared at him, her eyes enormous in the pallor of her face.

"I'm sorry," she whispered again. What could she say? He was right. He had given her no reason not to trust him since Henri. Why hadn't she trusted him? "I thought…you would have killed Katerina…I thought…"

He took a deep breath, let it out again. Katerina. Again. He had thought that was finished with.

"Let's get this over with, once and for all," he said. "Katerina was young and beautiful, and innocent, and aye, I might have killed her, at that moment, in that circumstance. Because at the time her life was set against the failure of the Stuart restoration, the death of hundreds, maybe thousands of Jacobites, and the certain betrayal of me, you and Angus. Henri had to die, and the best place to kill him was there, in the hothouse. We were verra lucky to find him in France, let alone get another chance to kill him. And, reluctant as I would have been, I couldna have let her live, with him dead. She knew Angus, knew whose servant he was. I wouldna have killed her for pleasure, because I enjoy violent solutions to problems, or for any reason other than to protect those I love, and I'm no' ashamed of that. Ye'd do the same, I'm sure. The boy was a completely different matter, as ye should have known. Now, either ye trust me and believe me, or ye dinna, but I'm no' going to spend the rest of my life explaining Katerina or having all my actions judged by what I might have done to her. Ye canna expect it of me, Beth."

"I don't," she said. "You're right. I've behaved as badly as you did. No, worse, much worse. You had reasons for not trusting me, even if they were wrong. I didn't. I'm sorry. I don't know what else to say, except I'll never do it again, I swear." A great hiccuping sob suddenly broke free, and she stopped, swallowed. "I don't expect you to believe me. I can't prove it," she finished hopelessly.

"Come here," he said, in a tone quite different from that he'd used by the boy's corpse. She stood, hesitantly, and he took her hand and drew her gently on to his knee.

"Beth my love," he began, and stopped as she suddenly burst into tears, sobbing convulsively, clinging to him as though she were drowning, mumbling the same incoherent words over and over again. It took several repetitions before he understood what she was saying, and when he did he felt the tears rise to his own eyes. He crushed her to him, feeling the fragility of her body, knowing the strength of her spirit, and what it was costing her to say what she was saying.

"Sshh, sshh, I willna leave you, *mo chridhe*," he said, in answer to her plea. "I'll never leave you. I couldna live without ye either, ye ken that, lassie, d'ye no'?"

While dusk deepened into night, they held each other tightly, both aware that the foundation of their relationship had finally settled and they could now build on this love and trust which would irrevocably bind them one to the other for the rest of their lives.

CHAPTER EIGHT

Edinburgh, Late October 1744

Dear Mr and Mrs Sennett,

It is with the utmost sorrow and regret that I write to inform you of the death of your son Nathan in a recent engagement with enemy forces.

He conducted himself with the utmost bravery during the conflict and will be sadly missed by his regiment. May I assure you that his death was instantaneous, and that he did not suffer. He was buried with full military honours on the 23rd inst.

Although I am aware that nothing can compensate you for the loss of a most exceptional son, I am nevertheless enclosing the sum of ten guineas, which I trust will at least alleviate any financial hardship caused by your beloved son's untimely demise. Please accept my most sincere condolences at your sad loss.

Assuring you that I am your humble and obedient servant,

The signature was impressive, but illegible.

"You can send them more than that if you want," said Beth, leaning over Alex's shoulder as he carefully blotted the letter before folding it. "I've hardly spent any of my dowry money."

"No," said Alex. "Ten guineas will make a difference to their lives, but will hopefully no' be enough for them to take the effort to get someone to write back. I dinna want them to find out their son was a deserter. The boy told me his mother was verra proud that he'd enlisted, and his father thought he was a bloody idiot. They canna write, so they'll have to get the minister or someone of that nature to read it for them. The whole village will think of

162

him as a hero. I canna do more for the laddie."

"Won't his commanding officer write to them anyway, to tell them he deserted?" Beth asked anxiously.

Alex smiled fondly at her innocence.

"If commanding officers wrote letters to every illiterate parent of deserting sons, they'd have nae time to command the army, and the village ministers'd have nae time to preach to their flock, they'd be so busy reading letters and writing replies. No, they'll maybe have a wee look round, especially if the sergeant realised how badly he'd wounded the boy, then they'll forget him. They'll keep a record of his name in case he gives himself up at the next general amnesty, and that'll be it."

"Is desertion a big problem in the British army, then?" Beth asked brightly.

"Aye, there are a lot of laddies like our Nathan here, who didna want to join and who make off at the first opportunity. Then there are a lot who enlist willingly for the uniform and the glamour, and havena a clue what they're letting themselves in for, and who run as soon as they realise how hard the life really is. But before ye start thinking that we'll have an easy time of it if there's an invasion, desertion's just as bad a problem amongst the Highlanders, too."

"What?" said Beth. "But I thought they'd follow their chief anywhere."

"Aye they will, but no' without question. Sometimes the methods the chiefs have to use to force their clan out is no' exactly gentle, shall we say. And the clans are what you would call irregular troops, that's to say they heed their chief before their regimental officer, and they're used to independent fighting. Which means they're good at thinking for themselves, but no' so good at following orders, or being disciplined. When they're happy you couldna wish for better fighting men. They're brave and loyal and ferocious fighters. When they're unhappy they say so, and if their complaints are no' dealt with, they vote wi' their feet and go home. That's why I dinna get my men tae follow me by threatening to burn their houses down. I'd rather have willing men fighting at my side. And if I've an unpopular order to give, I always explain why I'm giving it, so whether they agree or no', at least they ken my reasons. The Highlanders are no' mindless fighting machines like the British often are, and I wouldna have them any other way, for all the problems it can cause."

"What problems are those?" asked Beth, greatly interested.

"I'll tell ye later," said Alex, looking at the clock and standing up. "For now I've tae meet wi' Broughton and Lochiel and find out whether there's to be an invasion at all."

They had taken rooms on the third floor of a tenement in Riddel's Close, off the Land Market, and near enough to West Bow for the constant hammering of the smiths of all kinds whose workshops dominated that street to be heard, but not near enough for it to be too disturbing. Beth was entranced by Edinburgh, filthy and crowded as it was, with its impossibly narrow closes and wynds where a lady wearing full evening hoops would find her skirts brushing the buildings on both sides of the thoroughfare. The buildings were tall, the upper floors looming over the streets and blocking out the light, so that many of the closes were dark and gloomy even at midday. She had not believed Angus when he'd told her that it was common for a tradesman, an aristocrat and a labourer to all live in the same close, and sometimes even on different floors of the same building. She had told him that she might be naïve, but she was not stupid enough to believe that.

Nevertheless, here they were on the second floor of a tenement, below a highly respected doctor and above a milliner, whilst the whole top floor of the building belonged to an elderly baronet who Beth had not yet encountered. Regardless of status, the occupants of the tenements would greet each other with cheerful familiarity if they met on the narrow winding stairway that led to their apartments. These stairways were a nightmare to any lady of fashion; even with her hoops collapsed up under her armpits, negotiating the uneven stairs encumbered by countless yards of trailing material was no easy feat, and passing on the stairs was impossible. Beth was glad, therefore, as she strolled happily along Castle Hill Street with Duncan, that she had not yet had to adopt high fashion. The male members of the group, reluctant to a man to don the hated tight-fitting breeches and stockings after two months of genital freedom, had decided to retain their highland garb for the present, although they had removed the sprigs of pine from their bonnets which would identify them as

MacGregors. Alex had hoped there would be other Highlanders in Edinburgh, enough that their attire would not attract undue notice. Even when they discovered this not to be the case, most other Highland visitors having adopted lowland dress, they still decided to throw caution to the wind for a last few days of wearing their customary garb.

Alex and Angus had gone to the dingy club under the piazzas of Parliament Close where Broughton had established a meeting place for prominent Jacobites. Iain and Maggie had gone shopping, Maggie's eyes sparkling with excitement at the thought of spending money, a rare event for her. And Duncan and Beth were taking in the sights. They had wandered aimlessly round the tiny shops of the Luckenbooths without buying anything, and now made their way towards the castle, taking care to avoid the pigs that rooted around in the narrow streets, helping to clear up the piles of refuse that were deposited there every day by the citizens.

They joined the other people who were promenading and chatting in small groups on the esplanade of Castle Hill. Being one of the few open spaces in Edinburgh, it was a popular place to take the air and show off one's finery. Beth noted that there were no other Highlanders in evidence and that Duncan's incongruous dress was attracting some amused attention. Seemingly oblivious to this, Duncan stopped as they neared the gatehouse, all his attention on the cluster of buildings which made up Edinburgh Castle.

"Are you thinking what I'm thinking?" said Beth enigmatically as they stared up at the impressive edifice.

"I dinna ken what you're thinking," said Duncan, squinting upwards. "*I'm* thinking that it'd be awfu' hard to besiege the castle, if it had a good man in charge of it. The loch stretches right to its foot on the north. And d'ye see yon wall there?" he pointed up at a formidable curved stone wall studded with artillery emplacements which overlooked the approaches from the town. "That's the battery, and it's well-provisioned wi' cannon. It'd be awfu' difficult to get anywhere near the castle without being pulverised. Ye could starve them out if ye had the time, mind."

She looked at him with admiration.

"Do you look at everything you see with a view to fighting it?" she asked.

He grinned down at her.

"No," he said. "But if the prince invades via Scotland, this'll be one of the places he'll be looking to take, along wi' the forts along the Great Glen, Fort William in particular, and Stirling Castle, of course. That's no' what you were thinking about, was it?"

"No," she admitted, still staring up at the castle, its flag of the hated union with England fluttering merrily from the ramparts. "I was thinking that Iain and Maggie have become very secretive and giggly over the last few days. I wondered if Maggie was pregnant. Has she said anything to you?"

"No, she hasna," replied Duncan, tearing his attention away from the castle for a minute. "But you're likely right, Iain's being awfu' protective of her. It would be wonderful if she is. They've been married for three years wi' no sign of her womb quickening. Best we dinna say anything until they tell us, though." He winked at her and looked back up at the rock.

Beth and Alex had been married for over a year, with no sign of her womb quickening, either.

"I thought you'd have wanted to go to the meeting," she said, not wishing to pursue the subject she had started, or the thoughts that it was engendering in her mind.

"No, not at all," said Duncan. "I hate being in stuffy rooms in cities wi' crowds of people. Alex can tell me what happened later. I'm no' missing anything."

"You must really hate London, then," said Beth, suddenly gloomy at the thought of their imminent return.

"If I die and wake up in London, then I'll ken I've gone straight tae the deepest layers of Hell," said her brother-in-law with feeling. "Ye canna tell the seasons. Ye canna even breathe the air. I've nae idea why people choose to live there. Or here, for that matter,"

"It's fashionable," said Beth in her best society accent. "All the right people live in the town, don't you know?"

"Gie me all the wrong people then, and air that smells of green things instead of shit…look," he said suddenly, pointing to the sky, high above the castle walls. "An eagle. Can ye see him?"

She peered up into the cloudy sky. A couple of birds were flying by, specks in the distance, but much too small to be eagles, surely?

"No," she said. "Where is it?"

He bent his knees to bring himself down to her eye level, putting his cheek close to hers, and slung his arm round her neck in friendly fashion, his finger pointing diagonally upwards in front of her face. His hair brushed softly against her cheek.

"Follow my finger," he said. "There."

Now she had located it she couldn't understand why she hadn't seen it straight away. It was huge, or would have been, were it closer. Even at a distance it was impressive, soaring majestically above the castle, riding the thermals.

"Ohh!" she breathed, enraptured. "It's beautiful!"

"What a cosy picture of illicit romance! I am quite overcome!" came the comment from directly behind them.

Duncan straightened his knees and turned to face the man who was addressing them. There were several groups of people nearby, but no one else within earshot; yet the well-dressed young man with the mocking brown eyes standing in front of them was a stranger to him. Duncan kept his arm around Beth, moving it down to her shoulder, having no intention of removing it as if guilty and reinforcing the man's erroneous suspicions.

"Hello Daniel," said Beth coldly, having taken only a second or two to recover from the shock of seeing him in Edinburgh, of all places. "I see you have finally been released from the Fleet. Congratulations."

"Lord Barrington," he corrected, smiling. "No, I was never incarcerated. I have been away from London for a time, travelling. As have you, it seems."

"Ah," said Beth. "I trust your father paid your gambling debts then, once you realised you were not going to get your hands on my dowry?"

His smile faded. He turned his attention to Duncan, running his eyes insolently over him, from the leather-shod feet, up the powerful legs clad in checked hose, to the pleated kilt, the beautifully tooled swordbelt, the fine linen shirt and silver brooch holding the plaid in place at his shoulder. When he reached Duncan's cool grey eyes, his mouth tightened.

"It is customary to bow when you meet a gentleman, sir," he said tersely.

"Aye," said Duncan pleasantly. "It is."

The implication was clear, and Lord Daniel reddened slightly.

"What do you want, Daniel?" said Beth, aware of the mounting tension between the two men, and not wanting it to go any further.

The Englishman turned his attention back to her, smiling again.

"Why, nothing, Elizabeth! What could I possibly want from you? I merely wished to say hello, and to congratulate you on your speedy work."

"What are you talking about?" she said, genuinely puzzled.

"Well, your marriage bed is hardly warm, is it, and here you are proudly flaunting your barbarian lover around town! The least you could have done was to ensure he was decently attired. Sir Anthony will be distraught at you having taken such a filthy savage for a beau! Is he here, by the way?"

Beth's heart lurched as she saw, a couple of hundred yards or so behind Lord Daniel, the unmistakably tall figures of Alex and Angus emerge from a side street, heading in her direction. They took maybe a dozen steps or so before veering casually away to chat with a plainly-dressed man who had been trying to attract their attention. Her heart resumed its normal pace.

"No," she said, smiling sweetly at her former fiancé. "He is not here. But we will be returning to London soon. If you would care to call on him there, you can explain that you met me in the company of my kinsman and that your depraved mind led you to the wrong conclusion entirely." Duncan had taken his arm from around her shoulder now, and was standing loose-limbed and relaxed. Alex and Angus appeared to be haggling good-naturedly with the man, who was obviously a trader of some sort. She had no doubt they were watching every move of what was unfolding on the esplanade.

"Kinsman!" said Lord Daniel. "Ah, of course! I beg your pardon, Elizabeth. I had forgotten that your mother was from the northern wastes. No doubt she plied her trade most successfully in this fair city before moving south. There is always a great demand for whores in every populous borough, after all. I am sure you have a great many *kinsmen* here."

Duncan shifted position slightly.

"Lord Barrington," he said politely. "I can tell by your speech and your mannerisms that you're an Englishman, and havena been in Scotland long. I wouldna therefore expect you to have learned civilised ways as yet. Consequently I will forgive you your insulting remarks this time, but I would suggest you be on your way, immediately."

Lord Daniel's face flamed, his mouth twisting with rage.

"You will forgive me? Why you insolent swine!" he cried.

In the time it took for Daniel to locate the hilt of his sword with his right hand, Duncan had put Beth safely behind him and drawn his. He held it in readiness, the autumnal sunlight reflecting dully from the razor-sharp blade. People in the immediate vicinity hastily moved backwards out of danger, then formed a half-circle to watch the fun at a safe distance from the trio.

"Put it away, you ridiculous child, before he cuts you to pieces," came a commanding voice, whose owner now approached them at speed. He had been running, and had used his elbows to force a way through the onlookers. His wig was askew, his face flushed. For a moment Beth thought the man was speaking to Duncan and her blood ran cold at the thought of what was about to ensue. Then the man's hand closed over his son's, ramming his half-drawn sword back into the scabbard.

"The man challenged me!" protested Daniel, struggling to free his hand from his father's iron grip.

"That's right, he did!" lied a man in the crowd, still hoping to see a fight. There were several murmurs, both confirming and denying this statement. The Earl of Highbury ignored them.

"No, he did not challenge you. From what I saw, you insulted him and the Lady Elizabeth, and then you drew, or rather attempted to draw, first. Am I right?"

Daniel gave up the struggle and looked away.

"Yes," continued the earl, "I see I am. Very well then. If you persist in challenging this gentleman, I cannot stop you, but if you take even more than a cursory glance at him, you will see that you cannot possibly survive such an encounter."

"He called me uncivilised!" said the young man peevishly.

"And so you are, if you consider provoking a gentleman without cause and drawing your sword in the presence of a lady civilised behaviour. You will apologise, sir, to both the lady and the gentleman for your outrageous behaviour. You are bringing

JULIA BRANNAN

shame on the family name, Daniel, and I will not tolerate it." His voice was calm, but it was clear that he was very angry.

His son was equally angry, and was not about to apologise under any circumstances, that was obvious.

"I do not wish for an apology that is not freely given, my lord," said Beth, moving back to Duncan's side. "And I am sure my kinsman feels the same way."

Duncan nodded. His eyes had not left Daniel's, and he made no move to sheathe his own sword.

"Go home Daniel," said the earl icily. "Immediately. I will deal with you later."

The young man shot a furious glare at Beth and Duncan and turning on his heel, strode away through the laughing crowd, attempting unsuccessfully to gather the tattered remnants of his dignity around him as he went. In the distance Alex and Angus disappeared back up the street, following the enthusiastic trader. Duncan sheathed his sword. The crowd, disappointed at having been deprived of a spectacle, began to drift back into their original groupings. The earl sighed, and relaxed a little.

"My dear Lady Elizabeth, I am delighted to see you and to make the acquaintance of your kinsman, but it appears that every time we meet I am fated to apologise on behalf of my son for some outrage he has committed."

"If he behaves in such a manner to any other Highland gentleman, my lord, you will find yourself without a son to apologise for," observed Duncan grimly. "May I suggest with all due respect, that you teach him proper conduct, and that quickly, before someone else does?"

"You may, sir, although I have been trying unsuccessfully to do so for some time. He does, however, seem to hold a particular animosity towards yourself and your husband, Lady Elizabeth, although he has no reason to. He does not behave so rudely towards others."

"He does not respond well to failure, my lord," said Beth.

"No, he does not," said the earl, looking sadly after the retreating figure of his offspring. "Although one would think he would be accustomed to it by now, if his performance at the gaming tables is anything to go by. Well," he said, remembering himself, smiling and holding out his hand to Duncan, who accepted it and shook it. "I am sure you will not welcome my intruding any further into your day. I will take my leave of you both. Your servant, Mr MacDonald, Lady Elizabeth."

They watched him as he walked away, his erect, immaculately tailored figure attracting the attention of more than one lady as he passed.

"I really like him," said Beth. "Although I've never told him my mother was a MacDonald. I suppose Alex told him. He said they were good friends."

"Aye, he seems a fine man. Pity his son's such a wee gomerel. And he's the man ye nearly married, in place of Alex? Had you lost your senses entirely, lassie?"

"Yes, probably, but there are mitigating circumstances," Beth said. "Firstly, six months of living in the bosom of the Cunningham family would drive anyone insane. And secondly, I preferred Daniel to Sir Anthony, not Alex. There is a difference."

Duncan could not dispute that, and the newly christened Mr MacDonald and his kinswoman were smiling again as they walked down the hill to join Alex and Angus, who had both re-emerged onto Castle Hill Street carrying a small parcel.

Beth opened the one Alex had been carrying, which was intended for her, on the way to their lodgings.

"Oh, it's beautiful!" she said, taking out a delicately wrought silver bracelet, set with amethysts. She let him place it round her wrist, and held her hand up to admire it, putting the unpleasant scene of a few minutes ago from her mind. She looked with curiosity at Angus, who shoved his identical parcel hastily into his pocket.

"It's for Morag," he said. "It's a wee bit different to yours. I wanted to gie her something to remember me by."

"I doubt anyone who's been in your company for more than ten minutes would ever forget you, Angus, whether you gave them a bracelet or not," she replied.

Angus decided to take this ambiguous statement as a compliment, the corners of his mouth curling upwards.

"It's a sort of betrothal present, too," he said. "Two years is an awfu' long time to wait, when you're fourteen." They had agreed to marry when Morag turned sixteen, if she still wanted to at that time.

His voice made it clear that it was an awfully long time to wait when you were twenty, too.

"She'll wait for ye, laddie, I've nae doubt. She promised she would, did she no'?" said Alex.

"Aye," confirmed Angus, brightening. "And her da's no objections, which is good."

"And we're bound to be back there in less than two years, anyway," said Beth, hopefully.

"Next summer, it seems, if Charlie has his way," said Alex. Surprisingly, he did not sound overjoyed at this thought.

"How did the meeting go?" Beth asked, brought suddenly back down to earth.

"It was interesting, but it's no' over yet," said Alex. "Broughton and Lochiel are coming to our lodgings to clarify a few details."

"I'm thinking we need to be changing our clothes as well," Duncan said. "We're attracting too much attention as we are."

"Aye, you're right," said Alex. "And speaking of clothes, tomorrow morning I've an appointment wi' my tailor." He grimaced and looked at Beth. "And you've an appointment wi' a dressmaker."

Now it was Beth's turn to grimace.

"I'm sorry," said Alex sincerely. "But the holiday's over. Sir Anthony is needed in London, as soon as possible."

* * *

Sir Anthony Peters sat on one side of the hearth in the drawing room of his London house, resplendent in emerald green velvet breeches and frockcoat, set off by a buttercup yellow brocade waistcoat. His wig was curled and powdered, his heavy makeup expertly applied. His expression would have curdled milk.

His wife, wearing a similar expression, sat opposite him, clad in turquoise velvet, stays tightly laced, her hair swept up and secured with enamelled pins. Aquamarines sparkled in her ears and at her throat. The unhappy couple sat in silence for a time, staring moodily into the fire and thinking of the meeting in Edinburgh that had necessitated their immediate return to London without spending a week or two in Manchester on the way south as Beth had hoped they would.

They had met John Murray of Broughton at their Edinburgh lodgings, after the unfortunate episode with Lord Daniel. Dressed in brown frockcoat and breeches, he had looked quite different from the Highlander Beth remembered in Rome; smaller and slighter somehow, his fair hair hidden under a powdered wig. Donald Cameron of Lochiel, chief of Clan Cameron had turned up a few minutes later, also dressed in the sober garb of the lowlander rather than the Highland attire he preferred, although he wore his own thick light brown hair brushed ruthlessly back from his face and tied with a dark ribbon. He was a handsome man in his early forties, tall and athletically built, and his warm greeting of the MacGregors had endeared him to Beth immediately. The brandy having been poured, the men had got down to business straight away. Alex had given a brief resumé of the morning's proceedings for Duncan and Beth's benefit.

"John tellt us this morning that he had several meetings with Prince Charles in the Tuileries in spite of Balhaldy's trying to prevent it, and it seems that Balhaldy has been less than honest with the prince, exaggerating the level of support he could expect from his British supporters. He was under the impression that he could expect at least twenty thousand Scots to rise for him. He had no idea that Balhaldy has been keeping us in the dark about developments."

"I told the prince that the best he could expect from Scotland would be four thousand men if he came without a considerable body of French troops, as many of the clans have made French support a condition of them rising," Murray continued. "I doubt the Frasers will come out otherwise, and the MacLeods will be very reluctant too."

"MacLeod's no' the only one who'll be reluctant. So will I. It canna be done without French help, it's as simple as that," said Lochiel firmly, his handsome face grim. "The Campbells are an enormous clan, and wi' most of them on the government side, we need the support of the big northern clans, and we'll no' get it if the prince doesna have Louis' backing."

"What did the prince say to that?" asked Duncan.

"He said he would try to raise a body of French troops, but that he was determined to come to Scotland next summer, even if he had to come with a single footman," said Murray. "He's verra impatient, and frustrated at the aborted invasion. He's been dealt badly wi' by Louis too, which doesna help."

Beth groaned, and the men all looked at her.

"I've met the prince, you remember," she said by way of explanation. "He'll do it, won't he?"

"Aye, I've no doubt he will," said Broughton. "Unless we can persuade him otherwise. Which is why we're all here now." He paused to take a sip of his brandy. "Before I left France the prince gave me a letter for the Earl of Traquair, ordering him to go immediately to England, find out the state of affairs there and get some definite commitment from the English Jacobites. Traquair has refused to go."

"What?" said Duncan, amazed. "He's refused a direct order from Prince Charles?"

"He didna say no outright, but he's suddenly a verra busy man, and he did go so far as to say he was surprised the prince should think he had nothing better to do than run his errands."

There was a general gasp from the group at the thought that anyone who claimed loyalty to the Stuart cause could say such a thing.

"I can understand him," continued Broughton. "He's a friend of Balhaldy's. Balhaldy seems to want a rising at any price, and he's so desperate to keep the prince's favour that he'll tell him whatever he wants to hear, true or no. If Traquair goes to England and finds out that they willna rise without a French army behind them, as I suspect he will, it puts him in an awkward position. Either he betrays his prince by lying to him and telling him the English will join him without condition, or he betrays his friend by telling Charles the truth. So he's prevaricating."

"That's why Sir Anthony needs to return to London immediately," said Alex. "So that I can do what Traquair should be doing, and try to get a definite commitment from the English."

Beth glanced from Alex to Murray, who intercepted her look and smiled at her.

"Aye," he said. "Alex has told me about Sir Anthony. It's quite amazing. I never would have recognised him. I've revised my opinion of the baronet considerably from the last time we met. Dinna fret, Lady Elizabeth, the secret's safe with me."

"Dinna do it because you're feeling guilty, though," said

Lochiel to Alex. "Although Balhaldy's a MacGregor, he's also my cousin, but I dinna consider myself responsible for his stupidity."

"No more do I," said Alex. "We were on our way back to London anyway. And if Traquair doesna consider it necessary to help his prince, I do."

"We have to be sure of the support of the English and the French," said Lochiel. "And if we're not, we must, at all costs, prevent the prince from landing in Scotland next summer wi' his single footman."

Musing now in front of a London hearth, Beth wondered how anyone could stop the whirlwind prince from doing anything, once he had set his heart on it. She looked across at her husband, and discovered to her surprise that instead of gazing into the fire he was watching her instead. She had no idea how long she had been unknowingly observed, and coloured slightly.

"I'm awfu' glad I've got you," he said softly. "I dinna think I could have faced the prospect of being Sir Anthony again without you by my side."

She looked at him, thought of what she had almost lost and shivered suddenly, realising that she could not face the prospect of *anything* without him by her side. It was strange that less than two years ago she had not even known of his existence, and now the thought of life without him made her feel ill. *He knows what I'm thinking,* she realised as she saw his eyes soften.

"I meant what I said that night," he said.

An overwhelming desire to abandon the tedious visits and spend the day making love instead pulsed in the air, bridging the space between them. It had taken them two hours to get dressed. If they abandoned their outing now, they would never do it. Beth reluctantly swallowed back the invitation to him to tear all her clothes off and take her now, which she had been about to give voice to.

"Even though it now means you've got to call on my pompous boring cousin and his colourless sisters?" she said instead.

"Even if I had to call on the devil himself," Alex smiled. The sexual tension diminished, slightly. "Come on then, let's do it. It'll be easier once we've made our first formal call. We'll get back into the way of it then."

He stood and held out a hand to assist her to her feet, then put his arm around her. His head bent automatically to hers.

"You'll smudge your makeup," Beth reminded him, a second before their lips would have met.

He said something extremely obscene in Gaelic and released her reluctantly.

Beth smoothed her dress, tried to take a deep breath and failed due to the constricting stays, swept her way to the door and came to a shuddering halt.

"Oh damn it to hell!" she said viciously, moving back a few steps then hauling her hoops up gracelessly so that she could get through the doorway. She stopped in the hall and waited for her husband to join her.

"My cousins are not expecting us, are they?" she asked.

"No, they're just the first on a list of duty calls we'll have to make now we're back," Alex said. "Geordie should really be the first, but I've put him off until tomorrow. At least I didna have to endure his birthday celebrations."

They had arrived in London two days before on the second of November, three days after the bonfires and obligatory public demonstrations of loyalty to the Hanoverian king.

"In that case," suggested Beth, "let's forget the Elector and my stupid cousins for now. Loosen my stays a bit before I faint, and let's visit Edwin and Caroline first. At least we *want* to see them."

The drawing room was a study in familial bliss. Mother and father sat on opposite sides of the hearth, intent on their son, who was making his wobbly-legged way from one parent to the other, heavily supported by Caroline's arm. His small face was a picture of determination.

Edwin, arms held out to catch his son, looked round as the visitors entered.

"Where the hell have you two been?" he asked.

"Not quite the customary greeting, dear boy, but I suppose it shows you've missed us," Sir Anthony said, appropriating his customary place on the sofa. "Good God, he's changed, hasn't he? Or have you swapped Freddie for another child?"

The infant, who had indeed changed considerably, looked at the apparition placed before him in wonder, his eyes, which were now definitely hazel, opening wide, and his grip on Caroline's arm loosening. He took another faltering step unsupported, then toppled backward, landing on his bottom on the rug. His face wavered and Caroline scooped him up quickly before he could decide in favour of tears.

"Children do change over a three month period at this age, Anthony," Caroline said pointedly, kissing the child's fuzz of brown hair before commencing to bounce him gently up and down on her knee.

"Really, you two, it's not good enough," said Edwin sternly. "You could have told us you were going away for months. Caroline's been beside herself."

Caroline looked at him, lips pursed.

"Well, I've been a bit concerned as well," he admitted. "We knew you were going to a wedding in Manchester, but we had no idea you were going to stay away for so long. We thought you'd had an accident or been murdered or something, particularly when we had no word from you. Caroline finally wrote to you in Didsbury. I assume you haven't received her letter."

Beth and Sir Anthony looked at each other guiltily. It hadn't occurred to them that anyone would be worried about them.

"No, we haven't. I'm sorry," said Beth. "Lots of people go off to the country for a few months at a time. We thought you'd realise that was what we'd done."

"We did think that was what you'd done at first," said Caroline. "But when people go off to the country they usually correspond with their acquaintance in the city, regularly. Whereas you haven't written to anyone, have you? I even called on your cousins to see whether they'd heard from you, and had to endure Edward pontificating on for an hour about how to rear children, not to spoil the rod, cold baths twice a day, all that rot. It was appalling."

"I'm sorry," said Beth again.

"It was even worse when he started citing you as an example of what happens when a child is overindulged by its parents and becomes a headstrong, selfish adult with no consideration for others. I almost hit him, until I realised that the reason I was enduring his drivel at all was because he was right. Not about your upbringing, but about your lack of consideration. You two are our best friends. Why didn't you write?"

Beth looked at her husband helplessly. Maybe they would have been better going to Edward's first, after all. What could they say? *We're sorry, but we were charging half-naked around the Highlands of Scotland, making love in the heather, throwing each other in the loch and behaving like little children, and it was wonderful and we forgot all about you.*

"We've been in Scotland," said Sir Anthony, to Beth's utter astonishment.

"*Scotland?*" said Edwin incredulously. "Don't tell the king that, when you call on him. Or Cumberland. They're convinced the place is a hotbed of Jacobitism. All the prominent people there are being watched."

"Oh, that's the Highlanders," said Sir Anthony dismissively. "And only a small number of them, if rumour is to be believed. We were in Edinburgh. After we'd spent some time in Manchester, of course. Beth's ex-servants have bought a house together, and we stayed there. They really are excellent people. Of course we should have written. It was quite inexcusable. But it never occurred to us you'd be worried. We didn't forget you, of course; we've brought presents."

He fished in his pocket and brought out a ball made of four pieces of brightly-coloured leather sewn together and stuffed with cloth. He stood and presented it formally to the child, who was already reaching for it, attracted by the bright colours. It jingled softly as Freddie's hands closed around it, automatically transferring it to his mouth. Caroline reached to take it off him.

"It's quite all right," said the baronet. "I thought of that. It's sturdy enough for him to chew on without damaging it or himself, and too big for him to swallow. It's got some bells sewn inside it, too." He smiled, and Caroline softened before his eyes. "We've brought presents for you two as well," he continued. "They're in the coach. A bottle of excellent brandy, Edwin, which I was hoping you'd invite me to share with you, although I'll forgive you if you don't, in your present mood. And a length of silk, Caroline, which matches the colour of your eyes perfectly. And now you've got to forgive us, for we are really most contrite, and if we ever go away again we promise to write to you twice a day at least."

He adopted an expression of such utter distress that even Edwin, who had been determined to give his friend a hard time, gave in.

"How was Edinburgh?" he asked Beth.

"Interesting," she said uncertainly, wondering why Alex had revealed that they had been there at all. "Er…the castle is very impressive. And Anthony bought me the most delightful bracelet."

"Beth met Lord Daniel there," supplied Anthony. "It was the first time you'd seen him since our wedding eve, was it not, my dear?"

"Yes," she affirmed neutrally.

"He was travelling with his father, who is looking in superlative health," said Anthony, as though they had all enjoyed a pleasant chat together.

"I'm glad to hear it," said Edwin. "Highbury is an excellent fellow. Such a shame his only son is turning out to be a wastrel. You had a fortunate escape there, Beth."

"I certainly did," she said, shuddering.

Freddie dropped the ball on the rug, and Caroline popped him down beside it and reached for the servants' bell.

"How many calls have you made today?" she asked. "Have you had tea at Isabella's?"

"No, you're our first port of call," said Beth. "We couldn't bear to face my cousins first thing. We thought to ease our way back into London society gently."

"Then you haven't heard the news?" said Edwin. "I thought it was strange that you hadn't mentioned it, but then we have been making you eat humble pie for the last ten minutes."

"What news?" said Beth and Anthony together.

"Lord Redburn is dead," said Edwin. "He died three weeks ago. That's why Caroline wrote to you in Manchester, hoping you'd be there."

There was a shocked silence. Caroline rang the bell.

"Shall I call for something stronger than tea?" she asked.

"Aye," said Sir Anthony.

Caroline waited. Beth tried to catch his eye but he was looking away from her, distracted by the news.

"You what, Anthony?" she prompted gently. He looked at her, puzzled. "You said 'I…' and then stopped. What were you going to say?"

"I'm sorry," he said immediately, only the slight widening of his eyes showing that he had realised his slip and was appalled by it. "I can't believe it, was what I was thinking. I hadn't realised I'd spoken aloud. Yes, Caroline, some wine would be excellent, if you don't mind. God, what a shock. He seemed to be recovering his health under Anne's care."

"That's what everyone is saying," said Edwin. "I hated to admit it, but you two were right to coerce them into marriage. They were perfect for each other. He doted on Anne. She really blossomed, became a lot more confident. And she even managed to get him on to that milk diet you were so anxious to stop her talking about. He was losing weight, going for regular walks. We all thought he was getting better."

"How did he die?" asked Beth.

"The carriage had dropped them off at Birdcage Walk and they were strolling along together, when all of a sudden, according to Anne, he clutched at his chest, said something about not feeling quite the thing, and fell down on the path."

"The poor woman," said Anthony. "She must have been hysterical."

"Not a bit of it," put in Caroline. "She behaved admirably. She tried to revive him herself for a few minutes, and then she ordered some men who were passing to carry him to the carriage. After that she drove like the devil to Warwick Lane and demanded the attention of the most senior physician at the College. And got it. But there was nothing anyone could do. Lord Redburn was already dead."

"The funeral wasn't held until last Thursday, because she insisted on having an enormous send-off for him," said Edwin. "It cost a fortune. She gave out nearly two hundred mourning rings alone. There were four coaches, all covered in black, and a huge tea afterwards. I don't want to rub it in, but she was very upset that you couldn't be there."

Sir Anthony lifted his arm, stopping himself from rubbing his hand through his hair just in time. Instead he reached across to pick up his glass of wine from the tray which the servant had placed on the table.

"We will have to visit her, of course. We will go directly after we leave here," he said.

"I would go home and get changed first, if I were you," said

Caroline, eyeing her friend's clothing with a critical eye. "I don't think Anne will appreciate you turning up dressed like a daffodil, Anthony, delightful as you look. After the funeral she went to pieces, and Charlotte has been her almost constant companion ever since. Need I say more?"

Beth and Anthony both groaned in unison.

"I'm sure she'll come round in time, though," said Edwin. "After all, Charlotte was left with only memories of her poor dear Frederick. Redburn has left Anne stinking rich, as you pointed out when you were matchmaking, Beth. Once she realises that she's no longer dependent on anyone, I'm sure she'll regain the confidence she developed while she was married."

"Stinking rich is not all Stanley Redburn left her, though," Caroline said. "He also left her three months pregnant."

Beth was uncharacteristically silent on the way home.

"You're not that distressed about Lord Redburn, are you?" her husband asked. "It's not as though you knew him well, after all."

"No," said Beth. "I feel sorry for Anne, though. I never envisaged him dying so quickly. I was hoping she'd get the time to develop a little, away from the influence of the Winters."

"It sounds as though she did, from what Caroline and Edwin said."

Silence.

"Are you worried because of my slip?" he said. "I won't do it again. I'm going to speak only in English for the next two days, just to make sure."

"No, I'm sure you'll be fine," she said. "I couldn't understand at first why you told them about Edinburgh though, but of course if Daniel or his father talks about seeing us there, it would look strange if we hadn't mentioned it."

"Exactly. But I didn't think there was any need to mention the unpleasantness. William won't say anything and his son definitely won't be keen to chat about his humiliation."

Silence.

"I know what it is that's bothering you," said Alex as the coach pulled up outside the house. "You're regretting your choice of husband. You're thinking that if you'd known Lord Redburn was going to die this quickly, you'd have married him instead of me and have been a rich widow now, instead of being saddled with an impoverished fraudster who could live for another fifty years."

That made her smile, at least. He jumped down from the coach and she took his hand. They walked up the steps and into the house together.

"I'll go and change," said Beth, making for the stairs. Alex retained his grip on her hand and put his other hand under her chin, tilting her head up to his.

"Beth," he asked. "What's wrong?"

To his astonishment tears sprang instantly to her eyes.

"It's not fair. Everyone's pregnant!" she cried. "Everyone except me!"

"It's true," she sniffed a few minutes later, sitting on his knee in the library. "First Caroline, and then Janet – she's only just had one, and she's already pregnant again, and then Maggie, and now even Anne Maynard! Redburn," she amended. "What's wrong with me?"

"There's nothing wrong with you, Beth," said Alex.

"There must be!" she said. "We've been married for over a year, and it's hardly as though we haven't been trying."

"Caroline and Edwin were married for five years before they had Freddie," Alex pointed out. "And Maggie and Iain have been trying at least as much as us for the last three years."

"Anne must have fallen pregnant almost immediately," countered Beth, "and Janet was pregnant before she even got married! Are you very disappointed?" she asked. "I know you haven't said anything, but you must be." She had thought of little else since Maggie's expected announcement three days ago. The baby was due in April.

Alex's painted face creased in consternation.

"This is the first time I've thought about it, and that's the truth. I'm no' disappointed, not a bit of it," he said, forgetting his intention to speak only English. "We're young and healthy, and if God intends us to have bairns, he'll send us some."

"And if he doesn't?" she whispered.

"If he doesna, then I'll still thank him every day for giving me you," said Alex firmly.

"But what about the clan?" she said. "Won't they expect you

to have a son to take over the chieftainship?"

"Not at all," he said. "They'll accept sons of Duncan or Angus just as easily, if they're worthy. Aye, I ken Duncan isna likely to marry again, but I'm sure there are already one or two wee Anguses toddling around France and Italy and even London." He knew it was unlikely even as he said it, hoping to reassure her. Prostitutes were extremely knowledgeable in the art of terminating unwanted pregnancies, and Angus, reckless as he could be, normally took precautions to avoid getting the French pox. "Him and Morag will have a dozen, I'm certain of it," he finished, wiping a tear from her cheek with his finger.

"But you really like children," Beth persisted. She seemed determined not to be consoled. "You must want some of your own."

He shifted her on his knee a little to relieve the pressure of the cane hoop of her underskirt, which was digging painfully into his ribs. It had been quite a feat to get her on his knee at all, in this ridiculous dress.

"Beth," he said firmly. "I like children, aye. I would like some of my own, I'll no' deny that. You wouldna believe me if I did. But I'll have them with you, or with no one. Dinna forget, it takes two to make a baby. If we canna have them, and I say 'if' because we havena given it anywhere near enough time to be sure yet, then the fault is as likely to lie with me as with you. Now if ye want to go off and try wi' another man, that's up to you, but you'd better make sure I dinna catch you at it. Myself, I'll choose to stay wi' you, bairns or no'. If that's all right wi' yourself."

"Yes," she said, convinced at last. "That's all right with me."

She hugged him and clambered off his knee.

"Five years, you said. Are you sure?" Beth asked, as she reached the door.

"I'm sure. And they were trying. Ask Caroline yourself if you don't believe me."

"I believe you," she said, cheered. "I just didn't know it could take so long, that's all."

He knew it could. He also knew that most women became pregnant in their first year of marriage. He had meant every word he said to her. Nevertheless, he sent up a silent prayer that he would be allowed to have Beth and the joy of his own children too. It was greedy, he knew that, but there could be no harm in asking.

CHAPTER NINE

By the time Beth had washed away all traces of her distress and they had both changed into mourning dress it was after the accepted hour to make calls, but they were admitted by the Redburns' footman anyway and shown into the salon.

At first Beth thought she had gone blind, so great was the contrast between the afternoon sunlight outside and the darkness of the room into which they were shown. Then her eyes started to adjust, and she saw a figure rise and move to turn up the lamp. A thin yellow light dimly illuminated the three people inhabiting the room.

"Oh, how delightful to see you both, Sir Anthony, Lady Elizabeth!" gushed Lady Winter. "You have been away for such a long time." Her voice managed to hold reproach, curiosity and even a hint of genuine welcome, all at the same time.

Sir Anthony bowed, nodded his head to Lord Winter, who had also risen, and took two steps into the room.

"We have been travelling around this delightful isle, taking in its remarkable and diverse beauties, Lady Wilhelmina," he said politely before turning to Anne, who to Beth's alarm had not even stood to greet them, but remained slumped in her chair.

"My dear Anne, there are no words…" he began.

"We were just about to take our leave," announced Lord Winter, clearly intending to make a run for it whilst he could. He could not in good conscience leave his grief-stricken great-niece alone, much as he desired to. The Winters had called for ten minutes over an hour ago, expecting Charlotte to be present, and had been appalled to find Anne alone, and themselves trapped by politeness and familial obligation into indefinite attendance on the grieving widow. He saw the Peters' unexpected visit as a God-given opportunity to escape.

Lady Winter, who had been about to sit down, now stood again, wavering between taking advantage of the window of opportunity to go, and curiosity as to where the Peters' had been for three months.

"Do not let us keep you if you have an urgent appointment, my lord," said Beth. "I am sure we will meet again very soon."

"Indeed," said Lady Winter, brightening. "Now that you are back, you will of course be attending Clarissa's birthday celebrations next week. They promise to be most exciting. Dinner at their house followed by a visit to the opera, at which Mr Handel will be playing! Edward has reserved two boxes especially."

"Capital," sniffed Lord Winter without enthusiasm. "Now if you will excuse us." He sketched a bow at the company, tucked his wife's arm firmly under his own and left, as hastily as decorum would permit.

"My dear Anne," began Sir Anthony again as soon as the door had closed, moving to kneel by her side. "There are no words sufficient to express our distress on hearing the news of your tragic loss. We are distraught."

"You are very kind, Sir Anthony," said Anne in a monotone.

"It is not kindness which moves me, my dear, but concern for yourself. I am so terribly sorry." He sounded really genuine. "I cannot imagine how I would cope if anything were to happen to my dear wife. I would be beside myself." He took her limp hand in his and stroked it comfortingly.

For the first time since he had entered the room, Anne looked at him.

"Oh Sir Anthony," she breathed, her eyes filling with tears. "You cannot believe how horrible it has been." She looked down at the hand stroking hers, and a huge tear splashed onto the black silk of her dress.

"Oh God!" she wailed, throwing herself out of the chair and into his arms so unexpectedly that he almost toppled over backwards. "It was awful!" she wept into his shoulder. "Everybody has been so kind, but they keep reminding me that I am as rich as Croesus, as though that should be a consolation. I cannot bear it, I cannot!"

His arms came round her as she dissolved into a paroxysm of sobbing, and while her husband patted the bereaved woman's back and murmured words of comfort, Beth took the opportunity to turn the lamp up a little more. She looked around the room, appalled. The windows were tightly shuttered and every piece of furniture was draped in black crepe. No cheering fire burned in the grate in spite of the season, and the room was very cold. The air smelt old and stale. What was Charlotte thinking of? What were any of Anne's so-called friends thinking of, to allow her to bury herself like this?

Instinctively Beth moved towards the window, intending to open the shutters a little. Sir Anthony shook his head urgently; his stark white face was one of the few things clearly visible in the unrelieved black, and Beth abandoned her progress across the room.

After a time Anne's sobs gave way to mumbled apologies, which Sir Anthony brushed off, continuing to cradle her in his arms. *I must have looked like that*, thought Beth, *when I came home from France and threw myself at Duncan*. Poor Anne. She could not be reconciled with her husband. Beth sat down and waited for her to recover.

"I am so sorry," Anne was still saying, when the baronet finally considered her recovered enough to release her. She sat back into her chair, wiping her eyes with the tiny and useless scrap of lace which passed for a handkerchief in polite society.

"Anne," said the baronet, handing her his own more substantial handkerchief, "would you think me terribly impertinent if I were to ask for a fire to be lit? Only it is so dreadfully cold in here."

Anne started, and seemed to remember herself a little, which was what he had intended. Unused to considering her own needs, she had nevertheless been conditioned through years of sacrifice to caring for others, and now leapt into action.

"Oh, how remiss of me!" she cried, ringing the bell. "Of course. I have not thought of such things, since…and some refreshment, too. Are you hungry?"

"Yes, a little refreshment would be excellent," said Beth, who was not at all hungry but hoped that Anne would be persuaded to eat something, even if only out of politeness. She had always been thin, but seemed to have lost even more weight recently. She must hardly have eaten anything for the last three weeks.

The fire was lit, the refreshments brought, and Anne was persuaded with some difficulty to eat a small pastry.

"I do not want to sound unkind," she said, feeling a little better now she had made her guests comfortable, "but I often feel that, with the exception of Charlotte, and yourselves of course, nobody really has any understanding of what I am going through. I almost suspect that some people think I married Stanley only for his money. They seem surprised that I am not dancing with joy at the prospect of widowhood."

"I'm sure nobody would be so unkind as to think such a thing," said Beth, who was certain that was exactly what the majority of people were thinking. Lord Redburn had been over thirty years older than Anne. It would not occur to mercenary society that she might possibly have loved him. Beth wondered how long it would be before someone speculated aloud as to whether Anne had, in fact, poisoned her husband to get her hands on his wealth.

"It was quite clear to me, and I am sure to everyone else too, that you loved him dearly," Sir Anthony said.

"I did!" cried Anne. "I do! Oh what will I do without him! I do not know how I can continue living without him by my side. All the light has gone from my life!"

Beth silently cursed Charlotte, whose sentiments these no doubt were.

"Yet you must continue living, Anne," said Beth firmly. "And he has left you a most precious gift, which should be a comfort to you in this terrible time."

Anne looked at Beth, surprised.

"I am not interested in his money," she said. "I would give it all away just for the joy of one more day with him."

"I am not talking of money, Anne," said Beth. "I speak of the child you are carrying. His son or daughter."

"Oh yes," said Anne without enthusiasm. "Poor child! What it will be to be born into this world already fatherless!"

Sir Anthony almost laughed, clearly reading Beth's thoughts in her expression as she contemplated the joys of throttling her cousin. He lowered his head quickly as if pondering the truth of

Anne's, or rather Charlotte's, dramatic utterance.

"It will not be born into the world at all," Beth replied, keeping the exasperation from her voice with some difficulty, "if its mother doesn't start to take care of herself."

* * *

"Do I detect another plot brewing in your devious little mind, my dear Beth?" asked Sir Anthony on the way home, much later. They had finally left Anne ensconced in her salon in front of a roaring fire, feeling if nothing else a little warmer, and had paid a flying visit to Lord Edward's, whose complaints at their lack of consideration in calling at an irregular hour as well as not informing those dear to them of their whereabouts for three months were cut short by the appearance of dinner, to which Sir Anthony and his wife declined a begrudged invitation, stating that their own meal would be upon the table at home presently.

"No. Yes," said Beth. "Well, she can't be left like that, can she? She'll die of starvation or cold, or drown in sentimentality, if I leave her to Charlotte. It's bad enough having to put up with one widow rambling on incessantly about poor dear Frederick. I have no intention of allowing Anne to go the same way. It would be unbearable."

"And in any case, you like Anne," said her husband.

"Yes," she agreed, realising it fully for the first time. "Yes, I do. She's kind and caring, and obviously had a horrible selfish family. I think there's more to her than meets the eye. She had enough strength of personality to nurse her parents, and was forceful enough to stop Lord Redburn drinking, and she obviously loved him. What she needs now is some time to realise that she is capable of living alone, that she doesn't need to lean on anyone else. She's financially independent now. With encouragement, she'll learn to be emotionally independent too."

"You must remember though, that as well as being dependent on others, she needs to feel depended on," mused Sir Anthony. "She has a lot of love to give, too. The danger in you winkling her out of her mausoleum will be that she'll be vulnerable to anyone who shows her any affection, for quite some time."

"True. But she'll be in mourning for six months at least. That should be long enough for her to find her feet, with our help," said Beth, "by which time she will have had her baby, which will be completely dependent upon her. What better focus for love than a helpless reminder of poor dear Stanley?" She smiled, and her husband shook his head in despair.

"What do you intend to do?" he said.

"I intend to prise her away from Charlotte's influence, with Caroline's help," said Beth. "I'll get her to come to Clarissa's birthday party. It will be the ideal way for her to start facing the world again, in a large company where she doesn't have to contribute too much to the evening."

"What?" said Sir Anthony. "But that's only a week away. It isna possible. It's too soon."

"Would you care to make a wager on it?" she asked sweetly.

"No, I wouldna," he replied hastily, remembering the last wager he'd lost with his wife.

"Well," she said. "You concentrate on speaking only English for two days, then. You're not doing very well at the moment. And leave the plotting to me, for once."

* * *

"I hope you don't mind us calling on you unannounced Anne," said Beth as she entered the gloomy salon accompanied by Caroline and Freddie. "Only we were just passing, and thought we would pay our respects."

They had been 'just passing' for nearly three-quarters of an hour, Freddie thankfully remaining deeply asleep, the three of them ensconced in the carriage round the corner until Iain, acting as Beth's footman and lookout, came to tell them that Charlotte had left and the coast was clear.

There had been a slight improvement in the room since Beth's last visit. The lamp was already turned up, and there was a fire in the grate. That the shutters had not been opened was obvious from the air, or rather lack of air in the room. Caroline wrinkled her nose, but otherwise showed no reaction to the depressing atmosphere, having been forewarned as to what to expect by Beth.

Anne stood up to greet them. Another improvement.

"It's very kind of you to call," she said. "You've just missed Charlotte. She left only a few minutes ago."

"Oh what a shame," said Beth with such apparent sincerity that Caroline stared at her, shocked by her friend's effortless mendacity. "Still, it was you we came to see. We thought you would perhaps like to see how Freddie has grown. I was quite amazed by how much he changed in the time we were away. Caroline tells me you haven't seen him for some time, either."

"You are right, it was unforgivable of me," said Anne, taking Beth's words as a rebuke, although they hadn't been intended as such. She peered through the dimness at the comatose bundle of white lace in Caroline's arms. "He's beautiful. He looks like you," she said.

"Not at all," replied Caroline briskly. "He's turning into the image of his father, poor child. If we open the shutters a little, you will be able to see for yourself." Without waiting for Anne's reply, she dropped the dead weight of the child into Beth's arms and moving across the room, drew the curtains and threw open the shutters. Light streamed into the room. Beth, standing close to her hostess, repressed a gasp of shock at Anne's appearance.

She was almost skeletal, her arms mere sticks, her face pallid and sickly with grief and lack of sustenance, her eyes lifeless and deeply shadowed. She blinked in the sudden brightness, screwing up her face against the sun; and then, as her eyes became accustomed to the light, she turned her attention back to the baby.

"You are right," she said, looking at the sleeping features with rapture. "He does look like Mr Harlow, doesn't he?"

"Edwin, please. And I am Caroline. We are friends, after all," said Caroline, taking Freddie from Beth and pinching him gently and surreptitiously in the process to wake him up. The infant roused, blinked sleepily up at his mother, and yawned.

"Oh!" said Anne. "He's awake!"

"Would you like to hold him?" asked Caroline.

Anne smiled, held out her arms automatically, and then lowered them again.

"I…er…I…," she faltered.

"Are you not accustomed to children, Anne?" said Caroline kindly. "Don't be ashamed if you're not. Beth was positively prostrate with terror the first time Freddie was dropped in her lap."

"That's true," admitted Beth, sitting down without being asked

190

to. "I didn't have any experience of babies, being the youngest child of my family. I was frightened of breaking him. Of course he was a lot smaller then," she said.

"I don't have any younger brothers or sisters either," said Anne, also taking a seat, her eyes remaining fixed on Freddie, who was stretching in Caroline's arms and preparing for action. "But I love children. When I was young I used to make clothes in my spare time for the village children. Some of them had hardly anything to wear, poor mites, and used to run around in rags, even in the winter. I loved visiting them." A little animation came back into her face as she thought back. "There was one little girl I remember particularly. Alice. She was so beautiful, clouds of yellow hair and the sweetest little face! She was lame, some problem with her birthing, I think. But I used to play with her for hours. I made her a doll, and we used to spend a lot of time chatting together and making little clothes for it…" She stopped, realising that she'd been rambling. "I will call for tea," she said.

"Do you still keep in contact with her?" Beth asked.

"No. Father said it was not appropriate for a young lady of my breeding to be seen playing in the dirt with filthy urchins. He was right, of course," she said sadly. "It is sometimes hard to do the right thing, though. I missed her terribly."

Caroline put Freddie, now fully awake, down on the carpet, and threw his ball for him. It jingled merrily as it rolled across the room, coming to a halt at Anne's feet. She picked it up and held it out for the child, who crawled towards it. He sat up, took it from her with chubby little hands, and smiled winningly up at her. Caroline and Beth sent up a silent thank you to God for the perfect behaviour of the little boy, and watched with deep satisfaction as Anne melted before their eyes.

"Oh, he's adorable!" she said.

"He has my colour eyes," said Caroline. "But otherwise, as I am sure you can see now, he is his father to a T."

"It must be a great consolation to you at this terrible time to know that you will soon have a child of your own," said Beth. "A reminder of your husband to treasure and love."

Anne's hand fluttered automatically to her stomach, which was flat, concave, even.

"Of course," she said with awe, as though realising for the first time that she was pregnant. "It doesn't seem possible, somehow. I can't feel anything happening at all." She looked at Caroline, her eyes brimming. "Oh, do you think he will look like his father, too?" she asked passionately. "That would be wonderful!"

Remembering Lord Redburn's bulbous nose and less than prepossessing features, Caroline was inclined to disagree but was too sensible to say so.

"He won't look like anything unless you start to take care of yourself, Anne," Beth said. "If you continue to lock yourself away in this room with no air or light, and starve yourself as you have been doing, you will miscarry."

Her seemingly brutal words, combined with the angelic picture of lacy babyhood crawling round her skirts, had the desired effect. Anne flinched as though she had been hit.

"I hadn't thought…" she said.

"Of course you hadn't," said Beth consolingly. "You were stricken with grief. You still are. It's perfectly understandable. But you cannot afford to indulge yourself any more, Anne. You are carrying your husband's child. You owe it to Lord…to Stanley, and to your baby, to take the very best care of yourself. You must start eating, or you will starve your baby too."

"And you must try, hard as it will be, to be cheerful. A baby's growth in the womb is adversely affected by the mood of the mother, if she is excessively sad," added Caroline.

"Is it?" said Anne, her eyes widening.

"Most definitely," said Caroline firmly, who had made this fact up on the spot. "A healthy, happy child needs a healthy, happy mother. I will help you, of course. I know a good deal about babies now."

"And Anthony and I will help as well, in any way we can. We are your friends," said Beth. "And you must turn to us. We will be most upset if you do not."

* * *

"She's coming," announced Beth the night before Clarissa's birthday party.

"Why am I no' surprised?" said Alex, who had now fallen back into his dual role and felt no compunction about speaking Scots at home. "I suppose ye're going to regale us wi' the details of the campaign."

"Of course I am," said Beth smugly. "Caroline and I, after several visits, with the help of Freddie, who has behaved perfectly at all times in her presence, the little angel, have managed to persuade Anne that she owes it to her husband to ensure she has a healthy child. And that to do that she must cheer up and re-enter life a little."

"What my wife is trying to say," said Alex to his brothers, and Iain and Maggie, who were all draped in various relaxed poses around the drawing room, "is that she and her crony have terrified the poor woman into believing that if she has a moment's unhappiness between now and April, the bairn will be born with two heads."

"No we haven't!" protested Beth. "What we have done is got her eating again, and looking forward to the future a little. God, the woman was a skeleton! She'd have been dead in a month if I'd left her to Charlotte's tender ministrations. Sympathy is all well and good; encouraging someone to wallow for the rest of their life in self-pity is another thing altogether."

"It sustains Charlotte," pointed out Alex.

"True. But it was killing Anne."

"Well done," said Iain. "Now can ye turn your hand to *stopping* my wife eating, before she gets so big I canna fit in the bed wi' her?"

"Haud yer wheesht," said Maggie, who since becoming pregnant had indeed developed a prodigious appetite, but had not, in spite of Iain's dire predictions, put on any great amount of weight, although her stomach was starting to round nicely now she was in her fourth month. "I'm eating for the bairn too, remember."

"You must be having triplets then," said Angus cheerfully, moving to take up a supine position by the hearth. Maggie and Beth, both sitting on the sofa, used him as a footstool in perfect synchronicity, then laughed.

"As long as they're no' born on the sixteenth of April, I dinna care if there's ten of them in there," Maggie said.

"It'd be an awfu' bonny twenty-first present for me if they were," said Angus.

"Not for me it wouldna," said Maggie, wiggling her toes blissfully in the warmth of the fire. "I've nae intention of lying in my bed alone screaming wi' birthing pains, while you lot are all roistering away down here."

"I wouldna be!" said Iain indignantly. "I'd be with ye. Well, in spirit anyway," he amended, remembering with relief that men were not allowed in the birthing chamber. He put his arm around his wife's shoulder.

"Aye, it's the spirits I'm worried about," said Maggie

"Will ye be calling it Angus, then, if it's born on my birthday?" persisted the footstool.

"Only if it's a girl," replied Maggie. "I'd be too afraid of it turning out like you, else." She reached across to the plate on the table for the last biscuit, only to have it snatched from under her fingers by Duncan, who broke it in half, throwing one piece with perfect accuracy into his younger brother's open mouth, and munching happily on the other.

"It's all that excess fat, Maggie," Duncan said. "It's making ye slow." He ducked as a cushion sailed harmlessly past his head, glancing over his shoulder as it hit the wall behind him.

"See what I mean?" He grinned, turning back in time to receive the second one full in the face.

"Have the MacGregors no shame at all," said Beth amidst the general laughter. "Taking the bread from an innocent unborn child's mouth?"

"Speaking of the innocent, and gullible," said Alex. "I can see how ye got Anne tae eat again, but how the hell did ye talk her into going to a dinner party and the opera?"

"That's thanks to you," said Beth. "Once you told me that you couldn't come, because you're meeting with Sir all-the-double-u's…"

"Sir William Watkins Wynne," supplied Alex.

"Yes, him. And Sir John Cotton and the Earl of Barrymore, I realised that I would have no partner."

"I have to go, Beth," Alex said. "Wynne lives in Wales and rarely comes to London. If I dinna see him now, I'll have to travel two hundred miles to do it."

"No, it's perfectly all right. I'm glad, in fact." She was, for two reasons, only one of which she went on to reveal. "It means that I was able to persuade Anne that I needed her company if I was not to be the odd number at the party. Especially because Caroline won't be there. She's got to entertain some MPs to dinner that night. Edwin's parliamentary star is rising, it seems, and she's got to play her part. She's even looking to engage a nurse for Freddie, on a part-time basis."

"And Anne actually believed that you're so lacking in confidence you're afraid of attending a family dinner without me?" Alex said incredulously. "Christ, woman, if I dinna stop ye, I've nae doubt ye'll lead the MacGregors into battle single-handedly when the time comes."

"No, she willna," said Duncan. "She'll be at St. James's talking Geordie into believing that Hanover's particularly pleasant at this time of year, and helping him to pack his bags."

"That wouldn't exactly be a challenge," said Beth. "He spends more time in Hanover than he does in England as it is. I don't know why he persists in being king, when he obviously hates the place he's king of. Now if I could persuade his sons to go as well, and Cumberland to drown himself on the way across the Channel, that'd be more like it."

"Teach me some of your persuasive ways, then," said Alex. "If I can convince Wynne, Cotton and Barrymore to commit themselves to us, ye'll have nae need to persuade Geordie or his sons to go home. They'll be running as fast as their German legs can carry them."

"You're on your own there, I'm afraid," replied Beth. "You don't need any help from me, anyway. I learnt most of my devious ways from you. But persuading Anne to do things isn't very difficult. She could be talked into almost anything at the moment. It's up to us as her friends to make sure she's only pushed into doing the things that are right for her, until she's got the strength to make her own decisions."

* * *

Clarissa's birthday dinner was a success, although on a personal level Beth had not thought it was going to be at first. The table was set with the finest damask linen, delicate pink and white flowered china, and impressive displays of white chrysanthemums. The chandelier blazed with light, casting rainbows around the room, and the food promised to be at least edible, the Cunninghams having engaged a new and competent cook to replace the one who had run off with the French chef.

Clarissa had spent hours writing out place cards, embellishing each one with carefully painted flowers and foliage, and Beth had been horrified to discover that whilst Anne was seated at her left as she had hoped, the card on her right bore Richard's name. She had known that he was staying at his cousins' for the winter and would be present tonight; that was the other reason she had been glad her husband could not attend. Ever since she had lied to him about the identity of her assailant she had felt intermittent pangs of guilt. It would have been very difficult to watch Alex conversing with her brother, ignorant of what he had done.

But she had not expected to have to actually sit next to Richard, and as he took his place she nodded curtly to him and turned at once to Anne. He would not want to speak to her, she was sure, any more than she wished to converse with him.

"You are looking in excellent health, Elizabeth," he remarked, to her amazement. "Marriage seems to suit you."

She could not ignore him without arousing curiosity.

"Yes," she replied, turning her shoulder slightly towards him, "and the military life seems to suit you, Richard. You have such a skill with flowers, Charlotte," she continued without waiting for her brother to reply. "The displays are quite breathtaking."

"I was hoping for the opportunity to…" Richard began.

"Ah, Lieutenant Cunningham! I wonder if you and your delightful sister would do me a small favour?" came a familiar voice from behind them.

"Of course, my lord," replied Richard at once, standing and bowing.

"Excellent!" said the Earl of Highbury. "Then if Miss Clarissa does not object to me disrupting her seating plans, I would be most obliged if you would exchange seats with myself and allow me to sit next to your sister, sir. We are acquainted, and I see her so seldom. I am sure you understand."

Miss Clarissa, sitting for once at the head of the table in honour of her birthday, did not object, of course; she would not have objected if her highly exalted guest had chosen to eat his meal standing on his head in the middle of the table; but on glancing at Richard's face, Beth saw to her surprise that he most certainly would have liked to say no. He relinquished his chair and the earl sat down, shaking out his napkin with a flourish.

"Thank you," said Beth without thinking.

"Not at all, Lady Elizabeth. I owe you a favour far greater than that of relieving you of unpleasant company for an hour," he replied softly.

Beth looked at him. How much had Alex told him about her? A great deal, it seemed. She wondered again, not for the first time, how well these two men knew each other. She must ask Alex.

"Lady Redburn," the earl said, over Beth's head, "please accept my condolences on your tragic loss. I deeply regret that I was unable to be present at the funeral. Stanley Redburn was a fine man, and you made his last months the happiest of his life."

"Thank you, my lord," said Anne. Her eyes filled with tears, but she was smiling, too. Beth relaxed a little, especially when the soup came and Anne took her spoon and ate almost half a bowlful. Although still dreadfully thin, her pallor had been disguised by Sarah's expertise and her hair washed and swept stylishly on top of her head.

"Sir Anthony told us that you met him in Edinburgh, my Lord Highbury," said Isabella.

"Yes, Daniel and I were there on business. It was a chance meeting, but most interesting." He smiled. "Will Sir Anthony be joining us later, Lady Elizabeth?" he continued to Beth, thereby forestalling any awkward questions regarding the details of the encounter.

"No," she said. "He is meeting with some business acquaintance. He has neglected his financial affairs of late, due to our travels."

"One cannot afford to do that in these ever-changing times," replied the earl. "The world of business moves so quickly. It is all too easy to be left behind."

In spite of the innocuous nature of his words, Beth felt vaguely uncomfortable. Or was she imagining that he knew more of the business Sir Anthony was engaged in than he should? It was easy to read deeper meanings into the most innocent comments when married to a spy. *I am imagining it*, she thought as the conversation flowed around her, moving from business to Edwin's well-received speech in the commons regarding the need to keep some troops in Britain next spring to deter the Jacobites from rising.

She was not imagining the fact that Richard, from his place far down the table, was trying to attract her attention, though. She could feel his eyes on her as she drew Anne gently into the conversation, laughing and joking, at her light-hearted best. No doubt he wanted to provoke her in some way. She was determined not to be drawn into anything controversial, and refused to meet her brother's eye. This was Anne's night, more than Clarissa's, in Beth's view; she was not about to let anyone spoil it.

The meal over, and toasts drunk to Clarissa's long life and good health, the company departed for Covent Garden and a performance of Handel's *Ariodante*. Clarissa was beside herself with joy, for Mr Handel himself was to play. Even Anne, still dressed in deep mourning black, was smiling, and her eyes held a little lustre. The earl divided his attention between her and Beth, and as they settled into their boxes Beth realised that he had taken on the role her husband would have performed, had he been here.

Their box held eight people; Lord Edward and his sisters, Richard, Beth, Anne and the earl. The Winters and Fortesques had been consigned to the other box, to Lady Winter's annoyance and Beth's relief. The orchestra tuned their instruments. Footmen brought wine and cakes to the boxes. Beth ignored Richard, lavishing all her attention on Anne, and he was soon engaged in conversation with Edward. The Cunninghams continued to chat merrily, along with a good many of the people in the pit, even when the orchestra stood to denote that the performance was about to begin. There was a cheer from the audience as Handel walked on stage and took his seat at the organ. The overture started. Lady Winter leaned over the balcony to speak to Isabella. Lord Winter could be clearly heard explaining to a no doubt utterly uninterested Lydia that this was one of three operas by Handel based on Ariosto's *Orlando Furioso*. Beth smiled. At least she didn't have to put up with him this time. Clarissa moved to the front of the box, clearly hoping to hear some of the singing.

Suddenly the music stopped and an expectant hush descended on the theatre, followed by a resounding cheer, far louder than that which had greeted the entrance of the composer. Hats were thrown in the air.

"What's happening?" Beth asked.

"His Royal Highness Prince William Augustus has decided to grace us with his presence," said Lord Edward pompously, standing up and bowing deeply to the prince, who was taking his seat in the box on the opposite side of the stage from themselves, and did not respond to Edward's gesture, being too busy acknowledging the roar of the crowd.

There was a pause while the applause died down, then the performance began again.

"Really, it is quite an honour, to have such a hero attending the theatre on my birthday!" said Clarissa, as though the prince had come on her express invitation.

Beth sighed, and gave up hope of actually hearing any of the performance at all as the battle of Dettingen began to be re-hashed in great detail by Edward and Richard to the delight of Isabella and Charlotte, at least.

The first scene, in which the heroine Ginevra proclaimed her love for Ariodante and hatred of the Duke of Albany, came to an end to resounding applause.

"What do you think of the prince's exploits, my lady?" asked the earl *sotto voce* to Beth.

"I am sure he was very brave, my lord," replied Beth non-committally. "I am told it was a great victory."

"Yes, a victory indeed," agreed Highbury. "But not for Cumberland, I think, nor for his father either, truth be told. Did you know that George's horse ran away with him at the start of the engagement?"

"No, I do not recall reading that piece of information in the *London Gazette*," said Beth, wondering if the earl was a closet Jacobite.

"Well, of course you would not expect to. It is a somewhat partisan journal. Although credit must be given to the king. He did face danger without flinching, and the duke behaved most bravely when wounded. He still suffers pain from his injury, I believe."

Good, thought Beth, glancing across at Cumberland, who happened at that moment to be looking her way and nodded his head in her direction. Highbury stood at once, and bowed with the utmost servility, and Beth revised her opinion, remembering that there was a big difference between not liking the king and his family much, which few people did, and being a Jacobite. The earl was a Whig peer, after all.

Act One finished, and Beth leaned across to Anne.

"Are you all right, Anne?" she asked.

"Oh, yes. The scene in the garden between Ginevra and Ariodante was so romantic! I am actually quite enjoying myself," said Anne, smiling shyly. "You were right, of course. I owe it to Stanley to try to be as happy as possible, and to ensure he lives on in his son."

"A commendable attitude, my lady" said the earl. "But if you feel the need for a little air between acts, I would be delighted to accompany you to the foyer."

Anne blushed.

"You are too kind, my lord," she said.

"Not at all. I intend to take a short drive out into the countryside tomorrow. I was going to suggest, if you do not consider it too impertinent of me, that you accompany me. Would you like that?"

She looked at him, her eyes wide.

"You will of course, feel the need for a chaperone, as is only to be expected at such a delicate time," the earl continued smoothly before Anne could refuse, as she was clearly about to do. "My motives are of the purest kind, as I am sure you know, but unfortunately there are always those of a malicious nature who will see evil in the most innocent gesture. Clarissa, my dear, would you be so kind as to accompany myself and the Lady Anne on a short drive into the countryside tomorrow?"

Clarissa replied rapturously that she would be delighted, thereby trapping Anne into agreeing, in a move worthy of the devious Beth, or her husband. *What an excellent evening this is turning out to be,* Beth thought, smiling gratefully at the earl. She had planned on dragging Anne out somewhere herself tomorrow; now she would have it free to spend with Alex.

A footman entered the box, bowed, spoke a few words to Lord Edward, then moved forward to Beth, bowing again.

"My lady," he said. "His Royal Highness wishes to convey his compliments, and asks if you will do him the honour of joining him for the rest of the performance?"

She looked across at the opposite box, to see Prince William,

Duke of Cumberland smiling directly at her. Every fibre of her being wanted to say no, but she was as trapped as Anne had been a moment ago. Lord Edward had already stood to open the door of the box for her to leave, taking her acquiescence for granted, and she had no choice but to agree. Her cheerful mood of a few moments ago evaporated, and it was with some difficulty that she summoned a smile as the duke rose to greet her when she entered his box. He raised her from her curtsey and beckoned her to the seat next to his.

"What a coincidence that we should both choose to attend the opera this evening!" said the duke as soon as Beth was settled in her seat. He called for champagne, and the footman scurried away. "Do you enjoy the music of Handel, Lady Elizabeth?" he asked.

"Yes, very much, Your Highness," replied Beth, wishing Act Two would start so that she would have an excuse for not talking to this man. She rarely felt such antipathy for people, and it took all her acquired acting skills to mask the intense dislike she felt for him. Still, it was important to the cause that she retain the goodwill of the Elector's son. She must make an effort. She turned to him and smiled.

"Your husband is not partial to the opera then, I take it?" he continued. "He is not here tonight. Or is he joining you later?" The duke did not sound as though he relished that prospect.

"Sir Anthony is a great fan of the opera, Your Highness," said Beth. "But we have been away for a time, and he finds it necessary to pursue his business interests this evening."

"Ah!" said the duke, putting such delight into the syllable that Beth was instantly alert, and apprehensive.

Act Two began. Beth leaned forward, making it as clear as she could that she wished to give the performance her complete attention. The champagne arrived and was poured, and the duke handed her a glass, thereby forcing her to look away from the stage for a moment.

"My father tells me you travelled to Edinburgh recently," Cumberland said immediately, before she could feign absorption in the opera again. "How did you find the mood of the town?"

She knew exactly to what he was referring. Jacobite or Hanoverian?

JULIA BRANNAN

"Very merry," she replied, being deliberately obtuse. "It is quite a unique city. I think it is because people live in such close proximity to each other, that they have no pretensions. A lord may live in the same building as a haberdasher. People are most unaffected. It is quite amazing. I thought that it would seem quite provincial, but there are entertainments every night. And many taverns and coffee houses, just as in London."

The duke pursed his wet red lips slightly.

"And where do the loyalties of the populace stand?" he asked a little impatiently.

"Oh, with the king, of course," said Beth. "There are a great many toasts drunk to his health every night. I joined in more than one myself." She smiled, and raised her glass to him. There was a chink of crystal as he touched his glass to hers and drank, looking deep into her eyes as he did so.

There was one advantage of having nearly two thousand people watching your every move. He would not be able to force his attentions on her. All she had to do was to ensure he did not get her alone. Not difficult in itself, but she had to do it without offending him.

"You have the most beautiful eyes, Elizabeth," said Cumberland. "They are almost violet in this light."

And you have the eyes of a pig, she thought, noting he had dropped her title, indicating an intimacy she had not allowed him and did not feel, but at the same time could not object to.

"Why, thank you, Your Highness. My husband often makes the same remark," she said innocently, enjoying his fleeting expression of anger at Sir Anthony being brought into the conversation. "Indeed, that is one of the reasons I enjoy this opera so much," she continued. "Ginevra and Ariodante remind me of myself and Anthony, in more than one way."

"Really?" said Cumberland.

"Indeed. Our love has survived many trials. The unfortunate duelling accident in France, for example."

She wondered if Cumberland would pick up on the fact that the other way in which Ginevra reminded Beth of herself was in her hatred of the duke who fancied her.

"Yet you do not seem…particularly well-suited," Cumberland ventured.

Oh well, it was probably better that he had not picked up on the allusion. Alex would have done, but Cumberland was not renowned for his quick-wittedness.

"In what way, my lord?" she asked, giving up on the opera. Act Two was almost over. Only one to go and then she could rejoin the others to go home.

"You are so…feminine, Elizabeth, yet display quite an interest in military matters. I would have thought you to have preferred a more masculine and martial man."

Like myself. Though unspoken, the letters formed themselves in vivid colours over his head. He smiled and replenished her champagne, taking care to ensure his fingers brushed hers as he handed her the glass. She managed not to recoil, and sipped her drink slowly, using the applause as Ginevra took the stage for the final scene as an excuse not to respond to his statement.

The Act was over, the audience applauded and the interval began. Beth looked across to the other side of the stage. The Cunninghams were all looking her way, Edward and Richard radiating pride and approval. *All of a sudden I am in favour*, she thought disgustedly, *because the fat, repulsive son of a usurper to the throne is lavishing attention on me.* Lady Winter was bursting with questions already. Anne looked pale, but contented enough. Clarissa seemed a little disappointed. She, of all the family, was the only one truly interested in music. She must be disappointed that the company had talked all the way through the performance. *It is really inconsiderate of them*, Beth thought. *It is her birthday, after all.* Inspiration struck.

"It is my cousin Clarissa's birthday today, Your Highness," said Beth.

"Is it?" he said politely. "I will send her a bottle of champagne, with my compliments."

"That would be very kind of you," Beth replied, smiling winningly. "She does so love the opera, but my family have a habit of conversing throughout every performance. It would make her birthday unforgettable if you were to invite her to join us for the final Act."

"No," said Cumberland shortly, with such authority and finality that Beth was shocked into silence.

It is a warning, she thought. *I may think of him as a usurping slug, but he thinks himself a prince. He has the authority and power of a prince. For now, he is a prince. Do not forget it.* She looked at her lap, mulling over these thoughts, and he misunderstood her gesture.

"I am sorry," he said. "I did not wish to seem rude. But I have long hoped to have a little time alone with you." He placed his hand on her knee. "I had hoped," he said, his voice soft, "that you would join me for a little private supper after the performance."

Her heart banged against her ribs as adrenaline raced through her veins. The urge to hit him as hard as she could in his fat face was almost overpowering. She looked at the podgy hand resting on her knee, the short, fat beringed fingers curling proprietorially round the curve of her leg, and compared it with the broad muscular hand of her husband, the long, strong fingers. How dare he insult her and Alex in this way? She forced her temper and revulsion down by an enormous effort of will, looked up at him, smiled.

"You do me too much honour, Your Highness," she said. "But I regret most deeply that I cannot accept. I am acting as companion to Lady Redburn this evening. As I am sure you know, she was tragically widowed only a month ago, and this is her first outing since Lord Redburn's death. I have promised to escort her home."

"Oh, I am sure you need not concern yourself unduly," said Prince William dismissively. "After all, she is with friends. I have no doubt that any one of them will see her safely home."

The warmth of his hand was seeping through the silk of her dress.

"I am sure you are right," she said, sounding distressed without any effort at all. "But I also undertook to stay the night with her. She misses her husband so. The others will of course be going back to Lord Edward's house for liqueurs after the performance, but Anne does not feel capable, in her delicate state, of staying out so late. I must honour my promise, Your Highness. You, being a prince and a soldier of the highest calibre, will understand better than anybody the concept of honouring one's obligations, I am sure."

The hand was lifted from her knee.

"Of course. I understand," he said stiffly.

He *had* understood, that was clear. More than she wanted him to. She had offended him, and could not afford to. She needed to retain his favour, and his father's. They were an important source of information.

Act Three began, and she hardly heard any of it. She had to regain his regard, let him know she found him attractive, without encouraging him to think she was going to leap into bed with him at the first opportunity. He found her desirable, but he wanted no more than a fling, with no commitment. No commitment. That was the key.

"Oh, Your Royal Highness!" she cried suddenly, reaching across and seizing his hand, to his surprise. "Please do not be angry with me! I must fulfil my duty to Anne! Yet I am distraught that you might think I have anything other than the greatest regard for you!"

The hubbub of voices in the audience rose noticeably. It would be all over London tomorrow.

The duke, as she had hoped, was stunned by this outpouring of feminine distress, which, in common with many men of his nature, flummoxed him completely.

"I do assure you, my dear Elizabeth…" he began.

"Indeed, I am sure you know only too well how I feel for you," she continued, praying to God he didn't. "If only I were not married, things could be so different…"

She gazed pleadingly, adoringly into his eyes, seeing the instant alarm at her hint that she loved rather than lusted after him, followed by pride that she wanted him after all. She breathed a sigh of relief, which he misinterpreted as distress.

"I understand entirely," he said, squeezing her hand reassuringly. "Please do not distress yourself. I hold you in great esteem. Your consideration for your friend only raises you in my estimation. There will be other opportunities, I am sure."

Not if I have my way, thought Beth later, as the carriage made its way to the Redburn mansion.

"It's very kind of you to bring me home," Anne said from the other corner of the carriage. "Are you sure you wouldn't rather be having liqueurs with your cousins? I am after all not very good company at the moment."

"I had intended all along to accompany you home, Anne," said

Beth. "And I far prefer your company to that of my family."

Anne blushed, not realising what a slight compliment it was.

"I had no idea it was the latest thing at the Court to take liqueurs after an evening out," said Anne.

"Neither did I," replied her friend. "But the duke assured me that the king always insists on enjoying a liqueur with friends before bed, if he has been to the theatre. It relaxes one after the excitement of the evening, he feels."

Beth had shot back to the Cunningham box after the performance to reveal this invented royal custom, knowing that it would be immediately adopted by Edward and Isabella, who were always at pains to emulate royalty. Within a week everyone in London would be downing liqueurs by the bottle.

Details, she thought, Alex's voice echoing in her head. She would not put it past the duke having her and her family followed to make sure she had told him the truth. Maybe she was being over-cautious. Still…

"I don't need to relax," Anne said. "I am quite tired. I had forgotten how fatiguing a social occasion can be."

She still had to work out a way of getting into the Redburn house and staying there for a time. They drew up outside. Beth looked out. She didn't think they had been followed, but there were several carriages in the street. It was impossible to be sure.

"This will be the hardest part of the evening, I think," said Anne sadly. "It will be so strange to go in and not find Stanley there waiting for me. The house feels so empty without him. You must think me ridiculous," she finished, looking apprehensively out of the coach window at the front door.

"No, not at all," said Beth. "I understand exactly how you feel. After my father died I always felt his loss most keenly when I came into the salon where he used to sit. For months I half-expected to find him there, smiling at me. Sometimes when I came up the drive, I used to imagine I could see him at the window, waiting for me. It gets easier with time but even now, after over two years, I think it would still feel strange to enter his room and find it empty."

"Oh, you do understand!" cried Anne.

"Would you like me to come in with you for a while?" Beth asked, seizing the opportunity.

"Would you mind terribly?" said Anne. "Only it is the first time I have been out since Stanley…ah…I am sure it will be easier next time."

"I would be delighted," said Beth honestly.

In the end she managed to stay for several hours. Anne, reluctant to wake the servants, went to the kitchen and prepared tea herself, and the two women sat long into the night talking, of loss, of their childhoods, which had been so different, Beth's free and wild, Anne's restricted and dull, and of Anne's hopes for the future and for the child that she had now accepted she was carrying, and to which she was already starting to give her love.

It was three in the morning before Beth finally arrived home, opening the door very quietly so as not to disturb the household, who would all be asleep. She tiptoed into the hall, which was in darkness, and felt for the stair rail.

The library door opened suddenly, and a tall figure stepped into the hall, carrying a candle.

"Where the hell have you been?" said Alex.

CHAPTER TEN

Beth jumped violently.

"Jesus Christ, Alex," she said, clutching at her heart. "You frightened me to death. I thought you'd be in bed. How did your meeting with Sir Double-U go?"

"Where have you been?" he repeated. "Are you all right?" His voice managed to sound both angry and frightened at the same time. His face was in shadow, and she couldn't see his expression.

"Yes, of course I am. I've been at the opera. Had you forgotten I was going?" she asked, puzzled. Alex never forgot anything.

"The opera finished at eleven o'clock," he said, his voice cold now. "Where have you been since then?"

"At Anne's," said Beth. "She didn't want to go in the house alone, so I went in with her and we had some tea and talked for a while. What's going on?"

Alex closed his eyes and breathed out through his mouth.

"Anne's," he said, with utter relief. "Oh thank God for that."

"Why, where did you think I was?" she said.

"With Cumberland."

"What?!" Her voice rose, and he held up a hand.

"I'm no' angry wi' you," he said. "I didna think ye'd go wi' him willingly. But I knew he'd invited you into his box, and when ye didna come home I thought he'd invited ye somewhere else afterwards, and ye didna ken how to refuse him." He moved back into the library, putting the candle down on a small table, and she followed him.

"I find 'No' is usually pretty effective," she said.

"Aye, but I knew ye'd no' want to offend him. I've been sitting here for hours, tearing my hair out, because I wanted to find you and kill him, but I didna ken where he might have taken ye."

His hair was indeed sticking out in all directions, and she softened.

"I'm sorry," she said. "I could have sent word, if I'd known. I thought you'd just assume I'd gone back to Edward's."

"I would have done, if I hadna known about Cumberland."

"How *did* you know about him, anyway?" she asked, amazed. "I thought it'd be tomorrow at the earliest before that got round town."

"After I'd had my meeting, I went off wi' Barrymore to his club for a wee drink. Some of the other members had been tae the opera and were already blethering on about the beautiful blonde who the duke had invited intae his box. They said that ye'd thrown yourself at him and then gone off wi' him in his carriage afterwards. Well, I knew the first part couldna be true, but when ye didna come home, I thought the second part was, and… I was worried," he finished.

Beth looked around for signs of Alex's 'worry'. Smashed ornaments, fists crashed through furniture, Angus lying bloody in a corner, having provoked his brother into violence, as he was so good at doing…no. Alex had restrained himself well.

"Er, you actually got that the wrong way round," she admitted, emboldened by the lack of destruction in the room. "He did invite me to a private supper, which I refused, so I didn't go off in his carriage with him. I..er…did throw myself at him, though. A bit. I can explain," she added hurriedly, seeing the anger flare in his eyes instantly.

She sat down and explained, quickly.

"It was really difficult," she said. "I can't stand even being near the man, let alone touching him. But I thought that if I made him think I hoped for more than a brief fling, it might put him off altogether. It appeased him for now, anyway, which was the main thing."

"I see your point, and ye did well, taking all those precautions in case he followed ye, but I dinna think it'll put him off for long, Beth. After all, if he had an affair wi' you, and you fell completely in love wi' him, he could still discard ye whenever it suited him. He's a prince. Ye couldna do anything to hurt him, no matter how scorned ye felt. You must avoid being alone wi' him, Beth, at all costs."

"I know that already," said Beth. "I'm sorry, though. It seems as though the rumours already have me in bed with him. I hadn't expected that. It won't do your reputation any good." *Or mine either*, she thought. Although it seemed that giving your favours to royalty or the nobility was commendable as far as society was concerned, whereas giving them to anyone else made you a whore. It was ridiculous.

"Oh, Sir Anthony willna mind that at all," Alex said, cutting into Beth's thoughts. "No one'll say anything directly to him anyway, and he's awfu' good at ignoring broad hints and suggestions. I, on the other hand, would mind a great deal. I'll tell ye this now, Beth, so ye know it. If ever Cumberland manages to get you alone and propositions you, if it comes to it you say no directly, in whatever way ye have to, and tae hell wi' offending him."

"But we can't afford to offend…"

"Aye, we can, if the alternative is that bastard laying his hands on you. Christ!" he said through gritted teeth, clenching his fists at the thought of it. "You say no," he ordered, his face hard. "And if he doesna take no for an answer, ye hit him, or scream. I dinna think it'd come to that, though. He'd no' force a woman against her will, I'm sure. But ye dinna *ever* think ye're doing me or the Stuart cause a favour by taking him or any other man to your bed, Beth, because an ye do, I swear to ye now, I'll kill him. Do ye understand me?"

She looked at him, wide-eyed. He meant it. A shiver of fear ran down her spine, but it was overwhelmed by the realisation that his love for her outweighed his passion for the Jacobite cause and the consequent need to keep the Elector as a friend. He would risk it all rather than have her compromise herself.

She dismissed the fear. She would never be unfaithful to him. Neither with Cumberland nor anyone else, for any reason.

"Yes, I understand you. I will never go with any other man willingly, for the Stuart cause or not. You know that already, I think," she said.

His face relaxed and he smiled, his blue eyes suddenly warm.

"Aye, I ken that, *mo chridhe*," he said tenderly, taking her hand. "I'm sorry. I was just awfu' worried, and tired, too. It's been a long day. Let's away tae bed. It's verra late."

* * *

"Oh, I can't do this!" Beth said, throwing the cause of her frustration on the floor for the umpteenth time.

"Aye, ye can," said Duncan, picking the needles and wool up and expertly unravelling the mess she'd made. "It's easy when ye get the hang of it."

She glared at the tangled puzzle suspended from the two needles in his hands.

"Knitting is like making porridge," she said with such venom that Duncan burst out laughing. After a moment she saw the funny side and joined him.

"Why do ye no' just give up, and make Anne some baby clothes from material instead? Ye've an awfu' good hand wi' a needle and thread," he suggested. "Ye've made some lovely things for Maggie's bairn."

"I know, but it's annoying me that I can't get the hang of knitting, when you all find it so easy."

"It isna possible to be good at everything. Ye canna get the hang of wielding a claymore either, and we all find that easy too," he pointed out, placing the now untangled piece of work back on her knee.

"How do you know I couldn't wield a claymore?" she said mischievously. "I've never tried."

"Ye'd be sorry if ye did. They weigh a good fifteen pounds, and they're awfu' tiring if ye havena got the muscle for them," he said, looking doubtfully at her slender arms. "Remember Alex's scar."

"Yes, well, maybe I've not got the strength for a claymore, but I have for knitting. Do you mind if we have another go?"

"Not at all," said Duncan. "I've nothing else tae do."

The two of them were alone in the house. Iain and Maggie had gone shopping for food, and Angus was out in the shed at the bottom of the small garden, taking advantage of their absence to put in some more work on his present for the baby. He was making a crib, but wanted it to remain a secret until it was finished, which had resulted in much furtive behaviour on the part of the MacGregor brothers, and the rather interesting phenomenon of owls calling warningly across the garden in broad daylight if the mother or father in waiting showed any sign of visiting the shed. Maggie and Iain, whilst remaining ignorant of the reason for the conspiracy, were of course extremely suspicious, but were collaborating to the extent that they rarely went in the back garden any more, with the resultant diminishing of the diurnal owl population in the area.

Alex was out at yet another meeting with the principal English and Welsh Jacobites. These meetings were testing him to the full, because whilst he understood some of the objections the others had to committing openly to the Stuarts, he mistrusted them and doubted their stated intention to participate in a rebellion at any level. He often returned home tired and crabby, smelling of tobacco smoke and brandy, with little or no progress to report.

"I wonder how Alex is getting on," pondered Beth now, dropping three stitches without noticing. "I wish I could be with him."

"He'd take you if he could, ye ken that," said Duncan, taking the knitting gently off her and retrieving the stitches before they could unravel too far. Alex had said as much the previous day. It would be useful to have an ally quietly watching proceedings, picking up subtle reactions that he, fiercely negotiating, might miss. But he was neither attending these meetings as himself nor as Sir Anthony Peters. He did not trust the English Jacobites enough to reveal his true identity to them, and of course if he went as the foppish baronet, he would be revealing openly to people who were already under suspicion by the authorities that Sir Anthony was a spy. Instead he had taken on the role of Benjamin Johnson, a cloth merchant from Liverpool, complete with suitable accent, sombre clothing, a hideous light brown wig and brass-rimmed eyeglasses. No one would ever guess that the cloth merchant was Sir Anthony; and it would take some considerable scrutiny to recognise Alex MacGregor in the unprepossessing features of Mr Johnson.

Beth was another matter entirely. With her glorious hair and striking facial beauty, she would be far harder to disguise. The men Alex was meeting were of the nobility. There was a good chance they might run into Sir Anthony and his wife. It was not worth the risk of them recognising her, much as he would have liked to have her with him.

From the hall came the faint but unmistakable sound of someone knocking on the front door. Duncan and Beth looked at each other.

"Are ye expecting a caller?" he asked.

"No," she said. "But it could be Isabella, or Anne, I suppose. Or anyone who wants to find out how my affair with the Elector's son is going."

Duncan stood, smoothed down his dark blue velvet breeches, slipped into his shoes and retrieved his coat from the back of the chair. He looked down his nose at her with the utmost arrogance.

"How do I look?" he asked.

"A perfect footman." She smiled. "Except for the wig." She stood up, abandoning the knitting and helped him to put it on, tucking his own hair up under it. He moved to the door as the caller knocked again.

"Is my lady at home?" Duncan said formally.

"Yes." Beth sighed. "I might as well face the hordes. Unless it's Cumberland himself, in which case I have a particularly infectious disease of some sort. Leprosy. Plague. You decide."

She picked up the knitting again. Now, what was it? Hold the wool loosely. That was the problem. She felt that if she didn't keep a death grip on the yarn, all the stitches would fall off the needle, but of course that was ridiculous. All she had to do was relax. She draped the wool carefully over her fingers and knitted half a row. The library door opened and Duncan walked in.

"Who is it?" she asked without looking up.

"Lieutenant Cunningham to see you, my lady," said Duncan politely.

The needles jumped in her hand and half the stitches slid neatly off one of them.

"Oh damn it to hell!" she said angrily, referring to both the baby garment and the identity of the visitor, who now appeared behind Duncan in the doorway.

"Good morning, Elizabeth," he said hesitantly.

"What do you want, Richard?" she replied without preamble.

"Er…shall I tell cook to prepare tea, my lady?" asked Duncan.

"No, Murdo," said Beth. "Lieutenant Cunningham will not be staying long enough for tea."

Duncan nodded, bowed, and left the room. He would stay out

of earshot but close enough to hear if she shouted him, she knew that. She looked belligerently at her brother. She had no need to be polite; they were not in company.

"What do you want?" she repeated, enjoying his obvious discomfort at the lack of welcome. He stood in the doorway undecided for a moment, then took two steps into the room.

"I am making a social call," he said, attempting a smile. "It's quite normal for brothers and sisters to visit each other."

She looked at him coldly.

"It's gratifying to know that you've remembered I'm your sister, Richard," she said. "You have not always done so."

He flushed scarlet, destroying the flattering effect of his bottle-green outfit, which went well with his dark hair and colouring.

"But in remembering our familial connection, you've forgotten something else," she continued. "We have a bargain, you and I."

"A bargain?" he echoed.

"Yes. I agreed to marry Sir Anthony and get you your commission, and you agreed to get out of my life and have no further communication with me. I appreciate that whilst you are staying at Edward's we are bound to see each other from time to time. That is inevitable. But your presence here is not only unwelcome, it's also breaking your promise. Get out."

He stiffened at her rudeness, his face darkening with anger rather than shame this time, but he made a visible effort to keep his temper, and she knew then that he wanted something from her, badly.

"Is Sir Anthony at home?" he asked, looking round as though he expected the baronet to materialise magically in the room.

"No," answered Beth, rethinking her attitude. She did not want Richard to call again. She wished to avoid him and Alex talking together, as far as she could. "You can tell me what you want," she asked again, in a less belligerent tone.

He responded to it immediately, moving into the room and sitting down. He looked around.

"This is a beautiful house. You have done very well out of your marriage after all, Elizabeth," he said, smiling properly at her this time.

"So have you," she responded, not returning the smile. "You

got not one commission, but two."

"Are you happy?" he asked her unexpectedly.

"Do you care?" she said.

It was not the response he had expected; to say yes would be an outrageous lie, and he could hardly say no. She could see him searching round for another way of breaking the ice. She wondered whether to let him waste more time trying, then decided against it. She wanted him to leave, not to squirm.

"Richard," she said. "Small talk is not your forte, particularly when you don't like the person you're making it with. You've clearly come here to ask Sir Anthony something. He isn't here and I don't expect him back for some time, but if you tell me what you want I promise I'll inform him as soon as he returns."

He looked at the floor for a moment, undecided, fiddling with the hat in his hands. He had lost a little weight, she noticed, and it suited him.

"My colonel is to retire in January," he said finally, putting the hat down on the chair beside him. "I don't know if you know how the army commission system works, but…"

"Everyone moves up," she interrupted.

"It's not quite as simple as that, but basically, yes," he said. "If I want to be considered for captain, I have to say so now. It's like a chain; everyone depends on the one below or above, and it takes time to organise."

"So even though he doesn't retire for two months, you have to commit yourself now," Beth said.

"Yes," said Richard. His eyes were shining at the thought of another promotion. He looked almost handsome, in a saturnine sort of way.

"Well I don't know why you felt a need to tell me first, but congratulations," she said, knowing now exactly why he had come to see her. *His ambition has overcome his reason,* she thought. *He truly believes he can talk me, or more probably Alex, into paying for another commission for him.* He had put what happened between them to the back of his mind and was arrogant enough to believe that because he could forget, she would, too.

"This is a real chance for me to prove myself, Beth," he said, forgetting himself and using the diminutive of her name in his excitement. "As a captain, I'll command a troop of up to sixty men and officers. Once I've shown my competence in leading them, there'll be no stopping me."

"As I said, congratulations," she repeated. She was not going to anticipate his request for money, as he clearly hoped she would.

He blushed again, but kept his eyes on her, his face earnest.

"Beth, I swear to God that if Sir Anthony will loan me the money to get this promotion, I'll pay him back within the year. He can easily afford it. The jewels you wore to the opera the other night alone would nearly pay for it. It would be nothing to him, but it'll change my whole life."

She looked around at the sumptuous furnishings, thought about the expensive clothes in her wardrobe and the diamonds she'd worn to the opera, and wondered what Richard would say if he knew that not one scrap of it belonged to her husband. He didn't even have legal ownership of his name, or the land his clan lived on. He was penniless. The only money they had of their own was her dowry, and even that would be forfeit if the true identity of her husband was ever discovered.

"As I'm sure you can imagine, Richard, this lifestyle is very expensive to maintain. Appearances can be deceptive. Many society people are not rich, but actually heavily in debt," she said.

"Are you telling me that your husband is up to his eyes in debt?" Richard said, stunned.

She *had* thought for a moment to tell him that, but then realised that she had no need to make excuses for what she was about to say. She was not afraid of him. He could hit her, although he would have to answer for it to the authorities this time if he did; but he had no hold on her any more.

"No, I'm not telling you that," she said. "I'm telling you that Sir Anthony will not pay for your captain's commission."

He leaned forward as though to reach for her hand, and she recoiled from him. He dropped his hand.

"Beth, please," he said. "The man is in love with you, any fool can see that. You have him wrapped round your little finger. He will agree to anything you ask."

"Maybe," she said. "But I am not going to ask him. I promised I would tell him why you called, and I will, but I will not ask him to pay for your captain's commission."

"Can we not put the past behind us?" Richard asked, trying to put a pleading tone in his voice. "I know I pushed you into marrying Sir Anthony, but it was for your own good. You have done very well out of it; you're mixing with the cream of society and you're obviously happy. If it hadn't been for me you would still be in rags, struggling to make ends meet in that dilapidated house in Manchester. Surely that's worth something? If you do this for me, I will never ask for anything again, I swear it."

"You bastard," she said coldly. "You have the cheek to try to tell me you had my welfare at heart when you forced me into marriage with Anthony? You're forgetting something, Richard. I know you. Hatred is the only honest emotion between us. Nothing would have made you happier than if he'd kept me beaten and starved in a cupboard. It must really upset you to see me contented. I owe you nothing, and that's exactly what you'll get from me. Nothing."

He glared at her, the mask of civility slipping.

"He signed your dowry over to you, didn't he?" he said. "You can't have spent all that. You're careful with money. I only need a thousand pounds. I'll pay you back, with interest if you want."

God, would he not give up?

"No. No. Never," she stated flatly. "Is that clear enough? Ask someone else. Goodbye." She stood up as a signal that he should leave, and he rose as well.

"You've paid for those lazy servants of yours to buy their own house and lord it about, and for that bloody slut to rent a shop," he said, his voice rising, showing his true colours at last. "I'm the eldest, for God's sake, and the heir! That money should have been mine. You had no right to it!"

"Take it up with your lawyer, then," she said. "But leave right now, or I'll have you thrown out."

His hand moved automatically towards the hilt of his sword. It was the only thing he had in common with Alex, she thought. They both wore a sword as a practical item, not as decoration, as some men did.

"You think you're something special, don't you, just because you've got a pretty face?" he spat. "You sweet-talked father into cheating me out of my inheritance, and you've managed to charm that pathetic molly into giving you anything you want." His left hand formed into a fist. The muscle in his cheek pulsed and she backed away out of arm's reach, fetching up against a small table.

She didn't want to shout for Duncan and let Richard think she was afraid of him, but if he made a move to hit her she would have to.

"Yes," she said, smiling pleasantly because she knew that would annoy him more, although her voice shook with the effort of controlling her temper. "Life is unfair sometimes, isn't it? It gave me the looks *and* the charm of the family. Shame there wasn't much left over for you. Still, you're learning to plead quite well. You did a reasonable job today. If I didn't know you so well I might have been fooled. I'm sure you'll be able to persuade someone else into funding you, if you practice a bit more. Murdo!" she shouted, as though calling the footman to see Richard out rather than stop him murdering her as he clearly wanted to do. The door opened almost immediately, as she had expected it to. Richard unclenched his fist, retrieved his hat from the chair and slammed it onto his head. Then he turned back to her.

You mark my words, you bitch," he snarled, eyes blazing. "You'll be sorry you refused me this. I'll make you regret it, you see if I don't."

"I already do," she said icily. "I regret letting you into the house to waste twenty minutes of my time. I won't be doing it again."

He spun round and strode from the room. Duncan followed him out, returning a few moments later. Beth was still standing in the same spot.

"I take it that was no' exactly a congenial meeting, then," Duncan commented.

She stood for a moment more, breathing heavily. Her hands were trembling. Then she turned to the table behind her, picked up the vase of flowers standing on it and threw it at the wall. It shattered, water and flowers cascading everywhere.

"The bastard!" she screamed. "I hate him! Why can't he just leave me alone?"

Duncan eyed the mess of petals and glass for a moment, then turned back to her.

"Aye," he said calmly. "Brothers can have that effect on ye sometimes."

She looked at him for a moment, her body stiff, her face twisted with rage, and then she started laughing. Her body relaxed as her anger was transformed to mirth.

"Oh God," she said between somewhat hysterical giggles, as he guided her gently back into the chair. "What would I do without you?"

"Ye'd have to cope wi' Alex and Angus on your own, which is a fate devoutly no' to be wished for, believe me," he said, laughing with her, although he was somewhat concerned about what had caused her explosion of temper.

She was just starting to calm down and was outlining Richard's purpose for visiting, when Alex returned from his meeting.

"Christ," he said as he walked into the room, pulling the eyeglasses off and stuffing them into his coat pocket. He had a green indentation on the bridge of his nose from the brass rims. "What a bloody awful day!"

"I take it it was no' exactly a congenial meeting, then?" said Duncan, sending Beth off into renewed whoops of laughter.

Alex looked at his wife with curiosity.

"Sorry," she said guiltily, gulping and fishing in her pocket for her handkerchief.

"No, it wasna," said Alex, answering Duncan's question but still looking at Beth. "The glasses didna help. They're a bonny disguise, but I canna see a damn thing when I'm wearing them. I'm thinking I should ha' got the ones for young people, instead of for old ones. I thought I'd be able tae look over the top of them, but I look too arrogant if I do that, especially as I'm supposed tae only be a merchant. It was all right when I was sitting down, but I walked into the doorpost on the way intae the salon and nearly knocked myself senseless, and had to feel my way around for the doorhandle on the way out. I'm no' surprised the English are reluctant tae join us…what the hell's the matter wi' you?" he asked as Beth gave up all attempts at seriousness and collapsed into peals of helpless laughter at the thought of her husband crashing blindly around a room while three English aristocrats looked on in amazement.

"Ah… she's got a good imagination, I think," Duncan said, starting to laugh as well. Alex took off his wig and grinned himself, infected by the general hilarity even though he didn't fully understand the cause of it. She had already been laughing before he told her about his amusing problem with the spectacles.

"Oh God, I'm sorry," Beth tried to say, convulsed. "I've…hee hee,…had a few problems myself today." She wiped her eyes and tried to compose her face, unsuccessfully.

Alex looked around the room for clues as to the peculiar behaviour of his wife, took in the shattered vase, soaked floor and broken flowers. Understanding dawned.

"Ah," he said. "Angus. Did ye manage to actually hit him wi' the vase then, or did he get out of the way in time?"

Beth snorted, red in the face, but even so she might have been able to resist going off into another fit if Angus hadn't unfortunately chosen that moment to enter, having become aware of Alex's return.

He took in the scene of amusement before him, and opened his mouth to ask the cause of it. Alex looked up at him.

"What have ye been up to, ye wee gomerel?" he asked.

Angus's open-mouthed look of mingled confusion and outraged innocence was too much. Beth melted into helpless giggles again, joined by Duncan.

"Aye," she choked after a minute, almost unintelligibly, tears pouring down her face. "Brothers can have that effect…" she caught Duncan's eye, and they both set off again, while Angus and Alex looked on, giggling themselves even while they wondered why.

It took a full ten minutes for Beth and Duncan to calm down completely, during which time Angus, having convinced Alex of his complete ignorance as to what on earth was going on, went off to fetch tea and wine.

"How did your meeting go, then, when you'd stopped walking into walls?" Beth giggled, covering it up by taking a gulp of tea. She bit down hard on her lip.

"I'll wait until Iain and Maggie come back," Alex said. "I'd rather tell ye all together. Tell me what happened that was so amusing this afternoon. I could do wi' a laugh."

Duncan and Beth looked at each other.

"Dinna start again," Alex warned with mock severity.

"I'm not," Beth said. "It wasn't really funny at all."

She explained about Richard's visit, growing more serious as she did.

"I should have thrown the vase at him, instead of waiting until after he'd gone," she said. "I quite liked that vase. At least I'd have got some satisfaction by drenching him."

"D'ye think he'd have hit ye if ye had?" Alex said.

"Probably," she replied. "I'm surprised he didn't anyway, to be honest. He's not renowned for controlling his temper and I provoked him enough. He certainly wanted to."

"I'm glad he didna," said Alex thoughtfully. "I'd have had to call him out if he had."

"No you wouldn't," she said. "Sir Anthony would just wail and moan a lot, and maybe threaten to put in a bad word for him with his commanding officer."

"Let me rephrase it then," said Alex. "I *would* have called him out if he'd hit ye. But it'd be awkward, and I'd rather no' have to. I dinna think Sir Anthony could get away wi' two accidental duelling deaths, and I dinna think Richard's a man to give up if ye only wounded him."

"No he isn't," she agreed, shuddering. When she'd been arguing with her brother, she hadn't thought of the possibility of Alex calling Richard out. "No, I did call him a coward once, a long time ago, but I was wrong. He's a bully, certainly and most bullies *are* cowards, but I don't think Richard is. Anyway, he didn't hit me so there's no harm done. And I doubt he'll come back to be humiliated again."

"What do you think he will do?" asked Angus.

"Nothing," she said. "What can he do? He's got no hold over me any more. All my friends are independent of him now. The most he can do is find someone else to lend him the money for his commission, although he must have already asked everyone he can think of. He wouldn't have come to me except as a last resort, I'm sure of that. If he does manage to get the money though, he'll no doubt flaunt it in my face that he got his commission anyway, without my help. That won't bother me. I couldn't care less if he ends up a general, although I'd feel sorry for the soldiers under his command. Good," she said, as she heard the front door open. "That'll be Maggie and Iain. Now we can forget about Richard and have dinner, and then talk about your meeting instead."

"They willna commit themselves," said Alex later. "No' in the way that Charles wants. Broughton wanted to get their commitment in writing. Well, I knew I didna have a hope in hell of them putting their signatures to anything. They've already been questioned more than once by the authorities, and the only reason they havena been charged is that there isna any concrete evidence against them."

"Like bits of paper," said Beth.

"Exactly. So I gave up on that idea straight away. It's as well I did, because I've had the devil's own job to get them to agree to anything at all, even verbally."

"Why are they so reluctant?" asked Iain. "After all they agreed to rise last year, did they no', when the French made landfall?"

"Aye, they did," agreed Alex. "But the French *didna* make landfall, did they, so we've no way of knowing whether they'd have fulfilled their promise or no'."

"You mean you don't think the English will rise *at all*, no matter what happens?" Beth said, shocked.

"I didna say that, although I do sometimes wonder if they'll wait until Charles reaches London afore they do," Alex said. "Ye ken, there's a big difference between drinking toasts and singing songs to the King across the Water, and risking everything ye own and your life too."

"But look at what they've got to gain, if we win," said Angus.

"Aye, but look at what they've got to lose, if we fail," said Alex. "Life is different in England, and in lowland Scotland, too. People are more comfortable, and it never ceases to amaze me what enormous liberties people will allow themselves to be deprived of in order to hang on to wee comforts they've become accustomed to, but could do without. And it doesna matter to the English whether the Union's repealed or no', as it does tae us. They've no' got the same incentive to rise as the clans have, and that's one thing that worries me."

"What's the other?" asked Duncan.

"Barrymore, Cotton and Wynne themselves. They're all running scared since *Habeas Corpus* was suspended. Dinna forget, Cotton only escaped being arrested because another man was mistaken for him. He's a big man, taller than me even, but he's no' a fighter. He's awfu' fat, and soft. He even protested to the

French that they shouldna invade in January because it was too cold!" he said contemptuously. "Then there's Barrymore, who *was* arrested, of course, and who got out of trouble by telling parliament that he wouldna risk the loss of the poorest acre of his land to defend the title of any king in Europe, which is no' exactly reassuring."

"Yes, but people will say anything to get out of prison, won't they?" reasoned Beth. "I mean, he didn't give anyone else up, did he?"

"No, he didna," Alex conceded. "But he's nearly eighty, Beth. He must be thinking more of making his peace wi' God than leading a rebellion."

"What about Wynne, then?" said Iain.

"Ah, well now, he's a different matter. He's younger than Barrymore, in his fifties, and fitter than Cotton. And more powerful than both of them. He's the most powerful man in North Wales, as well as being the MP for Denbigh. He's raised a good following for the Stuarts among the Welsh. I think the Welsh are more likely to rise than the English. After all, there's a good deal of resentment that Wales is generally considered part of England instead of a principality in its own right, as it should be. That's the way Scotland'll go, too, if the English have their way," he said sourly.

"Well, that's good then, isn't it?" Beth said. "Not that Scotland will become part of England, I mean, but that the Welsh are for James."

"Aye, but Wynne's leading them. And while of the three, he's the one I like the most, he's awfu' cautious, too cautious for me. Maybe I'm misjudging the man, and he will rise as he says, although I think he'll wait until the rising's well under way afore he does, but he'll no' commit to it without French help, and I canna argue wi' him there, because the clans dinna want to, either. It seems Charles is on his own in thinking he can take the throne wi' his single footman."

"So what do we do now?" asked Maggie.

"I send a report of my negotiations to Broughton and the others, and tell them what I think. And then I think we've nae choice but to make it verra clear to the prince that he must not, under any circumstances, come to Britain without the French at his back."

CHAPTER ELEVEN

Christmas Eve 1744 passed by peacefully, even pleasantly, the MacGregor family having refused all social invitations, determined to enjoy the festive season ensconced in their warm and cosy rented London home.

Beth, who had been almost paranoiacally superstitious that, following the pattern of the previous two years, some unexpected violent event was going to occur, breathed a sigh of relief as the clock chimed midnight with no more disastrous occurrence than the burning of the morning's porridge, which, as Beth had been in charge of preparing it, was hardly unexpected.

Maggie, now starting her sixth month of pregnancy, often felt tired and breathless, and suffered spasmodically from severe backache which she tried stoically to ignore. Beth had taken to watching her carefully for excessive yawning or grimacing and massaging of her lower back, whereupon she would pack the protesting young woman off to sit in the library with a hot drink, and would take over whatever task she had been engaged in. Which had resulted in the burning of the Christmas Eve porridge and several long and increasingly heated arguments with Maggie, who protested that Beth was treating her as though she was made of glass.

"I'm not one of your pampered society women," she said one morning early in the New Year, when Beth had found her resolutely scrubbing the kitchen floor, dark shadows of fatigue under her eyes and one hand firmly clamped on the small of her back. "If we were at home, I'd no' be able to lie down in the library every day. I'd just have tae get on wi' it."

"I know, but you're not at home, and you don't have to get on with it," Beth protested, bending down and trying to wrest the scrubbing brush out of Maggie's hand.

Maggie, considerably taller and stronger than Beth, maintained a firm grip on the brush.

"I feel better if I'm doing something," she insisted. "I'm no' one for lying about in the middle of the day. It doesna feel right."

"You have to think of your baby, though," reasoned Beth, kneeling down beside Maggie, heedless of the wet floor. "And it's not the middle of the day. It's not even seven o'clock yet. It's still dark, for God's sake!"

"My baby's fine, he's kicking away merrily in there. And I was awake and didna want to disturb Iain, so I thought I might as well make myself useful."

"How much sleep have you had?" Beth asked, concerned.

"Almost none at all, if all her tossing and turning was anything to go by," said Iain sleepily from the doorway. "I know I didna get more than an hour or so."

"I'm sorry," said his wife, sitting back on her heels and brushing a strand of fiery red hair from her face. "But the bairn's lying strangely, and it's awfu' uncomfortable. He'll move soon, I'm sure, and I'll be fine." She dipped the brush in the bucket of soapy water and prepared to continue her task.

"Iain, will you reason with her?" said Beth. "She should be relaxing if she's tired and in pain, not scrubbing a floor that's already clean!"

"I tellt ye, I'm fine...hey!" she protested as Iain plucked the brush neatly from her hand, passed it to Beth, and then scooped his wife firmly up into his arms. "Put me down!"

"I'm wi' Beth on this," he said, ignoring his wife's struggles and protests as he carried her past a surprised Alex, who was coming down the stairs as Iain marched down the hall to the library. "Ye've no need tae wear yourself out, *a ghràidh*." He plonked her down on the sofa, plumping up some cushions behind her. "I'll make up the fire," he said, "and ye can have a wee rest."

"I've only just got up!" she protested angrily, making to rise. He pushed her back down firmly.

"Well find something else to do, then," he said. "Something that involves sitting down."

"There isna anything," she replied stubbornly. "Will ye stop treating me as though I'm going to break! I'm sick of it. I'm having a baby, that's all. Thousands of women do it. It's natural. I've lost my waistline, no' my senses. If I get tired, I'll go to bed."

"Maggie, please," Iain said pleadingly, his uncharacteristic burst of husbandly dominance exhausted. "Ye must be tired. There's nae harm in lying down occasionally."

"Aye, but if you had your way I'd have lost the use of my legs wi' lying down by now," she said. She got to her feet and glared at Beth. "You scrub the floor then, if ye've such a mind to," she said. "I'll make up the fire, then I'll come and start the porridge."

Iain looked helplessly at Beth. Much as he loved his wife, she was stubborn and unreasonable at times, and had become even more so as her pregnancy advanced. She seemed acutely aware that she was having it easy compared to her fellow clanswomen in Scotland and was determined not to let anyone pamper her in any way at all.

"Angus is making the porridge," Alex said, striding briskly into the room, carrying an armful of material. "And Iain is lighting the fire," he continued with such a tone of command that Iain turned to the task immediately, gratefully relinquishing his mutinous wife to the other man.

Alex dumped his burden down on the floor by the side of the sofa and turned to Maggie.

"I…" she started.

He took her by the shoulders and propelled her firmly back on to the sofa.

"And you," he said, "will do as ye're tellt for once. These," he gestured to the pile of shirts and stockings, "need mending. And that's what ye're going to do."

Maggie picked up one of the stockings, which sported a hole in the heel.

"These are Sir Anthony's," she said. "Sir Anthony doesna wear mended stockings. He buys new ones."

"He does wear mended stockings if ye canna see the darn," Alex said. "His sponsor's no' got a money tree growing in his garden. It's about time Sir Anthony economised a wee bit."

Maggie looked up at him, undaunted.

"You're just inventing work for me," she said. "And anyway, Beth's the one for the needlework, not me, as ye ken verra well."

"I've got other things for Beth to do the day," Alex said. "And her talents lie in fine embroidery, no' darning, which I ken well ye can do."

Iain blew carefully on the fire to encourage a blaze, ensuring that his back was turned to the confrontation. Maggie pursed her lips mutinously.

"I'll no' be humoured, Alex," she said, moving to the edge of the sofa.

"We're no' humouring ye, you stubborn wee besom," Alex replied angrily, leaning forward and placing his hands heavily on her shoulders again. "Christ, woman, ye're worse than Beth! We care about ye, and if we were at home we'd be doing the same. Some women carry their bairns easy, and some dinna. That's all there is tae it."

"But if I…"

Alex placed one finger over her lips.

"I'm your chieftain, and I'm ordering ye to sit here and mend these clothes. No arguments. If ye dinna, I'll have ye flogged and turn you out, and ye can have your bairn in the snow, if you're so determined to suffer unnecessarily!"

He straightened and strode out, leaving Maggie and Iain sitting open-mouthed in the library. Beth followed her husband to the kitchen, where to her relief Angus was, as Alex had said, making the porridge.

"Went well then, I see," he said, stirring merrily and eyeing his brother's set face.

"Wasn't that a bit extreme?" Beth commented, dropping the scrubbing brush in the bucket of cooling water and sitting down at the table. "There's not much point in threatening someone if they know you've no intention of carrying it out."

"I'm tempted to," Alex said. "Christ, she's always been stubborn, but she's nigh on impossible now. She seems determined to do the opposite of whatever ye tell her, regardless of how stupid it is."

"What did you mean, anyway, when you said she's worse than me?" Beth asked.

Alex shot her a dark look, and she decided suddenly that she'd rather not know.

"Is this what women are normally like when they're pregnant?" she said.

"They're all different, from what I've seen," Alex replied. "Some are a bit moody, some are a wee bit sharp-tempered, some," he gestured in the direction of the library, "are bloody impossible, and others are fine all the way through, like Anne, for example."

This was true. Anne Redburn, whose baby was due at the same time as Maggie's, in April, could not have been more different from the pale, heavy-eyed woman now resignedly threading her needle in the library. Anne was bursting with health and vitality, her skin glowing, her hair shining, and the weight she had lost following the death of her husband regained. At the moment she was in Manchester. Beth, knowing Anne's aversion to spending time at home alone, had contemplated inviting her to join them for Christmas, and had been relieved beyond words when Anne had told her that she had accepted an invitation from Isabella to accompany the Cunningham family to Raven Hall for the festive season. Among other things, it had meant that Alex had not had to play Sir Anthony throughout the holiday, for which he was immensely grateful.

Iain now returned to the kitchen.

"She's fine," he said in response to the unspoken question in the faces turned to him. "She's already nodding over her needle. I dinna ken why she canna admit she's tired. It's normal enough, after all."

"I don't think she sees it that way," Beth said. "I think she sees it as being weak. A bit like I did when I was in Scotland and felt I had to prove myself. She doesn't want us to feel sorry for her."

"She wanted the bairn to be born in Scotland, too, which doesna help her mood," Iain said.

"Does she?" asked Alex. "Why did ye no' stay up there, then, instead of coming back to England wi' us?"

"We didna think of it then," Iain said, yawning and combing his long hair with his fingers. "But she doesna want the baby to be a Sasannach."

"It'll be a Gordon, that's all that matters, surely?" Beth said.

"Aye, that's what I've tellt her, but she's no' happy about it. She's a wee bit worried too that she's no' carrying the baby right, I think, though she hasna said anything, even to me."

"She'll be fine, man, if she takes care of herself," Alex said reassuringly. "But she canna make the journey home now, she kens that, surely?"

"Aye, she does," Iain said, ladling a generous helping of porridge into a bowl. "I'll take her a bite tae eat through, if she's still awake."

Nobody mentioned the fact that Anne had made the journey to Manchester without a qualm, and had every intention of returning to London at the beginning of February. But the roads to Manchester were not the same as the rough and boggy trails and paths to Loch Lomond. And Anne's pregnancy was clearly not the same as Maggie's.

* * *

"Right then," said Sir Anthony as the Peters' carriage clattered into the frosty courtyard of St James's Palace on the last day of January. "I don't know if William will be there or not, but if he is, you stay close to me. Don't give him any opportunity to get you alone. If he tries to, refuse point blank to go with him. He's no shortage of willing mistresses, and he'll soon turn to someone else if he can't get you on your own. You'll just have to put up with George's German war talk, I'm afraid."

"I'd rather put up with a week of that than five minutes of Cumberland," Beth said, remembering the feel of the duke's hand on her knee at the opera with a shudder.

Two hours into the Court visit Beth still felt the same, just, although she was bored almost to distraction. To give King George his due, he had thoughtfully sent for refreshments, and did address a few polite comments to Beth in English. But as soon as he got onto talk of war, he became excited, and when he became excited, he spoke in his native tongue.

She watched him from the discomfort of an inadequately padded gilt chair, as he explained his intention to recommence the war in Flanders as soon as the thaw started, his hands gesticulating, his neat little physique dwarfed next to her husband's large frame in spite of Sir Anthony's ability to diminish himself.

How such a small and compact man had managed to father such a massively-built and corpulent son was beyond Beth. George's eldest son, Prince Frederick, seemed to have inherited his father's build at least, although whether he had inherited his features or personality she had no idea, having seen the prince only once, in Ranelagh gardens at a distance. Sir Anthony had expressed an intention to introduce her to him, but it was difficult at the moment, as relations between father and son, normally extremely hostile, had temporarily broken down altogether. A visit to Prince Frederick now could cause total ostracism from the rest of the royal family, and Sir Anthony wanted to keep up to date with the king's intentions in Europe. Beth sipped at a cup of rapidly cooling tea and tried to appear contented. At least Cumberland was not present, having gone riding with his sister Amelia. That was a blessing. And Maggie, still pale and permanently tired, seemed to have taken the family's concern to heart, at least a little, and was relaxing a bit more. That was a blessing too. Beth's stays, which were digging painfully into her sides, were not. She could do with loosening them a little.

Suddenly decided, she stood and curtseyed, thereby interrupting the male conversation.

"If you will excuse me for a moment, Your Majesty," she said, blushing prettily at the embarrassment of having to reveal a need to relieve herself and endearing the king to her, who granted permission to leave his presence, then forgot all about her the moment she'd left the room.

The privy was a long way away, down many yards of draughty corridors, and Beth took her time both getting there and back again. With luck they would be able to leave soon, she hoped, pausing by a glassed door which led on to an enclosed garden. The sun had come out, and the frost sparkled like diamonds on the bare branches of the shrubs and carefully pruned trees. She lingered a moment, reluctant to return to the stuffy atmosphere of the salon and the unending torrent of incomprehensible German.

"Are you fond of gardening, Lady Elizabeth?" came a voice from directly behind her. She let out her breath in a shocked gasp, and turned to find the person she least wanted to see at that moment standing directly behind her. He still wore his heavy outdoor coat and his face was flushed with cold and exercise. And pleasure at seeing her. She curtseyed deeply, taking the time to compose herself.

"Did you have a pleasant ride, Your Highness?" she said on rising, wondering if it would seem rude to edge past him and continue walking back to the salon.

"Indeed I did. The weather is most bracing, but I am glad I returned in time to see you."

Cumberland, deliberately or not, placed himself in a position in which in order to get past him, she would almost have to push him out of the way. She remained where she was, and answered his first question to her instead of commenting, as courtesy required, that she was glad to see him, too.

"I do not know much about gardening, Your Highness," she said. "In Manchester, my father employed a gardener and since I have been in London I have not had the time to indulge. But this garden seems very beautiful." She turned back to the view in order not to have to look at his beaming face.

"It is," he said. "I planted some of the shrubs myself, and when the war is over and I have a little more leisure and my own residence, I intend to take a personal interest in my own gardens. As for this one, although it is winter and most of the plants are therefore dormant, the holly is particularly delightful at the moment, as is the *helleborus niger*, a recent acquisition of ours."

"Very interesting," she said, having no idea to what plant the Latin name referred.

"It is, although you cannot see it from here. If you would care to accompany me in a turn about the garden, I will show it to you." Assuming acquiescence, he reached past her to open the door, and she moved back in alarm.

"I really must return to the salon," she said. "His Majesty and my husband will no doubt be wondering where I am."

"I am sure you will realise that I cast no aspersions on your considerable charms when I state that my father, if he is speaking of the forthcoming war, will hardly have marked your absence. And I'm sure Sir Anthony will not object to you taking the air for a few moments."

He wouldn't, but he would certainly object to the person she was taking it with. She looked out at the frosty garden.

"It's very cold," she said. "And I am just recovering from…"

In a gesture of the utmost gallantry he removed his coat and placed it tenderly around her shoulders, cutting off her excuse.

The coat still held the warmth of his body, and smelt of horses and fresh air. If it had been Alex's she would have snuggled gratefully into it, relishing the unique smell of healthy, active male. As it was, it took a great effort of will not to fling it off her shoulders and run.

"There," he said, opening the door and smiling down at her, clearly finding the fact that his coat engulfed her diminutive frame charming in the extreme. He tucked her arm under his and led her out. "Come," he said. "It is surprisingly warm in the sunshine, and the fresh air will do you good."

Faced with no choice apart from the point-blank refusal Alex had told her to make, which seemed inappropriate in view of Cumberland's courteous behaviour, she accompanied him. With luck he would talk about gardening, show her the *helleborus* whatever-it-was, and then she could plead fatigue or a blister, or anything, and make her escape.

"Your father seemed to be telling my husband that he plans to return to Flanders at the earliest opportunity," she said.

"Did he?" replied the duke, apparently surprised.

"Well, he was speaking in German," she admitted. "But I recognised a few words, and his gestures are very eloquent."

"Ah, I see. Papa does tend to forget himself somewhat when speaking of his campaigns. Poor thing, you must have been very bored," said Cumberland, patting her hand sympathetically.

Damn. That was not what she had intended.

"Not at all," she put in quickly. "I am very interested in languages, and German is so…"

coarse and guttural.

"…much like English," she said. "I am sure I could learn it quite easily, if I put my mind to it. I must ask Anthony to teach me."

The duke frowned at the mention of her husband. Good.

"My father does not intend, I think, to command his troops in person this time. I hope to play a part myself, however," he said.

"I am sure that after your great bravery at Dettingen His Majesty could not fail to give you an important command," she said, hoping to engage him in talk of war, as the allegedly delightful *helleborus* plant did not appear to be making itself known, and there was little else to comment on in the leafless garden.

"Yes, I think I am not being immodest if I say the army could do with a little young blood. It could certainly do with some tightening up of discipline."

"Really?" she said. "Everybody says the British Army is a most formidable fighting force. Look at their achievement at Dettingen."

Soldiers were also generally considered to be the scum of the earth, too, although Beth thought it politic not to mention this.

"You are right. The British soldier, properly trained and disciplined, is second to none. But they are hard men and prone to unruliness unless set a good example by their officers. When I take command of the forces I intend to set that good example, and ensure my officers do the same. If the officers maintain the highest standards of discipline, the men will automatically imitate them. Ah, here we are," he said, halting beside a border.

Why couldn't he have just said it was a Christmas rose instead of showing off his knowledge of Latin? Beth thought irritatedly, looking at the plant. Nevertheless, she bent to examine the blooms, taking the opportunity to detach her arm from his.

"Oh, they're beautiful!" she cried. They were, the delicate yellow stamens contrasting with the creamy white petals. There were some buds too, their furled petals tinged with pink.

"A testament to the fact that even the most delicate of blossoms can survive in a variety of conditions," he said, stooping beside her and deftly plucking a flower. Before she could stop him he had carefully tucked the stem into her hair, allowing his fingers to brush her cheek lingeringly as he lowered his hand. "It is lovely," he breathed, "but your beauty eclipses it utterly." He bent his head to hers, clearly intending to kiss her.

How had they moved so quickly from military discipline to seduction? She reached up in panic and placed both her palms on his chest.

"Your Highness!" she cried. "You forget yourself. I am a married woman!"

He lifted his head but did not move away, and she saw with a sinking heart that he was undaunted.

"I have not forgotten that you are married," he said. "Nor have I forgotten your words to me that night at the opera. 'If only I were not married,' you said. You gave me reason to believe that you returned my affection."

She had. Alex was right, it had been a mistake. He was not put off by her declaration. Quite the opposite, in fact.

"Indeed, I do have strong feelings for you, but I am married, Sir, indisputably so, and you would surely not have me be unfaithful to my husband?"

"Nobody's marriage is indisputable, Elizabeth," he said, smiling.

Her eyes widened in shock. Was he hinting that he would be willing to engineer a divorce for her, in order to make her his mistress?

"I am quite happy in my marriage, Your Highness," she said, putting as much ice as she dared into her tone. "My husband is considerate and generous and I could not wish for more."

"You are wrong," replied the duke, seizing her hand with uncharacteristic fervour. "You could, should wish for more. You should wish for love, and devotion, and passion. Mere kindness and generosity are not enough. You are a beautiful woman, Elizabeth; you need a man to awaken you to the sensual pleasures of life." He pressed her hand passionately to his lips.

She had a sudden urge to laugh, recognised that it was born of terror, and swallowed it back. She thought rapidly. He seemed to truly believe himself in love with her. He was younger than her in spite of his size and air of authority. Young enough to mistake lust for love.

What had Alex said? Hit him, or scream. No, it had not come to that, not yet. But she could see no way of extricating herself from this situation without offending him, and she hated him for putting her in this position.

"Your Highness," she said firmly. "I am overwhelmed by your affection for me. But I am married, and I take the sixth commandment most seriously, as I do the vows I made on my wedding day. As much as I regret it, I cannot deceive my husband. I am not accomplished in duplicity, my lord."

She tried to retrieve her hand from his, but he kept a firm grip on it. For the first time she wondered if she was in physical danger. Alex had said the duke would not force her against her will, but he was a big man and they were alone in the garden. He could easily overpower her if he chose to, and he was a prince. No one would take her word over his. Except Alex, who would, and would kill him without hesitation, regardless of the consequences. She swallowed down her rising panic. She could not lose her head now. She needed all her wits about her.

"I am not asking you to deceive your husband, Elizabeth," Cumberland was saying. "I am well acquainted with Sir Anthony. He is a most amenable man. I am sure we could come to some mutual arrangement, without the need for any underhand behaviour."

"No!" she cried, so loudly that the duke started in surprise. She took the opportunity to pull her hand from his grasp. "No," she repeated, more quietly, but with a marked tone of desperation in her voice. "I do not wish to contradict you, Your Highness, but in truth you do not know him as well as you think. He can be quite jealous, when roused." That was true, if something of an understatement.

"Are you telling me Sir Anthony is a tyrant in private?" said Cumberland, thunderstruck. "He seems so...docile. My God, he doesn't beat you, does he?"

Beth could see how the duke might think that. She was trembling and obviously distressed. She was tempted to say for a moment that he did, but realised that would only fuel the argument in favour of divorce, and could possibly result in the besotted young man calling Alex out.

"No," she said. "He does not beat me. As I said, he is considerate. But he would not be happy at the thought of sharing me with another man, however illustrious and discreet he might be. It would lead to a rift between us, which I doubt could be healed, and would lead to great awkwardness, once you tired of me. I'm sure you can appreciate that."

He couldn't, not at the moment.

"How could I ever tire of you?" he declared. "You are that most exceptional of women, a delicate beauty of great intelligence who shares all my interests and has a mind of her own!"

She played her final hand. If this failed, there *was* nothing left but to scream and hit him.

"Your Highness!" she said, breathlessly. "Are you proposing marriage to me?"

She watched as he took an involuntary step backwards, his face registering his shock momentarily before he composed himself, and knew she had the upper hand again. He could not marry her, an untitled, divorced woman, without defying his father. Prince William knew about duty. He was a slave to it. She was gambling on the fact that he would never go against the king's wishes, no matter how passionately he felt for her.

"Elizabeth," he said desperately. "There is nothing I would like more. But I am a prince. I cannot marry for love, you must know that. But I am sure, if you feel for me as I do for you, that some way can be found…"

"I am sorry," she said unhappily, interrupting him. "You put me in an impossible position. Whatever my feelings for you, I am a woman and am therefore vulnerable, in a way that you, as a man, and a prince, are not. If I did as you asked, I would have failed in my duty to my husband. I would be ostracised from society and my reputation would be in shreds. No one would have the temerity to say anything against me while I held your favour, but afterwards…I would be ruined. I could not bear it." She lowered her head modestly. "Please, Your Highness," she continued in a small, distraught voice. "If you care for me as you claim to, do not ask this of me, I beg you."

Arrogant, somewhat narrow-minded and a strict disciplinarian the Duke of Cumberland was; he was also intolerant of rebellion or disobedience in any form. But he was not an uncaring man by any means, and he believed himself at that moment to be in love with Beth. She had defeated him, although he did not realise it then, seeing only that he had distressed the object of his affections, which was the last thing he had intended to do. He took her hand again, tenderly, and this time she did not attempt to withdraw it.

"Please, I had no wish to upset you," he said, fighting to recover his poise. "Of course I understand your position. Your sense of duty and regard for your good name are truly commendable. I should have expected nothing less from such a woman as yourself. I am sorry. We will say no more about it."

They walked towards the house in silence, the beauty of the Christmas roses forgotten. He would not beg her to become his mistress, that was clear, but she was still unsure as to whether he was offended or not.

"May we at least remain friends, Your Highness?" she said

anxiously as they approached the door.

He looked down at her, the misery in his pale blue eyes quickly veiled.

"Of course," he said politely. "I would not have it any other way."

He was struggling to master himself, she realised, and as she watched him walk away to change out of his outdoor clothes, she felt a pang of sympathy and of guilt for having deceived him. It was not her fault that she was beautiful, she told herself determinedly as she returned to the salon. If she could switch off whatever it was that was so appealing to men she would, willingly. She had not encouraged him in any way. He had insulted the Highlanders, her people. He had insulted *her*, by proposing that she become, effectively, his whore. He was horrible, and fat, and pompous, and a usurper.

By the time she reached the salon, she had managed to revive all her feelings of revulsion for the Elector's son, and she entered the room flushed with emotion, her eyes sparkling with indignation, looking so lovely that even the king, looking up from his place on the sofa, smiled in appreciation.

Sir Anthony did not. He looked at the flower in her hair, which she had completely forgotten about, and then at her rosy face.

"You have been a very long time, my dear Elizabeth," he said. "I was starting to worry. Did you lose your way?" His voice was casual, perhaps slightly concerned. His eyes were cold. She shivered involuntarily and reached up to pluck the flower from her hair.

"Er, no," she said. "I met Prince William, who offered to show me the gardens."

"*Ach, so!*" said the king. "*Wilhelm interessiert sich sehr für gartenarbeit!*"

"I'm sure he does," said Sir Anthony, without translating. "And did you enjoy what he showed you?"

She could hardly say no in front of the king, and she didn't want to say yes, as his question clearly had a dual meaning, and it was obvious that Alex was singularly unimpressed that she had spent the last half hour strolling round the gardens with the man he had expressly told her to avoid being alone with at all costs.

"It was very interesting," she said, her eyes sending a silent plea for understanding. She fiddled nervously with the flower, and he moved towards her, taking it from her hand and replacing it in her hair.

"The duke has excellent taste," he said, smiling only with his mouth. "But you're shivering. You are hardly dressed for the outdoors, my dear."

She opened her mouth to say that the duke had lent her his coat, then closed it again. Better she explain later.

"Yes," she said, feeling suddenly annoyed. What right had he to behave so coldly towards her? She had just succeeded against all the odds in fending off the prince without incurring his displeasure, while Alex had been merrily quaffing wine and discussing military tactics. "I do feel somewhat cold, suddenly." Their eyes clashed, and then he turned away, towards the king.

"If Your Majesty would be so gracious as to allow us to leave?" Sir Anthony said, bowing deeply. "Pleasant as I am sure the gardens are, the season is somewhat inclement, and I would be distressed beyond measure if my dear wife were to catch a chill. I think it better if we return home as quickly as possible, with your permission, Sire?"

"*Ja, naturlich,*" said the king. "Of course. I cannot imagine what William was thinking of, my lady, to ask you to walk outdoors in such weather. I trust you will take no harm from it."

"I am sure I will not, Your Majesty," said Beth pleasantly. "My husband is too protective of me at times. I am not as weak and feeble as he seems to think."

Sir Anthony placed her cloak on her shoulders, folding it around her in a gesture that was tender, and then took her hand in a gesture that was not.

The moment they were out of the room, she freed her hand from his and they walked to the coach in frozen silence, which they maintained until they reached home and there was no danger of them being overheard.

"I tellt ye, I ordered ye, not to let him get you alone," Alex said hotly, the moment the front door was closed.

She rounded on him so quickly that he took an involuntary step backwards.

"Yes, you did," she said. "And I tried. I had no idea he'd even come home until he was standing behind me. And before you say that I should have pointed out how cold it was, I did, and he put his coat round me and then led me out before I could stop him."

"Ye should have refused to go out wi' him, like I said, Beth," he fumed, pulling off his wig. "And what the hell were ye doing, letting him put flowers in your hair? I tellt ye…"

"I know what you told me!" she shouted, tearing the rose from her hair and throwing it at him. "You told me to scream and hit him, but if I'd done that I'd have looked ridiculous, and you'd never have been invited back to the palace again. You weren't there, so you don't know a damned thing about how it was!"

"I know you looked bloody guilty when ye came back," he roared. "What else did ye let him do so that I could be invited back to the palace?"

"Nothing!" she cried. "I wasn't guilty, I was angry! Clearly you think as little of me as Cumberland does, if you assume I'd let him seduce me in the bushes!"

He had the grace to look shamefaced at this.

"I'm sorry," he said. "I shouldna have said that, but I canna stand the thought of ye letting him even touch you. I ken ye wouldna have let him go too far, even if it did mean risking our position at Court."

"No, you're wrong," she said, her eyes blazing. "I can't stand him. I wouldn't, I didn't, let him go anywhere at all. He put a flower in my hair and held my hand, briefly. That's all. The man thinks he's in love with me. What I *did* manage to do was to reject him in such a clever way, though I say so myself, that he's upset but not offended, and your position at Court is unaffected. It wasn't easy but I did it, and you should be congratulating me, not prancing about in a jealous rage!"

"I am not prancing about in a jealous rage!" he said indignantly.

"Yes you are," she replied. "You have no more right to be jealous of what I've done with Cumberland than I had to be jealous of you and Anne Maynard!"

"Anne Maynard?" he said incredulously. "That's a different matter entirely. I felt sorry for the lassie, that was all. There was never anything between us, as you well know!"

"Not on your side there wasn't," retorted Beth. "Any more than I have any feeling for Cumberland. But she was besotted with you, just as Cumberland is with me. The only difference was that she didn't have the courage to show it, and he did. And I wasn't stupid enough to be jealous, and you are!"

He looked at her for a moment, speechless.

"I've told you before, Alex," she said, in a normal voice this time. "I'm beautiful. Men are attracted to me. I can't help that. You're handsome. Even as Sir Anthony, women are attracted to you. You can't help that, either. But we can both help being jealous. It's ridiculous, when we're supposed to trust each other."

"Were you jealous of Anne, then?" he asked, his anger dissipating as quickly as it had flared. He moved closer, the corners of his mouth lifting in the beginnings of a smile.

"No," she said. "Of course not." She pushed firmly to the back of her mind the desire she had once had to punch Anne, before she had realised the woman deserved sympathy, not anger.

"Really?" he said, reaching out and pulling her to him. "Not even a wee bit?"

"No," she said. "Not even a wee bit."

"You're lying," he said confidently, bending to kiss her. "I can tell."

"How could you tell I was lying?" she asked some considerable time later, after they had both washed off the rouge and white paint they had become liberally smeared with, had raided the pantry, and repaired to bed for an extremely early night.

"If I tell ye that, ye'll be as wise as me," he said, straightening the bedclothes, which had become somewhat disarranged following the recent activity. "Congratulations, by the way."

"What for?"

"For appeasing Cumberland without giving anything in return. That was quite a feat. What would ye have done if he *had* proposed marriage?"

"Hung myself," she said. "I think it might be better if I don't go to the palace with you for a while, though. If we meet anywhere else and he comments on it, I can always say that I was too distressed to meet him, or something like that."

"And it saves you the tedium of listening to the Elector spout on about war for hours on end," Alex said.

"Yes it does, doesn't it?" said Beth with a grin. "I hadn't thought of that."

"You're lying again," he remarked.

"No, I'm not!" she protested. She wasn't, and he knew it, although she still didn't know how.

"Interesting what he let slip, though," mused Alex. "Are ye sure he didna mean you to know?"

"Yes," she said. "Because not a minute before he inadvertently revealed he was going to have command of the forces in Flanders, he told me that he was only hoping to play a part. Is it important?"

"Who gets command of the army? Of course it is."

"Do you think it'll be a good thing or not?"

"For us? I'm no' sure, but I can think of a lot of people I'd sooner have in command than Cumberland."

"Why?" she asked.

"Because what he tellt ye is right. The British Army is one of the best in the world. But it's often undisciplined, and badly trained. If Cumberland succeeds in bringing them into line, it'll make them harder to beat. Especially for the clans, who'll never be disciplined. But there are some points in our favour, too."

"Such as?"

"Cumberland's young and inexperienced. He showed bravery at Dettingen, and he's got the authority of royalty, but he'll have to tread carefully if he's no' to ruffle the feathers of the old men he'll be superior to. Hell, I dinna ken if he'll be a good commander or no'. I've got other things on my mind right now."

"Like what?" Beth said, leaning precariously out of bed to reach for the wine and inadvertently displaying her bare back and one firm white buttock.

"Like this," he said, making a lunge for the exposed part, causing her to shriek and miss her grab for the wine, almost tumbling out of bed altogether. He caught her neatly round the waist and gathered her back under the sheets.

"Don't you need to replenish your strength, after the last time?" she said, giggling.

"Christ, woman, d'ye take me for a man in his dotage?" he said indignantly, pinioning her to the mattress beneath him and demonstrating comprehensively that he was well and truly replenished. "That was a full half hour ago. I havena even warmed up yet."

Things had started to become extremely warm, to say the least, when there was a knock at the door, and before Alex or Beth could tell whoever it was to go away in no uncertain terms, the door opened and Iain walked in.

They both looked at him, stilled by his expression. He had barely noticed what they were doing and how comprehensively he was intruding, and his face was white and drawn.

"It's Maggie," he said, before they could ask. "She's started her pains."

CHAPTER TWELVE

"It's too soon," said Maggie despairingly when Beth appeared in the bedroom dressed only in her shift, closely followed by Iain. Maggie, to Beth's surprise, was pacing up and down the room, consciously making an effort to breathe slowly and steadily, small beads of sweat breaking out on her forehead. Beth had expected her to be lying down in bed, clutching the bedpost and screaming in agony.

I have no idea what to expect, really, she thought, panicking, realising that her expectations of what she would find in the room were based solely on Caroline's amusing retrospective account of Freddie's birth, which she said had mainly consisted of her screaming her head off, threatening to kill Edwin if he ever came within ten yards of her again, and uttering language that would have made a soldier blush. After which a small, slimy squirming creature had been placed carefully in her arms by the midwife, and her heart had immediately melted.

The midwife.

"Get the midwife," Beth said to Iain, who was hovering uncertainly in the doorway of his own bedroom, which had suddenly become alien territory to him. He nodded once, cast a worried glance at his wife and shot off, grateful to have a reason to leave. Beth, who wanted nothing more than to follow him, instead moved a few steps into the room, just as Maggie halted in her pacing and clutched her stomach, her face contorting as the spasm passed over her.

"Shouldn't you be in bed?" said Beth.

"It's wet," explained Maggie when the pain had receded. "My waters broke. I thought I'd wet myself at first. And it's better if ye move about while ye can." She looked at the other woman, her green eyes dark with anguish, "It's too soon, Beth. I canna have it now, it's too soon. It's no' due for another ten weeks or so."

Beth, completely at a loss for what to say to comfort her friend, instead turned to practicalities.

"I'll change the bed," she said briskly, pulling the wet bedclothes off the mattress and piling them in a corner. She patted the mattress, which was also wet. "There are clean sheets in our room," she said. "Will you be all right alone for a minute while I fetch them?"

Maggie attempted a smile, which turned into a grimace.

"Aye," she said. "The pains are no' close together yet. But they're getting stronger. Dinna be too long."

When Beth arrived back in her bedroom she found it full of male MacGregors. Duncan was already dressed, and was buttoning his waistcoat. Alex was sitting at the dressing table in his shirtsleeves, spreading white paint over his face, and Angus, dressed only in black woollen breeches, was rummaging in the wardrobe. Of Iain there was no sign.

"Has Iain gone for the midwife?" Beth asked.

"No," said Duncan. "He's gone to make some tea."

"*Tea!*" cried Beth. "To hell with tea! We need the midwife, now!"

Alex paused in his cosmetic endeavours, recognising the fear in his wife's voice.

"He has to stay here Beth, in case he's needed," he said, with a calmness of tone that made her want to hit him, even though she knew he was adopting it for her benefit. "And the midwife'd no' come out at this time of night for a servant. Iain's too upset to express himself properly. Likely he'd threaten to cut her throat if she refused, and land himself in jail." He went back to his preparations, smearing two spots of rouge on his cheeks, before standing and donning a lilac brocade waistcoat that Angus handed to him. He smiled at her reassuringly.

"I'll cut her throat myself if she refuses to come out," said Beth grimly.

Alex crammed his wig on his head, stuffing his feet into his shoes at the same time.

"There'll be no need for that, my dear," he said in a crisp English accent. "Who could refuse Sir Anthony Peters, when he smiles so winningly?" He gave a grotesque grin that ordinarily would have made Beth laugh. "And if that doesn't work," he finished, buckling on his sword, "my bottomless purse should."

He moved past her towards the door, followed by Duncan. Beth grabbed at his sleeve.

"For God's sake hurry, Alex," she said desperately. "I need you. I don't know what to do. You know a lot more about childbirth than I do."

He looked down at her, not without sympathy, and shook his head.

"No, Beth," he said gently. "I know a lot more about *children* than you do. About childbirth I know as much, if not less than you." He squeezed her shoulder. "You'll be fine," he said. "Just follow your instincts."

And then he was gone and Beth was left with Angus, who smiled helplessly at her. She remembered why she had come to the room and turned to the wooden chest, dragging two sheets out, and wondering how it was possible for Alex to know less than her about childbirth, when she knew nothing, nothing at all.

"I'll away off and help Iain wi' the tea then, shall I?" said Angus hopefully, preparing to flee.

Beth gritted her teeth in anger. It was ridiculous. All these grown men, who would cheerfully face ten attackers armed only with their fists, were reduced to jelly at the thought of the imminent arrival of a tiny baby. Why should it be assumed that she knew better than them what to do just because she was a woman? At that moment she would happily have faced ten men herself rather than cope with what was to come.

"No," she said. "You can come with me." She watched with malicious satisfaction as Angus's eyes widened in terror. "The mattress is wet and needs turning."

She had never seen a task accomplished with such speed in her life. Angus worked with the strength of a man possessed, turning the heavy mattress as though it were a feather, his muscles bulging with the strain. Then he vanished, and Beth was left alone with the pregnant woman. She changed the sheets quickly and helped Maggie into a clean nightgown. Then she waited helplessly while another spasm of pain doubled Maggie up, before assisting her gently into bed. Her face was as white as the pillow, her dark auburn hair as red as blood in the candlelight. Beth sat down carefully on the side of the bed.

"Maggie," she said, wondering how to explain that she had no idea what to do without panicking the young woman. She had to say something, though; she could not bluff her way through this, as she had through so much else in her life.

"Aye, I know," said Maggie, reading her thoughts. "Ye dinna ken what tae do. Ye've no experience wi' bairns. Dinna fash yourself, Beth, I think it'll be a while yet. Wi' luck the midwife'll be here by then."

The look of relief on Beth's face was so immense that Maggie laughed, in spite of her fear.

"I'm sorry, Maggie," Beth said. "I'll do anything you ask, but you'll have to tell me what to do."

"Pray," said Maggie, although she knew in her heart it was futile. "Pray as hard as you can that these are false pains. Because I want this bairn so much, Beth, and he canna live if he's born tonight. He's not ready." Tears trickled down her face. "I've waited so long," she cried. "Oh God, I've waited so long."

Beth leaned across and took the despairing woman in her arms, and they clung together, praying for a miracle that they both knew would not be granted.

"She ain't here," the sleepy voice called down from the window in answer to Sir Anthony's frantic banging on his door.

"What do you mean, she's not here?" cried Sir Anthony indignantly, clearly suspecting that the man was lying. "She must be here. I need her services, immediately. I'm willing to pay very handsomely for her trouble."

"Even if you was to offer twenty sovs, guv'nor, it wouldn't do no good," said the man disrespectfully, eyeing the dandy with disgust. "I told you, she ain't here. She's away over the river somewhere delivering twins."

"Where exactly over the river is she?" said the baronet impatiently.

"I've no idea," came the reply. "But I'll tell her you called when she gets back, in the morning, prob'ly."

"Ah. I see," said Sir Anthony. "Well, do you know of any other midwives in the area, my good man?"

"No," said the man curtly, annoyed at the term of address. He was nobody's 'good man', particularly not this powdered molly's. "That is, there's Sally Morgan in St. Giles, but I wouldn't trust her to deliver pups, let alone littl'uns, drunken old cow. And there's Ann O'Neill, but I know for a fact she's out, too. Uncommon night for babies." He withdrew his head, preparing to close the window, but stopped at the pleasant sound of coins jingling together. A great many coins, by the look of the leather bag which had appeared in the fop's hand as if by magic.

"What a shame," Sir Anthony said regretfully, turning away. "I was of course, prepared to pay up to fifty sovs, as you so enchantingly call them. I have twenty here, on account. But if you don't know where your good lady wife is, there's nothing to be done. Where exactly does Mrs Morgan live?"

The man leaned so far out of the window he was in danger of falling out of it.

"Now let us not be so hasty, my lord," he said, quickly revising his opinion of the gentleman below. "You woke me out of a deep sleep, and I was a little fuddled. But I remember now. I'll get dressed directly." The head disappeared and within moments a light came on in the room.

"Remarkable how refreshing to the memory gold can be," remarked Sir Anthony to his manservant.

It was remarkable how refreshing it could be to thieves, too. Especially in the maze of less than salubrious streets around Westminster Abbey. Three emerging shadowy figures faded quickly back into the darkness at the sight of Duncan flexing his broad shoulders and half-drawing his sword. They would go for reinforcements.

"We canna stay here," he whispered urgently to his brother just as the midwife's husband appeared at the door, somewhat haphazardly attired, but respectable at least.

"I quite agree, Murdo," replied the baronet. "It will take my boy at least a day to remove the filth from my shoes. And my stockings are utterly ruined!"

The man's look of contempt transformed itself into an unctuous smile as the baronet looked up from his contemplation of his bespattered hose.

"Now, my good man," said Sir Anthony. "I am sure I can entrust you with this purse, if you will just ride like the very devil to fetch your wife!"

"Er, no thank you, my lord," said the man, who, though his fingers were itching to count the bag's contents, knew the area and that his chances of leaving it in possession of such a sum were nil. "I am sure I can trust a gen'leman such as yourself to pay up fair and square later. I'll fetch my wife to your house directly, sir."

He set off in the direction of the river, and as soon as he was out of sight the baronet and his manservant vanished with remarkable alacrity in the opposite direction, Sir Anthony having very vociferously checked that his pistol was indeed primed and cocked. They rode for some time in silence, carefully watchful.

"Where are we going?" asked Duncan as Alex suddenly veered off the route home, heading instead for the Strand.

"If the midwife is worth her salt, as I'm sure she is, she won't leave her current patient until she's safely delivered, no matter what her husband says. The authorities will revoke her licence if she does. And Maggie needs help now." He turned down a small respectable street just off the main thoroughfare and knocked loudly at the door of a shop.

There was a short pause, and then a muffled voice came from behind the door.

"I'm closed," it said. "Who is it?"

Sir Anthony announced himself, and there was the sound of a bolt being hastily pulled back. The door opened and a young woman in a dressing gown peered cautiously round it.

"Sir Anthony?" said Sarah, her eyes wide with alarm. "What's wrong? Is it Beth?"

"No, not exactly," he replied, moving past her into the shop without asking permission. "What do you know about childbirth?"

"Lady Anne," said Sarah confidently, that being the only woman of Sir Anthony's acquaintance in the family way, as far as she knew. "I'll get dressed."

She turned away and he reached out and caught her arm, marking how she shrank from his touch, even though it offered no threat. He let her go.

"I'm sorry," he said. "No, it's not Anne. It's my cook. She's started her pains, but she's very early. Beth's with her, but she's no idea what to do, and the midwife has been sent for, but is at another delivery. I'm sorry to wake you, but I thought a woman of your... er...past experience might be able to help. Will you come?" His voice was tense and held none of the normal flowery affectations of the dandy.

"Yes, of course I'll come," she said, rushing off to dress. He had never alluded to her background before, had never treated her with anything less than the utmost respect, which was one of the reasons that she liked him so much. The fact that he had now, told her that he was more worried than he appeared to be. He was right, she did know something about childbirth. Midwives were often reluctant to attend women of ill-repute, and the prostitutes tended to help each other rather than call in the authorities, whom they instinctively, and generally with good reason, mistrusted.

They arrived home twenty minutes later, Sarah feeling somewhat shaken, having been mounted behind the grim-faced Duncan, to whom, in spite of her aversion to physical contact with the male sex, she had clung as though her life depended on it as they galloped through the deserted streets. He jumped down from the saddle and reached up, lifting her down as though she were a feather and placing her carefully on her none-too-steady legs. He smiled, and the grimness was gone.

"I take it you're no' accustomed to riding, lassie," he said.

"I've never been on a horse before in my life," she said shakily. "And will never go on one again, if I live to be a hundred." She detached herself from his steadying hand and followed Sir Anthony up the steps to the house.

Beth had never in her whole life been so grateful to see anyone as she was to see Sarah. So grateful that she didn't even question why she was here instead of the expected midwife. She had done everything that she could in the practical sense: the fire was blazing, soothing mulled wine was steaming by the bedside and Beth was sitting with Maggie, holding her hand and feeling utterly helpless. She looked up at Sarah with the same expression that men generally adopted in the face of childbirth.

"It's coming too soon," she said, Maggie being temporarily

incapable of speech.

"I know, Sir Anthony told me," said Sarah. "How too soon is it?"

"About ten weeks," gasped Maggie. Her face was white, her lips pale.

"Can we do anything to stop it being born now?" Beth asked desperately.

Sarah looked doubtfully at the pregnant woman. This was a new experience for her. The last time she had been present at a premature birth the mother had been glad it was coming too early, having tried unsuccessfully for four months to dislodge it from her womb. But then to prostitutes babies were often an inevitable but unwelcome side-effect of their profession. This one clearly wasn't.

"Well, we could raise the foot of the bed so her legs are higher than her head," she said tentatively. Beth shot off the bed as though from a cannon, ready to go and call the men. "Wait," said Sarah, "have your waters broken yet?"

Maggie nodded.

"It's coming," she said tearfully. "I hoped it was false pains, but it isna. Oh!"

Sarah nodded, watching as Maggie fought her way through another contraction, sweat pouring down her face. They were very close together, she noticed. It would not be long. Maybe an hour or two.

"I need towels or clean cloths," she said, thinking fast. "To put under her. When the baby's born it'll be very messy. And oil, warm water and something to wrap the baby in when it's born. And a sharp knife and string."

Beth ran from the room and Sarah took her place on the bed, taking Maggie's hand in hers. The woman was trembling, and Sarah's heart went out to her.

"Is it your first child?" she asked.

Maggie nodded.

"We've been trying for three years," she said. "I couldna bear it if…"

"Don't think about that now," interrupted Sarah hastily. "Concentrate on getting through this, and we'll worry about the baby when it arrives. Get used to the pains, because you'll probably be having them every year now your womb's discovered what it's there for." She saw Maggie's face light up as she grasped at the straw Sarah had given her and hoped God would forgive her the white lie.

"Try to breathe slowly," she said. "Can I have a look at you?"

At Maggie's nod she folded back the sheet and gently pushed the woman's legs apart.

"There's no point in keeping your legs together," she said gently. "It doesn't work anyway."

"It's burning," said Maggie indistinctly, her face contorted.

"I know," said Sarah. "It does. I'm not a midwife, but I've seen several born. When Beth brings the oil I'll feel to see if the baby's in the right position, but I think – oh shit!" she said, as the top of the baby's head suddenly appeared. She felt carefully with her fingers as she'd seen the midwives do, to see if the cord was looped around its neck, but before she could be sure, Maggie gave a strangled cry and the baby slithered out in a mess of blood and fluid into Sarah's hands.

Beth, choosing that moment to reappear, her arms full of the things Sarah had asked for, nearly fainted on the spot.

"It's all right," said Sarah frantically, glancing over her shoulder. "It's normal. Just a bit faster than I expected, that's all. Give me the knife."

She tied and cut the umbilical cord and reached for the jug of water, taking it and the baby over to the corner of the room, where there was a basin.

"Beth," she said, hooking her finger into its mouth to pull out any mucus and then gently washing the tiny infant, who showed no sign of life. "In a few minutes the afterbirth will come. You can help by pulling very gently on the cord, but only when the contractions start."

Hopefully that will occupy Beth and stop her from fainting, Sarah thought, although a quick glance told her that the colour had come back to her face. Not so Maggie's. The absence of a child's cry was deafening in the small room. Sarah kept her back carefully to the bed, gently rubbing the baby's limbs dry. It was a boy, but too small, much too small. His skin was wrinkled and almost transparent and he was very thin. At least she could clean him, and let Maggie hold him before his body cooled and she had to accept he was dead.

"It's a boy," Sarah said, feeling Maggie's eyes boring into her back.

"Let me see him," Maggie said, trying to accept the inevitable. "Please. Just once, before….please."

Sarah held the tiny baby easily in one arm, and picked up another cloth, intending to wrap him up before giving him to his mother. The little chest fluttered, and he suddenly opened his mouth and uttered a tiny, thin wail that stilled all activity in the room.

"He's alive!" Sarah breathed in awe, her eyes filling with tears.

"Let me see him!" cried Maggie desperately, struggling to rise. Beth pushed her back gently as Sarah hurriedly crossed the room, placing the minute bundle into his mother's arms.

"Oh, mother of God, oh God, he's beautiful," she said, bursting into tears. Her face screwed up as the contractions began again, but she hardly noticed, so intent was she on her son.

Beth left Sarah to the unpleasant business of dealing with the afterbirth and moved round the side of the bed to take a look at the new arrival.

She had never seen anything so tiny in her life. He was impossibly small, must weigh no more than three pounds or so at best. He had a shock of black hair like Iain's, and the tiny hand peeping out from the enfolding cloth was no bigger than the first joint of her thumb. His eyes were closed tight, but she knew enough about babies now to know that when they opened they would be blue. If they opened. She glanced at Maggie, and a look of sudden acceptance of the inevitable passed between them. Maggie lifted him gently off her chest.

"Baptise him," she said, holding him out to Beth. Beth's eyes widened in alarm and she backed away.

"I can't, Maggie, I'm not a priest!" she said.

"Midwives can baptise children in an emergency," Maggie replied, her voice trembling. "And you're of the faith, Beth. Please."

"I'm not a midwife, either," Beth pointed out. "But she'll be here soon. Or I could get Al…Anthony to fetch a priest."

Where would they get a Catholic priest at this hour? In these uncertain times? The thought ran through both their minds at the same moment.

"There isna time," Maggie said desperately. "Look at him, Beth. I'll no' have him die unbaptised, and go to Limbo. Please."

Beth made a decision, took the fragile bundle carefully, and moved across to the jug of water. It wasn't holy water, but it would have to do.

Sarah, aware that she had been all but forgotten at this intense moment, froze, not wishing to draw attention to the fact that she had just been effectively informed that Beth, as well as her cook, was a Roman Catholic.

Beth put one finger in the water and carefully made the sign of the cross on the baby's forehead.

"*In nomine Patris, et Filii, et Spiritus Sancti, amen*," she said, crossing herself. "I name this child," she stopped and turned to Maggie, "what do you want to call him?" she asked.

"Iain," said Maggie, gazing intently at her son and the woman who held him, her pain, her distress, the other occupant of the room, everything else forgotten. "Iain Charles Stuart."

Beth closed her eyes, then opened them again and looked at Sarah, whose expression of studied blankness told her that she'd understood only too well the implications of what she'd just heard. There was nothing she could do about it now. She turned, dipped her finger in the water again.

"I name this child Iain Charles Stuart..." She stopped. She could not say the child's surname. Sarah knew too much already. Sure that God would recognise the child when it came to Him, surname or no, she hastily wet the baby's forehead and blessed him again, before handing him hurriedly back to his mother. She pulled the sheet gently up over Maggie and turned to Sarah.

"We have to tell Iain," she said, remembering as she said it that his name was supposed to be John. She grabbed Sarah's hand and they left the room together.

"Don't say it," said Sarah as soon as the door was closed and Beth turned to her. "I won't say anything to anyone, ever. I haven't heard anything and I don't want to know any more."

"Sarah," began Beth.

"If it wasn't for you I'd be dead, or at best still selling myself to people like Richard, for pennies," Sarah interrupted. "I owe everything I am to you, and to Sir Anthony. And even if I didn't, you're my friend, Beth, the only true friend I've got. That means more to me than you know."

Beth grabbed Sarah by the shoulders, wrapped her arms round her and hugged her fiercely.

"Thank you," she said simply. They moved to the top of the stairs together. The men were in the drawing room; the door was slightly open and a patch of yellow light filtered into the hall, along with a murmur of conversation.

"Beth," Sarah said softly as they were about to descend the stairs. "I don't know if Sir Anthony knows or not, and I don't know what you're up to, if anything, but for God's sake, promise me you'll be careful."

"I will be," she said. "I promise."

She couldn't keep this from Alex, she realised. Better she tell him than wait until Maggie did, when all this was over and she remembered what she'd done. But for now the most important thing was to tell Iain that he had a son.

Their entrance into the drawing room was met by a sea of anxious male faces. They all paled when they saw Beth and Sarah together, assuming they were there because Maggie was beyond help.

"Is it…is she…?" Iain faltered.

"Maggie's fine," said Beth briskly. "There were no problems, and she's fine."

"Oh Christ," he said, and burst into tears.

She realised then that his shakiness was not merely due to fear for his wife, but to overindulgence in alcoholic comfort too, and she glared at her husband and his brothers, who all refused to meet her eye, before standing on tiptoe and seizing Iain by the shoulders. She shook him as hard as she could.

"Iain," she said firmly. "Get a hold of yourself. You have a son."

He stopped crying abruptly, and stared at her.

"A son?" he said. "But…"

"I know," she said, more gently. "He's alive, now. But you must go to them quickly, because…"

She got no further before he tore himself from her grasp and ran from the room. They heard him take the stairs three at a time and the sound of the bedroom door being wrenched open, then closing again, more softly.

"Sit down, both of you, before you fall down," said Sir Anthony gently. "I'll pour you a drink. You look as though you need it. You certainly deserve it, by the sound of things."

"We didn't really do that much," said Sarah, downing her first glass of wine as though it was water. Sir Anthony did no more than raise one eyebrow before pouring her another. Duncan and Angus, servants again, disappeared quietly from the room. "It was all over so quickly, I didn't even have time to examine her, or anything."

"Quickly?" said Beth. "She was in agony for ages! She was having really bad pains for at least an hour before you arrived."

Sarah looked at her friend.

"Beth," she said. "A woman's pains normally go on for about twelve hours before the baby's born. If there are problems, it can be a lot longer, days, even. That was the fastest, easiest delivery I've ever seen."

"Twelve hours!" echoed Beth.

"How is the baby?" Sir Anthony said, repressing a smile at his wife's horrified expression.

"Too small," Sarah said practically, firmly quenching the urge to scream at the unfairness of life. "I thought he was dead, but then while I was washing him he started crying. I nearly dropped him, I was that shocked. I hope I'm wrong, but I honestly don't see how he can live for more than a few minutes, Sir Anthony. I'm sorry."

"Don't be sorry, my dear," he said. "We are all immensely grateful to you for coming at all. I don't know what we'd have done without you, especially as the midwife still shows no sign of arriving, and it's almost dawn. How can we thank you?"

"You already have," she replied, casting a look at Beth. "It's nice to be able to do something to repay you in a small way for all you've done for me." She put her glass down. "But I must get home. If I'm quick I can get an hour's sleep before I have to open the shop."

"Of course," said Sir Anthony, standing. "I will ask Murdo to escort you home."

"No," she said firmly.

"He is quite harmless, I do assure you. You will come to no harm in his hands, and I will not allow you to go home unaccompanied at this hour."

"It's not his hands I'm worried about," she said. "It's the horse. I'll walk, thank you all the same."

In the end 'Murdo' walked Sarah home, and Beth and Alex, too tense to sleep, and deciding to await the arrival of the midwife, repaired to the cosier library, where Angus joined them and Beth recounted what had happened in the bedroom.

"It's not Maggie's fault," she said hurriedly, even though Alex showed no sign of accusing her. "She was in a terrible state. All she could think of was that the child mustn't die unchristened." She swallowed heavily, fighting back the tears.

"I dinna blame Maggie," said Alex thoughtfully. "But can Sarah be trusted?"

"Yes," said Beth with conviction. "She can. I'd stake my life on it."

"You are doing, Beth. Or Maggie and Iain's, at least. If she talks, I could deny any knowledge that my cook and footman were Jacobites, and claim that you were a soft-natured fool that didna have the heart to turn a pregnant woman over to the authorities when you found out what she was. But it would be very awkward for us all, Beth, and Iain and Maggie would go to prison, or worse. Are ye sure ye can trust her?"

"Yes," said Beth. "I'm sure. She's my friend, Alex, but if I thought for one moment she'd betray us, I'd tell you, I promise."

"Even though ye ken what I'd have to do?" he asked softly.

She looked at him.

"Yes," she said. "Even though I know what you'd have to do. You're more important to me than a thousand Sarahs. She's trustworthy, Alex."

He nodded, and smiled thinly.

"Well, then," he said, to Angus. "Let's away off up and see our new wee clansman, just for a minute."

The baby clung on to life long enough for Duncan, returning from Sarah's and stopping to pick up the mail on the way, to see him too. The midwife appeared at nine o'clock, exhausted and flustered, to be sent away twenty pounds richer for having done nothing, and Beth threw the mail, which consisted of a slim letter from Manchester addressed in Anne Redburn's neat hand, down on the hall table, too preoccupied to contemplate reading about the trivial affairs of her cousins at the moment.

Against everyone's expectations, Iain Charles Stuart Gordon held tenaciously on to life for another twenty-six hours, finally giving up the struggle at nine thirty the following morning and plunging the whole family, who had already become deeply attached to him, into mourning.

CHAPTER THIRTEEN

Over the next few days life in the MacGregor household regained some semblance of normality. Iain resumed his usual chores, saying he needed to work to give his hands something to do and his mind something to occupy itself with, although, judging by his closed, grim expression, the ploy was only a partial success. When not working, he spent a lot of time in the bedroom with Maggie, or with Duncan, walking in the fields to the north of the house or drinking and playing chess.

Angus, the morning that little Iain died, took an axe and went silently to the shed at the bottom of the garden, where he smashed the crib he had been making into such small pieces that it was impossible to tell that it had ever been anything other than a pile of kindling. Sifting through the ashes after he had burnt the remains in the yard, Beth found a fragment of beautifully carved celtic knotwork, which after examining she fed back into the embers in respect of Angus's wishes, the tears in her eyes due to more than just the woodsmoke.

Alex incarcerated himself in the library, where he wrote up a detailed report on his unsatisfactory negotiations with the English and Welsh Jacobites. He also included the information Beth had learnt about the Duke of Cumberland's expected promotion, and reiterated his firm belief that Prince Charles must not come to Britain without substantial French backing. He then put it all in code and sent it by special courier to John Murray of Broughton in Edinburgh.

Beth took up the household duties that Maggie would normally have done, except for making the morning porridge, which Angus did, wresting the spoon from her hand on the second morning as she was staring despairingly at the glutinous inedible mass in the pot. After the smashing and burning of the crib he had returned to his normal cheerful self, only a slight tightness around his mouth betraying that it would take him some time to recover from the loss.

Maggie stayed in bed. As it was customary for a woman to stay in bed for several days after the birth of a baby if she was privileged enough to be able to do so, nobody worried too much when Maggie did not appear downstairs, although they had half-expected her to. It was only after seven days had passed and she still showed no sign of rousing herself, that everyone started to become a bit concerned.

"She's eating," said Iain, when the others asked him when she would be likely to leave her bed. They were all sitting in the library waiting for Angus to return from the post. "No' as much as she should, maybe, but enough. But she willna talk about…she'll no' talk about it," he trailed off.

"Have you tried to talk to her about it?" asked Duncan gently.

"Aye," said Iain. "No. Well, it isna easy, ye ken. I tellt her that it's no' good just to lie about where you've got all the time in the world to brood. I said that it's helping me a wee bit to be keeping myself busy, and suggested she might like to just start by lying downstairs for a few days rather than in bed."

"What did she say?" asked Alex.

"That she wasna me, and she'd deal wi' it in her own way. She said she needs to think things through and sort it all out in her head, and she canna do that if she's downstairs wi' people coming in and out every minute. She said once she's ready she'll get up and no' before." He looked at the others, his face for the first time showing his concern.

"Aye, well, the stubbornness sounds like Maggie, right enough, but little else does," said Alex.

"She needs someone to talk to," Duncan said. "No' a man. Someone who kens what she's been through, and can approach it in the right way."

"No," said Beth, seeing that they were all now looking at her. "I know I'm a woman, but I've no more idea than you what she's been through, and she knows it."

This was true, but any further discussion of the situation was ended by the return of Angus with an envelope addressed to Benjamin Johnson, in Murray of Broughton's handwriting, delivered to the coffee-house.

"There wasna anything at the post," said Angus, taking off his footman's frockcoat and throwing himself down in a chair in his customary fashion. "So I thought I'd check the coffee house, though I thought it was a bit early for a reply."

Alex did a quick calculation.

"If the courier was fast both ways, it's possible," he said. They all crowded round as he opened it, eager to hear the contents.

"It's in cipher," he said. "I'll decode it as fast as I can." He went over to the writing desk in the corner and the others all sat back to wait. Angus poured some wine. They waited.

"What did the letter from Manchester have to say?" asked Duncan suddenly. "Have your cousins done anything interesting?"

Beth looked at him blankly.

"On the night…er…last week, I brought a letter from the post on the way back from seeing Sarah home," he elaborated.

"I'd forgotten all about that!" Beth said. "I left it in the hall. I'll go and get it."

She disappeared, returning a couple of minutes later.

"It had slipped down the back of the table," she said. "It's from Anne Mayn…Redburn." She slit the envelope. "It's probably really boring," she warned, unfolding the densely written sheet of paper.

"Even boring news'll pass the time until Alex is ready," said Angus.

"I'm working as fast as I can," Alex muttered from the desk, head down, quill scratching away.

"Her handwriting is so small I can hardly read it," Beth said. "I don't know why she can't write legibly, even if it does use more paper. After all, it's not as though she has to worry about the cost of the post any more, is it? Let me make sense of it, and then I'll read it out to you."

There was a general sigh, and the others settled back to wait again.

"I was thinking, now the thaw's set in, that we could maybe go up on the roof tomorrow and fix those loose tiles, before they start causing a problem," said Duncan.

"Let's see what Murray has to say first," replied Angus cheerfully. "We might all be riding north to join the prince and his huge French army."

Duncan looked at his brother, one eyebrow raised.

"Aye well, in the unlikely event of Louis getting off his arse and rousing an army for us, we'll forget the roof. Otherwise…"

"Oh, you bastard," said Beth unexpectedly.

Everyone stared at her. Even Alex stopped writing. She continued to pore over the letter, oblivious to everything else.

"Oh God, how could you?" she said, then looked up at Alex, who had risen from his chair. "What was it you once told me?" she said, her eyes brimming. "Don't underestimate your enemy." The tears spilled over, pouring unheeded down her cheeks.

"What's the matter?" asked Alex, thoroughly alarmed now.

"Don't underestimate your enemy, you said," she repeated. "I should have listened. But I would never have guessed…I didn't…" She swallowed hard, and swiped the tears angrily from her face. "God forgive me," she said softly, and standing, thrust the letter into Alex's hand before rushing from the room.

Alex stood for a moment, folding and unfolding the paper in his hands, unable to decide whether to follow his wife or read the letter.

"Read it," said Duncan. "Then you'll ken what's amiss, and how to mend it. She's gone upstairs, she'll be alright for a few minutes."

Reluctantly Alex sat down on the edge of the chair and haltingly, for the writing, though neat, was really very small, began to read;

Dearest Elizabeth,

I really hardly know how to begin this letter. I am so excited, and so happy that I am sure my hand is trembling, and that you will not be able to read the news that I am so eager to tell you. I was afraid that you would be angry with me for not observing the proprieties, and for not telling you sooner, but Lord Edward told me you have scant regard for proprieties, which I am sure you will not take amiss, dear Elizabeth, and I can explain the delay in telling you my news, if you will only promise to read to the end of this letter.

"Christ, she's long-winded," said Alex impatiently, wanting to find out what the news was that had made Anne so happy and Beth so desperate. He scanned a few lines. "The whole family are as happy as Anne by whatever it is, and Charlotte's beside herself, brainless wee lassie." He frowned, and carried on reading.

> *I wanted to write to you before, but Lord Edward and Richard advised me to wait, as we had so little time beforehand, and I really do not think I would have been capable of holding a pen at all until now, when the deed is done, and I am safely, and most happily…married!*

"Bloody hell!" said Alex.

"Married?" said Angus. "Is she no' the lassie whose husband just died?"

"Aye. What's she thinking of? She's no' even out of mourning yet."

> *And there, that is my wonderful news, and I know you will be shocked, but I hope the shock will be lessened, when I tell you who has made me the happiest of women. Of course, I am sure you have already guessed, and will welcome me into your family as your cousins already have, with open arms.*

"Has she married Lord Edward, then?" said Duncan.

Alex ignored him, continued reading, then scrubbed his hand through his hair as he came to the words which had prompted Beth's reaction.

"No," he said. "She hasna married Lord Edward. She's married Richard." He skimmed through the rest of the sheet silently, then stood. "I'll go to her," he said, and left, taking the letter with him.

"It's my fault," Beth said as soon as she heard him open the door. She was standing by the window, looking out over the garden to the fields beyond, and seeing nothing. He came to her, put his hand on her shoulder.

"No," he said. "It isna your fault."

"It is," she insisted. "I should have paid for his captain's commission. If he hadn't needed the money for that he would never have thought of marrying Anne. I'll never forgive myself."

"How do you know he hadna thought of it already? He's very ambitious."

"Because if he had he would never have humbled himself by coming to me to beg for money," Beth said. "No, he's done this because I wouldn't buy his commission. And he's done it quickly, while they were away, partly because of that, and partly because he knew I'd have stopped it if I'd known what he was up to."

"You couldna have stopped it," Alex pointed out quietly. "They're both of full age, Beth."

"I would have," she replied firmly. "I'd have told her what he is, what he's done. That would have made her think twice. God, how could she be so stupid? He's horrible!"

Alex turned her gently to face him.

"No, he isna, Beth. He's quite attractive, and he's learned a lot about social behaviour in the last two years. He's a lot more polished now."

"Attractive!" she cried. "How can you say that? He's ugly, and evil, and …and bow-legged!"

Alex laughed.

"Aye, I'll give you bow-legged. But he's no' ugly, Beth. You just see him that way because ye dinna like him."

"What did the will say?" she said suddenly, urgently. "You went to the reading with Anne. Will Richard become Lord Redburn now?"

"No. It's a hereditary title. It'll pass to Anne's baby if it's a boy, along with everything else, although Anne will have a generous allowance, and will be allowed to live in his London house and on one of his country estates until she dies, when they'll revert to her son."

"And if it's a girl?" Beth asked.

"If it's a girl, then Anne gets everything except a big dowry and a property in Sussex which will be held in trust until the girl marries or comes of age. Beth, I canna…"

"And if the child dies?" Beth persisted.

"Then Anne gets the lot. The title will be defunct, because there are no male relatives living."

"Was there any provision made in case she married again?"

"No," Alex said. "I dinna think Redburn expected her to marry again. He loved her, and thought she loved him enough to never consider another man."

"She did love him," said Beth. "Have you read the letter? She was coerced into marrying Richard. He managed to convince her that she needed looking after and the child needed a father, and that he would be the ideal choice."

"Aye, but we discussed the possibility of this, Beth, if you remember. We knew she was vulnerable."

"I know, but I thought she'd refuse all offers until she was at least out of mourning!" said Beth. "I know what's happened," she continued angrily. "The whole family have worn her down. It'll be to Edward's advantage to have so much money in the family, and all his sisters think it's impossible for any woman to live without a man to guide their every move. She has no idea what she's done, what she's married. He's evil, Alex. What can we do?" She looked up at him, her eyes pleading with him to find a solution.

"Accept it," he said. "There's nothing we can do. Maybe it'll all work out better than ye think. Maybe he's changed."

"No," she said, shaking her head. "He hasn't changed. He's always been bad, even when he was a child. He'll hurt her, Alex, and God help her and the child if it's a boy."

"Oh come on, Beth," said Alex. "As badly as ye think of him, surely ye dinna think he'd harm a wee bairn?"

"I don't know what he'd do. He beat John, repeatedly, and drove Martha from the house. He didn't care what happened to *her* child."

"Aye, but there's a big difference between beating and dismissing servants, who were probably sullen at best and defiant at worst, from what ye've tellt me, and hurting your wife and innocent stepchild," Alex reasoned.

"He hit me, too!" Beth cried, getting angry in spite of his reasonable tone. "And left me in the barn for Graeme to find. That's hardly the action of a caring brother!"

"No, it isna. But ye tellt me yourself, you'd just thrown a knife at him and called him a coward. I might have hit ye myself, if I'd been him." He smiled down at her, and her eyes softened.

"No, you wouldn't," she said, putting her arms round him.

"You'd have taken the knife off me before I could have thrown it, and dragged me off to bed." She froze momentarily, then continued speaking quickly before he could ask her what had crossed her mind. She couldn't tell him that, even if it would prove how reasonable her fears for Anne were. "You don't know him," she finished lamely.

"Maybe not," Alex admitted. "But I ken the woman he's married, and I hardly think she's likely to provoke him like you did. Even if the child is a boy, Richard'll still be wealthy. He'll get his captaincy and any other rank his commanding officer is daft enough to gie him, and he'll be able to entertain his officer friends to his heart's content. And Anne'll be happy to indulge his every whim and look after him and the child. She'll no' gie him reason to hit her, and if he's feeling vicious he'll be able to bully his men instead. It could all work out better than ye think, Beth. Let's look on the bright side."

He didn't add *because there's nothing else we can do, anyway*, but they both thought it.

"You're right," she said. "I'll look on the bright side. But while I'm looking on it, I'll keep an eye on her. When are they coming back to London?"

He looked at the letter, which had become a bit crumpled during their embrace.

"In two weeks. Less than one week, now," he said, because the letter had taken three days to arrive, and had lain neglected for another week.

"I think we'll throw a dinner for them," Beth said. "To welcome them back. That'll please Anne and annoy Richard, because he'll be expecting me to be angry and to ignore them. And it'll give me a chance to see if she's as happy as she says she is. Now, let's change the subject. What did Murray's letter say?"

* * *

Murray's letter said that he had received Alex's and had included the information in a packet he'd already prepared, signed by himself and many of the chiefs, stating that they were of the unanimous opinion that no rebellion was possible without French support. He had given this to the Earl of Traquair, who promised to forward it to the prince straight away and who intended to go to France himself soon in any case. All that remained to be done was to continue gathering information where possible and to wait for Charles' response. Because there was nothing more they could do to influence Charles, Beth was not thinking about that as she entered Sarah's shop, having turned her attention to more domestic problems.

She had paid a visit to Caroline and Edwin, although she had rightly assumed that Anne would also have written to them with her news. She had, but with the consideration that was one of her most endearing features, she'd posted the letter to Caroline two days after Beth's so that her 'dear sister' would receive the news before anyone else. The Harlows were of the same general opinion as Alex; it was a shock, but there was nothing anyone could do but hope all would turn out well. But then they didn't know Richard either. No one did. And she couldn't tell anyone. It was a lonely feeling, but she had been lonely before and had learnt to cope with it.

Sarah was just finishing off an elaborate and very youthful hairstyle for an elderly overpainted lady, and politely asked Beth if she would be so kind as to take a seat for a few moments, whilst at the same time demonstrating by way of an elaborate mime behind the woman's back that this ridiculous coiffure was not her idea and that the woman sporting it was really as stupid as she looked. Beth managed to refrain from laughing and sat down demurely, accepting the coffee offered by a very young girl she had not seen before, who then disappeared through the door leading into Sarah's private room.

"I haven't seen her before," said Beth as soon as the customer had gone.

"I take it you mean Emily and not the cantankerous old trout?" said Sarah irreverently. "Yes, she works for me a couple of days a week, cleaning, making coffee, that sort of thing. She's got a big family, so the money comes in useful. She's gone home now, you can come through."

"And you can afford a servant," Beth said, following Sarah through to her room.

"Yes I can," she replied proudly. "Wonderful, isn't it? And it's nice to help someone else out too. Mrs Marshall was my last client today, but I'm really busy normally. Business really picked up after

Anne married Lord Redburn. Which I assume is what you're here to tell me about. Richard and Anne, I mean."

"It isn't, actually. I thought you'd already know. You seem to know everything the moment it happens."

"Everybody in London knows about Anne and Richard, though. She wrote to Lady Winter." Sarah beckoned Beth to a seat and took one opposite. "Are you frightened for her?" she asked.

Beth looked around the room, which was simply but tastefully furnished. Two comfortable chairs and an oak table, cream-painted walls, a framed landscape hanging over the fireplace. A little rug by the fire.

"Yes," she admitted after a moment. "But everyone else seems to think I'm worrying unduly."

"Even Sir Anthony?"

"Yes, even Anthony. He thinks that Richard may be settling down, and doubts that Anne will provoke him like I did. Which is true. You have a nice room here. I haven't seen it before."

"Thank you," said Sarah. "Does Sir Anthony know that Richard tried to rape you?" She said it matter-of-factly, as though she were asking whether Anthony knew that Beth liked toast for breakfast.

The room vanished. Everything vanished except this young woman sitting opposite her, who knew what nobody knew. Beth stared at her, her eyes wide with shock.

"How do you know that?" she blurted out, before realising that she had now made any denial impossible. "Did Richard tell you?"

"No, of course he didn't," Sarah said. "No one told me."

"Then how...?" Beth was stunned, panicked. Her voice died in her throat. Sarah leaned forward.

"I'm sorry," she said. "Maybe I shouldn't have mentioned it. I know all about men and sex, as you're aware. I know what they're like when you please them and I know what they're like when you don't. I've also had those who'd already tried it on with another woman and been refused. The nice ones wanted you to make them feel handsome and virile, to soothe their hurt feelings. And the bastards wanted to take their frustration out on you, humiliate you like she'd done to them. That's what Richard did that night when he came to my room and I tried to comfort him. If he could he'd have raped me and beaten me, but as it was you'd kicked him so hard he wasn't capable."

"So he just beat you instead," Beth said.

"Yes. But I knew what had happened. I thought at first that he'd made a try for Jane, Grace, or even little Mary. I wouldn't put anything past him." Sarah grimaced. "Even I didn't think he'd try to swive his own sister, though. I couldn't believe it when you told me."

"I didn't tell you!" Beth protested.

"Yes, you did. You told me you'd had an argument with him and he was very angry with you when he left you."

She had. She remembered now, sitting on the foot of Sarah's bed, assessing the injuries Richard had inflicted on her. She had known, all this time. Over two years.

"You haven't told anyone, have you?" Beth said.

"No, of course I haven't. I think you should tell your husband though."

"No!" Beth almost shouted. "No, I can't."

"Why not? He doesn't seem the kind of man who'd blame you. He's nice, and he's obviously very fond of you."

"That's the problem," Beth said. "He wouldn't blame me. But he would kill Richard."

"Well, that would certainly sort out the problem of Anne's stupidity, if he did," Sarah said, considering. "Although Anne might be a bit upset at being widowed twice in a year. Are you worried that Richard might kill Sir Anthony instead of the other way round?"

She was completely serious. Beth looked at Sarah as if seeing her for the first time, realising how little she knew the woman who had once been her maid.

"No. Anthony is a good swordsman. But Richard's my brother, Sarah," she said. "I couldn't be responsible for his death."

"Well no, I suppose not," said Sarah doubtfully. "Everyone's different, I suppose. If my brother did that to me, I'd be happy to see him dead. I won't tell Sir Anthony though. It's not for me to do that. But I will keep an ear out for any rumours about Anne for you. Is that what you wanted to ask me?"

Beth had virtually forgotten what she *had* come to talk to Sarah about, she was so shocked by the direction the conversation had taken.

"That would be nice," she said now, dragging her mind back to the present day. "But no. I came to talk to you about Maggie."

She quickly outlined how Maggie was still in bed ten days after the birth, and how active she normally was. That she didn't even do anything in the bed, just lie or sit there pleating the bedsheets between her fingers for hours on end.

"Murdo thinks she needs someone to talk to. Someone who understands what she's been through."

"Murdo," said Sarah. "Is he the one who rides a horse like a madman?"

Beth laughed.

"Yes. But he's very sensitive as well. And I think he's right. She won't talk to her husband, and I've tried, too, but she won't talk to me either."

"And you think I might have more success because I've lost a child as well?" Sarah asked quietly.

"Yes," Beth admitted. "I know you haven't told me the details, but…"

"I haven't told anybody the details," Sarah said. "I've never talked to anyone about it, ever."

Beth nodded, bit her lip.

"I'm sorry," she said, standing up. "I shouldn't have asked you. It wasn't fair."

"Yes it was," Sarah said. "You want to help your friend. And maybe it's time I did talk about it. They say it helps to tell someone your problems, that by just talking about it you feel better, whether they offer any advice or not. I'll come tomorrow."

"It does help, if you can trust the person you're talking to," said Beth, sitting down again. "Can I tell *you* something?"

"Not if it's about the baptism. I just want to forget that."

"No, it's about Richard. That night, when he came to your room. Graeme thought I'd kicked him in the balls too, although he didn't guess why like you did. I didn't. What I really did was…"

It's true, Beth thought as she walked home later, her step light. *It does make you feel better, sharing something with someone you can trust. Much better.*

She saw things in a clearer perspective now that she'd laughed about it with Sarah. It would all be all right. Anne would not provoke Richard, ever. She was incapable of it. He was older now and had everything he wanted. He had no reason for violence. He would settle down. Anne would work wonders with him, as she had with Stanley Redburn, and in time would give Richard an heir too, which if Edward failed to marry, as seemed increasingly likely, would one day inherit the Cunningham title and fortune. Richard would certainly be pleased with her if she did that.

Everything would be all right.

* * *

When Sarah arrived at the Peters' residence the next day it was Sir Anthony himself who greeted her at the door, bowing to her with an exaggerated flourish that in anyone else would have been a sarcastic gesture, her status being so much inferior to his, but which in his case managed to convey genuine respect. He gallantly took her basket of beauty preparations and ushered her into the house.

"My dear Sarah!" he gushed, "I cannot tell you what an honour you do us, to agree to assist us at this difficult time! Acting the part of an angel of mercy is becoming a habit with you." His dark blue eyes sparkled with humour and beneath that, a genuine regard, and she returned his smile.

"I'm sorry, I'm a bit later than I agreed with Beth…Lady Elizabeth," Sarah corrected.

He waved his hand about impatiently, and the glass bottles tinkled merrily in the basket.

"I am sure I will not be offended if you call my wife by her diminutive name. After all you have known her for longer than I, and are a most trusted friend."

The emphasis on the word *trusted* made her pause in taking off her cloak and glance up at him. For a moment she saw a different man entirely; tall, menacing, and the cold warning look in his eyes made her shiver. Then it was gone, she must have imagined it, and he was fussily assisting her off with her cloak and leading her up the stairs, the trivial, harmless fop once more.

"It matters not a jot that you are late, as my cook is not expecting you," he said, turning back to whisper confidentially in her ear. "I thought your visit would come better as a surprise." He clapped his hands in ecstasy, nearly dropping the basket in the process. "I do so love surprises! When they are of a pleasant nature, of course. Now, let me introduce you."

He knocked politely on the door but then entered before Maggie had had time to respond, thereby spoiling the deferential effect somewhat.

"My dear Margaret!" he said, showing himself fully so that Maggie would instantly know that he was Sir Anthony, her employer, and not Alex, her friend and kinsman. "I have a visitor for you, and a most delightful surprise! I am sure you remember Miss Browne."

"Yes, sir, I do. I never had the chance to thank…" Maggie began, sitting up in bed. The shutters were open, but the curtains were drawn, and the room was bathed in a dull blue light.

"Miss Browne is here in quite a different capacity today, Margaret," he interrupted, moving across the room to open the curtains. "There! That's better!" he trilled as sunshine streamed into the room, lighting up the pallid face and lank tangled hair of his cook, who bestowed a venomous look on his brocade-clad back.

"Now," he said, turning from the window and beaming at the company, "Miss Browne is a woman of many talents, and her greatest is to make the very best of every woman, or man, who visits her establishment. Why, I have seen her take ten, even twenty years off an old lady at the mere stroke of a brush, and her reputation is unparalleled. The nobility flock to her in droves! But today she is here to devote her attentions exclusively to your good self!"

"That's very kind of you, Sir Anthony," Maggie said in a tone that expressed nothing more than the ardent wish to plunge a knife into him at the first opportunity, "but I really havena any need…"

"To thank me! As you know, I always like to take the very best care of my staff! Well, I will leave you two together. I am sure you will get along famously. Be sure to call in the library before you leave, Miss Browne. Murdo will take you home. In the carriage," he added.

In a flurry of lace and violets he was gone, leaving Sarah

standing uncertainly in front of her none-too-willing client. They regarded each other in silence for a moment.

"Miss Browne…" Maggie began.

"Sarah," said Sarah, moving to the foot of the bed. "You had no idea I was coming, did you?"

"No," said Maggie. "And I'm sorry for your trouble, but I really have no need of a fancy hairstyle and face paint. I dinna ken what he's up to, but you're wasting your time."

"I think he's worried about you," Sarah said, sensing that here was a blunt woman who would not appreciate prevarication. "I know Beth is. She's not used to being helpless, but she knows she can't help you."

"Nothing can," said Maggie, "least of all some fancy creams and scents. I'm sorry, I dinna mean to be rude, but I've tellt them all, I'll get up when I'm ready. In a few days. I just need a wee bit of time, that's all. Thank ye for what ye did for me. I appreciate that, all of it."

Sarah bent down and picked up her basket.

"Well now I'm here, I might as well make myself useful," she said. "I didn't think you'd want a fancy hairstyle, so I didn't bring any hairpieces, or paint for that matter. But I could at least wash your hair for you. That'd make you feel fresher at any rate, and make me feel as though I've earned a little of the fee Sir Anthony is paying me. I just need some warm water, if you agree, that is."

As if by magic, there was a dull thud at the door and then it opened to reveal Duncan, arms full of steaming buckets of water, his shoulders draped in towels.

"Sorry," he said, smiling apologetically. "I had to kick instead of knocking. Sir Anthony thought ye'd be in need of hot water. I can bring more if ye want."

"Christ!" said Maggie under her breath. "All right, I give in!" She glared at Duncan, who smiled and nodded at Sarah before backing out of the room hurriedly. "It seems they'll no' be satisfied until ye've done something tae me, at any rate."

Sarah got Maggie arranged on a chair with her back to the dressing table, and, filling a basin with warm water, asked her to lean her head over the back of the chair into the water. She worked silently, wetting the lank red hair and gently massaging the soft lavender-scented soap into her scalp, until she felt the tension leave Maggie's body. Then she waited a little more, until the green eyes closed and the mouth relaxed.

"You have beautiful hair," she said, eyeing the dark red locks floating in the basin with admiration. "It's a very unusual colour."

Maggie smiled, but didn't open her eyes.

"Aye, it's my best feature. My only good feature, in truth. I'm no' blessed wi' good looks, but then neither is Iain, so we make a fine pair."

"How is he coping?" Sarah asked. "He must be worried about you too."

"He's coping by being busy," Maggie said. "I'm coping by thinking it through. We're different."

Sarah closed her eyes. A spasm passed across her face at what she was about to do and then was gone, unseen by the other woman.

"When you're thinking it through, though, do you find yourself going over and over the same little detail until you think you're going mad?" she asked.

The eyes shot open and the mouth tightened again. Sarah looked into Maggie's eyes, continuing to massage her scalp in languid circles.

"That's what it was like for me, that's all," she said, marvelling at how casual she was managing to sound, when her stomach was screwed up in a little ball. "I thought it might be the same for you. I found myself going over and over every detail, trying to blame somebody, because I thought nothing so terrible could have happened without someone being at fault."

Maggie stared up at her, unblinking, silent.

"I couldn't blame the father, because he was long gone," Sarah continued. "As soon as he found out I was pregnant, he was running for the hills. And I couldn't blame the midwife, because I didn't have one. I had to do everything myself. And anyway, my daughter lived for a week after that." She swallowed heavily, and smiled sadly down at her client, her fingers moving more slowly. "So I blamed myself instead. For a long time."

Maggie reached up and gripped Sarah's wrist, stilling her motion.

"Do ye still blame yourself?" she whispered.

"No. There were lots of reasons why she didn't live. I couldn't get enough to eat, the father didn't help me as I'd thought he would. My father…" Her voice faltered, and she gently removed her wrist from Maggie's grip, taking her hand instead. "But the real reason she died was because she wasn't meant to live. That's what I think now. Her leg was…not right, sort of twisted. And the life I had after that wasn't what I'd have wanted my daughter to grow up with."

"Iain was perfect, though," Maggie said. "And he had two parents who loved him. He would have had a good life. It *was* my fault," she added with sudden passion. "Everyone kept telling me to rest, and I wouldna. I had to prove that I was strong. If I'd kent what I was doing, I'd have rested all the time. It's a punishment from God because I was too proud, that's what it is."

Sarah kept her hold on Maggie's hand but moved round to crouch down in front of her.

"Have you told your husband this?" she asked.

Maggie lifted her head out of the bowl and water poured down the back of the chair on to the floor. Neither woman noticed.

"No," she said. "I canna tell him that. If I do, he'll either try to persuade me I'm wrong, or he'll start to wonder what he did amiss, too. It wasna his fault."

"It wasn't yours either," Sarah said. "Let me tell you something about myself, although maybe you know already. Beth does, and so does Sir Anthony. Before she hired me as her maid and brought me to London where I could make a new start, I was a whore. I didn't have much choice, really. I didn't have any skills that I could earn money from. I couldn't go home, and I didn't really care what happened to me at that time. So I went to Liverpool at first and got in with a woman who set me up in a place near the docks. Am I shocking you?"

"Aye, a wee bit," Maggie admitted. "But go on."

"Well, then, I won't go into the life I had, you'll have an idea what whores do, I'm sure. And in spite of all the ways women try to avoid getting with child, it happens. And once the baby's in there, it's the devil's own job to get him out before he's ready, no matter what you do. I can't tell you the times I've seen a woman delivered of a normal healthy child when she's spent months sitting in hot baths, drinking gin, jumping up and down and even throwing herself downstairs. And I've seen women like you, who've done nothing, and whose child has been born early anyway, or full term like Lucy, and still died. And most times there was something wrong with them, especially the ones that came early. Twisted legs, withered arms, blind…it's as though God, if you believe in a God, has decided this one will be better off with Him instead of here, where life is hard enough even for perfect children. Iain looked perfect, true, but you wouldn't have known until he started to grow up. There was a reason he was taken, and it wasn't because you wouldn't rest, believe me. That had nothing to do with it."

"Did you try to get rid of your baby?" Maggie asked.

"No, I wanted her, like you wanted Iain. But it wasn't meant to be, and I accept that now. I do not believe that God punishes you by hurting innocent children."

"But the Bible says…" Maggie began.

"To hell with the Bible, and all the so-called men of God who twist its words," Sarah spat, with such hatred in her voice that Maggie was silenced. She turned away, picked up a towel and wrapped it round Maggie's shoulders. "I'm sorry," she continued after a moment, her voice calmer. "You're a Catholic, I know."

"D'ye no' believe in God at all, then?" Maggie said, shocked.

"Of course I do," Sarah replied acidly. "I'm the daughter of a minister, after all. I was brought up to believe in all of it, from Genesis and the sin of Eve that tainted all women forever, to St Paul and the fact that women must always be subservient and obey men, who are their superiors. I believed that all people are sinners, and must constantly pray, and fast, and beg for forgiveness on their knees on stone floors for hours at a time. And as I was already tainted with Eve's unforgivable sin, I didn't hold out much hope of going to Heaven, whatever I did. When I was really small, I accepted that father was beating and starving me for my own good, to drive the sin out of me and bring me to Christ's mercy. Now I just think he was a vicious bastard, like lots of men I've met since, who liked causing pain. And to answer your question more seriously, yes, I do believe in God, but not in men, and one day I'm going to learn to read and find out for myself what Christ said, and if it was that what my father did to us was right, then I won't believe in Him, either."

This wasn't how Sarah had meant the conversation to go. She

was supposed to be comforting Maggie, and here she was, blurting out things she had never told anyone and had never intended to tell anyone. But at least Maggie had forgotten her own troubles for the moment. She was pondering quite a different problem now.

"Christ didna say that you should beat bairns, I'm sure," she said. "I havena much in the way of the reading myself, but my da used to read the Bible to us when we were wee, and Father MacDonald, who used to come from time to time, used tae tell us all sorts of lovely stories about the Holy Family. The Old Testament's full of fearful stories, but our Lord Jesus was a kind, caring man. He loved children. He wouldna have beaten them, or starved them either."

Sarah looked at her.

"But you believe He killed your son, just to chastise you for not resting when you should have?" she said. "That sounds pretty vicious to me."

Maggie blinked, opened her mouth, then closed it again and thought for a while.

"It sounds awfu' daft when you put it like that," she said eventually.

"That's because it is," Sarah said gently. "Don't you think it more likely that Christ took him because he wasn't formed quite right, out of kindness?"

"Aye," said Maggie. "Maybe you're right."

"I know I am," said Sarah confidently. "And I'm also sure that you're not doing yourself or anyone else any favours by lying here in bed brooding, especially your husband, who must be worried sick about you whether he shows it or not. I'll admit to you, Beth came to see me because she was worried about you and thought I might be able to help, because I'd lost a child of my own. All that rubbish Sir Anthony made up was just a ploy to get you to let me in the room. Although I will finish washing your hair and make you look a bit fresher. I didn't want to come, to be honest."

"Why did ye, then, an ye didna want to?"

"Because I owe Sir Anthony and Beth a lot. And because I didn't like to think of you torturing yourself because you had no one to talk to. I got through it on my own, but it took a long time. A very long time. And now I'm glad I came."

"So am I," said Maggie. "Ye've helped me a lot. I think I might get up today, once my hair's dry."

Sarah smiled, and tipped Maggie's head back into the cooling water.

"You've helped me, too," she said. "I hadn't realised how much I needed to talk, even after all this time. I suppose you never get over it completely. But you come to terms with it and move on. You'll go on to have more children, I'm sure, and they'll be lucky, because they'll have parents who love them." She lifted the jug and started to rinse Maggie's hair.

"What about you?" said Maggie. "Are ye no' hoping to have more bairns?"

"Me? No, it's not for me. I'm a businesswoman now. And I'm not interested in men. I've had enough of them to last me a lifetime."

"They're no' all like your father. There's some awfu' good ones about."

"I know, but I'm not likely to meet one who's willing to accept what I've done. And I wouldn't lie to a man if I was going to marry him. Better just not to bother. I'm really quite happy as I am. I don't have to answer to anyone, and don't want to."

She towelled Maggie's hair dry and started to gently comb out the tangles. Some minutes passed in companionable silence, after which Angus appeared with some tea and slightly oddly-shaped biscuits which Beth had baked. He looked approvingly at Maggie, appreciatively at Sarah, winked at her, and left.

"Can I ask ye a question?" Maggie said when his footsteps had receded down the corridor.

"What?"

"How did ye get wi' child, if your father was so strict? And what did your father say when he found out ye were having a bairn? Or did ye no' tell him? Ye dinna have to tell me unless ye want to," she finished hurriedly.

"No, I don't mind," said Sarah, who as she said it, realised she didn't, really didn't. "No, I didn't tell him. I used to go out and take food and suchlike to the old people of the parish. Charitable works. It was the only time I went out, my father not being one for letting his children enjoy idle amusements. Village fairs, music, singing and dancing were the devil's way of tempting you into sin.

I quite enjoyed visiting because it got me out of the house, but my older brother always came with me after I was twelve, just in case I might take it into my head to tempt a man into sin with my evil womanly wiles." She laughed. "I didn't have a clue what a womanly wile was. My brother Philip did, though. He had his eye on a girl from the village, so what we took to doing was setting off together, then he'd disappear and go courting, and I'd do my visits. We'd meet up at the last house and come back together, demure as you please. Philip hated father, and we both got satisfaction out of fooling him.

Anyway, one day I went to visit Mrs Grimes. I didn't look forward to calling on her because she was really old and she'd gone a bit strange. She'd ask you the same thing over and over again, and half the time she didn't remember who I was at all. When I got there this day, though, there was a man with her. I'd never seen him before, but he said he was her son, and he lived over Liverpool way but he was travelling through and had come to see his mother."

"Was he the father of your bairn?" Maggie asked.

Sarah nodded.

"Every week I went to see Mrs Grimes after that he was there, except once or twice. He was handsome, or I thought he was then, and a lot older than me. I was fourteen and he was maybe twenty-five, thirty. And he had a way with words and something of the town about him, which made him seem really special to me, me having never been out of the village. He was just a sweet-talking shit, I know that now, I've met enough of them, but I didn't know anything then except that children were born out of evil, unspeakable acts. But when he kissed me, that was so nice I didn't think it could be evil, and then things went on from there and…well, you know how babies are made."

Both women moved over to the fire, where Maggie dried her hair by fanning it out over her shoulder, while Sarah nibbled on a biscuit.

"I didn't know what was going on at first," she continued. "When I was sick, I thought I'd just eaten something that didn't agree with me. And then I started getting fatter, and I couldn't understand it because I'd always been thin. I mentioned it to Robert, that was his name, because I was worried he wouldn't like me if I got fat, and he just got this sort of strange look on his face and said I shouldn't worry, it was just part of growing up. And then he stopped visiting his mother and disappeared and I never saw him again. I think that's why I went to Liverpool later. I was hoping to see him there, silly cow that I was.

"After a while, about six months, I couldn't hide it any more. Stupid as I was, even I knew what was happening then because the baby had started kicking and everything, but I just thought I could have it and not tell father somehow. When he found out he went mad. He made me tell him everything, and I did, except the bit about Philip sneaking off. He flogged my brother anyway, just for not watching over me well enough. And then he beat me, not with his belt like he usually did, but with his fists. I thought he was going to kill me."

"Did he turn ye out?" said Maggie. "Did your mother no' stop him?"

"My mother died when I was five," Sarah said. "No, he didn't turn me out. He dragged me to church on Sunday and made me stand in the pulpit in front of the whole village while he read a sermon on Delilah and Jezebel and how Satan can be found even at the very door of the house of the Lord. I assume I was Satan, and he thought he was the Lord by then, the bastard. I remember looking down at the sea of faces. I'd never been up on the pulpit before, and all of them were looking at me as though I was dirt. I was standing there, all crooked because he'd kicked me in the back and I couldn't stand up straight, with my nose broken and my face black and blue and nobody had a kind word or look for me, and I thought then, if this is the house of God and these are Christians, then I want none of it. That's when I started to hate, which has helped me a lot over the years, even if you're not supposed to. Hatred gives you strength. He never mentioned the father at all, except to say he was a married man with three children who had been led into temptation by his slut of a daughter, which was a bit of a shock, because I hadn't known Robert was married till then. He obviously didn't blame Robert at all, which seemed really unfair, but I still would have stayed at home to have the baby, I think. I didn't know what else to do. Until he told the congregation that although I was a sinner, and my child would be a sinner, it was his Christian duty as a minister of the Lord to show mercy and bring my bastard up to follow the right path, though it would be very hard, as the baby would be doubly cursed, with bastardy and an evil mother."

"Or trebly cursed, if it was a girl as well," said Maggie, who had now got the measure of the Reverend Browne, and whose own troubles had paled into insignificance beside this remarkable woman's.

"Yes. I hadn't thought of that," said Sarah. "Anyway, he never got the chance to beat my child to a pulp. It was knowing what he would do to her that gave me the courage to do what I did. I walked down from the pulpit, down the aisle and out of the door. He shouted for me to come back, but I just kept on, although I had no idea where I was going. And I walked and walked for miles, until it was night and I found a little hut in the woods, all falling down, and I slept there. Next morning I got up and had a look round, and then I decided to stay where I was, on my own. So I patched up the hut as best I could and lived on berries and stuff, and water from the river. Lucky it was summer, or I'd have starved to death. The rest you know."

"My God, you're amazing," breathed Maggie. "Does Beth know all this?"

"No," said Sarah. "Only you. And I'd rather she didn't know, or Sir Anthony either. I'm not amazing, I don't want you to think that. I was just desperate, that's all. And now I'm not. And I don't ever intend to let any man try to ruin my life again. Are you going to get dressed, then, if you're getting up? I could do your hair in a nice simple style."

"How could I no' get up now, when I havena been through half of what you have?" Maggie said, a little shame-faced.

"I didn't tell you this to make you feel pathetic," Sarah said. "I told you because you asked, and maybe because I needed to tell someone. And you need to get on with your life. You've got a good job and a nice husband. Have more children. Bring them up to be kind, gentle people."

"I'm no' sure if they'll be gentle," Maggie said, struggling into her stays. "But I'll make sure they're fair-minded and honest, at least. I've got another problem though, one I'll have to face as soon as I go downstairs. Maybe ye can advise me." She grinned.

"If I can," said Sarah smilingly, sensing that this was not going to be an Earth-shattering dilemma.

"How the hell am I going to cope wi' Sir Anthony and Beth's smug faces when they see that their wee plot worked?"

"Let them have the satisfaction. They deserve it," Sarah said. "They're lovely people."

"Aye, they are," said Maggie. "And you're no' so bad yourself, either."

CHAPTER FOURTEEN

Beth made a final inspection of the cream and gold dining room, eyeing the linen-covered table with approval. It was immaculate. The polished silver and crystal reflected the light from the chandelier and the scented candles on the table. A comfortable padded chair was provided for each diner. Clearly-written name cards were in each place. A huge fire had been burning in the hearth all day to ensure the room would be comfortably warm when the guests arrived.

In the kitchen Maggie was taking charge of the small army of helpers who had been drafted in to prepare the food for the dinner for twelve and the larger buffet meal that would follow for the extra guests who were joining the others in the evening to play cards in the drawing room.

Duncan was instructing the extra servants who had been discreetly hired to take guests' coats, serve the meal and generally hover, anticipating their every wish. Duncan, Iain and Angus were perfectly capable of dealing with twelve dinner guests and thirty or so card players without help, but it was a sign of wealth and prestige to have a superfluity of servants, and Beth, normally so careless of polite opinion, was out to make a good impression tonight.

She repositioned a knife, refolded a napkin, and looked anxiously at Caroline, who was standing in the doorway watching her friend with an amused smile on her face.

"Is it all right?" she said.

"It's beautiful," Caroline assured her. "Perfect."

"What about the flowers?" Beth persisted, frowning at the elaborate arrangements of white and yellow blooms.

"I've never really noticed this before, with you looking so different from the rest of your family," observed Caroline, "but you really are a Cunningham after all, aren't you?"

Beth looked up in surprise.

In what way?" she asked.

"In the way you're fussing and fretting about ridiculous details when everything is absolutely perfect. You'd give Isabella a run for her money at the moment. Stop it. It's lovely. It will be a perfect evening. Everyone will go away with the impression that Sir Anthony is rich and influential, not least because he *is* rich and influential. That's what you want them to think, isn't it?"

"Is it that obvious?" Beth said.

"Only to me, because I know you, and I know how much you hate entertaining and how little you care for the social niceties when you go to other people's entertainments. You hardly notice the floral arrangements and lighting, and you could be eating roasted ants off banana leaves for all you care, if the conversation is interesting. So the fact that you've now noticed that a knife is half an inch out of line is a sure sign you're up to something."

Beth laughed, and resisting the temptation to reposition a name card that was not quite central, joined her friend in the doorway.

"You're right," she said. "It doesn't do any harm to remind people of Anthony's status from time to time, though."

"True. But this statement is meant exclusively for your brother, isn't it? What are you trying to tell him?"

Beth cast a final glance round the room then led the way down the hall to the library, which was the favourite room for the family to be intimate and cosy in. She sat down, beckoning Caroline to another seat.

"I'm trying to tell him that even though he's now irrevocably married to a woman who is far richer than us, with his captaincy in the bag, he does not have either influence or the respect of society, both of which have to be earned, and both of which Anthony has. And that therefore he'd better not hurt Anne, because if he does I, through Anthony, will bring as much of that influence as possible to bear on him. I don't want him to think he can do anything he wants, without restraint."

"But he can, Beth," Caroline pointed out gently. "Within the boundaries of the law, of course. If he wants to hit his wife, within reason, he can. You know that. Every woman does."

"Yes," said Beth, "I do. I'm sure Anne does, too, although she's too sweet-natured to think any man she loved would ever beat her for pleasure. I also know Richard. I just want to warn him that there will be consequences when he does hit her, that's all."

"*When*? You're really convinced he will, aren't you?"

"Yes," said Beth, "I am. But I know you don't believe me."

"It's not that I don't believe you, exactly," said Caroline. "I just don't see it as inevitable, as you seem to. I couldn't imagine anybody hitting Anne. I don't think she's done one provocative thing in her whole life. You're worrying too much."

"I hope so. But at the very least Anne will appreciate the gesture I'm making in throwing a party for her. And she'll know she has a friend in me, if she needs one."

"Where is the rich, influential man, anyway?" asked Caroline.

"Upstairs, dousing himself in cologne and despairing over whether to wear the lime green or the sulphur yellow, most likely," said Beth. "I'd better go up myself and start to get ready."

"And I'll go home and remind Edwin that we're to be here at seven. He forgets everything now if it isn't about politics or Freddie. It's nice that he's starting to see the fruits of his labours, but it's hard sometimes to see so little of him. I'll see you later. And I'll let Anne know she has a friend in me as well. After all, my family are peppered with enough impressive titles to make Richard's eyes pop, even if they don't bother with me much, Aunt Harriet excepted. Although they are softening a bit, now Edwin's on the rise. Apparently cousin John actually grunted good morning to Edwin the other day when they passed each other in Westminster."

"What's cousin John, then?" said Beth, walking Caroline to the door.

"A viscount. We've got one of everything in the family, from duke to black sheep."

"The black sheep being you," Beth said.

"Yes." Caroline smiled. "Every ancient family has to have one. I'm just following tradition. See you at seven."

The dinner was a great success, as Caroline had predicted. The food was excellent, the wines expensive, the servants obsequious. Sir Anthony wore neither lime green nor sulphur yellow, but russet velvet, and the conversation sparkled as far as was possible given the qualities of the guests, which consisted of the entire Cunningham family, Lord and Lady Winter, Thomas Fortesque and his daughter, and the Harlows.

Anne, in the difficult position of being still within the mourning period for her late husband, whilst at the same time celebrating her recent marriage to her present one, had chosen to wear a soft dove-grey silk. Her burgeoning waistline was concealed by the hooped skirt, and she was radiant. There was no other word to describe her. She radiated happiness and good health, and had from the moment she entered the house and accepted Beth's congratulations by enfolding her in a warm, if awkward embrace, due to the voluminous skirts both women were wearing.

At the table, Beth utilised the espionage skills Alex had taught her, watching Anne carefully whilst effortlessly maintaining a vacuous conversation with Isabella and Clarissa regarding the rain which had fallen almost without pause during their stay in Manchester, and half-listening to the conversation at the other, male dominated end of the table, which was turning to politics and the war in Flanders.

No, she thought after half an hour of intense if subtle observation, *Richard hasn't been cruel to her yet.* True, he was not showing obvious signs of helpless infatuation as Anne was, blushing every time she mentioned his name, and casting demure glances at him from under her eyelashes every few minutes, but Beth would not expect any man to show slavish infatuation in public. Except Sir Anthony of course, who did it for effect when the need arose. But when Anne caught Richard's eye he returned her smile, and when she needed to leave the room for a few minutes he escorted her to the door with the utmost consideration. He even waited for her and led her back to her chair, tenderly kissing her hand before returning to his seat, which caused a little flutter of romantic sighs from the other ladies, Caroline and Beth excepted.

If Caroline was too practical to sigh, Beth was too stunned by this loving gesture. She had expected at best that he would be friendly towards his wife, vaguely attentive when the need arose. And at worst she had expected him to be indifferent, and to see signs of anxiety in Anne, a need to please born of fear rather than love. But she saw none of this, nothing other than a genuinely warm regard, affection even, on Richard's part, and complete infatuation on Anne's.

She ignored the I-told-you-so glance thrown down the table at her from her husband, who knew exactly what she was up to, and instead watched Richard as he ate his soup. He looked up suddenly as though aware of her scrutiny, and their eyes met. Instantly she smiled, conjuring up an expression of such sisterly warmth for him that he was, for a moment, completely flummoxed. Something dark flickered in his eyes, and then he smiled back at her before returning his attention to his plate.

For the first time then, she saw him as others did, saw that he was indeed quite a handsome man, with an athletic build, tanned skin, dark eyes and hair. His face was lean, with none of the plumpness of cheek and double chin which marred Edward's otherwise similar looks. She could still see brutality in the hard planes of his face, and in the habitual tightness of his mouth, but she also saw how irresistible that would be to women, who were attracted to the untamed quality of such men. She herself found that hint of ruthlessness and wildness deeply compelling in her own husband. Anne, and other women, would interpret this quality in Richard as a sign of strength and authority rather than of cruelty and vindictiveness as she, who had experienced it at first hand, did.

Had she imagined the smugness in his smile? She would give him the benefit of the doubt, for now. She had to; it was obvious that he had done nothing more than make Anne blissfully happy. She hoped it would long continue so.

"Will you go to the country to have your baby, Anne?" asked Caroline, when she had finished her soup. "It must be due very soon now."

"Not until April," replied Anne, blushing. "I have two months to wait yet. But I intend to stay in London now, and have it here. The midwife has already been arranged, and I am planning a nursery. The decorators will be coming next week." She glanced at Richard and smiled.

Was there a slight tightening of the skin around his eyes? A pursing of his lips?

"Yes," he said. "We have agreed that it would be better for Anne to be near her friends as the time approaches. I fear I will be recalled to Flanders before the child is born. I expect the summons any day, and it will give me the greatest relief to know she is surrounded by those who will care for her whilst I am away."

"Oh of course we will, Richard!" exclaimed Charlotte. "You can depend upon it!"

"Can't you defer your service until after the baby is born?" asked Caroline. "I'm sure if you explain the situation to your commanding officer he will understand."

"I am afraid that to generals, war takes precedence over everything else," said Richard. "Although my wife's safe delivery is a matter of the greatest importance to me, of course my commanding officer will see it in quite a different light."

"General Hawley is on excellent terms with my great-uncle Francis, if I'm not mistaken," Caroline persisted, observing Richard's smile become decidedly more forced as she continued. "He's an earl, you know. I'm sure I could ask him to put in a word for you if you want to stay at home for a while."

Edwin shot Caroline a puzzled look, but wisely forbore from commenting that as great-uncle Francis was one of the most outspoken and unwavering opponents of Caroline's marriage, the likelihood of him putting in a good word about anything at her request was remote to say the least.

"Oh no!" cried Anne, putting an end to Beth's anticipation as she waited for Richard's response to being forced into a corner. "I wouldn't hear of it! Richard is to take up his new commission, and needs to make the best possible impression. It would do his career no good if General Hawley thought him to be unreliable in his duty." He gave her a look of inexpressible gratitude, and she smiled. "It is quite enough to know that his thoughts and affection will be with me, and that I have good friends who will call on me occasionally while he is away."

"Of course we will," Beth said. "You can count on my support and help in anything at any time at all, you know that. I am always here for you." She cast a warning look in Richard's direction, but he was watching Anne, and his expression was, unbelievably, one of the deepest regard.

"Quite right," put in Lord Edward. "Ridiculous expecting a man to hang around and shirk his duty for a child that isn't even his. Women's business, that. No place for a man."

An uncomfortable silence greeted these tactless words for a moment. Anne looked down at her plate. Beth glared at Edward.

"When I married Anne, I agreed to look after the baby as though it is my own," said Richard. "It wasn't why we married, of course, although it was the reason why we married so quickly. I intend to do the best for the child. I will return to Flanders because my country demands it, and because my wife wishes me to." He smiled at Edward, who seemed to become suddenly aware of his faux pas.

"I certainly didn't mean…" he blustered.

"Of course you didn't," interrupted Sir Anthony, waving his hand at the servants to signify that the plates be removed. "When do you expect to embark, then, Captain Cunningham?"

Richard beamed at the baronet, obviously flattered by the premature title. He was still a lieutenant, although he did not enlighten the company.

"In March I expect, if we are to be ready to campaign in April. I await the king's command."

"We're all awaiting the king's command," said Thomas Fortesque. "It's rumoured that he has designs on making Cumberland Commander-in-Chief. It's ridiculous, if you ask me. He's a mere boy."

"He acquitted himself remarkably well at Dettingen, did he not?" said Sir Anthony.

"Yes. But it takes more than showing great bravery and getting shot to make a man fit to command more than forty thousand men. He has great potential, true, but he's too young and inexperienced for such a post."

"Is it not more of an honorific title than an executive one?" asked Sir Anthony. "After all the last time the army had a Captain-General was in '21, and it's done well enough without one since then. He will have no control in financial matters, and little say in the matter of appointments. That's the king's prerogative."

"Don't we know it," grumbled Thomas. "Cumberland would never be appointed otherwise. But you're right. He will have no defined responsibilities. But Prince William doesn't seem a man to be content with a mere empty title. And he has great influence with his father. That's what worries me."

"It's as well for you then, Richard, that your sister is on such excellent terms with the prince," said Lady Winter. "I'm sure she will have you a general in no time." She smiled at Beth before casting a sly glance down the table at Sir Anthony. "You *are* still on good terms with him, are you not, Lady Elizabeth? I hear you have not visited the palace recently."

Beth, who had been enjoying Richard's consternation at the disturbing thought that his sister might have influence with the C-in-C of the army, registered this barb belatedly.

"It's most unusual for you to be so misinformed, Wilhelmina," replied Sir Anthony mildly. "She accompanied me there only a month ago, and Prince William kindly entertained her whilst I discussed matters of state with His Majesty." He smiled warmly at his wife, throwing the conversational ball to her now she'd had time to prepare herself.

"Yes," she put in before Lady Winter could make any insinuations as to the nature of the entertainment Cumberland had provided. "We had a very interesting conversation. He took me for a walk in the gardens, which are very lovely even at this barren time of year. He is most partial to *helleborus niger*, and wished me to see it. Do you grow it yourself?" She looked at Lady Winter and smiled sweetly.

"Oh, of course," the lady affirmed uncomfortably, unwilling to admit she had never heard of it. "It is one of my favourites."

"I don't suppose the prince mentioned anything of his future appointment or his intentions to you, did he, as you seem to be in his confidence?" Thomas asked.

Sir Anthony shook his head slightly, but Beth didn't need that gesture to know she must not mention what Cumberland had said. On the other hand, she didn't want Richard to think that the duke never talked about military matters to her either.

"I'm sure you realise, Mr Fortesque, that even if the duke were to have discussed anything of the sort with me, I could not divulge anything that was said in confidence. We talked about gardening.

I am sure he would not mind me saying that he is a keen gardener, and hopes to pursue his hobby when he has his own household."

"Which reminds me, my dear," said Sir Anthony. "Whilst I was out today, who should I encounter but the Prince of Wales, who was taking a constitutional with his dear lady wife, the Princess Augusta, you know. He reproached me for not having visited him for some considerable time."

"You can't visit him, though, and remain on good terms with the king, can you?" said Edwin. "George even dismissed his own servants for lighting Frederick's lamps, didn't he? And Handel was ordered to refuse Frederick's invitation to a concert."

"Well, yes, but that was a long time ago. A lot of water has passed under the bridge since then."

"A lot of very dirty water," said Edwin. "There's no love lost between those two."

"Maybe not. But nevertheless the prince pointed out, quite rightly, that it was most remiss of me not to have introduced my wife to him. Like his brother, he takes a keen interest in gardening, and wishes me to see the progress he has made at Kew House. So I have accepted an invitation for Wednesday week. I'm sure I will be able to square it with the king. He and I are really the greatest of friends. He knows where my loyalties lie."

"Why didn't you tell me?" whispered Beth as the guests moved from the dining room to the drawing room, where card tables had been placed in readiness.

"Tell you what?" Sir Anthony said, carefully removing his wife's hand from his sleeve, and enfolding it in his own gloved one. "Please, my dear, you must remember, this velvet marks so when one touches it. I really regret having purchased this outfit. It was most remiss of the tailor not to warn me…"

"Stop trying to change the subject," she hissed. "The visit to Prince Frederick. Why?"

"I had no chance to. You spent all the time between me coming home and dinner either with Caroline, or droning endlessly on about the place settings and your worries that Richard was a murderous lunatic. Don't do it, by the way."

"Don't do what?"

"Warn him that if he touches her he'll be sorry, or tell him you think he's a gold-digger and that you intend to make his life hell."

"I wasn't going to!" she lied.

"Yes you were. I know you." He drew her carefully to one side, on the pretext of discussing the arrangements for the buffet. "If you do he'll take it as a challenge, and he'd be more likely to hurt her just to prove he can. Although to be honest, he seems quite fond of her, if not of the child she's carrying."

"So he hasn't fooled you completely then," Beth replied huffily, put out that he'd read her so well, and unwilling to admit that in spite of past experience his comment on Richard's attitude to Anne seemed to be well-founded.

"Not completely, no." He smiled and fussily rearranged a wayward strand of her hair, tucking it carefully back into place. Isabella and Clarissa, passing behind them, smiled at the intimate gesture and went to take their places at a table. He slid his arm around her waist and drew her towards him. She stiffened.

"Don't," she whispered.

"Why not?" he murmured into her ear. His breath was warm and soft against her neck. "You're my wife. We are allowed to embrace in public." He kissed the delicate earlobe and she shivered.

"You're being cruel," she whispered fiercely, maintaining her rigid posture and look of boredom with difficulty. "You know how hard it is for me. If it wasn't for that horrible cologne you wear I wouldn't be able to keep up the pretence that I find you distasteful. I'd leap on you and tear all those stupid clothes off you, and then you'd be sorry."

He smiled delightedly, and a mischievous look flickered in the blue depths of his eyes.

"I'd be sorry? You really think so?" he said quietly, his voice laced with seductive promise.

"Yes," she said more loudly, putting her palms flat on his chest as he attempted to draw her closer. She was aware of several pairs of amused or sentimental eyes observing them as they stood in the doorway. "Really, Anthony, you just warned me not to touch your outfit and now you're in danger of ruining it entirely!"

To stay in character he had no choice but to release her immediately and bemoan the spoiling of his coat, which was really too bad. What would the guests think? He would have words with his tailor the very next day. And more than words with her later, his eyes, warm and sensual, promised. She turned, intending to enter the card room.

"Wait," he said, taking her arm and drawing her to one side. "I haven't finished talking about your brother. I agree with you that he hasn't married Anne for her beauty, or because he's genuinely in love with her. I think his fondness for her is based on the fact that she's submissive, and has given him what he wants. If Anne tries to thwart him, she'll be sorry, I'm sure. But she won't. You've warned him that you have great influence with Cumberland, I've warned him that I have great influence with George, and your accomplice Caroline has warned him that she has great influence with his general's friend. He understood it. Leave it at that. Ah, Lord Thistlethwaite! So delighted you could make up our numbers! I am but a sorry player myself, and as the host of this little soiree…" He drifted off and Beth was left alone with all her senses tingling deliciously and the realisation that he had anticipated a barrage of questions about the prospective visit to Prince Frederick and had cleverly managed to deflect her from asking them.

She took his advice with regard to Richard and left it at that. Alex was right. To confront her brother head on would not be wise. The last thing she wanted to do was to provoke him into an act of violence. She looked across the room. Richard was sitting at a table, awaiting his deal of cards. Anne stood behind him, one small hand laid proudly on his shoulder. Even as Beth was watching them he beckoned to a servant, who hurried off and returned with another chair, so that Anne could sit down. Maybe she *was* worrying about nothing. She had changed a lot herself in the past two years. Maybe he had, too. Perhaps all he needed was someone to love him and indulge his every wish, as his mother had. If that was the case, Anne would be perfect for him.

* * *

"No," said Alex, observing Beth through the dressing-table mirror as she took the rose-pink velvet dress out of the wardrobe and laid it carefully on the bed. "Not that one."

"Which one, then?" she asked. "The green is dirty, and I can't wear the blue silk. If Prince Frederick's house is as poorly heated as St James's Palace, I'll freeze to death."

He put the hairbrush down and turned on the stool, his hair falling in soft burnished waves on his shoulders.

"The moss-green wool," he said. "Or the brown. Aye, the brown."

She stared at him in disbelief.

"I can't wear the brown to visit the Prince of Wales, even if he is a usurper!" she protested. "The skirts aren't full enough for a court hoop, for one thing. Wool is out of fashion, and it's too plain. It's more the sort of thing I'd wear to visit Caroline."

"It's warm and comfortable though, is it no'?" he said.

"Yes. Which is another reason why it's not suitable for a Court visit."

"The brown, then," he said, turning back to the mirror and deftly plaiting his hair.

"What are you wearing?" she asked suspiciously.

"The grey wool," he said, tying his hair and reaching across for the pot of white paint.

"The grey?!" exclaimed Beth. "What's going on? That's one of Abernathy's outfits. Sir Anthony never wears grey!"

"Today he does. Ye dinna ken the prince, Beth. He's no' like his father and brother."

"Maybe, but I still can't be introduced to him for the first time dressed like a tradesman's wife. Are you trying to insult him, so you won't be invited back?"

"Not at all," replied Alex, slathering white paint across his face. "I havena visited him for two years. He intends to punish me for it. I ken the man well. Trust me, the brown."

"Punish you?" said Beth, alarmed. "In what way?"

"I have an idea, but I'm no' telling ye," he replied mysteriously. "It'll be better that way. Ye'll act more naturally. Wear your riding gloves, too."

"What? Alex, you've got to tell me…"

"No, I havena," he interrupted. "But I will tell ye this. You'll enjoy yourself more than you're expecting to, I promise ye that."

Beth could not imagine how she could possibly enjoy herself visiting any member of the Elector's family. Particularly when she was dressed like a servant and had no idea what to expect. They drove along a tree-lined avenue, drawing up outside the house, and were greeted by a footman as they stepped down from the carriage.

"You see now my dear, why it is known as the White House," said Sir Anthony, taking her arm. She could. It was impressive, with its many sashed windows and newly refaced white stucco Palladian facade. The footman led them, not as Beth had expected, to a cavernous drawing-room or a gloomy salon, but along a path which ran round the side of the house to the gardens. He crossed the lawn, stopped at the top of some winding stone steps flanked by tall ruthlessly shaped evergreens and yelled at the top of his voice:

"Sir Anthony and Lady Elizabeth Peters!"

There was a short pause, and then a small, swarthy-skinned, somewhat grubby man dressed in brown woollen trousers and jacket came trotting up the steps. Presumably this was one of the under-gardeners, thought Beth, who would lead them on to a summer house of some sort in the gardens, where the prince and princess would meet them.

To her utter astonishment, her husband immediately made a deep and courteous bow.

"Your Royal Highness!" he declared.

For a moment Beth stared at the amused countenance of the man standing below them. He had a smear of dirt on his forehead and a hole in his stocking. Then a tug on her arm shook her from her stupor and she sank into a curtsey. When she rose, the prince had mounted the rest of the steps and was standing in front of them.

"Sir Anthony," he said, smiling. "I see you have come prepared after all. I cannot fool you."

"You would be disappointed if you could, Your Highness," the baronet replied, smiling.

"True, true. I see you have prepared your wife as well. *Enchanté*, Lady Elizabeth," said the prince, wiping his hand on his breeches before taking hers and raising it to his lips.

"I have only advised her as to the appropriate attire for the occasion, Your Highness," said Sir Anthony. "Nothing else."

"Ah," replied Prince Frederick, his eyes sparkling. "Well then, my lady," he reached past Sir Anthony and took her arm, tucking it familiarly under his and leading her down the steps, "we are in the process of transforming our little garden, and intend to plant a great many exotic plants, which even as I speak are making their way across the ocean to us. Of course there is a great deal of preparation to be done before they arrive."

They reached the bottom of the steps and the evergreen canopy finished, revealing the 'little garden', which stretched away into the distance. A series of rudimentary paths had been marked out with string and sand, and one had been half-laid with slabs of grey stone.

Beth looked around her with interest, and realised immediately why Alex had told her to wear the brown. Dotted about the garden were numerous courtiers of both sexes, richly clad in bright silks and velvets which were completely inappropriate for the tasks to which they had been assigned. Their faces wore expressions ranging from mildly disgruntled to positively outraged. All of them were armed with garden tools.

"As you see," continued the prince, leading Beth across the muddy, freshly dug soil as though he were showing her the paintings in his richly carpeted gallery, "the soil must be thoroughly turned and sieved for stones before being finely raked. It is a wearying task. But luckily I have a great many friends who have kindly agreed to assist me today, the weather being so clement."

The courtiers gathered around seemed neither to be particularly friendly or kindly disposed towards Frederick, but Beth did not think it politic to mention this.

"Now, I had thought to ask you to assist Lady Philippa in digging over this plot, but now I see how delicately built you are, I think it would be better if you start by raking the spot over there, which has just been cleared of stones." He gestured to a distant square of land. "Whereas you, Sir Anthony, with your magnificent physique, would be far more suited to laying the path, I think. The stones are quite heavy but that will pose no problem for you, I trust."

"Indeed not," smiled the baronet, who had followed his wife and prince. "Fresh air and exercise are always welcome. So invigorating! To be close to the soil is to commune with God himself!"

"You haven't changed at all, Anthony," said the prince warmly. "I will find you a rake, Lady Elizabeth, if you give me a moment."

He wandered off.

"I presume you've used a rake before, my dear?" asked Sir Anthony.

"Yes. I used to help Graeme sometimes when he was preparing the vegetable beds. And I had my own little plot when I was a child. You knew this was going to happen. Why didn't you warn me?" She looked up at him.

"I suspected something of the sort, when Frederick told me he wanted me to see the garden. But I knew he would prefer it if it came as a total surprise to you. Are you very unhappy at the thought of a little gardening?"

"No, not at all," she replied. "I'd much rather do that than make small talk with a lot of people I have nothing in common with. It's the last thing I expected, that's all."

"It was the last thing most of the others expected as well," her husband replied. "Frederick loves this sort of joke. It sorts out the sycophants from the friends, and brings those with too high an opinion of themselves down a peg or two."

"Why don't they just leave?" she asked, eyeing a very pretty woman about twenty yards away, who had obviously never used a spade before in her life and was struggling to push it into the soil. The hem of her pale yellow gown was covered in mud. She looked across at them and scowled. Sir Anthony smiled.

"You must place your foot on the spade and put your weight on it, my dear Helen!" he called, demonstrating by lifting his foot into the air and driving an imaginary spade into the soil. "Horrible woman," he continued under his breath. "Malicious. You'll see her in action later, no doubt. They don't leave, because one day Frederick will be King, and it's worth no end of humiliation to them to have the favour of the future monarch."

"But surely if Frederick knows they're sycophants he won't favour them anyway when he comes to the throne?" she said.

"*If* he comes to the throne," Sir Anthony said in a very low voice so as not to be overheard. They both watched as the man whose father they hoped to drive from the country came striding back towards them.

"Here you are," he said, handing Beth a rake. "Now Anthony, if you will just follow me. The stones must be laid out in a particular way…"

It took Beth a few minutes to establish a comfortable rhythm, after which she worked automatically, pulling the rake through the fine soil and making her way slowly and methodically along the plot. She let her mind wander, remembering the pleasant childhood afternoons when she had worked with Graeme, watching carefully as he showed her what to do, then copying him with the small rake he had made especially for her. Sometimes she would make wavy patterns in the soil, pretending it was the sea. And once, when she was very small, she had used a twig to demonstrate proudly that she could write her own name in the freshly-raked earth. She breathed in deeply, inhaling the loamy scent of the rich soil and felt a wave of nostalgia wash over her as she remembered that smell clinging to Graeme's well-worn leather waistcoat, along with the fresh green scents of the plants he grew. She missed his dour affection and wondered how his rheumatism was.

"So you're Sir Anthony's wife, then," a voice came from directly behind her, startling her out of her reverie. She turned to see a tall large-boned young woman standing directly behind her, leaning on the handle of a spade.

"Sorry. Didn't mean to frighten you. You were miles away. Just wanted to say hello. Heard of you but not seen you before."

"Hello," said Beth. "It's Lady Philippa, isn't it? I was supposed to be helping you with some digging."

"That's right," affirmed the young woman, taking Beth's proffered hand and shaking it vigorously. "Lucky bugger. Wish I was tiny. Raking's much easier."

"I'll swap with you if you like," Beth offered. "I'm stronger than I look."

"God, no! Fred'd never stand for that. Works it out carefully. Those with the really dirty jobs he can't stand at all."

Beth looked around.

"He must really hate that poor fat man over there, then," she said, pointing to an elderly, rather portly red-faced man in heavily soiled burgundy brocade, who was reluctantly spreading horse manure across one patch of soil.

"Exactly. Can't stand him. Damn good judge of character, Fred. Toadying old fool, Papa."

Although her staccato way of speaking was reminiscent of Edward, nothing else was. Beth liked Lady Philippa immediately. Even so, she was aware that she'd put her foot well and truly in her mouth.

"Oh God," she said. "I'm sorry, I didn't realise he was your father."

"That's all right," grinned Lady Philippa, her hazel eyes sparkling. "Agree with Fred. Can't stand him either. Can't wait to be married and away from the old fool. Serve him right. Just wish I'd known, that's all. You obviously did." She looked down ruefully at her aqua-coloured velvet dress and delicate slippers, which had presumably also been aqua-coloured at one time, but were now dark brown.

"No, not really," said Beth. "Anthony did. He told me what to wear, that's all. I had no idea what to expect. This is the first time I've visited the Prince of Wales."

"Sensible chap, Sir Anthony," remarked Philippa to Beth's surprise, who had heard Anthony called many things, but never sensible. "Told you enough, but not enough to spoil Fred's fun, eh? Clever. Wish *I'd* known. Bloody idiot told me we were coming to see a play. Papa, that is, not Fred. Should have known you don't see plays at two o'clock. Own fault. Enjoying yourself?"

It took Beth a moment to realise she'd been asked a question. It took some getting used to, this clipped manner of speaking.

"Yes," she admitted. "I am actually. I've always enjoyed the outdoors."

"Hmm. Thought so. Good hand with a rake. Ride? Hunt?"

"No," said Beth. "That is, I ride, yes, but I've never enjoyed hunting much. When are you getting married?"

"Summer. June. Have to watch bloody Helen then. Bitch. Try to take him off me. Watch out tonight."

"I'm sorry?" said Beth, who had not quite followed this.

"Watch out. You. Helen. Very pretty, yellow dress. Tries it with all the married men. Sir Anthony. Fine chap. Watch her. With him."

"Ah. I see," said Beth. "Thank you. I will."

Lady Philippa wandered off, and Beth watched her go, bemused. There was something vaguely familiar about her, and yet she had never met the woman before, she was sure of that. She would not have forgotten meeting someone like her. She looked across the garden to where her husband was, amazingly, managing to move stones quickly and efficiently whilst maintaining a foppish, somewhat limp-wristed attitude. He was quite remarkable. *He would make a good living on the stage,* she thought. He could certainly give Garrick a run for his money. He looked up, saw her, and waved merrily. She waved back, smiled, and returned to her work.

At five o'clock Prince Frederick finally took pity on his guests, or perhaps it was simply that the light was failing. He called a halt to the day's work, telling his grubby workforce that they had half an hour to freshen up before dinner was served.

"It had better be good, after all that," grumbled one of the guests as they made their way up the stairs behind the footman, who showed each guest to a different room, where hot water, soap and towels had been provided.

"Well, this is very nice, at least," said Beth gratefully, sitting on a well-padded chair and looking round the green and white room. The furniture was all made of walnut, and consisted of an old-fashioned carved four poster bed, a chest, dressing table, and the chair Beth was sitting on. An expensive Turkish carpet covered the floor and she sank her toes into it, wriggling them blissfully. "I thought we'd all have to wash under the pump in the yard. That's what I used to do when I'd been gardening with Graeme."

"Don't mention that to Fred, for God's sake," said Alex, taking off his shoes and throwing himself on the bed. He patted the space next to him and she went to lie beside him, her head on his shoulder. "Are you enjoying yourself, then?"

"Yes, immensely. It was very amusing, watching people try to use tools they've never seen before, avoid getting their ridiculous clothes muddy and still remember to smile when the prince walked past. Although I feel a bit guilty getting pleasure out of watching the discomfort of others."

"Don't. They all deserve it. Or nearly all, anyway. They spend most of their time with their noses in the air, thinking everyone else beneath contempt. They treat their servants appallingly. So

Fred does the same to them, because he can. They won't learn from it, though."

"Lady Philippa seemed pretty down to earth," Beth commented.

"Ah, yes. Saw you talking. Bloody fine woman. Like her," Alex said. Beth punched him playfully.

"Don't you start," she said. "It was quite hard to understand her at first. She fillets every sentence back to the bone. She doesn't seem to like her father much. Or Helen. She warned me to keep an eye on her with you."

"Really? Will you be jealous if she tries to seduce me?" he asked, smiling.

"No," said Beth. "I'll be angry, with her if she tries it, and with you if you let her."

"Oh dear. I was hoping to flirt with her a little, to make you jealous. I thought it might make you realise what a desirable man you married."

"I know exactly which man I married, thank you," said Beth. "And it wasn't Angus. So if you start behaving like him, I'll castrate you."

"But you're not jealous."

"No. Tell me about Philippa. She looks vaguely familiar."

"That's because she's Caroline's cousin. They've got the same eyes."

"Is she?" said Beth, surprised, sitting up.

"Yes. Her father is Caroline's great-uncle Francis. She mentioned him the other night, remember?"

"The friend of General Hawley," Beth said. "She doesn't seem like the sort of woman who'd disapprove of Caroline marrying Edwin."

"She didn't. But her father did so she's not allowed to mention Caroline, or visit her. They still see each other occasionally, though. Philippa spends a lot of time at Harriet's."

"Is she Caroline's mad old aunt?"

"That's the one. She's not so much mad though, as deeply eccentric. And forgetful, now she's old. But she virtually brought Philippa up after her mother died. They speak the same way, very staccato. I haven't seen Philippa for ages, but I suppose Caroline's mentioned me."

"Yes. She knew you were married. And she said you were sensible."

"Did she? Well, I suppose if I'm sensible I'd better try to brush this mud off before we go down to dinner. I want to look my best, for Helen."

Dinner was not at all what Beth had expected, although she was fast learning not to expect anything normal. Obviously from the incredulous looks on the faces of the guests, it was not what they had expected, either. There was no damask tablecloth, polished silver, crystal glasses or delicate porcelain. Instead on entering the dining room the guests were greeted with a large scrubbed oak table, in the centre of which were a quantity of large loaves of bread and several platters of cheese and cold meats. Jugs of red wine were dotted about the table.

"Help yourselves!" said Prince Frederick as they entered and took their seats uncertainly. "There's plenty for everyone! It is so pleasant to eat good simple but hearty fare after a day of hard work, isn't it?" He was still dressed in his working clothes, and Beth watched him as he merrily tore open a loaf of bread with his fingers before spreading it liberally with butter. He was a small man with the neat physique of his father. But there the similarity ended. If she hadn't known better, Beth would have thought him to be of near Eastern origin, with his thick lips, heavy nose and sallow complexion. How this man could be the brother of the podgy, fair-skinned Cumberland, she had no idea. He didn't look in the least Germanic like the rest of his family did.

He looked up and smiled at her.

"You've stayed remarkably clean, Lady Elizabeth," he remarked. "And you've used a rake before, I noticed."

"Yes, Your Highness," she replied, reaching over for a piece of bread. "I don't think I'm any cleaner than anyone else, though. It's just that this dress doesn't show the dirt."

"It's delightful to have Anthony back in the fold, as it were. I suppose you know that visiting me will probably put you out of favour with my father. Does that bother you?"

The question was casual, but she was not fooled. What had Alex said? That George hated his son. But he had not said that the reverse was true.

"I am enjoying myself a great deal today, Your Highness. I will pray for a reconciliation between you and your father so that I may enjoy the hospitality of your whole family."

He eyed her shrewdly.

"Hmm," he said after a moment. "What do you think of the wine?"

She said that she thought the wine was strong and rough, but well suited to the hearty peasant fare, and then his attention moved on to the next guest, and she had time to look around. She had never met any of the guests before, although she had seen some of them at a distance, at the theatre or pleasure gardens. It could not be more clear that the king and his eldest son moved in completely different circles, and she wondered what had happened to make George hate his heir so utterly. Now was not the time to ask, though, even though the prince had just excused himself and left the room.

There was a general sigh of relief.

"Next time I'm invited for dinner I shall borrow my gardener's clothes," said one young man in grubby blue velvet.

"If you do that, Percy, you'll find yourself in the middle of an high class ball, with people expecting you to open doors for them and take their coats. You know how unpredictable Fred is. He likes his little joke," replied an elegant man next to him. He took a sip of the wine and shuddered delicately. "I don't know how anyone can drink this stuff, I really don't. It's disgusting."

"Oh, I don't know, I am becoming quite accustomed to it," trilled Sir Anthony. "I feel quite the country rustic!"

"I see being married has sobered you somewhat, Anthony," said Percy, eyeing the baronet's sombre clothes.

Sir Anthony cast a rueful glance over his attire.

"I know, utterly dreadful, is it not? But no, my exquisite taste has not been at all dulled by marriage. Surely you only have to look at the woman I chose for my bride to see that!"

Everyone looked at the woman he chose for his bride, and Beth tried not to blush.

"Beautiful," observed the elegant young man, lifting his spectacles to his snub nose and eyeing her lasciviously with long-lashed brown eyes. "Quite a morsel. What on earth did you see in Anthony, my love? You could have had your pick of society, a beauty like you."

By that he obviously meant 'you could have had me,' and she was suddenly reminded of Daniel. These were the sort of people he would associate with.

Beth looked him up and down slowly, then smiled.

"True. But looks, money and an empty head are not enough to satisfy me, my lord. I require a man who possesses a modicum of intelligence and who knows how to behave courteously towards a lady as well."

The young lord flushed.

"She's got the measure of you, David," laughed Percy. "No hope of a conquest there. Speaking of ladies though, where's Helen? There'll be nothing left for her if she doesn't hurry up."

There was a general titter at the linking of the word 'lady' with Helen.

"She's brought a change of dress," said Caroline's great-uncle. "I saw one of the footmen taking a bag up to her room."

"Trust her to think of that, bloody cow," mumbled Philippa through a mouthful of bread. "Play afterwards though. Macbeth. Damn good. Lots of blood."

"There will be lots of blood if it consists of a recitation by the children, like it was last time," threatened her father. "I'll shoot the little buggers rather than endure that again. Awful, it was. And it went on for hours."

"They're not here," said Philippa more distinctly, having emptied her mouth. She reached for the wine. "Off with Augusta to Chelsea. Shame. Nice children."

"Nice children?" said Percy. "Stupid, more like. Little George can't even…"

He stopped speaking hurriedly as the door opened, expecting it to be the prince returning. Instead a lovely young woman entered the room in a flurry of scarlet satin. Rubies glowed at her throat and ears, and her glossy black hair was beautifully arranged in a becoming style. She smiled at the company, her blue eyes travelling round the room until they alighted on Sir Anthony. The smile grew wider.

There were four other women in the room, and all of them immediately felt dowdy. Beth surreptitiously tucked a stray lock of hair behind her ear.

"Ah, Helen," said David. "We were wondering where you were. You're just in time to enjoy the last of the repast our prince has kindly thought to provide." He waved his slender hand at a nearby empty chair. She smiled at him, ignored the chair, and went to sit next to Sir Anthony instead.

"Like Shakespeare?" barked Philippa.

"Yes," said Beth, one eye on the scarlet vision, who had laid her small white hand on the baronet's arm. "Although I haven't seen Macbeth. Isn't it unlucky to call it that, though?" Sir Anthony leaned across the table, carefully choosing a slice of meat, which he placed on a plate in front of Helen. He addressed a remark to Percy, and then Helen was commanding his attention again, leaning close to his ear to murmur something obviously confidential to him. She smiled seductively. Beth tried to ignore her and concentrate on Philippa.

"Only if you're an actor, I think," she was saying. "Superstitious lot. Call it the Scottish play. Ridiculous."

Sir Anthony bent his head and whispered something back. His lips were almost brushing Helen's ear, he was so close to her. Whatever he said was electrifying. The smile froze on the woman's face, then she stood abruptly and moved away, just as Prince Frederick re-entered the room.

"Ah, I see you're all here now," he said jovially. "If you've all eaten enough, we can make our way to the theatre. The players are nearly ready."

* * *

"Och, ye didna really say that, did ye, Alex?" said Maggie, aghast. "Puir wee lassie."

"Poor wee lassie?" replied Beth. "You didn't see her. She didn't even make preliminary conversation. She just went straight in for the kill. I'd have slapped her if she'd carried on."

"I thought you werena jealous," remarked Alex, who was devouring a large bowl of broth. "Christ, I'm starving. I hardly got tae eat anything before we were dragged off to the play. Verra good though, excellent players."

"I wasn't jealous, I was angry," insisted Beth. "I knew you weren't interested in Helen. But when a woman makes a play for your husband in front of you, it's really insulting. She must have been hit before if she always behaves like this."

"Probably. But I doubt she's been tellt that her breath smelt so bad it was putting her victim off his food. I feel sorry for her too," said Duncan.

"I said it verra tactfully," said Alex, mopping his bowl with a hunk of bread.

"No you didn't," said Beth. "There's no tactful way to say that, not even for Sir Anthony. Her face just froze. It was a picture."

"Talking of freezing, yon wee Sarah's a cold one, is she no'?" Angus commented. "I was passing by her shop on my way home frae the market today and dropped in tae say hello. I've never had such a frosty reception. I had icicles growing on me when I left."

"Her shop isna on the way back frae the market," said Duncan. "What were ye up to?"

"Nothing!" protested Angus. "She's a bonny woman. I just wanted to get to know her a wee bit better, that's all. Mr Gough has just bought an ostrich for his menagerie, and it's said tae be a fearsome strange beastie. I asked her if she'd like to walk out on Saturday and see it wi' me. I was verra polite. And she nearly froze the balls… she was verra cool."

"You keep away from her," warned Duncan. "She's a respectable wee lassie. No' for the likes of you."

"Christ, I wasna trying tae ravish her!" said Angus hotly.

"Were ye no'?" said Alex. "That'll be a first, then."

"I had only the purest intentions," said Angus defensively. "Though if I'd known ye were sweet on her, Duncan, I wouldna have gone anywhere near her."

"I'm no' sweet on her," replied Duncan coldly.

"Ye go and see her often enough, and I've no' seen ye coming back frozen solid," countered Angus. "She likes you well enough, it seems."

"Do you? I didn't know you were seeing Sarah," said Beth in surprise.

"I'm no' 'seeing her'," said Duncan. "I've called round a few times, that's all. She likes me because she kens I'm no' interested in seducing her. She doesna feel threatened by me."

"She's had some bad experiences with men," said Beth hesitantly, not wanting to reveal too much.

"Aye, I ken," replied Duncan, which surprised Beth even

more. "You keep away from her, Angus. She's no' setting ye a challenge. She isna interested."

"Aye, I'm sure that's true. Dinna fash yourself, I'll no' come between you and your wee sweetheart," his brother teased. "Dinna forget tae wear one o' they sheepskin condom thingies, though, when ye…"

Duncan half rose from his chair.

"Prince Frederick's very different from the rest of the family, isn't he?" put in Beth hurriedly. "Why does the Elector hate him so much?"

"It's a family tradition," said Alex. "George's father hated him as well. I dinna ken, rightly. I'm no' sure George does, either. Frederick was left over in Germany when the rest of the family moved to England. He didna see his parents from when he was seven until he came over to join them fourteen years later. That wouldna help. But he was popular wi' the public, too. He's got a nice easy way wi' him."

Duncan sat down again. Angus, grinning, wisely went to sit on the other side of the room.

"Yes, I saw that," said Beth.

"Aye, well. His da should have given him some responsibilities. He is the heir to the throne, after all, until we get the Stuarts back. But he wouldna, because he didna like the fact that Frederick was more popular than him. So he treated him like dirt and made him into an enemy. I'll gie Frederick his due though, he willna have a word said against his father, even though he's been treated verra badly."

"I enjoyed the visit today. It was a lot better than visiting St. James's."

"Aye, it sounded like it," said Iain.

"I'm not so keen on some of his friends, though," Beth added, thinking of David, and Helen.

"Aye, well, Fred was something of a rake before he got married, and he still likes to drink and gamble at times. And to play jokes on people, as ye saw today. He attracts aristocratic dandies like David and Percy, and people who dinna like George."

"Why don't you see more of him?" asked Beth. "He seems more Sir Anthony's type than the Elector is."

"Because I dinna want to alienate myself from Geordie. I'm

friendly wi' the Hanovers to collect information, that's all. Frederick isna privy to the latest developments. I like him, but that's no' important. I canna be seen to be a regular visitor there. But I canna refuse him all the time, either."

"And also it's harder to spy on people you like," said Beth.

"Aye, that too," admitted Alex. "We'll wait till we're personally invited before we go again. It's better that way."

Beth agreed. She had liked Prince Frederick and Lady Philippa. But if she never saw the others again, she would not be sorry. In general though, life was reasonably pleasant for Beth at the moment. She no longer had to visit St. James's and endure the attentions of Cumberland, Anne and Richard seemed really happy together, Maggie and Iain were slowly recovering from the loss of the baby, and Duncan seemed to have found a friend in Sarah. Things could not be better, unless the Stuarts were on the throne and the MacGregors back in Scotland, where they belonged. But there seemed to be no sign of that happening in the foreseeable future. In the meantime she was content with what she had.

CHAPTER FIFTEEN

March 1745

Captain Cunningham and his wife of just over a month were whiling away a pleasant hour after dinner in their newly redecorated blue and cream salon. Blue was not what Anne would personally have chosen for the decor; she thought it a somewhat cold colour. But with the lamps lit and a roaring fire blazing in the hearth it looked cosy enough, and she would have agreed to Richard painting the room black if that was what he wanted.

She was taking great pleasure in indulging her new husband's every whim without a murmur. He was young, fit and healthy; he could eat, drink and do anything he wished without his wife feeling the need to point out that cream would possibly aggravate his gout, and perhaps just one small glass of port would be wise, rather than a whole bottle? It was wonderful to be, for the first time in her life, cared for rather than being a carer. They had been to several functions since they had been married, and at all of them he had shown her the utmost consideration. If he seemed somewhat more indifferent when they were alone together, well, that was only to be expected; war was looming, and he had important things to think about. Anne, accustomed to taking last place in people's minds, was honoured to take only second place in Richard's.

She carefully cut the thread on the waistcoat she was embroidering for him, then laid it down on the table at her side. She looked across to where he was seated on the other side of the fire, one muscular leather-booted leg crossed over the other, deeply engrossed in the latest copy of *The Gentleman's Magazine*.

He looked very fine in his new uniform with its gleaming brass buttons and silver lace trim denoting his new rank.

"What are you reading?" she asked, not because she was really interested in hearing the latest episode of the political satire set in the senate of Lilliput, but just for the joy of hearing his rich mellow voice. She had never known what it was to be truly in love before, and it was marvellous.

"I'm reading an article as to what measures Britons ought to pursue in foreign wars," the object of her devotion replied. "But there is not much in here that would be of interest to you. The poetry perhaps."

"Oh, is there an interesting poem? Do read one to me, Richard!"

"Not now, Anne," he replied. "I really want to finish this before I go to the club."

She fell silent, and returned to her embroidery. She needed a new colour for the wings of the butterflies that were fluttering around the buttonholes. She heaved herself out of her chair, her body heavy and awkward in her last months of pregnancy, and moved across to the table where she kept her box of embroidery silks, opening it and surveying the range of colours inside. Brown, they had to be a shade of brown. He wouldn't wear it if it was garish. She lifted out a beige shade, considered it for a moment, then put it back. It was too light, and would not make a strong enough contrast with the cream of the silk.

Richard finished his article and turned the page.

"I have been thinking, my love, about what name we should give the baby when it is born," she ventured.

He did not reply, but he did not ask her to be quiet either, which she took as permission to continue.

"I thought to call it Arabella if it is a girl. If you have no objection, of course."

She took out a skein of chocolate brown silk.

"Yes, if you want," her husband replied indifferently, his nose still buried in the periodical.

"It is such a wonderful coincidence that Arabella was the name of your mother as well as of Stanley's," she said happily. "And if it is a boy, I thought perhaps…"

"It will not be a boy," he interrupted. He closed the paper and placed it on the small table next to him.

"Well, I am sure I am hoping for a girl, if that is what you would prefer, Richard. But really, we cannot be certain it will be." She held the silk up to the lamp.

"Are you arguing with me, Anne?" he asked quietly.

"No of course not, darling," she said. The silk was a warm, rich shade of brown, and would match his eyes perfectly. She smiled. "But it is not for us, but for God to choose the gender of a child. I thought it best to be prepared in case…"

She was lying on the floor, one arm instinctively curled around her swollen stomach, surrounded by a rainbow array of silks and with no clear recollection of how she had got there. She looked up dizzily, trying to focus on the splash of red and black looming above her. Then it bent down and became Richard. He put his hands under her arms and lifted her to her feet. She clung to him while he half-carried her back to her chair and settled her into it.

"Really, Anne," he said. "You see what happens when you overexcite yourself? You must be more careful now you are so close to your time. Arabella is an excellent name for the child. You need think no further than that. I will ask the maid to bring you a hot drink." He took a cushion and placed it carefully behind her. "Now," he said, "I really must go to the club. It will not do to keep the colonel waiting, when I am hoping to apply for membership tonight. I may be late home, so don't wait up for me."

He took his hat, settled it onto his head and left the room, closing the door quietly behind him. Anne sat back and waited until the white sparkles dancing across her vision diminished. The maid did not appear.

After a time, when she was sure the dizziness had passed, she stood and walked shakily over to the looking glass. The left side of her face was on fire, and as she examined herself in the mirror she could clearly see a dark bruise forming along her cheekbone. She gazed intently at her reflection, as though this other Anne could provide an explanation as to what had happened. She could not remember having gone dizzy before she fell. She had certainly suffered from giddy spells and nausea early in her pregnancy, but had had no problems at all since the fourth month. She stood there, trying to piece together what had happened.

She had been speaking to Richard about the baby, and then something had hit her in the face, hard, and she had fallen. No, that could not be right. She looked round at the silks scattered across the floor. She had gone dizzy, and had caught the table with her face as she fell, knocking the box to the floor. That would explain the bruise. And Richard, concerned, had leapt up immediately to assist her. Yes, that was the only logical explanation. He was right. She would have to be more careful.

She knelt down with difficulty and began to gather the embroidery silks together, replacing them in the box, pausing only to wipe her tears away from time to time. Then she went to bed and lay awake for a long time.

Richard did not return home until the following morning.

* * *

"Your sister-in-law was in here yesterday," Sarah said indistinctly, her mouth full of hairpins. She bent over Caroline, expertly winding a strand of shining brown hair into a curl and pinning it in place on top of her head.

"Anne?" asked Beth, as though she had a whole tribe of sisters-in-law rather than just the one.

"Mmm," came the reply. She pushed a few more pins into Caroline's hair and then stood back to admire the effect. "There," she said. "It's nice, but it would look a lot less severe if you let me pull a few strands out and curl them to frame your face."

"No," said Caroline. "I want to look severe tonight. It won't help me to be taken seriously by a houseful of politicians if I look like the romantic heroine from one of those silly novels everyone's reading these days."

"I'm not reading them, my dear, I do assure you," said Sir Anthony from the corner of the shop, where he was poking about in various jars and boxes.

"You have done though," Caroline pointed out. "I distinctly remember you discussing *Pamela* once."

Sir Anthony looked up and smiled.

"Ah, yes," he replied. "But that was a long time ago and I did have an ulterior motive for doing so. I wished to engage the affections of my wife. I succeeded. I have not read a romantic novel since."

"You fraud," said Caroline good-naturedly. "Marrying a woman under false pretences. You should be ashamed of yourself."

"I am, deeply," he said with complete insincerity, and went back to his perusal of Sarah's goods.

"How is Anne?" said Beth to Sarah.

"She said she was fine," Sarah replied. Sir Anthony looked up for a moment, then went back to his rummaging.

"I really must get round to visiting her," said Beth. "I've been hoping to see her at one of Isabella's evenings, but I suppose I'll have to bite the bullet and go and see her at home."

"I thought you liked her," said Caroline.

"I do. It's the thought of having to be civil to Richard without his company being diluted by lots of others that puts me off."

"She hasn't been out for three weeks," Sarah commented, casually. "She's been having dizzy spells, or so she says, and has decided to stay at home as much as possible until after the baby's born."

"Has she seen a physician?" asked Caroline. "She needs to take extra care of herself now. The baby could come at any time."

"I don't think she's seen one, no," said Sarah, gazing intently at Beth. "She was going to some regimental dinner of Richard's last night. It seems all the wives were expected to go and Richard was most adamant she attend. She came in to ask for something subtle to cover up a bruise over her eye."

"Did she?" said Beth, a strange tone in her voice.

"Yes. She said she'd had a dizzy spell and caught her face on the corner of the mantelpiece as she fell."

"Oh! How divine!" cried Sir Anthony rapturously from the corner.

"I managed to restyle her hair so that it covered the bruise," Sarah continued without paying the baronet the least attention. "With luck no one would have noticed it, especially in candlelight." She paused. "And I showed her how to apply rouge to cover up the other bruise on her cheek. It was a lot older than the one over her eye, because it had faded to yellow." The two women exchanged a private look of understanding, and then Sarah started to tidy away her pins and combs.

"Where on earth did you get these, my dear? I simply must

have some!" Sir Anthony called insistently. The three women looked round to where he was sitting, a small box open on his knee. He held up his hand; in the centre of his pale blue doveskin palm was a tiny black silk carriage, pulled by a minute horse. "Isn't it exquisite?" he said breathlessly.

"They're very expensive," said Sarah, abandoning all her expert sales techniques in the presence of friends. "They're all cut out by hand."

"By some poor half-starved woman going blind in a cellar and earning a penny for ten, I expect," said Beth, exasperated. "Anthony, did you hear…"

"Well, yes, maybe, but nevertheless they are incomparable! Look at that!" He held up a tiny cat, complete with whiskers. "What do you think of that?"

"I think that you'll look even more ridiculous than you already do if you're seen in public with a cat stuck on your face," his wife replied, looking at the silk patch with disgust.

"*Au contraire*, my love. I will be the envy of society." He rummaged through the pot. "I will have one of each, Sarah," he said, closing the box and getting to his feet.

"There are twenty different patches, Sir Anthony," warned Sarah. "It will cost…"

"Oh, what matters cost, where fashion is concerned?" he cried.

"Anthony," Beth said. "Did you hear what Sarah just said about Anne?"

"Of course I did, my dear, I am not deaf," he replied pleasantly, taking Caroline's cloak and helping her on with it. "Anne is having dizzy spells. Did you suffer from such an affliction with Freddie, my dear?"

"No," said Caroline. "But of course it is possible, I suppose."

"Quite. Well, we must go. You do not wish to be late for the Cabinet, Caroline. We will take you home immediately."

"She is *not* having dizzy spells!" exploded Beth the moment they were in the carriage.

"How can you be sure?" Sir Anthony replied calmly, looking out of the window.

"Oh come on, Anthony!" she cried. "Caroline, you said yourself you didn't have them with Freddie! It's Richard, not the corner of the fireplace that's hit her."

"I didn't have them," Caroline agreed doubtfully. "But every woman's different, Beth. She could be having dizzy spells, but if she is, she should see a physician."

"Exactly!" said Beth triumphantly. "And if she hasn't, it's because he'll know that the only thing wrong with her is the swine she's married to!"

"Perhaps we should go and see her," said Caroline, "and try to persuade her to see a doctor."

"Yes, we should. And that's exactly what I intend to do, the moment we've dropped you off."

"No," said Sir Anthony, his eyes warning her not to pursue this while they had company. He glanced out of the window again.

"What do you mean, 'no'?" cried Beth. "I can't just do nothing! I'm going to go round to the house and talk to her, that's all. Find out what really happened."

"And what will you do if Richard's there?" he said. "You said yourself you don't want to be in his undiluted company."

"I don't," she replied hotly. "But that's not because I'm afraid of him. If he's there I'll tell him exactly what I think of him and what I'll do if he hits her again."

"Very well," he said, his eyes angry, his tone calm. "Let us assume for the moment that Richard is, as you assert, beating Anne. Do you think it will help matters for you to enrage him by ordering him how to behave towards his own wife?"

Beth glared at him.

"I'll be tactful," she said through gritted teeth.

"No, you won't," he said. "You are incapable of tact where your brother is concerned, Beth. You're not going."

Caroline shifted uncomfortably in her seat, clearly wishing she was somewhere else.

"You are making Caroline feel awkward," Sir Anthony said warningly.

"I'm sorry, Caroline," Beth replied, before turning straight back to her husband. "But I am going to Anne's, now. If Richard is there, I'll leave, immediately. Does that satisfy you?"

"No, it doesn't," he replied coldly. "You're not going, Beth, and that's final. Ah! Slow the coach a moment, Murdo. I spy an old friend."

The coach slowed and Sir Anthony leaned out of the window.

"William!" he cried. "You are just the man I was hoping to see. May I beg the pleasure of a word or two?"

The coach came to a halt, and the horseman bent in the saddle to smile at the two ladies inside.

"Lady Elizabeth, Mrs Harlow, delighted to see you," the Earl of Highbury said politely, paying no attention to Beth's furious expression. "Of course, Anthony. What do you wish to discuss?"

"A private matter. If it is convenient, I will descend for a few moments."

He got down from the coach and the two men moved out of earshot.

"To hell with him," said Beth. "I'm going to find out what's going on."

"He has a point though, Beth," said Caroline hesitantly, somewhat stunned by Sir Anthony's uncharacteristic authoritarian attitude.

"What! You agree that we should do nothing?"

"No," Caroline replied hurriedly. "But I don't think you should go round there without thinking it through first. I know you mean well, but Anthony's right. You're more likely to make things worse if you go dashing to rescue Anne."

Before Beth could reply, Sir Anthony leaned in through the coach window.

"William has kindly invited me to dine with him, my dear," he said. "And then I think I may accompany him to his club this evening. There will be several important people there." He smiled winningly.

"How can you think of…?" Beth began.

"Beth," he said firmly, casting Caroline an apologetic glance. "I will deal with this situation. William's club is frequented by many military men. You will go home. I will see you later. Murdo," he continued, pulling his head out of the carriage, and looking up at Duncan, who was driving, "you will take Mrs Harlow to her house, and then will take Lady Elizabeth home, where she will remain until I return this evening. Is that clear?"

It was clear. Not daring to make a scene, and knowing it would be futile and undignified anyway if she did, Beth went home, where she alternated between worrying about what Richard might

315

be doing at that very moment to Anne and fuming that she had married a man whose servants were also his family and his clansmen, and that they could not be bribed or persuaded to disobey orders under any circumstances.

* * *

The members of Highbury's club met every Wednesday in a coffee house near St. Paul's. A table was provided, with apple pasties, wine and punch, and a large fire burned in the grate. The floor, though bare wood, was clean, and sufficient candles burned to drive the shadows to the corners of the room. The walls, originally painted cream, had now darkened to a light brown due to years of tobacco smoke.

It was an eclectic club, and the conversation was therefore more varied than in clubs whose members held a profession or a pursuit in common. Nevertheless, as Sir Anthony had informed Beth, a considerable number of military men frequented its environs, and as he entered he was gratified to see not only the newly promoted Captain Cunningham, but also his colonel, ensconced by the fire with a number of other uniformed men. The earl had told him that Colonel Hutchinson frequented the club regularly when not on campaign, and as Richard had been admitted as a member only a few weeks ago, there had been every likelihood he would be present too.

Ignoring the calls from the huddled group in the corner to come and join in the discussion on Aristotle, the earl and baronet made their way over to the fire on the pretence of warming themselves.

"Uncommonly cold night tonight," said Highbury, standing with his back to the fire and lifting the skirts of his coat to enable the warmth to penetrate. "Blowing a gale. I nearly lost my wig twice between the carriage and the club."

Sir Anthony pulled up a chair and sat down.

"Captain Cunningham," he said. "Delighted to see you here. You managed to tear yourself away from the loving arms of your bride, I see."

"Shilling in the pot, Anthony," barked a large man opposite before Richard could answer. "No titles allowed here, you know the rule. And he's your brother-in-law, for God's sake!"

"Ah, yes, I'm sorry. I'd quite forgotten," said Sir Anthony ruefully, delving into his pocket.

"Does captain count as a title, John?" asked the earl.

"Of course it does!" replied the large man. "Mister counts as a title here. No excuses. Everyone is equal."

"I'm surprised to see you here tonight, Richard," continued the baronet, flicking a silver coin with perfect accuracy into a pot on the mantelpiece. "I thought you'd be spending as much time as possible with your dear wife, as you will soon be sundered from each other."

"I told Anthony your orders are through," interpreted Highbury.

"Ah," said Richard. "Yes. At last. We have to be in Gravesend and ready to embark by the thirty-first."

"Oh my dear boy!" cried Sir Anthony. "That is a mere ten days away! You must be devastated."

"What rot you talk, Anthony," said the colonel amiably. "He's ecstatic. We all are. We can't wait to get to Flanders and teach those damn Frenchies a lesson. With luck we'll have the whole war over and done with by autumn."

"We were just discussing the forfeiture law for those accused of treason, and whether it's unfair or not. There was an article in the *Magazine* about it a few weeks ago," said John, a captain in the horseguards.

"Yes, I read that," put in Richard. "It said that the law was too harsh, as it punished innocent women and children. Ridiculous, in my view. A man will think twice before committing treason if he knows his whole estate will be forfeit if he does."

"Don't you think that hanging, drawing and quartering is a sufficient deterrent?" said Sir Anthony, shuddering delicately.

"Not for some, no," put in another man. "Some of them consider it an honour to die for their misguided principles. But if they know their wives and children will be reduced to beggary as a result, they will think again. Wouldn't you think seriously before you risked Daniel's inheritance, William?"

"Daniel's inheritance would be safer with the king than with him, though," laughed John. "He'd gamble the whole lot away in a week."

The earl shot the horseguard captain a look that made him fall immediately silent and squirm uncomfortably in his chair.

"It does seem somewhat heartless, though," Sir Anthony commented, "to punish the innocent. After all, a wife can hardly prevent her husband from committing treason if he wishes. And his children certainly can't. And it breeds resentment too. Such disinherited children are hardly likely to grow up with warm feelings towards the king and his government."

"Not all women are innocent of blame. I believe many encourage their men into folly," said Richard confidently. "And as for it breeding resentment, you only have to look at the aftermath of the '15. We were too soft on the rebels then. Most of them were pardoned and left to continue plotting in their castles, and were they grateful for such lenient treatment? No. Instead they and their sons are all rising again for the Pretender."

"Are they?" asked Sir Anthony in mock alarm, looking fearfully round the room. "Where? I see no Jacobite hordes marching on the Capital, Richard. Or are you privy to secret information?"

Richard flushed angrily and tried to think of a witty retort.

"If anyone was privy to secret information, Anthony, it would be you, with your finger in every pie, as you well know," said Highbury.

"I see your point, though, Richard. You take a severe view," said Colonel Hutchinson. Richard smiled. He had known his colonel would think this way. "But I think on the whole Anthony is right," the colonel continued. "This law is patently unfair. It is a man's duty to protect and cherish his wife and children, who are weaker than him, both in body and mind. If he callously abandons them, then it is for the authorities to protect them in his stead, not to penalise them further for a crime they have not committed. You said that many women encourage their men into folly, but any man who allows himself to be governed by women, who, for all their charms, are deficient in intellect, is not worthy to be called a man."

Sir Anthony watched with great satisfaction as Richard's confidence crumbled away.

"It is quite obvious you speak as a bachelor, Mark, if you think women are deficient in intellect," said John moodily, to a chorus of laughter.

"True," the colonel conceded with a smile. "But I also agree with Anthony that the forfeiture law will encourage resentment. It will also encourage false accusations by those who stand to profit from the forfeiture. And of course the mob will take the fact that the government feels it necessary to enact such laws as evidence that the country is full of Jacobites, ready to rise for the Pretender, which is clearly ridiculous. It creates unnecessary fear, and may even encourage the Pretender and his son to invade, thinking they have more support here than they actually do."

"What is the Pretender's son up to at the moment?" asked Highbury.

"Prancing round Paris, attending balls and seducing French noblemen's wives, the last we heard," said John dismissively. "No danger there, if you ask me."

"Hmm," said the colonel. "Even so, what we need is a decisive victory over the French – keep them occupied over in Flanders, and they'll never think about assisting Charles again."

"That shouldn't be difficult, if the fiasco of an invasion attempt last year is a measure of their martial ability," said Richard, in a tone markedly less confident than his previous one.

"Is it not already the law that convicted criminals forfeit their goods?" said Sir Anthony, seemingly oblivious to the fact that the conversation had moved on.

"Yes, but it's not the same thing at all," said Highbury. "Many men who commit treason are educated, men of fortune. Whereas common criminals usually have little or nothing to forfeit anyway. Their families are relatively unaffected by the law."

"Apart from losing the breadwinner of the family, of course," said Sir Anthony thoughtfully. "But I suppose sometimes the wife and children are better off without such a husband. I have heard that many criminals are drunks and wife beaters too."

"You're naïve if you think that such behaviour is only confined to the poor, Anthony," replied his friend. "Why, only the other day I heard the most appalling story of a very wealthy man who beats his wife regularly."

"That's hardly an appalling story, my lord…damn!" said the colonel.

Sir Anthony flicked another coin into the pot.

"Have that one on me, Mark," he said generously.

"Thank you. A man must keep his wife in line, William."

"You're right, of course. But this woman is a most docile lady and also in her last month of pregnancy. One could not imagine her disobeying her husband, or so I've heard."

"Ah," said the colonel. "Well, that is quite a different matter, if the lady is in a delicate state. One must indulge women at such a time. I have heard that they can become quite emotional, even more so than normal. Perhaps the man is a brute. Does he beat her very badly?"

"I'm not personally acquainted with the gentleman, Mark, but I believe he does, although he is endeavouring to keep it quiet. He has not considered, I think, that if she loses the child her friends will be most distressed and of course the whole story will then be made public."

"And serve him right, too," said Mark. "Such men deserve a flogging, in my opinion. It is a man's job to protect his wife, and reason with her if she is in error. Violence should be the very last resort. Women are such fragile creatures."

"Am I right in suspecting you to be in love, Mark? You are waxing very lyrical," said the baronet slyly.

The colonel flushed scarlet.

"Certainly not!" he lied. "I am, as John said earlier, a committed bachelor."

"What do you think of this story? After all, you are but recently married and your wife is also pregnant, is she not?" said Highbury to Richard, who had gone very quiet. He coloured slightly, and a small muscle in his cheek twitched.

"Well," he hesitated. "I could not condone a man beating his wife without reason…" He looked at his colonel, who was engaged in lighting his pipe, but was nevertheless listening. The room seemed to have suddenly become very warm.

"Or even with reason, at such a delicate time, surely?" persisted Highbury.

"No, of course not," he said. He shot a deeply suspicious look at Sir Anthony, who smiled innocently back at him.

"You have been very fortunate in your choice of wife, dear boy," he said. "Anne is the most delightful, inoffensive creature. Her only aim in life is to please. I am sure you will never have the slightest cause even to reprimand her, let alone beat her."

"Yes, I met her at the regimental dinner last night," said the colonel, unwittingly hammering another nail in Richard's coffin. "Very pleasant young lady, timid even. The sort that rouses all the protective instincts in a man. We talked for a couple of minutes. She noticed I had a slight cold, and advised me to take a tea of elderflower, yarrow and peppermint, I think it was."

"That is Anne all over. Considerate to a fault!" sighed Sir Anthony. "If only my wife were half so docile."

"Ah, but Elizabeth is an extraordinarily beautiful woman, isn't she?" said Highbury. "And very spirited."

"Spirited, yes, that's the word," the baronet replied. "I indulge her terribly, but I cannot help it. When one is in love one can deny one's darling nothing, as I'm sure you will understand, Richard. All I have is utterly at her disposal." He smiled at his brother-in-law, but his eyes held no warmth.

"Oh for God's sake, Anthony, that should be at least a guinea in the pot," said John in disgust. "Is there no club rule against making your friends vomit?"

"Thank you, William," said Sir Anthony as the two men walked home together later. They had sent the carriage on, as it was a fine night. "I owe you, again."

"It was an absolute pleasure," said the earl. "I don't like Richard at all, I must confess. It was nice to see him squirm a little. Did you know the colonel was in love, and therefore likely to feel particularly sentimental towards women at the moment?"

"Certainly not," said Sir Anthony, smiling. "His affair with Lord Eastwood's wife is a well-kept secret, known only to the lady and her beau. Even Lord Eastwood is unaware of it."

"You're unbelievable," said Highbury admiringly. "Do you think Richard's taken the warning on board?"

"I hope so," said the baronet. "Because it's becoming increasingly difficult to stop Beth charging round to his house and threatening him. She has no common sense where her brother's concerned. He's not a pleasant man by any means, but Beth hates him far more than his treatment of her deserves, in my opinion. After all, it all worked out for the best. We're very happily married."

The earl smiled.

"He doesn't look like a man who would respond well to confrontation, especially from a woman," he commented.

"No. But he is very ambitious. He has the chance now to stop hitting Anne, if he is doing, without losing face, because we didn't confront him head on. But he knows that if he doesn't, and it comes out, his colonel won't be impressed, which will hardly help his career, and he also knows I'm likely to indulge Beth in any revenge she wants to take. He's not stupid. I can't make Anne happy in her marriage, poor girl, but I have a feeling she's about to be cured of her dizzy spells, at least."

* * *

Anne was still awake when Richard returned home, although she pretended not to be. He was not fooled. He knew the pattern of her breathing when she slept and this was not it. He lit the lamp, and sat down heavily on the side of the bed to take off his boots, letting them fall to the floor with a clunk. He stood up and took off his coat, before turning to face her. Her eyes were open, wide awake. He took off his waistcoat. Then he went back over to the bed and sat down. She was sitting up now, smiling uncertainly, and he reached across to capture her hand.

"Why did you tell Sir Anthony that I'd beaten you?" he said very softly.

Her eyes widened immediately.

"I didn't!" she gasped.

"Then who?" he asked, turning her hand over in his and stroking it gently, his eyes remaining fixed on her face.

"No one!" she cried immediately, close to tears. "I swear I haven't told anybody!"

She was telling the truth, that was clear. She would not dare lie to him, he knew that, especially when he was looking at her so intently. He let go of her hand and stood again, pulling his shirt over his head, deliberately flexing the heavy muscles of his chest and back in the process so that she would be reminded of how powerful he was, and how helpless she was by comparison.

"Who have you visited in the past days?" he asked pleasantly.

She thought for a moment.

"I haven't visited anyone since I started having my…dizzy spells," she said. "I went to see Miss Browne yesterday, that's all, and then to the dinner with you last night."

Miss Browne. Sarah. The whore who was devoted to his bloody sister.

"Why did you go to Sarah's?"

"I had to get something for this bruise on my face. I didn't know how to cover it, and I knew you wouldn't want your friends asking me how I'd got it." She was gabbling in her fear. "I told her I'd fainted and that I hit the mantelpiece as I fell. I swear I did! You must believe me, Richard, please!"

Ah, what a transformation, from devoted ecstatic bride, to terrified cringing wreck, in just three weeks! It had been almost too easy to be pleasurable. Yet she still desired him. He could feel her eyes admiring his body even as she cowered in the bed. Beth had not been so easy to tame.

Beth had not been tamed at all.

His face hardened. She was still there in the background, interfering. And that ridiculous popinjay was taking her side, that was clear. He would have to be careful, for a time at least. One of the minor reasons he had married Anne was that Beth had a soft spot for her. He knew that if he hurt Anne, he would hurt Beth, and that she would be impotent to do anything about it.

Except that she was not, and tonight through the mouthpiece of Sir Anthony and the Earl of Highbury, of all people, she had shown him, subtly, that she would act if he gave her cause. Well, he could be subtle too.

He reached across and stroked Anne's cheek with one finger, smiling as she flinched instinctively from him.

"I can see I have been a little hard at times," he said. "I am a soldier; perhaps I have been a bit too rough with you. But I am not used to being argued with."

"I never meant to argue with you," she whispered. "I only want to make you happy, you know that."

He stripped off the rest of his clothes quickly, and climbed into bed.

"Good," he said. "Then you can make me happy now. Turn over."

She obeyed him, turning onto her side, her back to him; but she stiffened as he slid his arm round her, pulling her into his chest and roughly squeezing her breasts.

"Richard," her voice was trembling. "Please…the baby…"

He entered her roughly, heard her gasp of shock, and then he thought only of his own pleasure as he thrust into her, aroused by her fear both of him and for the safety of this child she wanted so much and which he already hated. Finally he emptied himself into her with a grunt of pleasure and lay still, one hand still lazily massaging her swollen breast, his dark hair falling softly over her tear-stained cheek.

"If you want to make me happy," he said when his breathing had returned to normal, "then hurry up and drop this brat you're carrying, and make sure it's a girl. Then I can get one of my own on you. That's why I married you, after all."

He moved away from her, turned over to sleep, and smiled as he heard her trying to stifle her sobs in the pillow.

He would not hit her again, not for the time being anyway. But there were other ways. And about those Beth and her effeminate fop of a husband could do nothing.

CHAPTER SIXTEEN

On the thirty-first of March 1745 Captain Richard Cunningham said goodbye to his wife and, together with sixteen thousand other British troops, made his way to the coast ready to sail to Flanders and join their mainly Dutch and Hanoverian allies, making a total of around forty-five thousand men. Although the French force which was being assembled against them numbered some eighty thousand, the British troops were, in the main, confident of victory, partly due to the fact that the majority of the soldiers had no idea of the numbers they were to face. Keeping your men in ignorance was one of the basic tenets of the army, and was generally a very effective strategy.

Richard left behind a very confused Anne, who no longer knew what to think of the man she had married, whose behaviour towards her ranged from the deeply considerate, even affectionate when in public, to indifferent or deliberately cruel when in private. By nature submissive and adaptable, she had tried desperately to play the chameleon and become whatever he wanted her to be, to anticipate his every wish, and not to antagonise him by any word or gesture.

When he left, riding out of the yard on his grey stallion without a backward glance, she cried, because she knew she had disappointed him in some way, in spite of all her efforts; she must have done, for why else would he be so cruel to her? She also cried because she felt guilty; guilty that she was secretly glad to see him leave, was looking forward to being alone, to not having to endure his vicious insults and brutal sexual assaults, and most of all guilty, because a tiny part of her, quickly stifled, hoped he would not come back.

He had not hit her since the night at the club, but she was not stupid; she knew that was due to something that had happened while he was out rather than anything she had done right. After two months of marriage she still had no idea what her husband wanted. She knew only what he did not want; he did not want this baby to be male. She had anticipated the birth with joy; now she felt only a dull dread that when the time came, it would, in spite of all her prayers, be the wrong sex.

If Richard left his wife feeling confused when he embarked for Europe, he also left his country vulnerable. On the fifteenth of April the Duke of Cumberland set off for Harwich amid much pomp and ceremony to take up his new position as Commander-in-Chief of the Army in Flanders. England now boasted fewer than twelve thousand troops with which she could defend herself against attack, with a further fourteen hundred situated in Scotland under General Cope.

This fact was not lost on the MacGregors, who assembled in the library on the evening of the sixteenth to discuss the situation.

"He should be coming now, while there isna anyone to stand in his way," said Angus excitedly, sitting on the edge of his chair and downing a glass of wine as though it was water. "He'll never get another opportunity like this."

"It wouldna do him any good if he did, I've already tellt ye that," replied Alex. "The clans'll no' rise for him without the French helping him. And the French are otherwise occupied at the moment." He was sitting next to Beth on the sofa, his arm resting along the back of it behind her. One long finger lazily stroked the side of her neck, sending delicious shivers through her body.

"Aye, but that's the whole point," insisted Angus. "The French *are* helping him. They're helping him by tying up nearly the whole army abroad."

"That's no' the point, man," said Duncan. "The clans'll no' see it that way."

"Neither will the English," said Beth. "You said they want a definite commitment from the French before they'll agree to rise, didn't you?"

"Aye, I did," said Alex. "It isna going to happen, Angus.

Charles will do better to stay in France, or go back to Rome for the present. I hope to God that he's taken heed of Broughton's letter to him. He must have had it for a while now, it's been three months since Murray gave it to Traquair. I just wish he'd write back and tell us what his intentions are. If he'll wait a wee while and stop antagonising Louis, wi' a bit of luck, when Louis has beaten the British, he'll be more willing to help us, and put an end to the Elector for good."

"Do you really think they'll beat the British?" said Beth.

"Christ, they should do. They've got twice the force, and a good general, too, in Marshall Saxe."

"Louis could easily afford to give Charles ten thousand troops and still beat Cumberland," grumbled Angus.

"True, but he willna," said Alex. "And I'm no' going tae argue with ye on your birthday. We can blether about this another day."

"Twenty-one," said Maggie proudly, as though she were his mother rather than only a few years older than the birthday boy. "Who'd hae thought it? A man at last! I never thought I'd see the day."

"Neither did I," said Alex. "I thought someone would hae done for him long since. Still, ye've made it, laddie. Congratulations. Maybe ye'll start acting like a man now, and if ye're lucky ye'll make it to twenty-two."

"I intend to act like a man," said Angus, leaning down to fasten the silver buckles on his shoes, "this very night. There," he said, standing up and performing a little pirouette for the company. The skirts of his coat swirled out, then settled back into perfect folds as he faced his audience. "How do I look?"

He looked very fine indeed, a true gentleman. The midnight blue velvet coat and breeches, a present from his eldest brother, were expertly cut and showed off his broad shoulders, slim waist and long muscular legs to devastating effect. His shirt was trimmed with lace at the collar and cuffs, his cream stockings were of the finest silk, his black leather shoes were polished to a high shine, and his hair, tied back with a blue ribbon, gleamed dark gold in the lamplight.

"Ye'll pass," said Alex gruffly, but he was smiling.

"You look wonderful, Angus, as you well know," said Beth. "You don't need us to tell you that."

He grinned, and winked at her.

"Aye, but it's nice to be reminded now and then. Right, are ye ready, then, Duncan?"

Duncan slipped on his coat and stood.

"Are ye sure ye'd no' rather stay in, Angus?" said Maggie. "We dinna mind, truly."

Maggie and Iain's baby had been due at this time, and before her miscarriage the family had regularly joked about the possibility of it being born on Angus's birthday. Although the couple were slowly returning to normal, the three brothers had discussed the matter of the celebration between themselves, and Angus had decided it would be kinder to go out for the evening.

"Are ye mad, woman?" said Iain. "Trying to keep Angus out of a whorehouse is like trying to keep a wasp frae sugar. It canna be done. Leave him be. He thinks it's all there is to being a man. Let's no' disillusion him, eh?"

"If that's all there was to it," replied Angus amiably, "then I've been a man since I was thirteen."

"Thirteen?" said Beth, turning to glare at Alex. "You let him…you know…at thirteen?"

Alex shrugged.

"Am I my brother's keeper?" he asked philosophically.

"No. Well, yes, you should have been, after your father died. Angus, how could you, at thirteen?"

Angus grinned, and sat down again.

"Well," he said, "I did think that being married, Beth, ye'd have kent how it was done by now. But I see my brother's no' performing his duty, so I'll tell ye. First of all ye…"

"Out," said Alex.

Duncan gripped his younger brother by the shoulder.

"Come on, man, I dinna want to have to throw water all over that bonny suit to split ye up."

Maggie leaned over and whispered something to Iain which made him recoil from her as though he'd been bitten.

"Christ, woman," he muttered fiercely back to her. "No. And dinna ye ever ask me such a thing again."

Maggie looked down shamefacedly at her lap, and after a moment Iain leaned over and took one of her hands in his.

"I'm no angry wi' ye, *mo chridhe*," he said. "I can wait, as long as I need to."

The rest of the company all remained determinedly unaware of this private moment, which was a considerable feat, as the room was not large.

"I'll see ye to the door," said Alex to his brothers, rising from the couch.

Once in the hall he turned to Angus.

"Angus, be careful tonight," he said.

"I'm always careful," said Angus. "Well, almost always," he amended, seeing his brothers' incredulous expressions. "And I'll no' get drunk. It doesna' affect me anyway, ye ken that."

"Aye, I do, but ye usually dress like a servant or a labourer, and tonight ye look the proper gentleman. It's different. Ye'll attract more attention, because ye look rich. When I'm Sir Anthony I always take a lot more care. Ye have to be aware of everyone around ye, and what they're doing, without seeming to be."

"Dinna fash yourself, Alex, I'll be careful, I promise. I'm armed, and there're two of us. Why are ye so worried?"

Alex looked at his brother for a moment, then smiled and relaxed.

"Christ, I dinna ken myself," he said. "It's strange to see my wee baby brother a man, at last. I guess I havena looked at you properly in a long time, and tonight…well, I suddenly noticed ye're grown, truly."

"Och, man, ye're no' gonna get sentimental on me, are ye?" said Angus.

"No. You just make me feel old, that's all."

Angus stepped forward and gave his brother a rib-cracking hug.

"That's no' because I'm a man the day," he whispered into Alex's ear. "It's because ye *are* old."

There was a flurry of light-hearted punches, then Angus smoothed down his coat and prepared to leave.

"We'll have a big party for ye next year, to make up for tonight," Alex promised.

"I'll have a fine time tonight," Angus said. "It's better I go out than have Iain and Maggie reminded of the fact that we should have been greeting a new member of the clan. They'd have put a good face on it, but it would have hurt them. I'll hold ye to that, though, next year. A big party, in Scotland, wi' the whole clan."

"Aye, and James on the throne," added Duncan.

Alex held his hands up.

"I'm no' God," he said. "I canna promise ye miracles. But I'll do my best to give ye a big party, and I dinna see why it couldna be at home."

"If we dinna get going, I'll have no party of any sort the night," said Angus. "Are ye sure ye dinna want to come too?"

"Me?" said Alex. "Beth'd flay me alive if I went to a brothel. Besides, one of the good things about being married is ye dinna have to pay for it. Away ye go, and celebrate your manhood in style."

Angus left, laughing, to enjoy a very pleasant evening, returning at six the following morning, dishevelled and exhausted, and smelling of brandy and cheap perfume.

* * *

"I wish you hadn't shown Anthony these patches," Beth said, idly sifting through the box of black silk shapes on Sarah's table. "You can't imagine how ridiculous he looked the other night at the theatre with a little bird stuck on his cheek. The stars and crescents he used to wear were bad enough, but at least everyone else wears those too."

They were ensconced in Sarah's small sitting room eating a hot pie which she had had delivered from the pie shop round the corner. Sarah sighed blissfully and put both her feet in a basin of warm water.

"Ahh, wonderful," she said. "That's the only problem with dressing hair for a living. You're on your feet all day. I didn't show Sir Anthony the patches, if you remember. He found them all by himself. What are you looking for?"

"A cat," said Beth. "He wants half a dozen of them. Apparently people have been positively fainting with ecstasy at the mere sight of them on his face."

"He's certainly started a trend," said Sarah. "I've sold them all. I've ordered more, though, they'll be here tomorrow."

Beth abandoned her search.

"You should put some peppermint in the water. It helps to soothe the aches, or so Anne tells me."

"How is Anne?" asked Sarah.

"A lot better since Richard left, I would imagine, although she won't talk about him to me. She just changes the subject, and I don't want to press her. I'm not sure whether he's warned her not to talk about him, or if she's just being loyal to him. The baby's due any day now, so she spends most of the time sitting sewing clothes for it. I've been teaching her some new embroidery stitches."

"I haven't seen her since he went," Sarah said, wiping a smear of gravy off her chin with a handkerchief.

"Have you seen Maggie recently?" Beth asked suddenly, although she already knew the answer to her question.

"Yes," replied Sarah. "She calls in now and again. If I'm not busy we have a cup of coffee."

"Does she talk to you?"

"Well, of course she does," said Sarah. "It would be pretty boring if she just sat there silently."

Beth laughed.

"I asked for that," she said. "You know what I meant. I wondered if she confided in you at all. I'm worried about her, because even though her and Iain are making a good attempt to appear normal, there's something not right, and the other night she said something really strange to him. It was Jim's twenty-first, you know, and him and Murdo went to Mother Meredith's for the evening. Maggie asked Iain if he wanted to go as well."

Sarah froze in the motion of taking another bite of pie and put it back down on the plate.

"Did he?" she asked softly.

"No," answered Beth, unaware that Sarah was not referring to Iain. "He got angry with her at first, and then said that he could wait as long as he needs to, which made me think…what's the matter?"

"Nothing," said Sarah hurriedly. "Yes, she does confide in me, and she said that Iain confides in Murdo. I can't tell you what she's told me, because I don't divulge confidences, you know that, but they'll be all right. It just takes time. They love each other, that'll get them through everything. Did Jim enjoy his birthday?" she finished with studied casualness.

"Yes, judging by the state he was in when he got home, and by the fact that he didn't get up until the following afternoon,"

Beth answered. "Unlike Murdo," she continued conversationally, watching Sarah carefully, "who was up bright and early. He didn't indulge in the pleasures of the house. He just went to keep an eye on Jim, and make sure he was safe. Anthony bought Jim a new suit for his birthday, and he looked a real dandy, which made him more of a target for robbers. You don't like him, do you?"

"What? Yes, of course I do," said Sarah automatically, then blushed.

"Ha! Got you!" said Beth triumphantly. "I meant Jim. It's pretty obvious you like Murdo."

"I *do* like him," Sarah replied crossly, "but not in the way you're thinking. He's one of the few genuinely decent men I've met, Sir Anthony being another. And no, I don't like Jim. I've only met him a couple of times, but he's far too sure of himself, in my opinion, and only after one thing. I suppose he's used to getting it easily. He is very handsome."

"Yes, but you've only seen one aspect of him, Sarah. He's young and careless at times, but he has a good heart." She refrained from commenting further, realising that it would seem strange if she defended her servant too vehemently. "Do you see Murdo a lot, then?" she asked.

"From time to time," said Sarah carefully. "He's taking me to see the ostrich at Mr Gough's menagerie on Saturday."

Beth smiled, thinking of what Angus would say when he found out that Duncan had stolen his idea for an outing. If he found out. Duncan was keeping this new friendship very close to his chest. And so was Sarah, who showed a distinct reluctance to converse any further on the subject.

Beth moved the conversation on to another topic. If Duncan and Sarah were becoming friends, that was good. If they wanted to keep it secret, that was up to them. She would pry no further.

* * *

Less than a week later Anne went into labour. As soon as they heard, Beth and Caroline dashed round to the house, where Isabella, Charlotte and Clarissa were already waiting excitedly for them in the salon.

"The baby's just been born!" Isabella cried as soon as they entered. "We distinctly heard it cry, just a few moments ago!" She was almost beside herself with excitement.

"Why aren't you upstairs with Anne?" asked Beth, who had expected them to be crowded round the bed. "Is she all right?"

Isabella looked at her cousin in shock.

"Oh, Elizabeth, that would never do," said Isabella. "We are unmarried, you know. It would not do for an unmarried lady to enter a birthing chamber."

Clarissa and Charlotte nodded agreement.

"Why not?" said Beth. This was the first she had heard of this social taboo.

Isabella looked confused.

"Well…Edward said that…" she faltered.

"Ah, Edward," said Beth. "Well if he said it, it must be right. Very well, you stay here. I'm married, so I assume I'm safe to enter the bedroom. Caroline?"

The two women mounted the stairs.

"You're from an ancient aristocratic family, Caroline," Beth said as they reached the landing. "Is it the norm for unmarried women not to enter the bedroom?"

"Not as far as I know," said Caroline. "Whenever any of us gave birth, the room was so full of chattering females that the midwife used to have to fight her way through to get to her patient. But you know Edward, he makes up rules at times just to show he can still wield authority."

"It's pathetic, it really is," said Beth crossly. "Those poor women know nothing about life, and they never will while they live with him."

A thin reedy wail came from behind the door to which the maid had led them, and Beth abandoned all thought of her downtrodden cousins and entered the room.

In spite of the fact that it was broad daylight, the shutters were closed, the curtains drawn, and the room lit only by candles. Anne was lying in the bed, her face almost as pale as the pillows which propped her up. In the corner the midwife was busily swaddling the newborn infant. The room was stiflingly hot, and a sour smell of blood and stale air permeated it.

Beth sat down on the bed, trying to drive away the memories of the last birth she'd attended, while Caroline moved straight to the window, drawing the curtains and opening the shutters, paying no heed to the midwife's protests that her patient would be sure to catch cold. A blast of fresh cool air entered the room, and Beth took a deep breath.

"Are you all right, Anne?" she said, reaching for the new mother's hand, alarmed by the tears that were pouring unchecked down her face.

Anne nodded miserably, but was unable to do anything else but sob brokenly. Beth took her in her arms, wondering whether it was normal for new mothers to behave in such a way. One look at Caroline's face told her it was not.

"Is the baby all right?" Caroline asked the midwife anxiously.

"He's perfect!" the middle-aged woman beamed, looking tenderly down at the squalling tightly-wrapped infant, the only visible part being the furious red face. "It was a perfect birth, very easy. The little poppet slid out all by himself, straight into my hands!"

"Anne, what's the matter?" asked Beth. "The baby's perfect. You'll be fine. You're just a bit tired, that's all. It's to be expected after what you've just gone through."

"Here," said Caroline, deftly taking the crying bundle from the midwife and laying it gently on Anne's chest. "Hold him. He's lovely."

Anne's arms instinctively moved to cradle the baby and she looked down at him in wonder, then up at Beth.

"He looks like Stanley," lied Beth smoothly. "That's what you told me you wanted, isn't it? A boy to remind you of Stanley."

"He's wonderful," Anne said, "but I wanted a girl. I had prayed so for a girl." She sniffed, and another tear spilled down her cheek. "What am I going to do?" she whispered, as though unaware there was anyone else in the room.

"You're going to feed him, if you want any peace," said Caroline practically. "Open the front of your nightdress and put him to your breast. He looks lusty enough, I think he'll get the idea straight away."

Anne looked up at her in horror.

"Oh, I can't do that!" she said, forgetting her tears. "I mustn't feed him myself! Richard was very definite about that. It will ruin my figure, he said. I must find a wet-nurse, or better still hand feed him. Yes, he said I should hand feed him. That would be the best."

Beth bit back the extremely shocking expletive she had been about to use regarding her brother. All had become clear. Anne did not want a boy because Richard didn't want one. She took a couple of deep breaths to calm herself before she spoke again.

"Anne," she said. "I'm sure Richard will come round when he sees the child, and he will not be disappointed at all that it's a boy. In the meantime," she continued firmly, "he is not here and is not likely to be here for some considerable time. I can't think of anyone likely to be a better mother than you." She shot a quick look of apology at Caroline. "You should be happy. You have a lovely, perfect son, one of many no doubt, and it was an easy birth."

Caroline came and sat down on the other side of the bed.

"And you should feed him yourself," she asserted. "I did, and I assure you my figure hasn't suffered at all. It's a wonderful feeling. It bonds you to your baby like nothing else."

Anne looked doubtfully from Caroline to the baby.

"I have read that it is the best thing for a child," she said hesitantly.

"Of course it is," said Caroline brusquely. "You of all people, with your great knowledge of ailments and cures should know that."

"But when I told Richard that, he said it was a lot of new-fangled nonsense, and that there is nothing wrong with hand feeding, if it's done correctly."

"There's everything wrong with hand feeding," said Caroline. "Believe me, I know all about it. I read all the latest reports before Freddie was born, including some figures that Edwin got for me that aren't available to the general public. Almost all the children who are hand fed die. If you really don't want to feed him yourself, get a wet nurse. But even then your baby's got a higher chance of dying before he's weaned."

By the time they left, Anne had breastfed her child for the first time, had smiled weakly and had tentatively expressed the hope that Richard would not be too disappointed when she wrote to tell him he was the stepfather of a boy.

* * *

"Of course he'll be disappointed!" Beth raged once she was at home. "He'll be absolutely furious that Anne has not only had a boy, but that she's also decided not to murder it by following his advice!"

"Do you no' think you're being a wee bit hard on the man?" Duncan suggested carefully. "Ye do seem to think the worst of him all the time."

"That's because there's nothing good to think about him," she fumed. "He did it deliberately. He did his best to beat her into miscarrying, and now that hasn't worked he's trying to kill the baby by insisting she hand feed it, knowing full well that it has no chance of surviving if she does!"

"Did *you* know?" asked Alex, who was sitting on a chair watching his wife pace angrily up and down.

"Did I know what?" she said.

"That hand-reared bairns almost invariably die?"

She stopped pacing.

"No, I didn't. Not until Caroline told me just now. She was magnificent, really authoritarian. But that's not the point."

"It is, Beth," Alex said wearily. "You're a woman, you talk to other women who've an interest in that sort of thing, and you didna ken. Why do ye think that Richard would?"

She paused, thought for a moment.

"Because the child's going to disinherit him and he doesn't want it," she said. "But he can't murder it outright, because even he can't bring himself that low, so he's made it his business to find out how to kill it without anyone suspecting anything."

Alex buried his head in his hands.

"I give up," he said.

"I've only met your brother a couple of times," said Duncan. "But it seems to me that he's no' a particularly devious man, that he's accustomed to getting what he wants by force, mainly. That's why he beat your stableboy, rather than using more subtle means, is it no'?"

"Yes," Beth said. "That's why he hit me too, because I was too clever for him, and I wouldn't give in to him."

"Aye. And I can see that he might have beaten Anne hoping that she'd lose the bairn. But now ye're giving me quite a different picture of the man," he continued calmly. "Ye're telling me that he's subtle enough to have thought of killing a child by getting his mother to unknowingly deprive it of the nourishment it needs."

"Even I wouldna have thought o' that," Alex added, "And I'll admit to being as devious as they come. And ye tellt me that some of the stuff Caroline read about breastfeeding isna even available to the public. How the hell d'ye think Richard came by it, then?"

Beth sat down. The two men watched her searching for a way to still paint her brother black. Alex took her hand.

"Beth," he said gently. "I know your brother's cruel, and I know he's ambitious, too. But he's a man. He isna the devil incarnate, in spite of the fact that ye're trying to make him so. Maybe the bairn will disinherit him, but he's still rich. The allowance Redburn left Anne was generous to say the least, and it's all Richard's now. It's more money than he'll ever need, and the bairn'll make no difference to that."

"But he's…" Beth began.

"No, let me finish, Beth," he said. "I'm no' defending him. I dinna like the man, and I canna forgive him for hurting ye. I also agree that he probably hurt Anne, which was why I did what I did at the club. But you're unreasonable about him and you're more likely to cause him to commit violence than restrain him. Ye're like flint and tinder, the two of you, when you're together."

"Like you and Angus," Duncan said wryly.

"Aye, a bit like that," Alex admitted. "Except Angus and I are well-matched in size and strength, and we love each other, whereas you and Richard dinna, and that makes all the difference. As angry as I get wi' Angus at times, I never forget that, no' for a minute. Richard's no' responsible for everything bad that's happened to ye, Beth. In fact, if it hadna been for him, we wouldna have met. You should be grateful to the laddie."

Beth smiled, to his relief. Her constant ravings about her brother since his marriage were wearing Alex's patience thin. He was sorry for Anne, and would help her if he could, but ultimately there was little he could do. Anne had married Richard of her own free will; now she would have to learn to live with him, and Alex had tried unsuccessfully to make Beth see that for weeks.

"Maybe I was wrong about the breastfeeding," she admitted reluctantly. "Maybe he didn't know about that. But you don't know what he's capable of. He can't stand to be thwarted in anything. He never could, even as a child. And he's really ambitious. He wants power, and he wants money because the more money you have, the more power you have. And he'll stop at nothing to get it. You don't know him, Alex."

"Well, no, clearly I dinna," replied Alex, somewhat more sharply than he'd intended. "Because all I see is a somewhat brutal career soldier of average wit who wants to be a general one day, and maybe win a great battle. I canna understand why ye hate him so badly, Beth. Ye dinna rant on day and night about Lord Daniel, though ye've far more reason to. He threatened to cut your fingers off, and would have married ye and raped ye if I hadna got there in time! Is there something ye're no' telling me about Richard?"

She looked down at his hand, still clasping hers.

"No," she said. "Maybe you're right. Maybe I should let the past lie."

"I dinna want you to stop talking about him to me, Beth, if there's cause to," Alex said, surprised by her sudden capitulation.

"No, I will. But I have been ranting on about him, I realise that. I'm just worried about Anne, that's all."

He pulled her into his arms and kissed her.

"So am I," he said. "But I'll keep an eye on her, I promise."

To his relief, Beth stopped talking about her brother after that, except in the most casual way. Alex put it down to the fact that Richard was in Flanders, and therefore could do nothing to give her cause for comment until he came home. Hopefully it would be a long time before that happened, and in the meantime Alex was grateful for the return of his good-natured, loving wife.

CHAPTER SEVENTEEN

Flanders, May 1745

Richard was angry. He was angry in spite of the fact that he had managed to acquire warm and comfortable lodgings in the village wine merchant's house, to the envy of his men, many of whom were under canvas in driving rain in the sodden fields surrounding the village. He was angry even though the Belgian merchant was most accommodating, providing the best claret and port from his cellar and the finest food, expertly cooked, for a very reasonable fee.

He was angry because the slight wound he had received in his leg during the battle of Fontenoy, fought and lost ten days ago, was not healing as quickly as his impatience desired it to. He was angry because on the day of the battle Brigadier Ingoldsby, in spite of being ordered repeatedly by Prince William to attack the French fortified position in the wood near Fontenoy, had instead prevaricated, with the result that the foot soldiers had been subjected to devastating cannon fire as they advanced up the incline to face the whole French army. He was angry because in spite of all the odds, the British had actually been getting the better of the enemy until the damn traitorous Irish Foot, Jacobites to a man, had entered the fight on the French side and forced the British to retreat.

But most of all he was angry because the musket wound which itched and burned as he limped up and down the comfortable sitting room he had been allocated had not been inflicted on him during the actual battle of Fontenoy itself, but on the day before, when the cavalry had ventured forward and Lieutenant General

Campbell, leading the Horse, had been careless enough to get his leg shot off by a cannon. This had resulted in the death of the general and many others and the withdrawal of the cavalry from all further action, apart from helping to cover the retreating infantry. And it had also resulted in the end of Richard's dreams of achieving glory in his first battle as a captain, for now at any rate.

And to top it all, he had today received a letter from his pathetic little wife, which now lay open on the small escritoire and which he had read with disbelief. In it she not only told him the joyful news that she had produced a boy, who was hale and hearty and perfect in every way, but also that she had decided to disobey his specific order and nurse it herself. Of course she hadn't worded the letter that simply; it was full of gushing endearments and hopes that he would forgive her; he could almost see her cringing in fear as she wrote, anticipating his reaction when he read it.

Although she was obviously not fearful enough, or she would not have the temerity to nurse the brat herself. His sister was behind this. Anne hadn't mentioned Beth in the letter, but he could see her stamp all over this little rebellion of his wife's. What he wouldn't give to have them both here now, in this room, so that he could take all the frustration, rage and pain he'd endured in the past days out on them.

Someone knocked tentatively at the door.

"What?" snarled Richard, halting in his pacing. The door opened, and a nervous ruddy-faced young man poked his head round it.

"Er…you called for me, sir," he ventured hesitantly.

"Ah. Yes. Smith. I would like some tea," said the captain, in a more moderate tone.

"Tea, sir?" echoed Smith incredulously.

"Yes, tea," said Richard impatiently. "I take it you have heard of the beverage?"

"Yes, of course, sir. Straight away."

He started to duck back out of the door, with obvious relief.

"Sergeant," said Richard, halting the man in his retreat.

"Yes, sir?"

"How is Titan?"

The sergeant swallowed nervously.

"Er…the surgeon managed to get the ball out of his leg, sir, and he thinks it might heal in time, with luck."

"Good. You will ensure he gets the best of care. Did the surgeon say when he will be fit to ride again?"

"He's…not sure if he will be, sir. He said it will be a few weeks before he knows. The ball caused quite a bit of damage, he said, sir."

The sergeant closed his eyes and waited for the explosion.

"Ah. I see," said Richard quietly. "Well, we will have to wait then, and see what happens. And how are you, Smith?"

"Me, sir?" said the sergeant, stunned.

"Yes, you," replied Richard with something that looked almost like a smile. "You were wounded, were you not, in the battle? How are you?"

"I'm fine, sir," stammered the sergeant. "It was just a scratch."

"It was a lot more than that," said Richard. "You fought very bravely. All the men did. Ask the landlord to give a bottle of wine to each man, at my expense. I should have done that immediately after the battle, but I've had other things on my mind."

Now Richard did smile, at the sergeant's expression of unbelieving wonder. He looked as though he'd wandered into the mouth of Hell and instead of the expected cloven-hoofed demon with a pitchfork, had encountered a golden, fluffy-winged angel. It was good to keep the men on their toes, and one way to do that was to sometimes behave in the way they least expected you to. A gesture of appreciation now and then went a long way too, especially when it was bestowed by a normally harsh officer like himself. And his men *had* fought well. They deserved his praise.

"Yes, sir, at once, sir. Thank you. Very much. Sir." Smith said, beaming now. He made to leave the room again.

"Don't forget the tea, sergeant," Richard called.

"No, sir."

"And a woman. For the whole night. You know the sort I like."

Once the door was closed, Sergeant Smith drew out his handkerchief and mopped the nervous sweat from his brow. Captain Cunningham was the most unpredictable man he'd ever met. You never knew how he was going to react from one day to the next. He would have a man flogged if he even imagined he was not being shown sufficient respect; he expected all his orders to be followed without question; he had no sympathy with weakness or any display of nerves in his men; and if he wanted something he expected it to be provided for him, and would accept no excuses. He had, as far as the sergeant was aware, no discernible sense of humour.

On the other hand, his bravery was beyond question. He would not expect any of his men to face anything that he himself would shrink from. Which was fine, except that there was nothing he *would* shrink from. He was reckless in his courage, which the sergeant personally considered a dangerous quality in an officer, particularly as it endangered his men, of which the sergeant was one. Since he had married well and come into money the captain was showing that he could be extremely generous to his men, if he felt they deserved it. His men feared their captain and some of them hated him. No one admitted to liking him.

The sergeant started down the stairs. Tea. Why the hell would anyone who was in the enviable position of having a wine merchant for a landlord ask for tea? Still, it should be easy enough to procure. The woman was a different matter. Richard's reputation with women was already becoming notorious, and once a whore had spent one night with him she was not eager to repeat the experience, in spite of his generosity, and the word was spreading. There had been some whispered speculation in the mess as to whether the captain was a secret molly, who tried to hide the fact by buying women then taking his frustration out on them when he couldn't rise to the occasion, but neither the sergeant nor the men really thought this to be the case. Captain Cunningham showed no sexual interest whatsoever in his own gender. No, the captain was a normal red-blooded male, although he certainly seemed to hold women in deep contempt, to hate them even. It would not be easy to find a whore who was willing to spend a whole night with him. The sergeant would have to find one, though, or face the consequences.

He set off to accomplish his task. He felt sorry for the poor cow, whoever she was going to be, but the sergeant was a practical man; whores were whores, and better one of them be beaten half to death than him for failing to provide one.

In his room, Richard had already forgotten the sergeant. He sat down at the escritoire, scanned Anne's letter again, and picking up a sheet of paper and a quill, prepared to reply to it. It was most annoying that he couldn't write what he wanted to, and instead would have to send the sort of letter that everyone would expect a loving new husband parted from his dear wife for the first time to write. She might show the letter to others; she would certainly keep it, along with all the other ridiculous souvenirs she was already accumulating; a lock of his hair, a pressed flower from her wedding bouquet.

He sighed, adjusted position slightly to take the weight off his injured leg and settled down to write.

* * *

"So obviously she feels a great deal happier now, and the christening will go ahead next week," said Caroline. Her voice was coming out a little jerkily, as she was bouncing Freddie on her knee as she spoke. The little boy chuckled with delight, waving his chubby fists about.

"Good," Edwin murmured into his brandy.

"Have you listened to one word I've said?" his wife asked.

Edwin started and looked up.

"Yes!" he said. "Of course I have. Richard wrote to say he thinks that George William is an excellent patriotic name for the child and…er…"

Caroline shook her head in mock despair.

"I'm sorry," he said. "I'm just a bit preoccupied, that's all. I'm not sure it's wise for us to commit another six thousand troops to Flanders. It leaves us terribly vulnerable at home."

"There's no choice, though, is there?" said Caroline. "We have to replace the men who were killed at Fontenoy last month."

"Yes," said Edwin. "But if there were to be a Jacobite rising now, we'd be unable to defend ourselves."

"Do you really think there will be?" she asked. "The French army's as tied up as ours, and the Pretender's son is still whoring his way round France, isn't he? We're hardly in any immediate danger."

"Hmm," said Edwin moodily.

"Edwin, you have to relax at some point," she said with

concern. "Worrying yourself into an early grave isn't going to solve anything."

"You're right," he agreed, putting his glass down and reaching over to relieve her of the child. "So, the christening, then. Are we invited?"

"Yes, although the whole thing was nearly delayed again when Anne realised she'd forgotten to ask Richard who he wanted for godparents. I honestly think he couldn't care less. He's just been in a battle, and he was wounded; he's probably got a lot more on his mind than the christening of a child he's not that interested in."

"Who did she ask?"

"She asked Anthony and Beth, and Bartholomew Winter."

"Really?" Edwin raised one eyebrow. "Did Anthony agree?"

"Of course he didn't. He gave the same excuse he gave us for not being Freddie's godfather. Beth refused as well, but I think that's more because she knows Richard would be annoyed if he knew Anne had asked her, than because of any superstitious beliefs. She suggested Charlotte might be a better choice, as she helped Anne so much after Stanley died. Charlotte nearly died on the spot from excitement."

"I bet she did," said Edwin. "It must be the most exciting thing that's happened to her since poor dear Frederick died."

"The only exciting thing, I should think. What is it about the Cunningham men that they have to make sure they're surrounded by feeble women, and then still feel a need to trample all over them?"

"Insecurity," said Edwin. "It takes a man of great strength and personality to marry a firebrand and survive intact."

"Or not so intact, if you're referring to us in that statement," warned his wife.

"Not at all," said Edwin, with the polished insincere candour of the born politician. "I was thinking of Anthony and Beth."

"Of course you were. Anyway, it's nice to see Anne relaxed and happy again. She was terrified that Richard wouldn't forgive her for nursing the baby herself, but he seemed fine about it. Beth still thinks that he was trying to murder the baby by insisting Anne hand-rear it, but she always does think the worst of him. He had no idea it was so dangerous; he said as much in his letter."

"He did, actually," said Edwin.

"Did what?"

"Know it was dangerous," said Edwin, cradling his son, who was desperately trying to keep his eyes open, with diminishing success. "I told him myself one night, just before he left for Gravesend."

"Did you now?" said Caroline, a strange tone in her voice.

"Yes. We were playing cards, at the Winters. I can't recall how the topic came up, but I remembered all the statistics and stuff I got for you, because I found it appalling, to be honest, that it hasn't been made more public that you're effectively sentencing your child to death if you hand feed it. I'm trying to get the House to take some action over it, in fact. Anyway, I thought I'd mention it to Richard. It was a pretty noisy party, though. I expect he didn't hear me properly, or forgot."

"Yes, maybe he did," said Caroline. "I'm sure you're right." She leaned across and rang the bell for the nurse to come and take Freddie to bed. "I assume you can be present on Sunday, then? Only the most tedious and superficial people will be there, guaranteed. And the firebrand and Anthony, of course."

"And us," said Edwin. "And if you tell Beth I said she's a firebrand, I won't be responsible for the consequences."

"I'm sure you won't," said Caroline. "Don't worry, I'll spare no expense on your funeral."

* * *

Late June, 1745

"*Mhic an Diabhal!* I still canna believe it," said Alex, half to himself. "Why would he do such a thing? Has he turned traitor?"

The fact that Alex was breaking his golden rule of always remaining in character when he was dressed as Sir Anthony was a measure of how disturbed he had been by Murray of Broughton's letter, received today. In it Murray had said that the letter which he had entrusted to the Earl of Traquair four months ago, stating that the clans were unanimously against any rising in Britain without French support, had never been delivered to Prince Charles. He could be planning anything, assuming the clans would rise for him when they had no intention of doing so.

"Do you really think Traquair has turned traitor?" asked Beth.

"I dinna ken," said Alex moodily. "But what other reason could he have for holding on to Murray's letter for four months before returning it to him? If he couldna find anyone to deliver it as he says, he should have tellt us long since. Maybe he wants Charles to fail."

"Or maybe he thinks that if Charles waits for French support there will never be a rising," Beth suggested.

"Aye, possibly, but it's no' up to him to decide for us, or to keep information from his prince, either, the bastard."

"Still, at least the letter's on its way now, isn't it?" said Beth, trying to reassure Alex, although she was worried too. She looked out of the carriage window. They were close to Kew now; within a few minutes they would be entering the driveway of the White House. "Murray said Glengarry's taking it to Charles in person."

"Aye, I just hope it gets there this time, that's all." He sighed.

"Why shouldn't it? You don't suspect Glengarry, do you?" Beth asked.

"No, I'm just worried, that's all. And angry."

"Well, you'll have to stop being angry, and stop being Alex too," she said softly. "We're there." The coach rattled to a halt and Duncan jumped down to open the door.

Alex closed his eyes for a moment and took a couple of deep breaths.

"Christ, I hate this. I'm sick of it," he muttered, and then he straightened and stepped down from the carriage, and at once became Sir Anthony Peters, only his dark blue eyes retaining a vestige of his distaste for the role.

"Now Murdo, you will carry our trunk up to the room the footman shows you to," he said, fussily arranging his lace and smoothing his wig. "And you must take the greatest care that you keep it upright. It would be an absolute calamity if our clothes were to become creased!"

This time they had been warned that the lavish dinner and card party was to be preceded by a game of rounders in the garden, and the Peters had dressed accordingly, but taking a leaf from Helen's book, had brought along a change of clothes this time.

Prince Frederick and most of the other guests were already assembled on the lawn, where he had been explaining the rules of the game they were about to play and allocating them to teams.

Sir Anthony scanned the group, then drew Beth to one side.

"You see the two small boys?" he said softly.

She looked. Standing by the prince, arm in arm, were two little boys, aged around seven and five, dressed in miniature versions of adult costume; breeches and stockings, tiny embroidered brocade waistcoats and frockcoats. They even sported miniature powdered wigs.

"They're his two eldest sons, George and Edward. You must remember they're princes. Also George is a little backward. He can't read or write, and he clings to his brother all the time. Edward's odd too."

Beth was about to ask in what way, but then Frederick had seen them and was beckoning them over.

"Ah! Sir Anthony and Lady Elizabeth! So glad you could come! Hopefully we'll see more of you now that my father has departed on his annual jaunt to Hanover. Are you familiar with the game of rounders?"

"I am, Your Highness, although it is some time since I've played," said Sir Anthony, leading his wife across the grass. "But my wife, alas, has never even seen the game before."

"No matter," said the prince, waving his hand dismissively. "We are not playing too strictly by the rules today. You will learn as you go along. Now, Sir Anthony, if you would care to field this time, and Lady Elizabeth can join the batting side."

Sir Anthony trotted obediently off, disappearing to a distant part of the field, where several other brightly-dressed figures were dotted about at intervals. Beth could see Percy and the arrogant David, and surely that could not be Lord Daniel over by the tree? She strained her eyes to see, and then was distracted by a hand pulling at her skirt. She looked down.

"Papa says I must take care of you, and explain things," said Prince George from the level of her waist. "It's really easy though. When it's your turn to bat, Papa will throw the ball to you and you must hit it as hard as you can, and then run round those posts." He pointed to four posts set in the grass at intervals of about fifteen strides to form a large square. "We sometimes have five or six posts, but today we only have four. If you watch the others, you will see how it is done."

He led her across to where a line of people displaying various degrees of lack of enthusiasm were waiting to bat. Prince Edward trailed silently along in their wake, looking around him at the players.

"Are you going to play as well, Your Highness?" Beth asked.

"Oh, yes," the little boy beamed. "Edward and I both play. It is one of our favourite games."

"I prefer cricket," said Prince Edward. "But it has a lot of rules and isn't any good for people who don't really want to play."

Beth looked down at the top of the boy's head in surprise. Before she could think of a suitable response to this remark Prince George was talking again.

"Now, you see, the Lady Helen is going to bat." He lowered his voice. "Watch her, because she isn't very good and you can learn from her."

Beth grinned. The boy might be backward in academic matters, but he was clearly on the ball when it came to sport, and people. She watched as Helen took her place and gripped the bat. Prince Frederick waited until she was ready, and threw the ball. She swung the bat lazily and missed. Earl Francis, standing a few yards behind her, caught the ball and threw it back to Frederick.

"You can miss twice," explained George, "But on the third time you must run, whether you hit the ball or not. She doesn't hold the bat firmly enough, see."

"She doesn't look at the ball. She looks at the men instead," put in Prince Edward in his piping voice, which carried some distance. Helen frowned. Beth laughed.

"Edward!" whispered George. "Remember what Papa said."

Presumably Papa had tried to teach the remarkably astute five-year-old the rudiments of diplomacy, and had failed.

Philippa, a few places in front of Beth, turned round and grinned a greeting.

"Hello again. Not played before?"

"No," said Beth. "But I have good tutors here, I think."

Prince George glowed. Prince Edward looked distractedly around the field, seeming unable to concentrate on anything for more than a couple of seconds. Most of the men had taken their coats off and rolled their shirt sleeves up, and he proceeded to do the same.

"Damn good game. Better than digging. Got the right dress on, too." Philippa had obviously borrowed the blue and white striped muslin dress off someone who was of normal height. Tall as she was, the dress was too short for her, and the consequent display of neat ankles was not lost on the men. She followed Beth's gaze downwards.

"Practical," she said. "Intend to win. Bloody Percy, David and Daniel on the other side. And Papa. Obligatory to win."

Suddenly it was. Beth concentrated, watched as Helen clipped the ball with the bat and was caught out. The next player stepped forward, hit the ball and ran. The ball bounced once and Percy caught it, throwing it quickly to David who was already running towards the third post. He caught it, threw himself full-length and touched the post with the ball just before the unfortunate batter reached it.

"Oh bad luck, James!" shouted Prince Frederick.

"See, he is out now," said George. "The fielder can also get you out by hitting you with the ball while you're running between bases. It's called a stinger, because it hurts sometimes. James should have stayed at the second base. Then he would have had a chance to run on when the next person batted. He would not have scored a rounder, but he would have had another chance later. Now we have lost him."

Beth wondered how many of the players were deliberately getting themselves out so they could lie on the grass in the sun and watch. Certainly Helen looked deeply relieved, although James was scowling.

Philippa moved up into place, took the bat and braced herself, locking her gaze belligerently with the prince. He raised his arm.

"That man don't like you at all," came a small voice from beside Beth. She looked down, and then followed Edward's gaze to Daniel, who was still lounging nonchalantly by the tree. He was so far away she could hardly make out his features at all, let alone whether he was wearing a hostile expression. "He's going to hurt you," the child added indifferently, screwing his eyes up and focussing on the young lord.

Edward's odd, Anthony had said, and now Beth had an inkling of what he meant. The boy had been making a casual observation. He didn't seem to expect a reply. There was a crack of leather on wood and Beth looked up to see the ball sailing off into the distance. Philippa dropped the bat, hauled her skirts up to her knees and ran like the wind, careless of decorum. There was a flurry of activity on the field, but she had made it round the posts before the ball had been recovered.

"Damn!" said Frederick. "I knew I should have had you on my team, Philippa. Well done."

She walked to the back of the line, flushed and pleased, and sat down.

The game continued. To Beth's surprise no one made any concessions for the age of the little princes, apart from the fact that they had their own small bats. Their father bowled almost as hard as he had to the adults, and both of them did well. George scored a rounder; Edward made it to third base.

It was Beth's turn. She moved into position, feeling far more nervous than she should over a mere game. It didn't really matter whether they won or not, but Philippa was right. Winning, or at least doing your best, was important.

She braced herself as she'd watched Philippa do. Prince Frederick drew back his arm and threw, kindly aiming directly at the bat. She moved and the ball sailed past her into the earl's waiting hands.

"Bad luck," said the prince. He threw again. This time she clipped the ball as Helen had done, sending it straight forward. Frederick caught it.

"Oh," she said, feeling astonishingly disappointed. "That means I'm out, doesn't it?"

"No," said the prince, smiling. "It means you're improving. We'll allow you another go, as it's the first time you've ever played."

He threw the ball, and this time she hit it, so hard that she felt the reverberation all the way up her arms. She watched ecstatically as the ball went sailing over the heads of Anthony, David and, oh yes! Daniel, and then someone shouted "Run!" and she remembered what she was supposed to be doing, dropped the bat, grabbed her skirts and ran as fast as she could. It was a lucky strike, but as she tore past the last post to a round of applause she felt invincible.

She was not. The next round of batting got her out, and then it was the other team's turn to bat.

"Haven't a hope, really," Philippa commented as they moved to fan out across the field. "Helen will slope off somewhere, Papa lie down under a tree, and the boys aren't big enough to throw the ball any distance. Up to us, and James. Anthony and Daniel bloody good, too. Shame. Still, proper food tonight. Changing?"

"Yes," said Beth, who was starting to get the hang of Philippa's staccato speech and thought patterns.

"Damn good idea of Helen's, bringing a change. She won't be pleased, though. You especially, very beautiful. Competition."

Beth grinned.

"Thanks," she said.

As soon as the batting started Beth knew that Philippa was right. Her husband, as she'd expected was an excellent player, as was Prince Frederick. David and Percy were more interested in keeping their clothes in pristine condition, and consequently ensured that they were out almost immediately. Beth, who was positioned reasonably close to the batters, caught Percy out herself, and also caught his look of relief.

After that she found there was no need to concentrate on the batting. The ball sailed repeatedly over her head as Anthony, Daniel and Frederick scored rounder after rounder, and she started to think about the letter Murray had sent and its implications, her body half-turned to the back of the field, from where the ball would be thrown to her after one of the distant fielders had retrieved it.

Therefore it came as a complete shock when the solid ball hit her in the thigh with enough force to send her stumbling sideways. She bent down to pick up the ball, which had come to a halt at her feet, and looked across to where Daniel was standing, still holding the bat. He had made no attempt to run and was smiling at her. In spite of the protective layers of clothing, the ball had hit her with enough force to bruise.

"I'm sorry, Elizabeth," he said, looking anything but. "I didn't mean to hit you. I expected you to catch me out. I would have thought a woman with your background would have had extensive experience in handling balls."

He did it deliberately, she thought, instantly annoyed. *I'm sure of it.* She glanced at her husband, who had been sitting down, but now rose to his feet. Then she looked down at the ball in her hand and smiled.

"I do have some little experience," she said, focussing pointedly on his crotch, "but I am not accustomed to handling such very small ones." She threw the ball to the bowler and watched with satisfaction as Percy laughed and Daniel reddened slightly. "You should make sure your equipment is clean, my lord," she added, wiping her muddy hands on her skirt. "One can pick up such nasty diseases if one does not take good care of it."

"I would have thought that to be something Sir Anthony would be more concerned about, considering where he puts his equipment," Daniel said.

Beth felt her temper rise, and swallowed it down with an effort. Everyone was watching the altercation with interest, and the only ones who were unaware of the innuendoes were the children.

"Oh no, my dear boy, you are mistaken," said Sir Anthony, smiling innocently. "I do not play rounders or any other game of that sort at home. My grounds are not large enough. I possess no balls at all."

Several people laughed out loud at this, and Sir Anthony smiled around the group in a slightly perplexed way, clearly uncertain as to what he had said that was so humorous.

But it had worked, Beth thought as everyone walked back to the house a short time later. He had defused the situation, making it impossible for Daniel to continue his attack without becoming belligerent about it.

"He's up to something," said Alex as soon as they were alone in the changing room.

"Don't you think he's just being rude, like he was in Edinburgh?" Beth asked.

Alex thought for a moment while he pulled up his clean ivory silk stockings, gartering them neatly above the knee.

"Maybe. Did he hurt you?"

"Just a bit. My skirts saved me from being injured. It might bruise a little. I'm angry rather than hurt, though."

"He's not worth your anger. He's a fool, that's all. I doubt he'll ever learn. William should have let him rot in the Fleet for a year or two instead of paying his debts off this last time. The young idiot wasn't even grateful, just went straight back out and carried on gambling."

"Why doesn't the earl disinherit him?" Beth asked.

"He can't. The estate's entailed. And he wouldn't anyway. William loves his son. He's always spoilt him and protected him, which is a good part of the problem."

"Prince Edward said Daniel was going to hurt me, about half an hour before he did," Beth said, suddenly remembering. "You said he was odd. He is, isn't he?"

"Yes. I think it was Walpole, Horace that is, not Robert, who said Edward is a 'sayer of things'. He can be really amusing at times, because he's very astute, or embarrassing if you're the person he happens to comment on."

"It's more than that, though," said Beth.

"Yes, it is. He's got the sight, I think. I keep expecting him to point at me and say 'that man's a spy!' or something of the sort. No one would pay any heed to him if he did though, thank God. You look beautiful in that dress," he finished, appreciatively eyeing the royal blue taffeta gown she had changed into. He stood up to help her fasten the tiny hooks and eyes running up the back, dropping a kiss on her bare shoulder as he did.

"I can't say the same for you, unfortunately," she said, looking at the violent purple silk breeches and emerald green waistcoat with disgust. "But you are the epitome of Sir Anthony. Your patch has fallen off," she added with relief.

"Ah," he replied, immediately delving in his pocket and producing an identical little silk cat, to her dismay. "Thank you, my dear. Now, I am sure there must be some gum arabic somewhere…"

During dinner Lord Daniel sat with David at the other end of the table from the Peters, and the meal went very well, although Beth was unable to enjoy herself fully, as she kept expecting further insults to be hurled down the table. The two men were whispering together and every so often would glance in her direction. It was very childish, but it made her feel edgy and irritable. The food was plentiful, with venison in a rich sauce, mutton pasties, oysters and salamangundy, a highly colourful and varied salad, and the conversation was animated. The earlier game was thoroughly dissected, the clothes of the various guests complimented, and the latest staging of *King Lear* by Garrick commented upon.

It was refreshing to see Sir Anthony given a run for his money in the fashion stakes, thought Beth as the party removed to the card room. Percy and David, resplendent in crimson and gold respectively, had applauded the baronet's unique patches, which would shortly result in more profit for Sarah.

Beth, who did not want to play cards, went instead to sit in a corner, where a small group of non-players had gathered to chat. After a few minutes Sir Anthony joined her.

"Not playing, Anthony?" said Philippa. "Not like you."

"I am not in the mood, my dear," he said, flopping down limply next to his wife. "And they are playing loo. I really have no desire to lose my entire estate in one evening."

"Papa is playing," said Philippa. Sir Anthony smiled.

"Your papa is as rich as Croesus, he can afford to lose a fortune without blinking," he said. He stretched his purple legs out in front of him and admired the sparkling diamante buckles on his shoes. "Besides, I really feel quite fatigued."

"Shouldn't have played so well this afternoon then, should you," grumbled Philippa. "Would have won but for you."

"There's a spare seat here for you, Anthony," called Percy. Sir Anthony glanced round. David, Percy and Lord Daniel were seated at a nearby table. Percy beckoned to the remaining empty chair.

"No, no, but thank you," he said. "I will decline tonight. Loo is not my game."

"Oh, come on, Anthony, surely you are not afraid to play?" said Daniel mockingly.

"Indeed I am," said the baronet. "The stakes are too high. Why, in mere minutes I could lose the cost of the new coat I have ordered from my tailor! It is exquisite, scarlet figured silk," he said, turning back to his conversational companions. "Every button has a diamond in the centre! And to match it I am having the most delightful…"

"Will you play whist instead, then?" called Daniel.

"No, do not change your game on my account, dear boy. I am quite decided not to play this evening."

"And I am quite decided you will, sir," said Daniel firmly. "Choose your game. I can't say fairer than that."

Sir Anthony straightened in his seat and turned round to face the young man.

"You are most persistent," he said amiably. "But I will not play cards with you, my lord, not tonight or any other night. I wish you luck with your game."

"Why are you refusing to play with me specifically?" persisted Daniel. "Is my money not good enough for you?"

The baronet's expression remained good-humoured, his eyes friendly. Only Beth, who knew him so well, felt the slight tension quivering through his body, matching her own.

"Indeed, if you were in possession of any money of your own, it would certainly be good enough for me, my lord," he replied. "But your father is my friend and I will not render him any more impecunious than you have already done, by playing cards with you tonight."

Daniel leapt to his feet at once, his face flushed, a curiously triumphant look in his eye.

"By God, sir, how dare you insult me so!" he cried. "I demand satisfaction!"

"Anthony's only spoken the truth, you fool," said Philippa bluntly. "Common knowledge. No money of your own, have you? Normal for heirs. Hardly an insult."

"Nevertheless," said the lord. "I repeat, Sir Anthony, I demand satisfaction!"

"Really, this is most tiresome," said the baronet wearily. "I have already told you I do not wish to play. I am sure Lady Philippa will play. She should satisfy you; she is an excellent player, and quite ruthless."

"It is not cards of which I speak, sir, as you well know!"

"No? Ah. I see. You seek satisfaction of a more…ah…carnal nature. Well, I can recommend an excellent establishment not far from here. My footman spent an exhausting night there quite recently. He could not recommend the ladies highly enough and he is a most virile young man." The baronet winked knowingly and grotesquely at the company, eliciting a chorus of laughter.

"If I wished to seek the services of a whore, Sir Anthony, I need look no further than the woman by your side," Lord Daniel said coldly as soon as the laughter had diminished. "I see I must put it plainly. I challenge you, sir. Name your weapon."

Beth had stiffened and made to rise, but her husband's hand closed firmly around her arm, pulling her back down into her seat.

"I see I must also put it plainly, Daniel," Sir Anthony said into the sudden silence that had fallen over the corner of the room, and which was slowly spreading as others realised something was amiss. "I will not gamble with you, as I hold your father in too much esteem to bankrupt him, even if you do not. On the same basis I will not duel with you, as I will not leave your father without an heir, worthless as that heir may be."

"My God!" cried Daniel. "When you said you possessed no balls earlier, I thought you were joking! Now I see it is true. You are a coward!"

Everyone looked at Sir Anthony. He could not refuse now. No gentleman could allow himself to be publicly called a coward without retaliating.

"Why are you so determined to fight a duel with me?" asked the baronet. "You have deliberately tried to provoke me, when I wished only to relax in the corner and enjoy some light conversation. I will not play your game. Seek your death elsewhere, if you must. I will not oblige you."

"Anthony," whispered James urgently. "You cannot let this go. He has called you a coward! You must answer!"

"I have answered," he replied. Beth was trembling, but displayed no signs of imminent retaliation. Her husband let go of her arm. "I will say no more on the matter."

"You may not, but I will!" persisted Daniel hotly. "I say you are a coward, and a fool too. You have been emasculated by your peasant of a wife."

David was laughing, but Percy had paled.

"For God's sake, Daniel, you have gone too far. Leave it!" he urged.

"I will not," said the lord. "The rest of you may find it acceptable that the daughter of a disgraced lord's son and a common Scotch prostitute could so bewitch a baronet with her sexual ploys as to persuade him to marry her, but I find it appalling that we should have to endure the company of a gutter whore as though she were our equal."

"You will apologise to the lady, immediately," said a commanding voice. Daniel turned to see the diminutive but irate form of the Prince of Wales standing directly behind him.

"With all due respect, Your Highness, I will not," said Daniel recklessly. "I speak only the truth. It's common knowledge that she's the daughter of a whore. Even her husband agrees! He must, else why would he refuse to defend her?"

Beth had turned round in her seat to face Daniel's mocking face, her mouth twisted with rage. Sir Anthony smiled resignedly.

"Oh my dear boy, I see you are determined to…"

There was a flash of movement by the baronet's side, and Daniel cried out suddenly, taking a step backwards and clutching at his shoulder.

"I don't need my husband to defend me, my lord," Beth said, standing now, her fists clenched by her sides, her eyes sparking blue fire in the pallor of her face. "I am quite capable of defending myself. You say it is common knowledge that my mother was a whore. I say it is common knowledge that you are a wastrel and a fool, who demeans yourself by slandering me because you have never forgiven me for rejecting you when you begged me on your knees to marry you. And you have never forgiven my husband, who is worth a hundred of you, for rescuing me when you abducted me and tried to marry me against my will."

She glanced around at the sea of shocked faces, and then back at her enemy. The silence in the room was profound. Daniel still clutched at his shoulder. His face was as white as Beth's, his brown eyes wide with shock and pain.

"You dare to call my husband coward, sir," she said, her voice thick with contempt. "You, who showed what a true and brave gentleman you are by threatening to sever my fingers one by one until I agreed to marry you. You disgrace the name of Highbury, and the aristocracy you belong to."

She turned to the prince, and curtsied briefly.

"You will excuse me if I take my leave, Your Highness. I will wait for you in the coach, Anthony."

She bent down, picked up her reticule from the chair and then walked out of the room, head high, looking neither to right nor left, the soft rustling of her gown clearly audible in the silence. The door closed quietly behind her.

"Bloody hell!" breathed Philippa in awe. "That was magnificent!"

Daniel sat down suddenly. David moved round to his side.

"I would not remove the knife from his shoulder until you have something with which to staunch the blood," suggested the baronet calmly. "It will probably be terribly messy otherwise. I don't think His Highness will appreciate it if you bleed all over his aubusson carpet."

"Indeed I will not," said the prince coldly. "In fact the only thing I will appreciate, once your wound is tended, Lord Daniel, is that you leave my house immediately and do not return."

A servant appeared, carrying a bowl of water and a cloth. Carefully he cut away the sleeve of Daniel's coat and shirt, which were already soaked with blood.

"Such a pity my wife chose that moment to interrupt, when I was about to tell you that you had convinced me of the need to accept your challenge after all. If, once your wound has healed of course, you are still determined to duel with me, I shall oblige you, providing it is only to first blood and not to the death."

"I will gladly act as your second, Sir Anthony," offered Prince Frederick.

Sir Anthony had not thought it possible for Daniel to blanch any more, but he did at this news, and so did David. Interesting.

"Unless, of course, you wish to concede first blood to my wife and end the matter there," continued the baronet. "I will leave it up to you. Now, with your permission, Your Highness, I will also take my leave."

At the door he stopped, and turned round.

"Ah, may I request the return of the knife, my lord, if you have finished with it? I believe it holds some sentimental value for my wife."

"I'm not going to apologise," Beth said, the moment he climbed into the carriage.

"No more do I expect you to," said her husband, handing her the knife. "It will need cleaning. You behaved admirably, my dear. I'm proud of you. Now, I need to think. Please, let us take the time to calm ourselves a little and wait until we get home before we discuss this any further."

At home, they went straight upstairs to change.

"Aren't you angry with me at all?" Beth asked, eyeing him warily as he took off his wig and coat and sat down at the dressing table to remove his paint.

"No," said Alex. "He goaded us beyond endurance. I couldna expect you to put up wi' it, although I'd hoped ye would. Ye were lucky, though. If ye'd missed ye'd hae killed him, or worse, hit the prince. Did ye no' realise he was standing right next to Daniel when you threw the knife?"

"Of course I did," she said. "Luck had nothing to do with it. I wanted to hurt him, and I knew you didn't want to fight him, for some reason. I realised that if I hit him in the right shoulder I'd have my revenge for his insults and also stop him duelling for a few weeks until it heals."

Alex stopped wiping his makeup off and looked at her.

"Are ye telling me you aimed exactly for that spot on his shoulder?" he asked.

"Yes. I'd rather have gone for the heart, mind you, but I wouldn't want the earl to be childless either. I really like him. Why are you surprised? You know I can use a knife." She paused in her undressing to look at him. His eyes were sparkling.

"Well, aye, I kent ye wouldna hesitate to stab a man if there was need. Ye proved that wi' Duncan. But I didna ken ye could throw them as well."

"I told you I threw a knife at Richard once, remember."

"Aye. But ye missed."

"I intended to miss. I wanted to get his attention."

"Truly?" said Alex, completely forgetting about the situation with Daniel in his excitement at discovering this new skill of his wife's. "Could ye put your knife straight through that picture there?" He pointed to an indifferently executed painting of two small children which hung above the fire, and which they both disliked.

"Yes, if you want," said Beth. "Which bit of the picture do you want me to hit?"

"How about the boy's shoulder?" suggested Alex with a grin.

She stood, dressed only in her stays and shift, and took aim. Then her hand came back over her shoulder and forward with lightning speed, and the knife was quivering in the picture.

Alex went over to examine it.

"*Bas mallaichte!*" he breathed. "Ye did it! Could you teach me, and the others?"

"Yes of course, if you want," she said. "But you're so skilled with weapons I assumed you'd be able to do it already."

"No. That is, I can throw knives and make them stick in things. But I couldna aim wi' that accuracy. That's amazing! Your mother taught ye that?"

"Yes."

"What an awfu' fine woman," he said admiringly.

"I'm glad you think so, after all the insults she received this evening. Why did you let him do that, Alex, call me a whore and you a coward too? Why didn't you accept his challenge? You didn't have to kill him."

Alex pulled the knife out of the picture and handed it back to Beth, then ran his hands through his hair.

"He was up to something, Beth. He wanted me to accept the challenge. He was desperate for me to. If I'd agreed to play cards he'd hae accused me of cheating or some such thing. He was determined to get me to duel wi' him. Did ye no' see that? He'd never have refused a direct order from Prince Frederick to apologise otherwise. I wasna sure at first, but after ye'd left the room I accepted the challenge, when his arm's healed, and Fred volunteered to be my second. Daniel went white as snow, and so did David. I'll bet he'd already agreed to second Daniel."

"What do you think he was going to do?" said Beth.

It's my guess that they intended to get me to a private spot for the duel, and kill both myself and my second. They could always say there'd been some sort of accident wi' the pistols, or that my second tried to kill Daniel after he'd shot me, and had to be killed in self-defence. Of course, they assumed my second would be one of my servants. They could hardly kill the heir to the throne. That's why they blanched when Fred offered."

"Why does Daniel want to kill you, though?"

"I dinna ken, rightly. It's probably nothing more than spite. He's never forgiven you for not marrying him, and me for rescuing ye, as ye rightly said. I expect he'll hate us even more, now ye've tellt the whole of society the details. It wasna widely known that he'd abducted you."

"It is now," Beth said dryly. "Do you think he'll take up the challenge, then? Will you have to kill him?"

"I canna kill him, Beth. I've promised his father I'll no' hurt him, that I'll look out for him when I can."

"You've what?" said Beth, incredulously.

"Aye. Why d'ye think I didna kill him at the Fleet when he abducted ye? I wanted to, God knows."

"I never thought about it," said Beth. "But I thought you were Sir Anthony then, and he's a bit squeamish about blood."

Alex laughed.

"Aye, it's a devil to get out of silk and velvet," he said. "I'm going to have tae watch Daniel now, though. I dinna think he'll take up the challenge to a fair duel. It wasna what he was after. If he does I'll accept Frederick's offer, and wound the young gomerel enough tae put him out of action for a wee while. I'm more worried that he'll try something more underhand. Ye'll have to be careful for a while, too, Beth. Dinna go out without Angus or Duncan, if I'm no' with ye."

"Why?" said Beth, thoroughly worried now. "What do you think he might do?"

"Nothing, until his shoulder's healed, I hope. After that, I dinna ken. But I dinna want him to hurt you, because if he does, I'll kill him, promise or no, and I wouldna feel good about that. I want to avoid that, I must avoid that, at all costs."

"The earl must be a very good friend to you," said Beth, knowing that Alex did not make promises lightly, and hoping he would now elaborate on the details of his friendship with this man he saw only seldom.

"Aye, he is" said Alex, and then he changed the subject to arranging times for Beth to give the others knife-throwing lessons, and would be drawn no further.

CHAPTER EIGHTEEN

August, 1745

The atmosphere inside the stagecoach to London was somewhat merry, or at least as merry as it is possible to be when one has been closed up with one's fellow passengers for several days in a contrivance with hard seats and ventilation only from inconvenient draughts, and then jounced along the rutted and sometimes dangerous roadways of England for over twelve hours a day.

Still, as this was the normal state of affairs when travelling by stagecoach, and as the journey was almost at an end and no one had been killed or even injured, the extremely malodorous clerk had dismounted at Birmingham, the coach had not lost a wheel, and the driver, whilst fond of his ale, was at least not *permanently* inebriated, there was cause for merriment indeed.

The company, overall, had been pretty good too, and the evenings in the indifferent inns along the way had passed reasonably well. The sprightly octogenarian widow travelling to attend her youngest granddaughter's marriage, had had some interesting tales to tell of the old days, when Catholic James was on the throne, before the Glorious Revolution of 1688. She even remembered, as a small child, being held up to see Charles the Second as he drove past in his gilt carriage. The mirror-maker claimed to have travelled all over Europe, and told lavish stories of the Palace of Versailles and of the streets of Venice, which were not really streets at all, but canals, on which one could make love to dark-eyed beauties whilst floating along in strangely-shaped boats hung with glittering lanterns.

Only the young man with the strange accent who had boarded at Carlisle had nothing of interest to add to the conversation. In fact within an hour or so of him joining the stage, his fellow-travellers had come to the unanimous conclusion that there was nothing interesting about him at all. His clothes, though clean enough, were of a dull grey wool with no decoration, his hair (he wore his own hair, unpowdered too, which told a good deal about the lowliness of his birth) was a nondescript shade of brown, and he gave away nothing about himself, other than that he was from Carlisle, and was going to London to join his brother, who had already been living there for some time. He was pleasant enough, and courteous to the ladies; but clearly he had not had an eventful day in his life, and although he listened to his fellow passengers' tales with polite interest, he asked no questions, nor did he supply any stories of his own.

Once they entered London, he spent most of his time looking out of the window, observing the press of people, traders, horses and coaches which crowded the streets and brought the stagecoach's speed down to a crawling pace. After a while he announced that he thought it would be quicker for him to walk the rest of the way rather than remain cooped up in the coach for another hour or so until it reached the terminus at Holborn, and taking his (very small) bag from the floor between his legs, he leapt down from the coach and disappeared into the throng.

The young man had not wanted to take the stage at all; he would have preferred to ride. But he was travelling alone, and his journey had been a very long one, and to have made it on horseback without ending with his throat cut in a ditch would have been a miracle. His message was important. He could not risk it not being delivered. He smiled, glad to be almost at his destination. He was grateful to be in the air again; the adjective fresh could in no way be ascribed to the stuff which he inhaled as he made his way along the street. He had smelt all the odours which assailed his nostrils before; sweat, horses, various foodstuffs both fresh and rotting, urine, perfume, halitosis; but never in such concentrations as they now were. He tried not to wrinkle his nose with distaste, and, remembering the instructions he'd been given and occasionally asking the way, he slowly made his way to the north of the city, until he finally entered streets where the thoroughfares were wider, and less populous, and the hint of a smell of green fields refreshed him.

He stopped outside a large cream-coloured house surrounded by ornate iron railings. Several freshly-scrubbed steps led up to a green-painted door. The young man hesitated, excitement building in him, and took a moment to brush the dust from his coat, although he knew the people he was about to meet wouldn't care about his appearance. Then he moved to the bottom of the steps, and as he did so the door opened and a man appeared at the threshold, his head turned back over his shoulder to address someone in the hall behind him.

The young man halted, his mouth slightly open. He had never seen such a sight in his life before. The vision before him sported a peacock-blue frockcoat lavishly embroidered with gold leaves and flowers, and matching satin breeches, fastened with silver buckles at the knees. His stockings and waistcoat were of a scarlet so bright it hurt the eyes, and expensive Brussels lace frothed at the man's wrists and throat. Then the vision laughed lightly, and turning his white mask of a face forward, saw the young man at the foot of the steps; and froze.

"Holy Mother of God," the vision said, and took an involuntary step backwards, colliding with and treading on the foot of his wife, who was right behind him. She cried out in pain and he reached back automatically to steady her, never taking his eyes off the young grey-clad man all the while.

Then he recovered himself, and glancing quickly up the street observed that there were a good many people about; people who would note and comment if a young man of low birth were admitted through the front door of the house of such an important gentleman as himself.

"Ah, I had all but given up on your ever arriving!" the fop called, holding up his hand to stop the man mounting the steps. "You will go round the back of the house to the kitchen immediately, where John will meet you and show you your duties." He paid the man no further attention and turned back into the hall, where his wife was attempting to fight her way through yards of pink silk to assess the damage to her crushed toes.

"Now my dear, if you are really feeling so ill, then of course we will not go," he said in a peevish voice which carried halfway up the street. "But I wish you had thought to tell me before I spent an hour dressing. Really, it is most inconsiderate of you. No of course not," he continued, as though Beth was speaking to him, rather than merely staring at him as though he'd gone mad. "I would not dream of leaving you alone if you are ill." He pushed her gently backwards into the hall, and, after glancing back quickly to ascertain that the young man had gone, he shut the door.

"What on earth's going on?" said Beth as Alex made to run past her in the direction of the kitchen.

"Alasdair," he said. "Alasdair's here."

"What? Peigi's Alasdair? Are you expecting him?" She lifted her skirts and ran after him as he tore into the kitchen, her squashed toes forgotten.

"No," he said. "There must be something wrong."

In the kitchen Maggie and Iain had been sitting chatting at the table, but were now standing, looking at Alasdair with the same shocked expression that Alex, or rather Sir Anthony, had.

"What's amiss, man?" Alex said as soon as he was through the door.

Alasdair stared at him for a moment. He had heard of Sir Anthony, of course, from other clan members who had seen Alex's alter ego; but nothing could have prepared him for the real thing. If it wasn't for the unmistakable rich deep voice that had just addressed him, Alasdair wouldn't have believed his chieftain could be present under all the silk and paint. Certainly the fop at the door had neither sounded nor looked anything like Alex. It was remarkable.

Angus and then Duncan appeared behind their brother and Beth, and Alasdair remembered why he was here.

"He's landed," he said simply. "On the twenty-third, at Eriskay."

No one asked who had landed. Alex sat down heavily at the table and removed his wig. Beth remained standing, unable to sit at the narrow bench in her hooped skirts. Duncan and Angus hovered behind her. The oven fire crackled merrily. The stew bubbled in the pot. Time stood still.

"Has he brought the French?" Alex asked finally.

"No," said Alasdair.

Alex swore, fluently, in three languages. Time moved on.

"Has he brought anything? Except himself?" he asked hopefully.

Alasdair smiled wearily.

"He brought seven men wi' him," he said.

"Jesus," said Duncan.

"No, he wasna among them, unfortunately," Alasdair said irreverently.

"Neither was King Louis, I take it?" said Alex.

"No. He did have another ship, wi' seven hundred Irish troops, and a whole load of weapons, but it had a wee set-to wi' an English warship, and had to turn back to France."

Alex scrubbed his fingers through his hair, violently.

"So he landed in Scotland last month, wi' seven men and nothing else. Tell me he's on his way home again, please," said Alex, knowing already that if this was the case Alasdair would not have come over three hundred miles to tell him so.

"That's what MacDonald of Boisdale tellt him tae do," Alasdair said. "He went straight to see him, and tell him that the MacLeods and the MacDonalds of Sleat willna rise for him, as he hadna brought the French wi' him. Boisdale tellt him to go straight home. Charles said that he *was* come home. He's sent his ship back to France."

This so clearly matched what Beth would expect the dynamic young prince who had won her affections in Rome to do, that she laughed. Everyone looked at her. Alex scowled.

"I'm sorry," she said, blushing. "It's just so typical of him though, isn't it?"

"Aye, it is, the bloody idiot," Alex said. "Tae arrive in Scotland wi' no men, no weapons, and be told that two of the biggest clans willna support ye, and then refuse to see sense. That's just what we need in a leader." He stood up. "Let's get out of these stupid clothes, Beth. Duncan, you take a message to Isabella to say that Lady Elizabeth is indisposed, but it's nothing serious. Alasdair, have yourself a wash and a bite, and then we'll all meet back here in half an hour or so."

"Right, then," Alex said later. "Tell us everything. Then we can decide what we're going to do."

They were all seated round the kitchen table, bowls of stew in front of them, cups of ale at their elbows. Alasdair, having already demolished one bowl while the others were changing or delivering messages, gratefully accepted a second helping. The food at the inns had been indifferent, to say the least, and his funds meagre.

"Aye. Well, as I said, he landed wi' his seven men, and then the news spread like wildfire. Boisdale came tae him the next day, and then Charles moved on to Borrodale, to a farmhouse there. He sent letters out to all the chiefs, and a good few came and tellt him the same thing Boisdale did, to away off hame. But he wouldna go, and then Clanranald declared for him. Once he'd done it Glencoe and Keppoch joined too."

"Glencoe?" Beth said, her eyes wide.

"Aye. It was from your cousins at Glencoe that we heard about the prince landing in the first place. Kenneth was all for me riding down to ye that night, but then we thought he might still go hame, so we waited a wee while to see what transpired."

Alex was counting furiously.

"That's still only six hundred men," he said. "It isna enough to inspire the rest. Ye said MacLeod and Sleat willna commit. Lochiel willna either, and Lovat'll no' bring out the Frasers unless…"

"Lochiel's declared for the prince," Alasdair interrupted.

Alex stared at him in shock. The Camerons were a big clan, and powerful.

"No," he said after a minute. "No. I dinna believe it. Donald wouldna do that, no' without the French."

"He has, though," insisted Alasdair. "He rode up himself to see Charles, and they had an awfu' long talk, so I heard, and Lochiel wasna keen, tae say the least. But the prince won him round, and he's bringing the Camerons out. That's when we decided to come and tell ye, because once Lochiel agreed, we knew others'd join. Glengarry already has. Charles is raising his standard at Glenfinnan on the nineteenth, and they're all meeting him there, wi' their men."

The nineteenth. And today was the tenth. Nine days.

"This is it, then," said Iain in wonder. "After all these years of waiting, this is finally it."

"When do we leave?" asked Angus, his eyes bright with fervour.

"Wait," said Alex, holding up his hand. "I need tae think."

"Think?" cried Angus. "What's there tae think about? The whole of Scotland's rising for Charles!"

"No, it isna, ye bloody fool," said Alex, rounding on Angus so fiercely that he flinched backwards. "I wouldna hesitate for a second if it was. A wee bit o' Scotland's rising for him, that's all. I canna believe Lochiel's been bewitched by him. Christ, we're no' ready. It's suicide."

"Aye, well I'm sure it will be, if everyone thinks like you," retorted Angus scornfully. "If we wait for the French, we'll all die of old age, wi' our swords rusting under our beds and Geordie mouldering on the throne till he's ninety."

Alex lunged, grabbing Angus by his shirt with such force that he lifted him from his seat.

"And if we rise now, when we havena sufficient arms or the northern clans behind us, and no support frae the French or the English, we'll all die in the field, wi' our weapons rusting in the mud and Geordie's kin ruling forever, wi' no one to stop them." He threw Angus back down on the bench with a thud, and only Duncan's arms wrapped round the young man's chest stopped him from retaliating.

"It's no' the time, Angus," Duncan said quietly. "Leave it."

There was silence for a few minutes. Alex rubbed his hand through his hair again. Angus's breathing slowly returned to normal. Everyone looked at their chieftain with anticipation.

"Have ye no' heard anything of what's going on, down here?" Alasdair asked.

"There have been rumours," Beth said. "But there are rumours all the time. If we believed them, then we'd be in a permanent state of readiness for war. A couple of days ago the Elector put up a reward of thirty thousand pounds for anyone who captured the prince, and it was said there were vague rumours he'd embarked from France. Otherwise, no, there's been nothing substantial."

"It's no' such a stupid time as it seems, though, is it?" said Iain. "Wi' most of the British troops in Flanders, and losing, too. They're being pushed back all the time. Cumberland's away, and Geordie's in Hanover. If we strike fast we could be in London before they can get the army back to stop us."

"That's true," said Maggie. "Ye said yourself, Alex, that there's no more than seven thousand troops in the whole of Britain right now."

Alex showed no sign of having heard any of this. He sat at the table, head bowed, soup congealing in his bowl.

"If we leave tomorrow, we could make it tae Glenfinnan in time, just," said Angus.

"I canna go," Alex said quietly.

Angus shot to his feet.

"What do you mean, ye canna go!" said Angus.

"What I said." Alex looked up at his brother. "I canna go. Nor can Beth. No' yet. We'll have to stay a while, and see what the British intend to do when they find out what's happening. I've got arms coming in too, that I've tae pay for and arrange to get up to Scotland." He sighed. "Duncan, it'll be up to you to raise the clan for Charles. But only those that really want to go, ye ken. No one's to be coerced, and no boys under fifteen, no matter how they plead. And if ye get to Charles and find he's only got a handful of men after all, I want ye to go home, taking all the men with ye." He looked pointedly at Angus.

"We canna do that!" said Angus. "We've sworn to support him. We canna betray him now!"

The others half expected Alex to go for his brother again, but he merely looked at him, and when he spoke, his tone was calm.

"Angus, you're a man now. Think like one. Aye, I swore to support him, if he had French backing. And I'll support him without that, if I think we've a chance of success. But it's no betrayal to prevent a man from killing himself when he hasna a hope in hell of winning. James will never come to claim the throne himself, now. He's too old and sick. Charles is all we've got. And he'll only get the one chance. If he canna see when the time is wrong, it'll be up to his friends to do it for him."

"Do you think the time is wrong?" asked Beth.

"I dinna ken. Iain and Angus have a point. The French may never give us troops, and most of the British army is tied up abroad right now. But if enough of the clans willna commit, then I'll no' get my men killed out of misguided loyalty. We've had enough aborted attempts at a rising before. The next one must be a success, or the Stuart cause is lost. That's my view."

"What will you do then, if Duncan takes the men home?" asked Beth.

"I'll go up there and tell Charles myself why we'll no' fight for him. I owe him that at least. I wouldna expect anyone else to tell him such a thing to his face."

"Would he be awfu' angry, do ye think?" said Maggie apprehensively.

"No," smiled Alex. "He'd be awfu' persuasive. He is. I've nae doubt that's how he's won Lochiel over. He could persuade the devil himself to sing psalms if he'd a mind to. That's why he's so dangerous. If he'd as much sense as he's got charm, I'd no' be worried."

"I'll stay here too, Alex," said Maggie. "Ye canna keep up the pretence of Sir Anthony wi' no servants at all. I can at least do the cooking, and keep the important rooms clean. Ye'll have to hire a man for the heavy stuff, though."

"No," said Iain. "I'll stay with ye."

Everyone looked at him in surprise.

"It'll no' be for long, I'm sure," he said. "Duncan has to go, he's the next in line after Alex, and the men'll listen to him, and wild horses wouldna keep Angus away, that's obvious. I can wait until ye're ready, Alex."

"It could be a few weeks," Alex said.

"Aye, well, ye'll be needing a footman, I'm thinking. If ye hire a coachman, he can live out, and then ye'll no' need to be Sir Anthony all the time when you're at home."

Alex smiled, slapped him on the back by way of thanks, then lifted his spoon, looked at the soup, and put it back down on the table. There was another short silence, during which Angus positively fizzed with excitement, and the others displayed various expressions, beneath all of which was the dawning realisation that it seemed the rising was, at last, finally about to happen.

"Well, then," burst out Angus after ten seconds, when he could stand the endless contemplation no more. "Are we going to celebrate, or is it a nice wee cup of chocolate and an early night?"

As nobody felt partial to chocolate, but everyone felt the need, one way or another, for alternative liquid refreshment, it turned out to be a very late night indeed.

* * *

In the end it was a few days before Duncan, Angus and Alasdair left, because once they realised that it wouldn't be possible to raise the clan and get to Glenfinnan in time for the unfurling of the standard on the nineteenth, the need for haste diminished somewhat.

Alex, driven to distraction by Angus's boundless optimism, coupled with continual reassurances that his brother was no more than a Job's comforter and reflections on what it would be like to march triumphantly into London a few weeks hence, finally dispatched the unquenchable bundle of energy off to the coast to arrange shipment of the arms to Leith, and advise the smuggler Gabriel Foley of what was transpiring, if he didn't already know. Once Angus was gone, everyone could get down to packing, and discussing the situation in a more practical relaxed manner. Certainly Alex and Duncan were more relaxed, the former because the temptation to strangle his brother was at least temporarily removed, and the latter because holding yourself continually in a state of readiness to throw yourself between your siblings to prevent fratricide was somewhat wearing after a while.

Over the next day or so the plan took shape, on the assumption that the rising would not be another abortive one. It had been decided that the men would leave quietly by night, in the hopes that their absence would not be noted. The elevated circles in which Sir Anthony moved hardly registered servants at all, and wouldn't notice if his coachman suddenly changed. Or his footman. Or his whole household, for that matter. In the meantime, to cover up the sudden lack of staff, Sir Anthony would declare that he had just received his tailor's bill and had decided to retrench and give no entertainments for a while in an attempt to save money. His friends would see it as one of his little moods, soon to pass, Beth could moan in public about how frugal he had become about ridiculous things, whilst not economising at all on his wardrobe, and everyone would laugh at Sir Anthony's little foibles. In the meantime, as letters from Scotland to London would certainly be viewed with suspicion by the authorities, any coded missives from Duncan would be routed to Gabriel Foley via John Holker, a respectable and trustworthy Manchester cloth merchant who Beth had met briefly once in an alleyway room over two years ago. At a convenient time, when there was no more useful information to be gleaned in London, the Peters would pack their bags, announce their intention to go for a short trip abroad, and disappear. Then the MacGregor chieftain would rejoin his men, hopefully in plenty of time to engage in some interesting fighting before the triumphal entry into London which Angus was so enamoured of. And once Charles was safely installed as Regent for King James in London, Alex would send for his wife, who would of course be waiting safely and patiently with the other women at Loch Lomond for his summons.

Beth had her own views regarding her prospective role in this plan, but recognised that now was not the best time to discuss them, with Alex in a state of heightened tension. He was already worried about committing his clansmen to a rising he was unsure of, concerned for the safety of his over-enthusiastic youngest brother, and frustrated that he could not abandon Sir Anthony immediately and charge off to battle as he wanted. It was unlikely that he would receive with equanimity the news that his wife had no intention of meekly sitting in a Highland hut for months awaiting his summons to join him. Time for that later. Right now there was something more pressing to attend to.

"Duncan," Beth said, having finally succeeded in catching him on his own in his room. "I need to speak with you alone."

He looked up in surprise as she closed the door behind her. On his bed was a small pile of favourite books, from which he was trying to select one to take with him.

"Aye, what is it?" he said, obviously expecting her to ask him to look after Angus, or something of the sort.

"What are you going to do about Sarah?" she asked.

The emotion only revealed itself on his face for a fraction of a second, but she was observing him closely, and saw it. He looked away.

"Nothing," he said. "We're friends, that's all."

She snorted derisively, and he looked back at her, saw there was no point in continuing this line.

"Aye, well," he said. "What can I do? I can hardly go and tell her I'm away off tae fight for Prince Charlie, can I now?"

"She'll be terribly hurt if you leave without saying goodbye, Duncan," Beth said softly. "She really likes you."

He ran his hand through his hair in the way of his brother.

"Better that than she suspect something and go to the authorities," he said.

"She won't do that," Beth said. "And you know it. She already knows Maggie's a Jacobite, and that I'm a Catholic at the very least."

"And that's more than she should ken," he said. He held a hand up as Beth made to speak again. "Ye dinna need to defend Sarah to me, Beth," he continued. "I was being unfair. She willna go to the authorities. But they may well come to her at some point, if you and Alex disappear. And the less she kens the better. If they believe she has no information, they'll no' harm her. If they find out she kens a little, they'll want more. I wouldna have her hurt."

"What will I tell her? She'll notice you've gone. She'll ask."

He sat down on the bed to think, and she went and sat next to him.

"Tell her I've had to go home, on family business. That my granny's died or something of the sort, and I've tae go to the funeral, sort out her affairs. And that I'll come back, when it's all over," he added softly.

"Will you?" she asked, taking his hand, which had been smoothing the sheet. He closed his fingers around hers and looked at her, his grey eyes clouded with unexpressed emotion, and behind that, apprehension.

"Aye, I will," he said. "If it all goes well. And if it doesna…well, I daresay she'd no' want to see me anyway, in that case. Tell her, will ye?"

"No," Beth said. "Tell her yourself. It'll come better from you. You can call in on your way to Scotland, explain you've got to rush to get there for the funeral, that it could take some time to sort out everything, with all the cousins and suchlike. But you tell her, Duncan, or she'll be hurt. You're the first man she's trusted in years, and you owe it to her…"

"Tae tell her a pack of lies," Duncan interrupted.

"She'll understand that, later, when you come back and tell her the truth. But she won't understand if you leave without saying goodbye. She'll harden her heart against you, and you'll never get her back."

In the end, he didn't go on his way to Scotland, but the evening before, and he didn't rush off, but stayed for a few hours. When he came back in the early hours of the morning he seemed happier. And sadder, too. What he said, and what Sarah replied, remained a mystery, because neither of them ever spoke of it to anyone else.

* * *

"Ridiculous upstart!" Lord Edward announced, inadvertently interrupting Beth, who had just been assuring the Earl of Highbury in a low voice that there was really no need for him to apologise yet again for the behaviour of his wayward son. The earl glanced coolly across at Edward, awaiting further comment before he defended his son from what appeared to be, in Beth's view, a fair accusation.

"Cope will soon send him packing, never fear," said Lord Winter. "All a storm in a teacup, if you ask me."

The earl relaxed, gathered his bishop's robes about him, and turned his attention back to Beth.

"I am surprised you didn't choose to attend this little masquerade as an Amazon warrior, Lady Elizabeth," he said. "It would be more fitting than a demure mediaeval lady, surely?"

"Mediaeval ladies did not wear corsets, my lord," Beth smiled "I have chosen comfort over aptness. And it is always better to hide one's light under a bushel. It gives one the element of surprise."

"Yes, well, you certainly had that with Daniel. If you won't accept my apologies, then at least accept my thanks for not killing him. Anthony tells me you're remarkably accurate with a knife."

Beth shifted uncomfortably. How much did her husband tell Highbury?

"How is Daniel?" she asked.

"Healing. And licking his wounds over in France. Or possibly Switzerland by now."

"Oh, my lord!" cried Isabella. "Surely you have not let your only son travel abroad in these dreadful times!"

Lord Edward and his sisters, considering it beneath their dignity to adopt costume, but wishing to attend the party, had paid lip service to the spirit of the masquerade by wearing normal attire and adopting black velvet masks which covered their faces and were kept in place by a button held between the lips. Isabella's voice was somewhat muffled as a result, and it took the earl a moment to interpret her utterance.

"Ah, no, it is perfectly safe," he said after the requisite pause. "Travel is never affected by something as trivial as warfare, Isabella. The French are perfectly courteous towards the British in their own country, unless one dons a scarlet coat and waves a sword around. I doubt even Daniel will be indiscreet enough to do that."

"You really would call this little skirmish warfare?" asked Lord Winter, sweating heavily in the fur-lined robes of a judge.

"Good God, no, I was referring to the war in Flanders," replied Highbury. "That pack of ragged Highlanders will soon be seen off by General Cope, as you so wisely said. Why, he has over fourteen hundred men under his command, does he not?"

"Oh, no, my lord, he has far more than that," said Lord Winter proudly. "You should have been in the Lords today when we were discussing it. I have it on authority that Cope has now a total of three thousand, eight hundred and fifty men at his disposal."

"As many as that?" trilled Sir Anthony, appearing from nowhere, jingling merrily and delivering the lord a smart smack on the back of the head with an inflated sheep's bladder.

"He, at least has come in suitable costume," muttered Lydia Fortesque to her father under her breath, causing Beth, who was standing within earshot, to grin.

"For God's sake, Anthony, it's a masquerade, not a bloody play!" shouted Lord Winter, rubbing his abused head. "You're only supposed to look like a fool, not act the part too."

"Why break the habit of a lifetime?" said Beth nastily. "He spent enough on the costume, he might as well live up to it."

Sir Anthony shot his wife a withering look. The red and yellow belled jester's hat drooped over one eye.

"I thought you were retrenching, Sir Anthony," said Lady Winter. "No more fun, that sort of thing."

"Second-rate claret, no redecoration of the drawing room, no…"

"Oh, but my dear ladies! There is fun, and then there are clothes!" cried Sir Anthony, cutting off his wife's protests. "One must keep up appearances, you know. I am only economising on luxury items. Like newspapers. What were you saying about Cope, Bartholomew? I am sorry if I hurt you, do please accept my most profuse and heartfelt…"

"I was saying that he has a much larger force than is generally known at his disposal," Lord Winter interrupted.

"Ah, but that force will be to no avail if the Highlanders vanish into the mountains, as men of that craven type have always done when asked to stand and fight," pointed out the baronet.

"They will have no chance to. Cope is going north to meet them. He has already consulted with the Lord President and others who know the country well, and is assured of help from the clans loyal to the crown, who of course also know the territory. Initially he wanted to meet the rebels in the lowlands…"

"If they get that far," said Highbury disparagingly.

"Indeed," smiled the lord. "But the Marquis of Tweedale insisted Cope march north. He is heading for Fort Augustus, which is near to the seat of the rebellion, you know, and has a considerable number of arms to give to the loyal clans."

"Is this common knowledge?" asked Lord Edward.

"No, of course not," said Lord Winter, with the important look of one who is privy to all manner of secret information. "But I am sure I can rely on you not to spread the word. I only tell you so that the ladies will not be unduly worried about what is only an insignificant, trivial matter."

"Indeed," said Sir Anthony. "It is well known that peers of the realm spend the bulk of their days in the Lords debating insignificant, trivial matters. I am joking, sir," he said, seeing Lord Winter's imminent explosion. "If I am later to endure my wife castigating me over my expenditure, you will at least allow me to enjoy my costume to the full now."

He swung his bladder once more at Lord Winter, who ducked, with the result that Lord Edward received a faceful of sheep's innards, and then bowed, extending his parti-coloured leg to the company before prancing off into the crowd of revellers that thronged the pleasure gardens.

"How on earth you endure him I have no idea, Elizabeth," said Lord Edward in a rare moment of sympathy with his cousin.

"Neither do I, Edward," she replied. "I sometimes wish I had allowed you to force me to marry Lord Redburn instead of Anthony, after all."

"Was it important, what Bartholomew told us today?" Beth asked later. The merry hat drooped on the bedpost; its formerly merry wearer drooped on the bed.

"Aye, it was. If Charles kent about it tomorrow, it'd be verra useful to him in planning whether to face Cope or avoid him. But while I'm at least five days hard riding away from him, no, it's no bloody use at all."

Today he had received his first letter from Duncan, saying that he had raised the clan, and fifty men were marching with him to join the prince and see how the land lay. She knew that Alex was torn between wanting to lead his men himself, as was his duty and desire, and knowing that he was in a unique position to hear possibly crucial information here.

She went over and sat next to him on the bed.

"It must be very frustrating, hearing all this news and knowing that by the time you can get it to Charles, it'll be worthless."

"It is," he admitted, "I canna wait to be wi' my men, fighting, but right now it's necessary that I bide here. And I did find out some other useful information while I was cavorting about hitting people. Iain's on his way to Foley with it as we speak, and wi' luck it'll be in Scotland by the week's end."

"What's that?"

"The Duke of Newcastle's taking the rebellion seriously. And the Elector's starting to. He's going to cut short his visit to Hanover and come home. And he's asked for six thousand Dutch troops to be sent to Scotland. They're due under treaty anyway, and if they're as useless here as they were at Fontenoy, we've nae need to fear. Cumberland's written to Newcastle asking for command of the home forces if the Jacobite invasion becomes serious, but for now George wants him to continue losing in Flanders."

"And you found all that out today?" Beth asked incredulously.

"Aye," he grinned, pulling her close to him. "It's amazing what people will tell a ridiculous fool covered in bells, or rather what they'll say in his presence. There'd be no point in telling him directly of course, him being too stupid to comprehend the import of what they say."

"But clever enough to ask lots of questions to draw them out."

"Exactly. People love to be the first to ken momentous information. It makes them feel important. And in telling other people, they feel even more important. That's why spies are usually discreet, apparent nonentities. It's because they ken well when to keep their mouths shut."

"Discreet. Like Sir Anthony," Beth laughed.

"Aye, like Sir Anthony," Alex agreed. "And when he's gone, as I hope he will be verra soon, everyone will remember the clothes, and the patches, and the paint. And no one will recall a damn thing about the colourless forgettable man hiding inside."

"Hardly colourless," Beth said, fingering the soft curls of bright russet hair growing in a place normally well and truly hidden from everyone. He sighed happily, then turned over suddenly, trapping her underneath him.

"Nor forgettable, either, I hope," he murmured, and in the next hours proved to his wife that whatever adjectives could be ascribed to him, and there were many, forgettable was definitely not one of them.

* * *

Early September 1745

When Beth awoke, Alex was still fast asleep, curled on his side. She lay and watched him sleeping for a few minutes, then slid slowly out of bed, hoping not to disturb him. For a moment she thought she'd succeeded, but then his eyes snapped open, instantly alert for any danger.

"Shhh," she said softly. "It's early. Go back to sleep for a while."

He smiled, sighed, and then his eyes closed again, and he was instantly asleep.

Throwing a dressing gown over her nightgown, she left the bedroom and made her way downstairs to the kitchen. He could sleep as late as he wanted to this morning. They had no visits planned for today.

Last night he'd been at Highbury's club and hadn't returned until the early hours, exhausted and smelling of brandy and tobacco. She'd half-roused when he came in, and had been vaguely aware of him yawning and removing his makeup by the light of one candle so as not to disturb her too much, before sliding into bed next to her, wrapping his arm round her waist, and falling immediately into a deep sleep.

He was spending more and more evenings out at various gentlemen's clubs these days. Beth understood why; they were the best places to hear about the latest military manoeuvres. She also understood that she could not accompany him to these exclusively male domains.

Understanding was not, however, the same as liking. She was seeing a lot less of him as he strove to learn as much as possible about the Hanoverian reaction to the increasingly serious threat the Jacobite rebellion was now posing. Any useful information was immediately put into code and relayed, via Iain and Gabriel Foley, northward to Scotland, where more and more men were joining Prince Charles.

It was necessary. But she missed her husband. It was as simple as that. However today, she determined, would be theirs. He needed some relaxation and she intended to ensure that he got it, if only for a few hours.

Maggie and Iain had gone shopping for provisions, so after a solitary breakfast she repaired to the library, intending to write a letter to Thomas and Jane, but instead was distracted by the unusual title of the book someone, presumably Iain, as Maggie was not much for the reading, had left on the table. *The Sofa – A Moral Tale*. Leafing through it, she noticed the unusual chapter headings too: *Chapter I – The least tedious chapter in the book*. Intrigued, she curled up in a corner of the sofa and started to read, soon becoming caught up in the story, which appeared to be about a gentleman whom, upon dying, had been reincarnated as a series of sofas, and was now telling stories to a Sultan, who bore more than a passing resemblance to King Louis of France, about the people who had sat upon him, and, it seemed, had proceeded to do a great deal more than merely sit.

After a while she heard Iain and Maggie return from their errands and head for the kitchen. She stretched and yawned, and looked out of the window. It was a beautiful day, sunny and warm, a perfect day for a walk. Not for the first time she longed to do what Iain and Maggie took for granted; to dress in casual clothes, and go for a stroll, hand in hand with her spouse. A simple pleasure, but not one she could enjoy whilst they continued to live in this Godforsaken city as Sir Anthony and Lady Elizabeth.

She sighed. If she was feeling frustrated at the restrictions of her current life, how much worse must it be for Alex? Now that his clan had joined Prince Charles, Alex was growing increasingly impatient with the endless round of society calls and meetings, desperate to be with his clan, fighting for the Stuarts. Soon, he kept telling her, and himself, soon they would pack and leave, and when they returned to London, it would be with a victorious army, and as Alex and Beth MacGregor.

She wondered if there had been any mail. Iain called in at the coffee house twice weekly, where any letters for Benjamin Johnson would be held. She finished her chapter and then headed down to the kitchen to find out. Alex was probably up by now. If any letters had arrived, they'd be in code, and it would take him a good few minutes to decipher them anyway.

She was halfway along the corridor which led to the kitchen when a masculine expletive followed by a sudden crashing sound made her quicken her steps, and she almost ran into the kitchen, skidding to a halt in the doorway at the sight which met her eyes.

Alex, dressed only in breeches, was leaning over the table, breathing heavily, his hair falling over his face, his arms braced on the scrubbed wood. The crashing noise had presumably come from the table being swept clean of crockery and cutlery, which was now scattered across the floor. Beth exchanged a glance with Iain and Maggie, ascertaining by their expressions that they were no wiser than she was as to what had caused this outburst of violence against the breakfast utensils.

For a full minute no one spoke, the only sound being that of Alex's breathing as he sought to bring his emotions under control.

"What's wrong?" Beth finally broke the silence, unable to wait any longer to find out what the hell was going on.

Alex remained as he was, and after another few moments, Beth opened her mouth to ask again, when he suddenly looked up at her, and to her horror, his eyes were brimming with tears.

"There was a letter," Iain said. He looked down at the floor, and Beth, following his gaze, saw the single sheet of paper lying amongst the broken crockery. She bent to pick it up, intending to read it, but as she had expected, it was in code.

"What's wrong?" she repeated, frantic now. "Have we lost? Did Cope win? Are Duncan and Angus…?"

"No," Alex interrupted. "No, they're fine. We havena lost. Well, no' as far as I ken. Charles is riding to meet Cope now. I'm sorry," he continued. "I shouldna have…" He waved a hand at the mess he'd made.

"Nae bother," put in Maggie. "I'll clean it up."

"To hell with that," Beth said hotly. "If everyone's alright, and we haven't lost, then what's going on?"

"He wants me to stay," Alex replied. He'd regained some measure of control now, had blinked away the tears, although his breathing was still a little ragged.

"Stay? Who wants you to stay? Where?"

"Charles. He wants me to stay here, as Sir Anthony."

"We know that already," she said, puzzled. "We're staying for a few weeks, and then we're off to join him in Scotland, as soon as we can."

"No," Alex broke in. "He wants me to *stay* here. He's worried about the lack of good information about troop movements and suchlike, and he's asked me to continue gathering and passing information on. He says I'm in a unique position to find out intelligence crucial to the success of the cause, that no one else can do it."

Prince Charles had a point. Beth sat down at the bench, and put the letter on the table.

"How long does he want you to stay for?" she asked.

"Until he arrives in London to take the throne for his father," Alex replied desolately.

They abandoned the kitchen as it was, and repaired to the library with a bottle of wine to discuss the matter further. Alex picked up the book that Beth had abandoned on the sofa and glanced from it to her. It was not the sort of reading matter she usually chose.

"It was on the table," she said by way of explanation. "I was just passing time until you woke up."

He sat down and flicked through the opening pages whilst they were waiting for Maggie to bring some glasses for the wine.

"'…my soul entered that of a young man,'" he read aloud. "'And as he was an egregious fop, a busybody, a scandal-monger, a vain butterfly, an authority in trifles, serious only about his dress, his complexion, and a hundred other vapid nothings'…Christ!" he exclaimed, throwing the book down. "Is this what I'm tae be? When Angus and Duncan are telling their bairns about their great deeds in the glorious battles of the revolution that put Jamie back on the throne, am I tae tell mine about how I pranced around London dressed as a fucking molly? I'm sorry," he said.

That he'd used such a word in front of her and Maggie, who had now appeared with the glasses, told Beth more than anything just how upset he was.

"Charles does have a point," she ventured. "Lots of people can fight, but not many can do what you're doing. I think it takes a lot more courage to spend every day putting on an act, walking a tightrope, never knowing if you're going to be discovered, than it does to charge across a battlefield when your blood's up, hacking at the enemy."

"I was reared tae charge across battlefields and hack at the enemy, Beth," Alex countered. "There's nae glory in sitting in drawing rooms drinking tea and eating cake while ye blether on about the latest fashions. I canna tell ye how tired I am of it. The only thing that's kept me going these last weeks is knowing that it'd soon be over. I dinna think I can keep this up much longer." He looked across at his wife. "Is that how ye feel about what we're doing?"

"Well, I've never hacked at the enemy on a battlefield," she admitted. "I expect that takes a lot of courage, but only for a few minutes at a time, and then once the battle's over, you can go back to doing whatever you do afterwards, marching about and suchlike. With all your friends, who are doing the same as you. What we're doing is a lonely thing, and dangerous all the time. Or most of the time, anyway. We have to think about every word we say."

"Beth's right," Iain put in. "I ken ye're upset, Alex, and what ye're about may no' make such a good story, but it's important to the cause."

"Are ye no' wanting tae be fighting yourself, laddie?" Alex asked.

"Aye, of course I am, but there's nothing tae be done. We canna go against the prince."

From the look on Alex's face, it was very clear that he'd been intending to do just that. Maggie filled the glasses and handed them round. They all drank in morose silence for a few minutes as they variously contemplated months of formal visits, gentlemen's clubs, evenings alone with books entitled *The Sofa*, and dashing cross-country in all weathers with coded messages.

"Well," Alex said finally, "I might have to stay, and you too, Beth, but I see nae reason why you and Maggie canna go and join the rest o' the clan."

"Are ye mad?" Maggie asked bluntly. "Who'll take the messages tae Foley if Iain's no' here? Who'll do all the cleaning and cooking if I'm no' here?"

"I'm no' happy wi' Iain taking the messages as it is," Alex replied. "He's a Scot and he canna pretend otherwise, which puts him under suspicion straight away. If he's caught wi' a coded message on him, he'll hang, after they torture him tae find out what's in it. I've never been happy with it, but I thought it was worth the risk for a week or two, a month at most. But now...we could be here for months. I canna expect ye to keep taking such a risk. I'll take the messages from now on. It's safer. I can be any nationality I want."

"What?" Beth cried. "Just when exactly are you going to do that? You're already exhausted as it is, staying out most of the night, and then going half-blind writing coded letters by candlelight! You're not getting more than four hours sleep a night now! I'll do it," she continued. "Foley knows me, and if I'm stopped I can pretend to be a maid carrying a letter from my mistress to her lover."

"Ye canna ride across country alone in the middle of the night!" Alex countered hotly.

"I won't do it at night. I'll do it in the morning, or in the afternoon, after we've visited," she said. "We can send out to a pie shop for dinner, that'll save some time, and I can do a bit of cleaning in the evenings when you're out at the clubs."

Alex tore his fingers through his hair.

"Ye'll no'..."

"Will the pair of ye haud yer wheesht?" Iain shouted. "I'm no' going anywhere. I ken what I'm doing, and I ken the danger. I dinna need tae be telling my bairns about my brave deeds on the battlefield. Tae hell wi' that. Charlie's my prince, and you're my chieftain, and if he wants ye tae stay here, then I'm staying here with ye. And so is Maggie. For as long as it takes. And there's an end of it."

He banged the glass down on the table, stood, and walked out of the room, slamming the door behind him and leaving the other three occupants sitting open-mouthed at this uncharacteristic display of temper.

"Aye, well," said Maggie calmly after a few moments. "That's settled then. I'll away and see tae the dinner." She rose and followed her husband, closing the door quietly.

Silence reigned for a minute or so.

"Is that how ye feel?" Alex repeated his earlier question. "Are ye afraid and lonely?"

"No," she replied. "I didn't say that. I said it's a dangerous and lonely thing that we're doing, and it is. But I knew what I was getting myself into when I married you. Well, just after I married you, anyway. The only time I've felt lonely was when I thought you didn't trust me, after Henri. But we're past that now."

"Ye didna think that we'd be staying here forever, though, did ye?"

"We won't be staying here forever. Once this is all over, we'll go home. To Scotland," she clarified. "And if we have children…"

"When we have children," he corrected her.

"…when we have children, I'll be proud to tell them what their father did to restore King James to his rightful place, and to allow the MacGregors to use their rightful name. And if we've brought them up properly, they'll understand that there's more than one way to win a war, and that their father's a great hero, every bit as brave as any soldier on the battlefield. More so, in fact."

He smiled then in spite of himself, and reaching across the sofa, took her arm and pulled her on to his knee.

"I'm no' the only great hero in the room tonight," he said softly. "When ye put it like that, I can see that ye're in the right. But I wanted so much tae fight at my prince's side. I've spent my whole life waiting for this moment, and I'm sore disappointed,

Beth. I canna pretend otherwise."

She put her arms round his neck and buried her face in his shoulder, inhaling the fresh, clean male smell of him, this man she adored.

"But there's one thing ye're wrong about, *mo chridhe*," he continued. "This path we're on, it is dangerous, for all four of us. And it was lonely at first, for me. But I'm no' lonely now, no' while I've got you." He bent his head and tenderly kissed the top of her head.

"I'm not going anywhere," she said, her lips against his neck, her voice muffled slightly. "Whatever happens, we're in this together, for as long as it takes."

After that they sat quietly, embracing and drawing strength from each other to face the months ahead. And downstairs, in the kitchen, Iain and Maggie were doing the same.

HISTORICAL NOTE

In view of the interest many of my readers have shown in the historical events portrayed in The Jacobite Chronicles, I thought some of you might find it interesting to learn that quite a few of the more unlikely scenes in my books, are in fact taken from historical record.

In Chapter One, at the dinner party, Beth disturbs the family by stating that the Old Pretender had a Protestant chapel. Although one of the main reasons the Hanoverians put forward against a Stuart restoration was that it would plunge the country back into popery, King James VIII and III, in spite of being a Roman Catholic, did have an Anglican chapel and retained two Anglican chaplains at his Court in exile in the Palazzo Muti in Rome, to minister to his Protestant subjects. He also believed that if his son, Prince Charles, was to one day become the king of a Protestant country, he should grow up surrounded by Protestants as well as Catholics. When Prince Charles, at the age of four, was presented to the pope, he steadfastly refused to kneel, leading some to believe that he would become Protestant someday. This does cast into doubt the somewhat hysterical anti-Catholic pronouncements of the Hanoverian supporters.

Also in Chapter One, Gabriel Foley talks about 'Mr Red'. As unlikely as this sounds, Mr Red was a real person. His real name was Henry Read, and he agreed to bring English pilots over to Dunkirk to guide the French flotilla. However the English Jacobites became afraid when some of them were arrested, so sent Read to France alone, telling him to find suitable pilots there. But because his French was very poor, he couldn't do this without help, and was unable to find either the prince or any other English contacts, so after a few days of wandering aimlessly about, he returned to England.

Chapter Five - washing of the feet. This is an old Scottish custom which still persists in some parts of Scotland. Traditionally the bride had her feet washed by the womenfolk, and the man's feet were washed with soot and cinders. I've just adapted the genuine custom a little!

Chapters Fourteen and Seventeen - Prince Frederick, Prince of Wales, did have a very bad relationship with his father, and his shadow Court became a magnet for anyone who was in opposition to King George II. Numerous reasons have been put forward as to why father and son hated each other, but the fact remains that their acrimonious relationship was well-known and continued until the prince's death. Prince Frederick was renowned for playing practical jokes on his friends and sycophantic followers. As he was heir to the ageing king, people wishing to curry favour would put up with his pranks in the hope of future preferment. I've taken liberties with this character trait to write some scenes in my book, such as the gardening scene. Although there's no record of him actually being quite so horrible to his guests as to make them spread manure, Frederick *was* a keen gardener and also a lover of plays, even writing one himself under a pseudonym. So dire was the result that it ran for only two nights at Drury Lane before closing. He was also a great fan of cricket, and in fact died after being hit by a cricket ball in 1751, although this was not the direct cause of death.

As for Frederick's sons, the eldest, Prince George (later George III) was thought by his tutors to be 'lethargic and incapable of concentration'. He did not learn to read properly until he was eleven. He was very shy, and at times silent and morose.

Prince Edward, George's younger brother, was described by Horace Walpole as 'a very plain boy, with strange loose eyes…he is a sayer of things!' As Walpole did not elaborate on the things Edward said, I put my own interpretation on this, and gave him the second sight, hence the premonition that Daniel will hurt Beth.

In Chapter Sixteen Anne tells us that Richard has ordered her to hand feed her baby. Whilst it was common for wealthier women to employ wet nurses to feed their children, there was an increasing concern that the characteristics of the nurse could be somehow transported through the breast milk to the infant, and because of this, wet nurses were carefully vetted. An alternative to wet nurses was hand-feeding, which increased in popularity in the 18th century, both amongst poorer women who needed to go to work, and the more elite who felt breastfeeding was beneath them, but were unwilling to entrust their offspring to a wet nurse. By mid-century men of science started to become interested in the subject of childbirth, and in investigating the high mortality rates of children who were hand-reared. Natural scientists such as Carl Linnaeus began to argue that women should nurse their own children, as other mammals do. In 1739 Thomas Coram founded the Foundling Hospital in London, and in the 1740s, William Cadogan became an honorary medical attendant. He was a firm believer in breastfeeding, and believed mothers' milk was essential to child health. The exceptionally high mortality rate of infants was of great concern to the government, as these children would soon constitute the workforce, and the issue was debated in Parliament. To give an example of the seriousness of the situation, statistics show that out of ten thousand babies hand-fed in the Dublin Foundling Hospital over a twenty year period, only forty-five survived infancy.

In Chapter Eighteen, Alasdair arrives with the news that Prince Charles has landed in Scotland with just seven men. As foolhardy as this sounds, it's true. He actually set out with two ships. One was the *Doutelle*, in which he travelled with his seven men: four Irishmen, two Scots and an Englishman. Three of them were elderly men, and only one of them would play an important role in the rebellion – Colonel John William O'Sullivan. The other ship was the *Elizabeth*, which had 700 soldiers on board, as well as 1500 muskets with ammunition and 1800 broadswords. Unfortunately they were intercepted by an English warship, and a battle ensued in which the *Elizabeth* sustained heavy damage, and had to return to France. Consequently, Prince Charles did land in Scotland with just seven men, although he was not daunted by this.

And finally, also in Chapter Eighteen, I wanted to point out that *The Sofa – A Moral Tale,* was in fact a real book, and the quotation Alex reads out is taken directly from the book. It was published in France in 1742, and was by Claude Prosper Jolyot de Crébillon. It was a libertine tale, and a lot of the characters were satirical portraits of Parisians of the time – including King Louis XV. The author was temporarily exiled from Paris after its publication, due to this. It was translated into English the same year, so it's conceivable that Beth would have had a copy.

ABOUT THE AUTHOR

Julia has been a voracious reader since childhood, using books to escape the miseries of a turbulent adolescence. After leaving university with a degree in English Language and Literature, she spent her twenties trying to be a sensible and responsible person, even going so far as to work for the Civil Service. The book escape came in very useful there too.

And then she gave up trying to conform and resolved to spend the rest of her life living as she wanted to, not as others would like her to. She has since had a variety of jobs, including telesales, teaching and gilding and is currently a transcriber, copy editor and proofreader. In her spare time she is still a voracious reader, and enjoys keeping fit and travelling the world. Life hasn't always been good, but it has rarely been boring. She lives in rural Wales with her cat Constantine, and her wonderful partner sensibly lives four miles away in the next village.

Now she has decided that rather than just escape into other people's books, she would actually quite like to create some of her own, in the hopes that people will enjoy reading them as much as she does writing them.

Follow her on:

Facebook:
www.facebook.com/pages/Julia-Brannan/727743920650760

Twitter:
https://twitter.com/BrannanJulia

Pinterest:
http://www.pinterest.com/juliabrannan

Also by Julia Brannan

The Jacobite Chronicles

Book One: Mask of Duplicity
Book Two: The Mask Revealed

Made in the USA
Columbia, SC
03 January 2018